D0760403

THE CIVIL SERVANT'S
NOTEBOOK

Wang Xiaofang began his career in the civil service, which culminated in a position as private secretary to the Deputy Mayor of Shenyang Province Ma Xiangdong who, in 2001, was sentenced to death for gambling away over 3.6 million US dollars of public money in Macanese casinos. Since leaving his position in 1999, Wang Xiaofang has published over thirteen novels about corruption and politics in China. *The Civil Servant's Notebook* was his first novel to be translated into English.

THE CIVIL SERVANT'S NOTEBOOK

WANG XIAOFANG

Translated from the Chinese by Eric Abrahamsen

CHINA LIBRARY

PENGUIN BOOKS

UK | USA | Canada | Ireland | Australia
India | New Zealand | South Africa | China

Penguin Books is part of the Penguin Random House group of companies
whose addresses can be found at global.penguinrandomhouse.com.

| Penguin
| Random House
| PENGUIN BOOKS CHINA

This paperback edition published by Penguin Group (Australia)
in association with Penguin (Beijing) Ltd, 2015

1 3 5 7 9 10 8 6 4 2

Cover design by Di Suo © Penguin Group (Australia)
Text design by Steffan Leyshon-Jones © Penguin Group (Australia)
Printed and bound in China by South China Printing Company

National Library of Australia
Cataloguing-in-Publication data:

Wang, Xiaofang.
The Civil Servant's Notebook/Wang Xiaofang
9780734399588 (paperback)
Corruption—China—Fiction.
China—Officials and employees—Fiction.

895.1352

penguin.com.cn

A NOTE ON CHINESE USAGE AND NAMES

In Chinese, a person's given name always follows their surname. Therefore, the character Yang Hengda has the surname Yang and the given name Hengda. Lower ranked government officials will always refer to senior officials by their surname preceeded by official title. Vice-ranked officials will occasionally be referred to without the vice-prefix, especially by lower ranked officials, as a show of respect. Vice-Mayor Peng would then simply be shortened to Mayor Peng.

Pinyin, the standard Romanisation method for Chinese characters, has been used throughout this novel except where the Chinese is more commonly known by its former Wade-Giles spelling (e.g. Chuang-tzu).

THE
CIVIL
SERVANT'S
NOTEBOOK

Number Two Department, Department Head, Yang Hengda

'EVERYONE WANTS TO go to heaven, but the gate of heaven isn't like the gate of hell, which opens with a push. I confused the gate of hell with the gate of heaven.'

I read that in a report about the downfall of a high-level official.

I have to admit the statement shook me. I've always wondered: besides the doors of heaven and hell, might there be a third door? If not, then what is it we're struggling for? Is it merely to push open the door to hell?

Thinking this over I realise that in the course of my whole life, there's only been one door I've been compelled to push open every day, and that's the door to my office: Number Two Department, Combined Affairs, Dongzhou Municipal Government.

I am the department head. Every day when I open this door I am at my most smug and complacent – and my soul is at its most empty.

Last night I paid a visit to the Old Leader, whom I served for many years. He is ill with uric poisoning. Yes, that's uric poisoning, not uraemia. Many who visit him assume it's uraemia and can't see how it could be uric poisoning, but the moment the Old Leader explains, they understand.

He has uric poisoning because he's been drinking his own urine for years, and despite the fact that the habit has landed him in hospital, he

1

misses no opportunity to recommend his long-practised cure to his visitors. Tirelessly, he expounds its benefits, reciting from the *Compendium of Materia Medica*: 'Urine, *urina*, aka "karmic liquor" or "essential decoction". Salty of savour, cooling, non-poisonous. Principally used in curing chronic cough and congestion, cholera, injuries sustained in falls, haemorrhoids, etc.'

He'll add something about the urine cure being a quintessential part of Chinese culture. He hasn't changed a whit since I was in his service five years ago. He's still a devoted practitioner of the cure, even after he collapsed and was hospitalised.

Just the thought of the urine cure turns my stomach.

Though the Old Leader has been retired for many years, he is still a leading light in Dongzhou City, both by rank and record of service. He chose me as his secretary when I was a principal-level researcher in the office of the Retired Cadres Bureau of the Municipal Party Committee. He had read an article I published in the *Dongzhou Government Report* magazine about how retired cadres could maintain their health. The Old Leader liked my writing style as well as my firm grounding in health issues. Fact is I didn't have a firm grounding. I'd simply been asked to contribute to the *Dongzhou Government Report* and wrote something off the cuff. But the article earned his appreciation, and out of the blue he chose me to be his secretary.

Once I had assumed my post I learned the Old Leader was hoping to use my skill with the pen to produce an important manuscript. It hadn't yet taken shape. It was merely a notion in his head. The work was not completed until five years after I assumed my post, under the title, *Philosophical Reflections on the Urine Cure*.

Though I wrote the manuscript, it naturally appeared under the name of the Old Leader. He had poured five years of his heart's blood into the work; not for public consumption, but to record his experiences and share them with the retired cadres, and, of course, as a legacy for younger ones.

At first I had difficulty understanding what the Old Leader told me about his insights into the urine cure, so he was dissatisfied with what I wrote. He also believed that experience was the only true method of testing a theory.

So it was – after his repeated urgings and to better fulfil my duty – that I began the urine cure myself.

I never thought I would drink urine for a full five years.

In addition to transcribing the Old Leader's thoughts on the cure, I was also under strict instructions to record my own ponderings, two thousand characters per day, minimum. Come rain or shine he reviewed and annotated my notes as if he were reviewing government documents, with a red pen no less. So over the course of those five years I not only wrote the Old Leader's *Philosophical Reflections on the Urine Cure*, but I also accumulated nearly one million characters of my own *Reflections*.

I never imagined the Old Leader would be struck down by his urine drinking habit. This was the diagnosis of Western medicine, of course, and he had a staunch faith in Chinese medicine. He insisted that his illness was caused not by drinking urine, but, on the contrary, because there'd been a couple of days when he had *stopped* drinking urine. He had stopped because, being over seventy, he was having problems with his prostate and was unable to urinate, leading to a hiatus in his cure. Last night he still held fast to his opinion, saying he would continue his cure and 'Let them say what they will!'

I drank my own urine for five years and I think I'm qualified to say something about the cure. In the beginning, with the Old Leader's assurances, I too believed drinking urine would 'strengthen one's body and extend one's life'.

But after a long period of practice I realised that urine is a waste product, painstakingly filtered from the blood by the kidneys, and putting it back into the body was simply making the kidneys and liver do their work over again. No wonder he was poisoned!

3

Regardless what you believe, urine is not water, though water may be its major component. Urine is toxic. It is a waste by-product of the body's metabolism.

You can liken society to a human body, from which the metabolism of history expels cultural waste. This cultural waste is terribly dangerous, but we often confuse what is dangerous with what is great and enshrine these things as our traditional cultural heritage.

My reflections on urine drinking were precisely this kind of trash.

The day I left the Old Leader to become head of Number Two Department, my friends treated me to a proper send-off. I sniffled as I watched the yellow, white-frothed beer being poured into my cup. My friends thought I was weeping for joy at being made a department head. Little did they know those were tears of suffering. I had drunk my own urine for five years to get this position. I felt like a newly released prisoner.

That night I drank too much, and when one of my friends drove me home I was overcome by nausea. I ignored it, however, and once I got indoors I rummaged around for my reflections on the urine cure. It was a full ten thousand pages. The sections written during the first two years were already yellowing like dried leaves. I found a quiet place in the apartment compound and burnt them all, my face lit red by the fire, the flames hissing their mockery.

After my five years with the Old Leader, by rights, I should have returned to my position in the Retired Cadres Bureau but, similar to the way the Old Leader had selected me, a theoretical article I'd published in the *Dongzhou Daily* about the urban development of Dongzhou won the appreciation of Vice-Mayor Peng Guoliang, who had just taken office.

Prior to this, of course, Mayor Peng had visited the Old Leader on various occasions and holidays. The old man was extremely concerned with the progress of his career and had expressed great interest and solicitude as the Mayor first got to bureau-level and had then gone on to the position of vice-mayor. So Mayor Peng had become familiar with me. It was a Spring Festival when he came to visit the Old Leader in this case. He started complaining about the lack of talented writers and went on to an appreciation of my literary skills. Finally, he proposed I be transferred to the Number Two Department as department head. The Old Leader acceded with happiness.

And so I became the department head.

Including myself there are only five people in Number Two, but the state of affairs is complicated, and no wonder: Number Two Department is a policy-making core of the Municipal Government. It is also responsible for the day-to-day operations of the vice-mayor. In effect, I am Mayor Peng's office director. It is a good position.

My predecessor's deputy wanted it most, of course. His name is Xu Zhitai.

Xu is short and has a face like a brick and when he gets to scheming he's not to be trifled with. I heartily dislike the opaque and sinister smile that always hangs on his face. It reminds me of the phrase 'a smile that conceals the knife'. But just as well: that way I am constantly reminded to be on my guard. I am particularly wary of him because it was Xu who did away with my predecessor, with a proper office coup. But I soon worked out that all he wants is his daily bread, so that's what I've given him.

Not long after I took up my post, an opportunity arose to visit America with an investment recruitment team led by Mayor Peng himself. I passed it to Xu Zhitai and his brick-like face broke into a bready smile.

In Number Two Department, although I no longer suffer the daily dose of urine, I'm beset with the sense of being lost at sea. On the office wall hangs a quartz clock, and every time I see it I feel it is a white pit, a trap. I feel like I am falling into it. Other times it seems like a face, one that undergoes many changes. It cycles through my colleagues in the department. Sometimes it's Xu Zhitai's skin-deep grin. Sometimes it's Department-Level Researcher Huang Xiaoming's sunny visage. This is the face I envy most because it contains a touch of noble arrogance. Sometimes it's Junior Department-Level Researcher Ou Beibei's alluring, coquettish face, which turns my thoughts impure. Sometimes it's the apparently pure face of section member Zhu Dawei, one I could make most use of. Most often, of course, it is a face much like my own; a face that has drunk urine, a face that swings like a clock's pendulum.

I only met my predecessor, Zhao Zhong, after I had taken his position. He invited me to dinner. The reason I accepted was to discover more about conditions in the department, and in particular about the coup that had forced him out.

Zhao Zhong knew what I wanted and took the opportunity to slander and denigrate everyone. I kept my wits about me and took what he said with a grain of salt. He gave me one piece of information that startled me, however: the leader of the coup hadn't been Xu Zhitai. Shocked, I said, 'If not Xu Zhitai, then who?'

Zhao Zhong, a cigarette stuck into his grin, said, 'Tsk tsk, Yang Hengda, I thought you were cleverer than I, but it turns out that still waters run shallow! Let me ask you: if Xu Zhitai became department head, who would be vice-head?'

As the realisation hit me, I murmured to myself, 'But surely . . .'

Zhao Zhong nodded and revealed another startling piece of news. 'Hengda, terms are up at the end of this year. The old mayor is going to be Director of the Municipal People's Congress. Do you know who will take his place?'

I didn't need to guess. 'No matter how you look at it, it has to be Vice-Mayor Peng.'

I said this because Mayor Peng had been actively jockeying for the position and had often intimated to me that there was a good chance he would get it. Of course I sincerely hoped that he would be successful, as my boat would naturally rise along with the tide.

Zhao Zhong laughed with scorn. 'Hengda, have you learned noth-

6

ing from your years in the corridors of power? Do you understand nothing of politics? When has a standing vice-mayor of Dongzhou ever been promoted directly to mayor?'

I thought back over the last few mayors. None of them had. Growing impatient, I said, 'Enough suspense, Zhao Zhong, who will it be?'

With a look of enormous smugness, Zhao Zhong took a deep drag on his cigarette and said, 'Why, Vice-Governor Liu, of course.'

'Liu Yihe?' I blurted.

'Think about it carefully, Hengda.' Zhao Zhong smiled obsequiously. 'Is there anyone better suited to it than Governor Liu?'

Looking at Zhao Zhong's fat, smug face, a secret worry began to gnaw within me. The year Liu Yihe became standing Vice-Mayor of Dongzhou City, he had fought Peng Guoliang tooth and nail for the position. Now the two of them were in contest to become mayor, and if Peng Guoliang were defeated once more, was he likely to go quietly? Liu Yihe returning would mean storms within Dongzhou's official circles. There is nothing more important than your allies. If you backed the wrong person, all your efforts would come to nought.

During the meal Zhao Zhong hinted that I should switch my allegiance to Liu Yihe. I immediately became wary. I couldn't tell if this idea was his own or Liu Yihe's, but Zhao intimated that his advice was not offered lightly. I found myself in a dilemma. Loyalty was paramount within officialdom, but at every changing of the guard it was disloyalty that proved victorious, and loyalty empty.

I have always seen the civil service as a means of making a living, as a labourer labours, a farmer ploughs, a businessman makes deals or a teacher teaches. But traditional culture places so many burdens of high idealism and ethics within the pursuit of politics. The words 'public service' lie like a crushing weight on one's shoulders. I have served one leader or another ever since I began my government career, first in the Retired Cadres Bureau, then helping the Old Leader with his five years of research into the urine cure, and now cudgelling my brains to write reports for Peng Guoliang; a million characters' worth of material within a year, all signed with his name, with me ever the bridesmaid. Better to be a novelist, who can reach fame and fortune through his own work. Just look at me: my writing never earned me a penny. Even the cigarettes I smoked while I worked were paid for out of my pocket. And this was 'public service'? More like 'private service'!

Though I kept my cool in the face of Zhao Zhong's temptations, he could see that I was hesitating, and honestly, who wouldn't want to throw in their lot with the next Number One?

Zhao made an analogy that was very vivid, though a little crude: Number One was the cock, and Number Two was the balls. It may look like they have equal standing, inseparable as they are, but when it comes time for lovemaking, one gets the prize, and the other just watches the door. No wonder everyone wants to be Number One! Zhao Zhong broke into loud guffaws, and I grinned so broadly I almost spat out my abalone.

But what he said affected me deeply. Every clique has a core and a periphery. The core doesn't like the periphery weaselling inwards. Meanwhile the periphery isn't satisfied with its status. Struggle is inevitable, and in the course of that struggle, small fry like me have to fight just to keep from being sacrificed by the big fish. No wonder so many within officialdom follow the doctrine of 'what have you done for me lately?' The career of the official is like Li Bai's poem, 'The Road to Shu', beset with insurmountable peaks and passes, and treacherous fords and rapids, pitfalls concealed with flowers, and submerged reefs and rocks. Only by one's own wits can one reach the other side, if indeed there is an 'other side'.

I declined Zhao Zhong's offer to drive me home after the meal. I felt the desire to walk alone. The fresh air was comforting. Girls stood in twos and threes beneath the roadside trees, looking like the sketches of a third-rate painter. 'Poor little hookers,' I thought.

It was a real pleasure, walking through the night. After sitting in an office so long I had nearly forgotten that people are meant to walk – perhaps into eternity? The road to heaven is long but the road of man is short. Why choose the long over the short?

A 'beauty' approached, simpering, 'come and play, big boy!' I waved her off.

We come into life experiencing lust, and so we see all that promotes life as good. We fear death, and so we see all avoidance of death as good, little imagining that good and evil are both the children of freedom, both irrational. The path of humanity is evil, and the secret of evil is goodness. Evil is hidden in the hearts of all, a second self. True evil arises from freedom, but true goodness does as well. Freedom is a peculiar, incredible and uncertain thing. If given full rein it becomes evil. Why does absolute power corrupt absolutely? Because absolute power results in absolute freedom! When freedom is given full rein it holds nothing sacred, it accepts no boundaries.

My wife was still awake when I got home. She always waits up for me, mostly because she gets suspicious, and no wonder when the world outside is so full of temptations. The small fry has small temptations and the big fish has big temptations, and both fish and fry would have to be made of something special to resist those temptations.

I've never believed in that 'something special', though my wife is always preparing me something special – no, I should call it 'special medicine' – that she boils into soup for me to drink. Never mind that she studied Western medicine – she's never lost her faith in Chinese medicine.

Since becoming department head, I often stay up late writing or am obliged to go out drinking, and, as I rarely exercise, I have grown flabbier by the day. That 'cable of all flesh' has also become increasingly intractable, to the point where it no longer does my bidding. It bothers my wife no end, and she's dug up all sorts of folk remedies to try out on me, with no success.

She had found a new one that day. It had finished stewing and was awaiting experimentation.

Sure enough, the moment I walked in the door, she carried a bowl of black liquid out of the kitchen and handed it to me with a sly glance, saying it was a secret remedy handed down through six generations of Chinese doctors. I didn't want to disappoint her. Who wouldn't want more staying power? So I took the bowl and drained it with a flick of the wrist. My wife may not be a ravishing goddess, but I think she's just right: thin everywhere except her well-maintained bosom. Before I started at Number Two, she was the apple of my eye. But now I can't help comparing her to Ou Beibei, and after everything I've seen in the karaoke and sauna joints, even her bosom is no longer special.

Down the medicine went and I felt a heat rising in my chest. Seeing my wife's coquettish glances, I knew I'd be unable to avoid further experiments that night. Sure enough, the moment I slid into bed, her soft tongue began roaming over my sensitive parts, her white breasts firm and buoyant, as if it were she, not I, who'd drunk the medicine. I honestly did want to pleasure her, but the more I thought about it the more I felt that lovemaking had become a responsibility, a duty, a job no different from a day's writing. I was generally able to put on a show, but for some reason my fires were well and truly quenched that day. My wife worked herself into a sweat before finally giving up, wiping away tears. Seeing her so disappointed, I wanted to castrate myself on the spot.

The price of that day's exhaustion was that she demanded, starting the next morning, I go back to drinking urine. Nothing for it but to drink, then. I drank my urine for a week, with no change. My wife gave me no mercy, though, and every night tugged my manhood as though she were tugging a kite string.

One evening, however, when I was in a hurry to try some experiments of my own, my wife believed it was a week of the urine cure that had restored my 'Asian Mighty Winds'. Her moans were particularly titillating, and when I imagined them issuing from Ou Beibei I instantly began to swell. Not only that, I managed more than one hundred thrusts of the spear, as though I'd eaten goddamned Viagra.

The Office Chair

DO YOU KNOW what it means to be an office chair? Let me tell you. An office chair not only represents location, but it also represents status.

We might be lowly chairs, but our ancestry can be traced back to the dynasties of the Han and Wei. Do you know what our ancestors were called?

When I tell you, you'll kneel in homage, prostrate yourself even, for only our ancestors can reveal the secrets of the changing dynasties.

Why?

Isn't it obvious?

Our ancestors themselves were the secret. They were thrones, graded according to the rank of who sat in them.

Anyone who hears the word 'throne' feels a thrill, because once you sit on one, even your friends and relatives will ascend to heaven. When the emperor sits on a throne, the rivers and mountains are his. When a minister sits on one, wealth and honour accrue to him. It's no exaggeration that since the throne became a symbol of identity, status and power among the barbarian tribes, it has become something of a phallic symbol.

The office chair is a grand arena. Once you've sat on it you're a human being, an official, you've got a career. Keep your seat and your future will be glorious and rich. Lose your seat, and I become the tiger's maw! Don't believe me? Give it a try!

We office chairs are most particular about order. In ancient times we were called First Throne and Second Throne. In the modern day this has become First, Second and Third Hand, and so on. The 'hand' refers to the armrest. Never mind these 'hands' differ only by a single degree. That degree represents a vast difference in power. 'First Hand' means 'absolute'. Do you know what absolute means? It's the tail of the tiger, which none may tug.

The First Hand's chair is like a vast vortex, or an enormous magnetic field, into which people of all shapes and sizes are sucked. That's how cliques are formed. It's also how black holes are formed. I'm not boasting here. I believe that among all First Hands the most important is the county bureau-level First Hand.

Why?

Because, naturally, the county bureau is closest to the common people. It's the foundation of everything else. If the foundations are weak, the mountains will sway. So the county bureau-level First Hand is pretty important, right?

It's this importance that makes me proud to be the office chair of the head of the Number Two Department, Combined Affairs, Dongzhou Municipal Government, because Dongzhou is the county capital.

I've served under three successive department heads of Number Two Department. The first was Xiao Furen, who has gone on to become Deputy Chief Secretary and Director of the Municipal Government. Xiao Furen sat on me over the course of many sleepless nights of writing. When he first sat down his hair was sleek and shiny. When he stood up to take a higher post it was his bald pate that was sleek and shiny. That was to be expected. Xiao Furen worked doggedly and tirelessly, and after only a few years as department head his hair fell out entirely, leaving him with a 'Lenin pate'. Now he wears a hairpiece.

The second department head was Zhao Zhong, a man who looked like a water barrel. When he sat on me my joints squeaked and creaked. Of the three department heads I've served, Zhao Zhong was most apt to the title. He played his role as department head as if he was a bureau head. Not bad, eh?

Zhao had a habit of bouncing a leg. He'd start shaking it the moment he sat down, as if I were somehow electrified. He would also fart silently – long, foul farts that nearly killed me. There were only two circumstances under which he wouldn't shake his leg. The first was during department meetings. He liked meetings and he would run them as if he were a municipal leader on an inspection visit. The other circumstance when his leg fell still is known to no one else in the department but me, and that was when a woman was sitting on it. Zhao Zhong liked women. A pretty one could stop him in his tracks. The most beautiful in the department was Ou Beibei, and Zhao coveted her. But he was only a department head, after all. Ou Beibei hardly gave him a second glance and that bothered him. But department head of Number Two Department was equivalent to a director of the standing vice-mayor's office, and women who needed something from that office but couldn't reach it, particularly beautiful women, almost all ended up in his hands. On many occasions, when no one was in the office, these women would sit docilely on his thigh, and when that happened, Zhao Zhong's leg was still. Some other less decorous movements I will pass over in silence.

Zhao has been replaced by Yang Hengda, who was the Old Leader's secretary for five years.

This Yang Hengda is a careful and conscientious fellow. He works doggedly and uncomplainingly, and often stays late at the office. Don't fall for his hardworking demeanour, however, or his circumspect manner. At heart he's not content with his place. Not only does he have low tastes, but he also has wild fancies. I've always suspected that he's a bit of a voyeur, and he likes to peep into people's privacy. When alone in the office, he often goes through other people's drawers, particularly Ou Beibei's. He likes Ou Beibei every bit as much as Zhao did, and he's always glancing at her when she's not looking. But Yang doesn't have guts to match his libido, and keeps himself in check. My guess is he won't sit on me for long before he's promoted.

From ancient times to the modern day, no small number of civil servants have spent their days being frustrated by the seat beneath their rear ends. Some don't like where they're sitting, others fear losing their seats. Those sitting up front fear those sitting behind. Those sitting behind hanker after those sitting in front. Even those who never wanted a throne aren't willing to pass their whole lives without one, and then they stop at nothing to wrest one for themselves. Those who were born believing a throne should be theirs burn even more hotly to acquire one.

Lordy lord, the invention of the throne threw heaven and earth into darkness!

Number Two Department, Department Vice-Head, Xu Zhitai

MY PHILOSOPHY IS this: first board a ship, then worry about where you're going. Finding a goal is easy. Boarding a ship is hard. That's not a painting you see before you. It's the boundless ocean. Everyone wants to reach their ideal shore, but where is it? It's merely a utopia. Intuition tells me that the far shore itself is actually on board the ship anyway. The problem is, of course, that the ship is crammed full, and the shore is teeming with people craning their necks for an opportunity to squeeze on board. It's not a small ship, but there are too many people who want to be on it. This tells us that there is no other world but this one – none at all!

This is what I've learned from my ten years as a vice department head. Ten years I've held this position and I know that everyone in the Municipal Government laughs at me. I can't blame them. I can only blame myself for reaching understanding too late. Life is nothing but a process of exchanging one want for another. Those who have chased after their ideals, mistaking them for reality, will only ever be grains of sand on the shore.

After Zhao Zhong's departure, Number Two Department entered an age of democracy. I found myself 'acting' department head. Full of aspirations, I decided to get a few things accomplished while I was 'acting'. But what to accomplish? I was at a loss. I hardly knew how I kept myself busy each day. I just knew that something was not right in my spirit. I still felt the need to report to someone. Report what, to whom? It didn't matter.

An 'acting' department head must have a leader. I knew there was something wrong with me. I'd been vice-head for ten years and was accustomed to it. It had become a way of life. It was too much to expect that the word 'acting' could change my habits, my way of life. I even began to think fondly of the days when Zhao Zhong was department head and I was his deputy. At least I knew who to present my reports to. Becoming 'acting' department head had brought me no sense of novelty. Instead it felt as uncomfortable as putting on someone's old shirt. If there's no one higher up watching out for you, then no one lower down will follow you. Isolated like that, you're unable to create your own ecosystem, nor can you work towards your aspirations. What then?

Like I say, if you want to go far you must board a ship. Even if it's a ship of thieves, you must take the gamble or you'll linger forever on the shore.

I lost my father when I was young and my mother struggled to raise me. She had one dream for me: that I hoist a flag and make my own journey like a man.

I've disappointed her. Far from making a journey, when I was reassigned from the *Qingjiang Daily* to the Municipal Government, I made my nest in Number Two Department. I feel like the rooster my neighbour keeps in a cage. Lately I've noticed that the rooster crows not only at dusk, but any time of day, and sometimes all day long. In the middle of the night it might give a burst too. I never understood why the rooster crowed at random. Perhaps it has some nervous disorder. But when I became 'acting' department head, I understood the rooster wasn't crowing. It was asking for help, calling out, 'Save me! Let me out, I want to be free!' Number Two

Department became that rooster's cage for me, my own plight that of the rooster itself. I began to feel fate had been unkind to me.

Don't we all know that the longest rafter beam rots first, that the hunter aims for the bird that leads the flock? In the 'coup' at Number Two Department I was the longest rafter, and although I had yet to rot, the danger was real. What could I do? The rafter could not be allowed to rot. That rafter would be my gangplank onto a ship.

Clearly the only ship I had a chance of getting on was that of Mayor Peng, just as Zhao Zhong had once boarded Mayor Liu's. But I had the sense that I wasn't the shipmate Mayor Peng was looking for. And although Zhao Zhong left the department for the Municipal Service Centre and then resigned from the government altogether to make his own way in the world, he was still on Liu's ship, and his position was likely more important than before. I so wanted to be one of Mayor Peng's new crew, but it's impossible to force your way on board. Nonetheless, I did everything I could to demonstrate my competence, hoping he would give me a chance.

Everything went back to the beginning, however. After Peng Guoliang had been standing vice-mayor for a month he chose a new head for Number Two Department and the 'acting' in my title reverted once again to 'vice'. The new head, Yang Hengda, had been the Old Leader's secretary for five years, and though he was a bit unprepossessing, he was easy enough to get along with. You'd learn a lot from five years as secretary to someone like the Old Leader.

Yang Hengda outclassed me from the moment he arrived. He set the whole office to work creating a library of Peng Guoliang's material, the most thorough item of which, *The Sayings of Peng Guoliang*, won Peng's sincere approval. After reading through this library I realised the reason I'd remained vice-head for ten years wasn't because I had never been appreciated. It was because I didn't understand how to serve my leaders. I didn't know how to think like they thought or concern myself with their concerns. Instead I poured my energy into promoting my own ideas and displaying my own talent. I never changed my ideas to match their ideas, or subsumed my talents within theirs. I was constantly trying to outdo my leaders. How could I possibly outdo the leaders? How could I ever be more talented than them? If your leaders were your inferiors, then how would they ever have become your leaders? Unfortunately for me, this realisation came too late.

If I were asked, in the interviewing style popular at the time, 'Mr Xu Zhitai, what are your thoughts on suffering?'

I would answer with no hesitation, 'If I suffer, it means I am alive. Suffering is a proof of life.'

If pressed further: 'What is the greatest source of suffering to you?' I wouldn't need to consider the answer.

'A monotonous life.'

If the questions continued: 'Life should be full of colour and variety – how can it become monotonous? What exactly is a monotonous life?'

I would give my pained answer: 'It is a life in which you climb upwards, with only one goal. Always climbing, climbing upwards like a snake.'

If the interviewer doubted my answer and asked again, 'Why do you say it's climbing upwards, not moving forward?'

I would answer, in even more pain, 'Because I feel that I'm being seared in the fire pots of purgatory, and only by climbing upwards do I have a hope of life.'

If the interviewer still didn't grasp my meaning and asked, 'In your eyes, what is man?'

I would answer firmly, 'In my eyes there is no "man", there is only the people. I am not a man, I am a civil servant, and in my eyes a civil servant is a kind of statue. All of the office buildings that stand in Dongzhou are in fact statues of civil servants. I live in a world of statues, and in my eyes there are only two types of human being moving amongst them: public servants, and the people.'

I know that no interviewer would be satisfied with my answers, but this is truly how I feel. Every day I yearn to embrace everything within my reach, but I've never actually been able to reach anything. I don't know why I have such miserable luck, worse than Xiao Furen or Zhao Zhong, and now worse than Yang Hengda, who can drink his own piss.

My never having worked like Yang Hengda as secretary for such a powerful person as the Old Leader was another handicap. I hear the Old Leader is interested in health preservation techniques and is always recommending his urine cure to the retired cadres of Dongzhou. The urine cure has become something of a fad among them, and the primary text they study is the Old Leader's *Philosophical Reflections on the Urine Cure*. This was produced by Yang Hengda. I hear he drank a cup of urine every morning along with the Old Leader, to gain a deeper insight. That spirit of self-sacrifice and commitment is impressive! No wonder the Old Leader is so fond of him.

I related the story of Yang Hengda and the Old Leader to my mother. She asked me a question: if the Old Leader had been interested in a faecal cure, would Yang Hengda have thrown himself so willingly into his task? The question interested me.

I went to the library and sure enough there is such a thing as a faecal cure. It first appears in the *Twenty-Four Filial Exemplars*, in the chapter entitled '*He Tasted Dung With an Anxious Heart*' which recounts the story of a filial son who tasted his father's shit. It's quite moving. Here's the gist of it.

Yu Qianlou, a scholar of the Southern Qi, was appointed magistrate of Qianling. He was there for less than ten days when he felt a deep panic and began to perspire. Feeling something must be wrong at home, he left his post and returned. He found his father had been gravely ill for two days. The doctor told him, 'To know whether a sickness is improving or worsening, one need only taste the patient's excrement. If it is bitter, all is well.' Yu tasted his father's excrement and found it was sweet, whereupon he became anxious. That night he kowtowed to the North Star, begging to let him die in his father's place. A few days later his father died, after which Yu buried him and observed three years of mourning. This story moved countless filial children, many of whom followed Yu's example. Some of these children, themselves ill, tasted their parents' shit and although the parents themselves did not recover, the children's illnesses were cured. Deeply grateful to their parents, these children believed they had discovered the medicinal properties of shit. Thus, the faecal cure came into being.

This story made a terrific impression on me. If I could find the courage to 'eat shit', then my worries about boarding a ship would be over.

You might have made the sacrifice of the urine cure, Hengda, but I could make the sacrifice of the faecal cure. Who then would deny me passage on Mayor Peng's ship?

My chance came. When Zhao Zhong was department head he'd kept all opportunities to go abroad for himself, but Yang Hengda, hoping to make some friends, passed the first opportunity to me, a trip to America no less, with Mayor Peng.

As it happened, the Mayor, perhaps unaccustomed to the environment, fell ill in Los Angeles, attacked by vomiting and diarrhoea. Luckily his secretary Hu Zhanfa had brought medicine and was able to halt the vomiting and diarrhoea, but his fever still raged. Hu Zhanfa and I were obliged to take turns watching over him through the night. Not only did I bring him water and medicine as if I were caring for my own mother, but I also washed his soiled undergarments. After his fever abated, he asked to speak with me. He told me to work together with Yang Hengda. Anyone who worked with him was Peng's man, and he never forgot his men. He guaranteed that we would be treated well. Though we only spoke for twenty minutes, I was so worked up I could hardly sleep. Mayor Peng had told me himself that I was one of his men, and what did that mean? That meant he was allowing me onto his ship. Of course I was thrilled!

So getting on board a ship wasn't that hard after all. It only required you to see yourself as a cog. There was no need for a cog to think, of course, only obey. My mistake in the past had been to think of myself as a person, and to ponder everything that happened too deeply. I had never thought of myself as a cog. A cog didn't need to examine its conscience, of course. So I would abandon my habit of examining my conscience. You say it was a deep lesson I was learning? Luckily I hadn't learned it too late.

The Office Desk

THE SUN IS in the west and the building is empty, but the Number Two Department, Combined Affairs, Dongzhou Municipal Government, is noisy and bustling. The evening, once the civil servants have left, is the happiest time of the day for the office desks. A ray of light from the setting sun comes in the window. The quartz clock listens to the office desks as they pour out their feelings and share their secrets.

Cast

BIG MAN, back to the wall, window on the left, door on the right. The desk is a dingy shade of red sandalwood with a sheet of glass atop a green felt cloth and nearly half a metre of documents piled on the left-hand side, some in pleather envelopes, some loose-leaf. Yellowing newspapers are interspersed among them.

NUMBER TWO, back to the door, facing the window, yellowish colour. Cups have left heat stains in the varnish of the desktop and the ashtray is full. Documents stacked to left and right.

NUMBER THREE, opposite Number Two, back to the window, facing the door. Yellowing. Meticulously orderly, despite the quantities of documents. A small, fishtail-shaped cactus, bearing a few red blossoms, is placed in the upper right-hand corner.

LITTLE LADY, standard computer desk in the right corner of the office, grey colour. Desktop is tidy, three or four classy fashion magazines piled on the right, small round mirror on the left. In the middle a box of fruit-and-green-tea scented tissues.

LITTLE MAN, similar to Little Lady. Standard grey computer desk, half a metre high stack of newspapers on the left, manual of Chinese chess on top. Desktop slightly messy, bears a few cigarette burns.

Scene

BIG MAN: *Heaves a long sigh.* They're gone. Today nearly drove me crazy. Out of everyone in here, Number Two hates the sunlight most, and there they put you in front of the window.

NUMBER TWO: You've got it wrong, Big Man. It's my master who dislikes sunlight, not me.

BIG MAN: Number Two, do you know why your master has never gotten beyond the position of vice-head?

NUMBER TWO: Why?

BIG MAN: Because of the spot you're in: plenty of sunlight but bad *fengshui*. Look where I am: a strong, solid wall behind me and a window to the left where you can see the beautiful office yard. You know what this wall represents? A mountain. Now look again at where you are. You've got a door behind you. Not only nothing to bolster you up, but people can also spy on you easily. No one would sit easy if they were sitting in front of you.

NUMBER THREE: Don't listen to his stories. To hear him tell it, a desk that's in the wrong position would turn the Virgin Mary towards Sodom.

LITTLE MAN: Quit showing off your knowledge, Number Three. What's Sodom, anyway?

LITTLE LADY: *Jumping in.* I know; it's a city from the Bible, at the mouth of the River Jordan.

BIG MAN: But it's not just a city, is it Little Lady? From what Number

Three said, it sounds like some kind of parable. Right, Number Three?

NUMBER THREE: The people lived in lascivious sin, so Heaven destroyed the city with fire.

LITTLE MAN: So Sodom signifies a corrupt and degenerate life!

NUMBER TWO: Big Man, you're saying that as long as an office desk has good *fengshui*, a Sodomite who sat there would not only live morally, but might even turn into the Virgin Mary?

LITTLE LADY: *Resentfully.* Number Two, are you trying to make a comment about my mistress?

BIG MAN: Little Lady, your mistress has a diary hidden in you, isn't that right? Why don't you take it out and read it for us?

LITTLE LADY: *Hesitating.* Well, all right. I've read it in secret many times, but I've never understood how she's feeling.

Streetlights come on. The building's spotlights converge with neon lights in the yard to fill the office with a warm, blurred light. The middle drawer of the Little Lady desk opens and a notebook with yellow plastic covers, printed with a lotus pattern, flies out as if blown on a wind. The office grows still. The ticking of the quartz clock is the only sound.

LITTLE LADY: *Clears her throat.* 'I wasn't raped by him. I was raped by desire. I wasn't raped by his desire. I was raped by my own desire. One time is called rape. Twice is cohabitation. I have been raped more than once, but while I feel deeply revolted, I never try to resist my desire . . .' Do you understand this? What is happening to my mistress?

BIG MAN: *Indignant.* Whatever it is, it's degenerate!

LITTLE MAN: *Sympathetic.* Degeneracy, thy name is woman!

NUMBER TWO: *Mocking.* 'The eternal feminine draws us ever onward and upward.'

BIG MAN: *Matter-of-fact.* Little Lady, does the diary say who the rapist was?

25

LITTLE LADY: *Despondent.* You've got the most experience of all of us, Big Man, so tell us your deduction. Who do you think it is?

LITTLE MAN: *Haughty.* Big Man might command the respect of all, but I'm your Sherlock Holmes! Since she didn't dare mention the name in her diary, the man must be an important figure. Lady, your mistress might hate this fellow, but desire has pushed her into his arms, and that means she's not only succumbed to his mastery, but also has designs of her own.

NUMBER TWO: *Disdainful.* What designs could she have besides power, position, status, glory, wealth and pleasure; all the usual fatal things.

NUMBER THREE: *Meditative.* There's nothing simple about this business. It seems to me to be a quite peculiar case.

BIG MAN: Stop trying to turn everything into a 'case', Number Three. Don't you know that 'cases' are our ancestors?

LITTLE MAN: *Curious.* Big Man knows the most about history. Let's hear what he has to say.

BIG MAN: The earliest desks were small and short-legged. Before the Han Dynasty, when someone wanted to read, write or eat, they would put one of these desks on their low bed. In the late Han, when foreign-style chairs came to the central Chinese plain, rudimentary tables appeared. Those tables might have been taller than the bed-top desks, but those desks held the higher place in people's hearts.

NUMBER THREE: Big Man, what occupies the place of honour in people's hearts now are no longer desks, nor even tables, but podiums.

NUMBER TWO: *Doubtfully.* Number Three, you talking about writing podiums?

NUMBER THREE: Not just writing podiums, but also leaders' podiums and speech-making podiums, and of course chairman's podiums. What do we call it when leaders are promoted? We call it 'ascending the podium'. It's quite clear that the podium long ago replaced the desk.

LITTLE LADY: I don't think that's entirely true.

BIG MAN: In the end, an office desk is like a book. What our masters have in their heads is only as much as what we've got in our guts. You can tell a person's character from their office desk, and their attitude to life.

LITTLE MAN: You can tell a person's status by the quality of their desk too.

NUMBER THREE: *Disdainful.* People only live for status and reputation. They've never understood how to live for life itself.

LITTLE LADY: *Playful.* That means we office desks are like secret bases. Our masters' questions of style, feeling and interest are all concentrated in us.

LITTLE MAN: *Excited.* Lady, why don't you lead us in a song!

LITTLE LADY: *Enthusiastic.* OK, what shall we sing?

BIG MAN: How about the one Number Three wrote: '*Song of the Office Desks*'?

All the office desks' drawers open and the office is filled with joyful song.

LITTLE LADY:

Little office desk, grand stage of life,

Where all of life's great dramas play,

If you don't believe us, join the civil service.

Sit down before us, destiny won't hesitate.

'Stop fretting over your unique destiny',

Just you sit down quietly,

You have a 'duty to exist',

And duty's the same as service,

'Even just for a moment', be happy and content!

Number Two Department, Department-Level Researcher, Huang Xiaoming

I WAS TRANSFERRED to Number Two Department from the Municipal Research Office. It was Liu Yihe, then a standing vice-mayor, who appreciated my talents, so I've always felt grateful to him.

The Research Office may well be called the mayors' brain trust, but apart from a few directors, none of the brains ever got the chance to meet a mayor or vice-mayor in person. Never mind a mayor, we never got a look in with so much as a chief secretary or even a deputy chief secretary. I wrote plenty of strategy papers, all under the names of municipal leaders of course, but no one ever came knocking at my door.

So I waited, I prepared and I watched out for an opportunity to prove myself.

It finally came.

Mayor Liu, when he was a standing vice-mayor, assigned an important project to my office, a survey of the progress of the municipal investment attraction plan. The project was to be co-ordinated by my boss. I was one of only two researchers with a higher education degree and I also happened to be a member of the Foreign Investment Department, so I became the principal author. During the course of research I discovered severe falsification of the figures related to investment and business promotion. But my boss directed me to treat these lightly and focus on successes and achievements. The report was likely to be published in the *Dongzhou Daily*.

I quite understood. There was a rumour that Mayor Liu was considering promoting my boss. If true, this particular report could determine the outcome.

I always prepare for all eventualities. I surmised that if Mayor Liu was merely hoping to place an article praising his brilliant achievements in attracting investment in the *Dongzhou Daily*, there would be no need to mobilise our entire Research Office. Number Two Department, Combined Affairs in the Municipal Government could produce that kind of article in their sleep. Mayor Liu must have actually wanted to get a grasp of real conditions, resolve some problems and move the entire city's investment attraction work onto a new level.

So while I wrote the research report as per instructions, I wrote another copy in private that reflected my actual findings, condensing my knowledge about business promotion and investment attraction in the city. I intended to keep this alternative version to myself, though of course in secret I hoped it might one day become the basis for Mayor Liu's strategising.

When the report was complete, Mayor Liu broke with precedent by asking my boss to bring the principal author to his office when he delivered it.

This was the first time I'd come face to face with Mayor Liu. He gave me an impression of easy approachability. Zhao Zhong was also present, and in contrast to Mayor Liu's friendliness, he betrayed the tensions of a man facing an enemy. The air conditioning was on, but, perhaps due to his corpulence, he continually mopped sweat from his face.

While my boss delivered his report, I watched the smile on Mayor Liu's face gradually disappear, and while he remained as amiable as ever, that amiability became tinged with severity. When the report was concluded, he remained silent for a moment, then asked a few questions, to which my boss replied in an offhand manner.

When I heard Mayor Liu's questions, I exulted because they touched directly on the central problems of investment attraction, the very reason Mayor Liu had given this work to the Research Office. By strenuously praising the progress that had been made, my boss was obviously missing his leader's intent. I, on the other hand, already had a grasp of the causes, background and solutions to his questions.

Mayor Liu took the unusual step of asking me to add my remarks. This was my first chance to display my talents before the Mayor in person. I was a mere department-level researcher. Of all the civil servants in the city, how many would ever get an opportunity to deliver a work report to Mayor Liu in person?

None. That's how many. Yet the opportunity had landed in my lap.

I settled my nerves then launched into a ten-minute soliloquy, laying bare the ills of the system and proposing effective remedies. Liu was elated and asked me to write up what I'd said as a report. Then he did something that surprised me. He asked my boss and Zhao Zhong to leave his office and told me to stay behind.

At that instant I would have given anything to become a mouse and dive into a hole. I would have gladly leapt into a mousetrap even, but there was nowhere to hide. I steeled myself. Hadn't I already leapt into the cat's mouth? The only way I was going to stay alive would be to pull his teeth.

I handed over the research report I'd prepared in secret.

Fearing Mayor Liu might get the wrong idea, I gave elaborate explanations, but the more I explained, the worse I made myself appear.

Mayor Liu didn't pay the slightest attention to me. The more he read, the brighter his eyes shone. He slapped the table and said, 'Comrade Huang Xiaoming, you've saved the best for last. This is exactly the report I was hoping for, not only factually accurate but also perfectly positioned. Xiaoming, do you know why I asked you to stay behind?'

I didn't dare speak. I shook my head. Mayor Liu laughed and said kindly, 'Xiaoming, there are more than seven hundred people in the

Municipal Government, and plenty of them have false degrees. I know exactly where those degrees come from. What I need are real scholars, with real abilities.'

Hesitantly I said, 'Mayor Liu, isn't your Number Two Department full of brilliant writers?'

Mayor Liu said earnestly, 'That's right, each one of them is a master of the formal style, but they have no ideas. I don't mean moral dogma, I mean creativity. That report from your office was written according to the formal style, but what you've given me here displays real creativity. You were the author of both reports, so I can tell you're adaptable! What do you think: would you be interested in a transfer to Number Two Department?'

I'd seen and heard plenty in my five years at the Research Office. 'Liberation of thought' had been a constant refrain since the beginning of the era of reform and opening up, which must mean that we'd previously been fettered by unliberated thought. There was nothing strange about hearing the words 'liberation of thought' from a standing vice-mayor who was accustomed to reading official documents. All leaders said things like that.

But now Mayor Liu was talking about creativity in addition to thought, and that made me see him in a new light. I've always believed that Chinese philosophy is more a collection of empirical observations about the world rather than a complete theoretical system of ideas and values. That's the reason why we feel so keenly that we are still a developing country in terms of economic growth, yet don't seem to realise that we're also a developing country in terms of politics, culture and society. The theme of 'thought' has become nothing more than a political tool, but 'creativity' is still something new.

Now, as Mayor Liu spoke of 'creativity', I felt a sudden 'snow sweeps the sky, changing the face of the world' sort of impulse, and nodded vigorously. I said, 'Mayor Liu, a nation always needs someone who could break off one of their own ribs and use it as a torch. Those sorts

31

of people are usually scholars. I hadn't expected a politician such as you would also have the courage to gaze up at the stars. It's not only a stroke of good fortune for the people of Dongzhou, it's also good fortune for myself!'

This was flattery, but it was sincere. A large part of what people live for is simply 'recognition'. Why else strive for success?

Thus, I was transferred to Number Two Department.

Having heard his reputation, I was worried about Department Head Zhao Zhong, so once I had moved into Number Two I played the role of the bonded servant, standing on his side in all things and exerting every effort to protect his interests.

As time passed, I discovered that under Zhao's leadership Number Two Department was not only entirely hostile to creative thought, but it was completely bogged down by his authoritarianism. Believing he had played a role in my transfer, Zhao Zhong acted like a benefactor and treated me – a scholar personally appreciated by Mayor Liu – as his personal secretary, his lackey even. He bossed me about and I passed the days swallowing bile. I lost not only the leisure that I'd had in the Research Office, but I also lost my dignity.

Zhao Zhong's most authoritarian treatment was his refusal to allow me to have any contact whatsoever with Mayor Liu, despite the fact that the responsibility for writing Liu's speeches still fell squarely to me. Zhao Zhong was clearly putting up defences. Though I made absolutely certain to keep myself under restraint, he knew perfectly well that if he gave me a chance to make frequent contact with the Mayor, then I would most likely become his replacement. I may have been a lowly department-level researcher, but if Mayor Liu wanted to change that 'researcher' to a 'head', he could do it as easily as blinking.

As it turned out, Mayor Liu seemed to forget me completely after my transfer. Everything I wrote went to Zhao Zhong, who took the materials I had laboured over and claimed the credit without so much as a nod of thanks. Intuition told me that Mayor Liu understood the situation, but why did he never call me in again? I couldn't solve that riddle, but one thing did attract my attention. When I first arrived at Number Two, Xu Zhitai, Ou Beibei and Zhu Dawei hardly gave me the time of day. At first I thought they were jealous of my high education level, and since I was department-level to boot, I was likely to get in the way of their own advancement. As time passed, however, I found I was wrong. They were giving me the cold shoulder because I was too close to Zhao Zhong. They thought I had been transferred in by Zhao Zhong, that I was Zhao's man.

I couldn't survive without friends, so I tried to get closer to my new colleagues. None of them responded to my warmth. My mood turned gloomy. Though I was not an animal, I was being stuffed into a cage to make up a number. The most meaningful thing that could be done was to resist Zhao Zhong. I needed to wage an underground war, create a unified front.

I decided Xu Zhitai was the person who wanted most to overthrow Zhao. He had long brooded over the ossified state of the department. Xu was without a doubt the most ideal of torches. All he needed was a match to set him alight. And that match could be me. Once I got Xu Zhitai burning I could rest assured that Ou Beibei and Zhu Dawei would be fuel to the fire.

Timing would be everything, however. Opportunity, strategic advantage and human support would need to be in place. We could ill afford to lose. We would have to bide our time for now.

My opportunity finally presented itself when Mayor Liu was abruptly transferred to be the Vice-Governor of Qingjiang Province. Zhao Zhong was on an overseas trip. The next standing vice-mayor would perhaps be Peng Guoliang, but no reliable news had been released. The opportunity might not come again. Xu Zhitai had long since grown tired of waiting.

I invented a pretext to invite him for a drink and discovered that liquid courage is especially efficient. Once he'd gotten a little in him,

Xu Zhitai started speaking his mind, and our discussion ranged widely. In the end we decided that, as far as politicians or conspirators were concerned, politics was the desire for and pursuit of power. It consisted of the tricks and techniques used to control others. But to a real statesman, politics was one method of leading a meaningful life, a method of protecting and serving people. Politics began with people of character. It is the conscience that calls to us. Since the days of Machiavelli, Western political theory has defined politics as a power game, but I believed that its beginning and end was ethics and conscience. Xu Zhitai brought up a question: seeing as Westerners had defined politics as a power game, how was one to master that game? Specifically, every civil servant wanted to find the way of officialdom, but what exactly was that 'Way'? We debated for a long time but neither could persuade the other. In the end we compromised. For now at least, the 'Way' was to get rid of Zhao Zhong.

We'd finally gotten to the crux of the matter. Xu Zhitai had long kept himself in check, and as soon as the topic changed to Zhao Zhong, his face took on a look of disgust and he started saying 'that hog' this and 'that hog' that. He was obviously desperate to get rid of Zhao and feared nothing except that I might sound the retreat. He had even higher hopes for what would happen afterwards. Xu had been vice-head of the department for ten years and his greatest wish was to become head.

I felt that the reason he had spent so much time treading water was that he didn't understand politics. Take this 'coup' as an example. If we drove off Zhao Zhong, the position of department head wouldn't necessarily be his. In fact it almost certainly wouldn't be. He wouldn't end up any better off than he was now. The most basic law of politics was obedience, and obedience was determined by degrees of power. If you tried to disobey the law of politics – spoken or unspoken law – you wouldn't get away with it. Politics required rules and was unworkable without them. How can the game be played if no one follows the rules?

Wearing your heart on your sleeve like Xu Zhitai was the last thing you wanted to do.

Xu Zhitai would make a fine weapon, however. I could use him to get rid of Zhao Zhong and worry about the rest later. All revolutions needed their martyrs. Of course, Xu believed that I was participating in the coup in order to become vice department head – that's how narrow his thinking was. I was actually worried he wouldn't think that way. He believed that an ally was the same as a brother. That's another thing he didn't understand.

You can't say the coup didn't come off smoothly, nor that the result wasn't as we desired. It progressed according to plan. Zhao Zhong was driven out and sent to work as a secretary for a few days in the Municipal Service Centre. He soon resigned.

After he was gone, Xu Zhitai's satisfaction lasted less than a month, ending when the new standing vice-mayor, Peng Guoliang, selected a new head, Yang Hengda, for the department.

I had heard about the initial struggle between Vice-Mayor Peng and Vice-Mayor Liu for the position of standing vice-mayor. Relations between the two had always been strained. Now Vice-Mayor Peng had gotten his wish, but Vice-Mayor Liu had been elevated even higher, to Vice-Governor of the province. Peng Guoliang was sure to be unhappy, and he had to have his own reasons for choosing the Old Leader's secretary to direct his own office.

Peng Guoliang was a previous chief of the Municipal Youth League of Dongzhou City and had made bureau-level by the age of twenty-nine. I'd never had much contact with him. I'd just heard that he was straightforward and deeply loyal to those who worked under him. They say that 'the lakeside pavilion gets the moonlight first'. Being near to power has its advantages. Working in the combined affairs departments of the Municipal Government was good in that you were constantly in the company of the mayors. Zhao Zhong used to block our access, and had ruined any chances I might have had with Liu Yihe. Though

I hadn't yet figured out Yang Hengda, he seemed broad-minded, as you might expect of someone who'd been the Old Leader's secretary, and was not simply treading water.

Hu Zhanfa, Peng's secretary, had been with him for five years. You could tell by the awe with which Zhu Dawei treated Hu Zhanfa that he was planning to become Hu's replacement. I'd never really thought about becoming secretary to a mayor, but given how little chance I had of becoming vice-head or head of the department, being a mayoral secretary was my last hope. Zhu Dawei and I each had our strengths. It would come down to which of us gained greater appreciation from Mayor Peng.

Zhu Dawei was obviously thinking to use Hu Zhanfa to 'save the country by roundabout means'. This was an ill-advised move from the start. No matter how close he was, Hu Zhanfa wasn't Mayor Peng himself, though of course he could put a very effective bug in his ear. There was no doubt that anyone who wanted to replace Hu Zhanfa in the lofty position of mayor's secretary would have to work both ends at once, and at the very least keep Hu Zhanfa from saying anything bad about him.

Zhu Dawei got a leg up on me by rendering a great service to Hu Zhanfa. Hu was studying for an in-office master's degree and was having a terrible time preparing for the foreign language test. Zhu Dawei took it for him, scoring a surprising eighty-seven per cent.

Even Ou Beibei's thoughts and efforts were bent on Mayor Peng. In recent days, there was a certain glow in her eyes when she looked at him.

When Yang Hengda first arrived he gave Ou Beibei, who had only ever had an administrative position in the department, a chance to try her pen. If you worked in Combined Affairs and couldn't write, you'd never get to advance. Ou Beibei didn't think she was a particularly bad writer and had always been troubled by the fact that she wasn't given writing assignments. Yang Hengda, not wanting to be accused of holding talent back, assigned Ou Beibei to write an article entitled

'A Year-to-date Summary of Export-Oriented Economy in Dongzhou, and Prediction of Rest-of-year Development Trends'.

Ou Beibei took the opportunity very seriously, hoping to show her talents in front of everyone, but when the article was done and handed to Yang Hengda, he actually started laughing, and couldn't help reading a bit out loud: 'Export-oriented economy in Dongzhou is developing like a tiger descending from the hills, with bamboo-bursting force.'

Zhu Dawei and I couldn't help laughing. Ou Beibei knew she'd become a joke, and her embarrassment turned to fury. She stalked up to Yang Hengda, snatched the article back and tore it to shreds.

Ou Beibei was still different from the female administrative workers in other offices, though. She could speak fluent English and was often taken by various vice-mayors to meet foreign guests, to the point where the director of foreign affairs had lodged a protest with Xiao Furen. When Vice-Mayor Peng became standing vice-mayor, he asked Ou Beibei to interpret every time he met a foreign guest. She'd more or less become his personal interpreter, and she seemed transformed because of it, particularly the light in her eyes when she looked at him. It was already leading to rumours.

The Fountain Pen

IF THE SERVANTS of the people are unable to think with their fountain pens, then what use do they have for the heads on their shoulders? The world might be conquered with the barrel of a gun, but it is ruled with the barrel of a pen, though you all seem to have forgotten what a pen is for.

Let me tell you: I am the embodiment of thought itself. I'm not for drawing idle circles. A great Western thinker once said that all human dignity arises from thought. Thought begins with a pen, and thus I am your dignity. But you seem to have forgotten me altogether.

Wake up! I am the torch that lights the way of your official career. Without my illumination, you'll be led astray! I'm not trying to frighten you. Just browse through history – history is written with a pen. You all want to go down in history, right? Well, without me you'll be denied the tiniest share of immortality! Those who cannot think with a pen are mediocre. Civil servants who cannot think with a pen will never become politicians, much less statesmen. Don't bother telling me you don't want to be a statesman or a politician, that you're happy being a regular old civil servant. I know you could never be satisfied with being ordinary. If you could, you'd have your choice of careers. Why insist on being a civil servant? Even as a plain civil servant, if you want to carry out your duties successfully, you will need to learn to think with a pen.

You are the executors of the nation's policies, you are promulgators, you are sowers, you are service personnel. It is not only official documents you author (state policy and law), but it is human relationships, it is righteousness, fairness and justice. Use your pens to write the beauty of human life, to scourge its ugliness and evil!

I am a ship that can take you to your ideal far shore. I am an ocean that can broaden your minds and hearts. I am a mountain that can elevate your souls. I am medicine that can cure the mediocrity of your heart. Don't you yearn for the heights? You won't be able to climb up there. You can only fly up like an eagle. Spread your wings. I am the pinions of your soul.

I should remind you, however, that if you don't have lofty aspirations you should never perch above the abyss like a bird. Soaring into the sky can bring joy to the heart, but it can also bring terror to the soul. Ambition is not enough in politics. You also need wisdom. It's a game of both heart and head.

You public servants who have lost the pen, how will you travel with me? Don't ask me whence you've come; I care only for where you are going. But I can tell you where I've come from. Remember well: I come from truth. I am at once the author of truth and its servant. I would never dare place myself above truth. Would you?

I will help you, of course. Don't think that I'm merely a pen. I tell you, my ancestors and all the rest of my kind are your mirrors. Don't you often say that history will be the measure? You could also say that the pen will be the measure, and if you regularly use me to inspect yourself, that self will not be lost.

Power will not only spin your head, but it will distort your soul. Public servants who have forgotten what a pen is are already standing at the edge of a cliff. The mountain across from you rears up into the clouds and a pyramid gleams at its peak. It lures you with its glow, but without me as your wings, don't even think of taking a single step forward! Do you think there's still time to pull up short? Just try it! That stone beside you has already tumbled down, and by the time you hear the echo it will already be shattered into dust. Do you want to plunge after that stone? Feel your heart and see if it is still beating!

Why are your expressions so cold? Because you have lost me, you have lost thought, lost your intelligence, lost your wisdom, and have nothing left but a cold heart. How can your flesh remain warm when your blood has cooled? If you aren't warm-blooded you'll never understand what is meant by 'the people'. I'll tell you, 'the people' consists of both you and the common folk. Collectively, you are fish and water, you are one. Don't ever think of yourselves as officials, otherwise 'the people' will no longer be whole.

It's been a while since you wrote the words 'the people', hasn't it? I mean since you wrote them with feeling, since you engraved them on your heart. Simply writing the words down is meaningless. Since you call yourselves the servants of the people, 'the people' must be the entirety of your soul!

The ambitious will say that 'soul' is simply a synonym for the body. Those who are numb of spirit will agree: the soul is simply another form of the body. True public servants would snort in disdain, because they use pens as scalpels, to cut open the body – how much more so the soul – under the shadowless light of the spirit. One thing is for sure: those ambitious people who have forgotten the people have no souls, and the souls of the numb of spirit will truly become their bodies. There's something I want to say to those who scorn the soul: they scorn it because they are prostrated before it in worship. But who is it who has created this scorn and this worship? It is those who abhor the pen, of course. They worship the soul because they themselves have none, and because they have no soul they naturally scorn it. If only you were to use a pen to illuminate these soulless bodies, they would instantly regain their original form, and that mad, pitiful ambition would vanish like smoke.

Do you know the difference between greatness and insignificance? It's no more than a pen; a single fountain pen. You may laugh at my presumption, but that's because you've never troubled to look to the stars. A nation needs someone to be looking to the stars. Maybe you did once. So which is more insignificant: political power or the stars? Your answer is perfectly obvious, and that's the lure of politics. Only now do I understand why you would enter politics: because politics is mesmerising. But politics is meant to be sought, not pursued. The world is divided into a near shore and a far shore. The near shore is reality, the far shore the ideal. Pursuers will never depart this shore, and only seekers can hoist the sail of idealism.

By what means do we seek? You will say 'thought', which is quite correct, but what do we use to think? Now we're talking about me again. Some take my meaning and are quietly exultant, thinking I will bring them glory. But they're dreaming. No matter how important I may be, I will never become a shortcut for those who pursue. I should warn you: there has never been such a thing as a shortcut to success. Why should you use me to think? Because I am the feeler, the root, that your own brain was too lazy to send forth. If you want to really think, you'll need to root yourself in the soil of the people's practical lives. The poet Ai Qing once said, 'Why are my eyes so oft full of tears? Because I love the land so deeply.' That's land, remember. Not mud, not marble, not floorboards, and definitely not the flooring of your sedan. 'Land' can mean many things, of course. It can mean fields, it can mean factories, it can mean schools and communities and oil fields and mines. Do you understand? It means real life, real experience! Only by standing on that kind of land can I send forth my feeler of thought into the soil and allow you public servants to experience real knowledge.

How long has it been since you stood upon the land? Do you remember the fragrance of the soil? I know that the ignorant and ambitious have long since forgotten. If your speeches never stray from the script, why not pick up the pen and try writing them yourself? I've already said a pen is not for marking circles or writing signatures. You're not superstars, so why pretend? Learn from practical experience, but think with the pen.

Remember what a great man once said: 'Leadership can be extended most broadly with the pen. What is written travels farthest, and the process of writing refines and concentrates the thoughts. The pen is the primary tool of leadership.'

Plainspoken words to be sure, but that's real insight. Who said that? It was the master architect of China's 'Reform and Opening Up'. He insisted time and again that the pen is the primary instrument of leadership, one that would have to be mastered in order to lead one's comrades. I'll tell you, wielding the pen is not a technical issue, but rather a basic principle of leadership, and a crucial influence upon peace and prosperity. Don't think I'm making too much of this. The lessons of history should be heeded. Grasping power means grasping a pen. The authoring of essays has long been known as 'the heart of statecraft, and the work of immortality'.

Throughout history, around the world, great statesmen have always taken care to cultivate their literacy. Ancient political documents bore strict professional demands. What were those demands? It was required that an official with a particular function must personally author all documents connected to that function. No ghostwriting or cheating would be brooked. It would result at least in demotion, possibly in further punishment.

Use the pen to unearth the deepest treasures of your heart. The thoughts of one can influence the many, and the thoughts of the many can influence a nation, or even the world.

Now you see what the way of politics is, don't you? It's simply the way of the pen. Never mind the black cap of office. I am your true crown. But not everyone can wield this crown. They say that whoever has popular support has the realm, and it is those who have thought that have popular support! I am the incarnation of thought. Stop raising up your monuments. I am already in your hand!

It's a shame that I and my brethren have been locked so long within your drawer. Those who have forgotten us are now seated sanctimoniously at office desks, in conference rooms, on sofas, in cars. They speak endless false words and spew forth empty phrases, and don't realise that in losing their pens they have lost their lives. You're laughing once again at my self-importance . . .

They are still breathing, to be sure, but life is more than just breathing. I have never drawn breath, yet I live forever.

Number Two Department, Junior Department-Level Researcher, Ou Beibei

IN *DREAM OF the Red Chamber*, Jia Baoyu says, 'Girls are in essence pure as water, and men are in essence muddled as mud. When I see a girl I feel light and refreshed. When I see a boy I feel repulsed and disgusted.'

Girls are made of water so that they might wash the world clean. I don't actually like Jia Baoyu's words. Comparing women to water makes their virtue seem too easy. I think women are made of jade. At least, beautiful women are made of jade, and beautiful civil servants are the most costly and exquisite jades of all. Jades like those concentrate the essences of heaven and earth, of the sun and the moon. Firm yet mellow, delicate yet wise, pure and retiring, enticing and beautiful.

I am known as Ou Beibei but my proper name is Feng Xinyu, *yu* for jade, stone of the spirits, of fate. After five years of marriage, however, my husband hasn't given me so much as a pebble. He's caught up in his work all day long. Yet for all his scurrying, he's only a director-level section member in the Foreign Investment Bureau office. Watching other women's husbands rise in the world while my own can barely manage to hold his head up – how can I be content as a wife? If I were just an ordinary person that would be one thing, but I was an outstanding student at the Language Academy and the one all the boys kept an eye on, and now I am the most beautiful civil servant in the Municipal Government. How can a woman like me be married to a mere director-level section member? It's demeaning!

Wang Chaoquan started out quite promising. During military training at college he hit the target every time and even the drillmaster was impressed. He told him that if he joined the army he could be a general. Chaoquan was head of the class all four years of college, the best in every subject. He was a miracle student, and what's more, he wrote wonderful poems that were often published in the school paper. He began pursuing me our sophomore year and his love poems were awfully sentimental. One in particular I remember perfectly. It started, 'My dear, I am vexed at my inability to press you in my arms, your cherry lips have brought me magic, so let me love you, embrace you, kiss you!' What kind of poem is that? It's barefaced seduction! I just don't understand how, if he can pursue a woman so single-mindedly, he is still so hopeless at forwarding his career.

He speaks three foreign languages fluently: English, Russian and German. German isn't spoken by more than a handful of people in the Dongzhou Government. Even the Foreign Affairs Office has no qualified German interpreters. This alone has let him accompany municipal and department leaders on several trips to Germany. Anyone else would have used the opportunity to get closer to the leaders, but he doesn't know how to turn these things to his advantage.

I've always wondered if he once took a knock to the head that somehow rendered him unfit for officialdom. Never mind official rank, if you spend all that time around consuls and commercial counsellors and get friendly with them, you can leave the service and start a commercial empire based on your foreign investment contacts. But Chaoquan seems to have no interest in money whatsoever. I don't know what he spends his days thinking about, either. When other people read books, they read *Romance of the Three Kingdoms*, *On Politics* or *Thick Black Theory* – things that at least might have some benefit to your political career. But he's always got his nose in something like *A History of the KGB*, or *Delta Force: Anti-Terrorism Unit*, *The Future of the War on Terror*, *A History of Global Anti-Drug Law* or *Black Triangle*. We can't even agree on TV shows to watch. I like soaps and romances and he likes mysteries and thrillers, buying complete sets of *James Bond*, *Mission Impossible* or *Infernal Affairs*. It's as though he works in the Public Security Bureau, not the investment promotion one. It looks like I'm bound to become a bitter old woman. I won't let that happen!

It's not that I no longer feel love. I am in love, just not with my husband. The love I feel, I must keep buried in my heart. The one I love is so lofty I hardly dare look at him. I can only gaze upon him from a distance. I want to scald him, to freeze him, to warm him. I want to kiss his heart, listen to its beating. In my own heart I repeat a line of poetry: 'My dearest, don't be angry. I only wish to sleep next to you!'

This is the most physical of poetry, and my physical body is all I have. Why are there people in this world who only love the soul and not the body? The soul is not to be loved, it is only to be praised. Why are we forced to choose between love and praise? Why do they almost seem opposed to one another?

I look forward most of all to being his interpreter. He never asks for an interpreter from the Foreign Affairs Office. Every time he meets foreign guests he requests me as his personal interpreter. Those are the times that I am happiest, because then I am closest to him. He is like a grand mountain and I am a limpid spring at the foot of that mountain. What a perfect pair we make! But I cannot even call his name. I can only think to myself, Mayor, why can't you cast a single tender gaze at me? Are you afraid I'll seduce you? But I do want to seduce you! Don't you love the soul and detest the body? Well, let's see if I can use my body to seduce your soul!

You're no fool, Mayor Liu. You ought to know. My body is a ship upon which you may explore. It is a bed where you may rest. It is a desk where you may work. My existence is for your life. I want to use existence to slip inside you, to make you think about existence, need existence, love existence. And yet you disregard existence. You disregard *my* existence. Though I send you glances as inviting as the summer sky, you seem to look right through me.

A mayor needs the love of his people, but he needs the love of a woman even more. I want to be his woman. What's so wrong about that? I know why you're laughing at me. It's because I love a mayor, not a man, right?

I am a swan, not a toad, though there is a toad among us: Zhao Zhong, head of Number Two Department. That damned hog, fat as a ball and rolling around the office all day long with a bellyful of malice. He dares have designs on me! A mere department head, a cringing dog that wags its tail and fawns over Mayor Liu – you dare try your luck with me?

I can't bear him, particularly when he comes over all smiles, like sticky cow manure crushing a flower!

The two of us were alone in the office one day and he saw his chance, walking over with a book of jokes written in the Qing Dynasty, saying how terribly funny it was, and starting to read without so much as a by-your-leave:

'An official was promoted, and said to his wife, "My position is now greater." His wife said, "That being so, I wonder if *that* has become greater?" He replied, "Naturally so." They busied themselves, and the wife complained that he was as small as before. He said, "It is much larger, but you cannot feel it." She asked, "Why can't I feel it?" He answered, "When a man is promoted, is his wife not elevated with him? Mine has grown larger; yours has grown larger as well."'

Isn't that sexual harassment? And if it were true that it did get bigger with promotion, well, Liu Yihe is a mayor and Zhao Zhong you're only a department head, so he must be plenty bigger than you!

No wonder when corrupt officials are exposed they usually turn out to have a crowd of mistresses. If *that* gets bigger along with promotion, but their mistresses grow larger right along with them, of course those officials would never be satisfied! It ought to be that the mistresses get progressively smaller, otherwise the corrupt officials would start abandoning their loosening mistresses!

Zhao Zhong could tell I wasn't amused, and read another one.

'A husband and wife had both grown quite fat, and every time they were together their bellies got in the way. An old woman told them, "I'll tell you a trick. Try going in from the rear." The couple tried it, and found it was quite pleasurable. The next day they asked the woman, "Where did you learn that trick you told us?" Her answer was, "From watching dogs and bitches."'

This joke I found tremendously funny, because Zhao Zhong's wife is as fat as he is.

My love for Mayor Liu was stymied when he was promoted to Vice-Governor of Qingjiang Province. A vice-mayor was already high enough. A vice-governor was way out of my reach.

Peng Guoliang, the youngest member of the Municipal Party Committee, stepped up as standing vice-mayor. I'd always had a good impression of Peng Guoliang since he, like Liu, asked me to be his interpreter when meeting foreign guests rather than using the Foreign Affairs Office. He was different than Mayor Liu in one sense though: he never avoided my gaze. Peng Guoliang was younger and more handsome than Mayor Liu, and my heart began to stir once more.

Then came the coup in Number Two Department. Xu Zhitai and Huang Xiaoming gave fatty Zhao the shove and we got a new department head, Yang Hengda. Yang gave Xu all the overseas trips and made Huang Xiaoming responsible for all articles and materials. What's more, he let Huang deliver them to Mayor Peng in person. At first I couldn't understand what Yang Hengda was doing. Then I realised he was aware that Xu and Huang had teamed up to dispose of Zhao Zhong. They couldn't be allowed to continue their alliance. It was best that they be divided.

Zhu Dawei and I had our opportunities, of course, though we weren't put in charge of any major projects. But I couldn't complain about that. I've always thought the ability to write was a matter of natural talent. I don't have that talent and neither does Zhu Dawei. When I arrived at the department, like him I dreamed of becoming secretary to a mayor, but male mayors were never given female secretaries. They said it was to avoid unhealthy relationships.

Of the mayor and nine vice-mayors, only one was female, served by Number Four Department. She was in charge of all municipal organs of public security – hardly prestigious work – but if I became her secretary, I could possibly go from there to become director of the political arm of the municipal Public Security Bureau. There were no women working in Number Four Department and the term of the present secretary was nearly up. The female vice-mayor needed a new secretary, selected from the staff in all combined affairs departments. I was the most likely choice, and the female vice-mayor liked me, but then someone began talking behind my back, saying I was too pretty and she would look poor by comparison. The vice-mayor really was average looking, though she had a fine, imposing air. But I had too many competitors. My heaven-sent opportunity was snatched up by a girl from Number Five Department. My opportunity to become a mayor's secretary was lost because of my beauty. Is beauty a sin?

That was the end of my opportunities. I couldn't count on my husband, much less my parents. I could only rely on myself. I had two major resources. The first was my beauty, the second was my foreign language abilities, and if these two advantages were to change my future, it would need to be by means of love.

I would never have dreamed that my love would waver between wealth and power.

It began with a trip to burn incense at Ci'en Temple, on the West Mountain.

Tales of the efficacy of the Mother Goddess of Ci'en Temple had been making the rounds of public citizens and civil servants. The stories were eerie: no matter what you asked for, you would get it, so long as you asked sincerely.

At first I didn't believe them, but Huang Xiaoming said his brother's son, a poor student, had gone with his family before the high school entrance exams to burn incense at the temple. Sure enough, he got an excellent score and was admitted to a provincial-level experimental high school, the best in Qingjiang Province.

I hadn't had any luck in my career for years. If I went to Ci'en Temple to make a wish, perhaps that would change. So on a brilliant, windy Sunday I went.

Ci'en Temple is surrounded by looming peaks and deep gulches, twisted pines and eerie rocks. The temple buildings are set off by white clouds and green water, and the winding staircase threads enchantingly through forests and past cliffs.

Along the highway there were at least twenty or thirty billboards advertising the Mother Goddess of West Mountain. The crowd that had come to burn incense formed a line a kilometre in length and it was a good while before I had my turn. Just as I was about to light my incense, someone slapped me on the shoulder and I turned to see a fat, shaven figure wearing an old-style robe and handmade cloth shoes on his feet, holding a string of sandalwood prayer beads and grinning at me.

At first I didn't recognise him. He didn't seem like a boss, nor did he seem like a monk. When I got a good look, I was stunned. It was Zhao Zhong!

I asked involuntarily, 'Department Head Zhao, what are you doing here? Have you come to make a wish?'

Zhao Zhong pulled me aside and said, 'Beibei, fate brings us together again. Why don't we go down the mountain and I'll treat you to dinner, then I'll tell what wish I made.'

Flustered, I followed him and discovered to my surprise that he was driving a Benz 600. Stunned, I said, 'Not bad, Zhao! How'd you get rich so quick?'

Zhao put his hands together and said in a false voice, 'Amitabha, my job is the daily accumulation of good karma, and the deliverance of souls from torment.' He motioned me into the car.

The Benz carried us out of the mountains. I asked him directly, 'They say all business is dirty business. You wouldn't be cheating the devout, would you?'

He answered in tones of self-satisfaction, 'Beibei, Chinese culture has little to say about good and evil. It's all about success and failure. If you succeed, that's good. If you fail, that's evil.'

Seeing Zhao's face shining with satisfaction and thinking back to his crestfallen appearance as he was driven out of the Municipal Government, I was filled with emotion. I decided I would learn from Zhao Zhong, and see if I couldn't replicate just a bit of his success.

He took me to dinner at Jinchongcao, Dongzhou's most famous restaurant for bird's nest, shark fin and abalone. Though he kept his hands to himself during the meal, I could see he'd never entirely given up hope. He drew out a long red box and opened it to reveal an exquisite jade necklace with a gilded Guanyin Buddha. It filled me with longing.

Zhao Zhong insisted on hanging it around my neck and said in tones of the deepest sincerity, 'Beibei, I bought you this present six months ago. I knew then we have a common destiny, and that one day I would hang it around your neck. And look, my wish has come true.'

Zhao Zhong had truly never abandoned his plans for me. For some reason I'd always seen him as an ugly toad, hoping for a mouthful of swan's meat, but perhaps frogs really could become princes. After I'd heard him expound on his theory and philosophy of running temples, I practically worshipped him, but I still gently and tactfully rejected his present. I couldn't let him in so quickly. I would play him out on a long line.

The biggest revelation that came from my chance encounter with Zhao Zhong was the fact that most people who worship Buddha do not believe in Buddhism but are simply hoping to further their own interests. Zhao Zhong was getting rich from people's willingness to turn to Buddhism for the things they couldn't get by themselves. All the stories of the efficacy of the Mother Goddess were fabricated by him as part of his business strategy. Even the abbot of the temple was hired by him, with a salary. He was the CEO of Ci'en Temple Ltd.

Zhao's success lay in his grasp of timing and opportunity, his ability to advance with the times, to hold firm while all else is in flux. In a world as changeable as ours, the only thing I see remaining stable is human greed. Greed knows no limits. It is eternal and unchangeable. But how to turn that greed into reality, a reality of success and fame?

I attended a department-level cadre training session at the Municipal Administrative Academy. A leader of the Academy spoke at the start of the session, and that was the first time I beheld the glorious visage of Peng Guoliang's wife, Zhang Peifen. She was Vice-President of the Academy. My reaction can be summed up in one word: ugly! It was an immeasurable boost to my confidence.

When I returned to the office from the training session, Hu Zhanfa gave me a job: go to Mayor Peng's office and help him arrange some photographs. It was a heaven-sent opportunity, and my heart immediately started thumping.

My life had always resembled a pool of stagnant water, without the slightest ripples. I was determined to hurl a stone into its centre, to make myself known. I had neither the ambition nor the ability to save the world, but I could save one man. I didn't mean Wang Chaoquan, of course. He was beyond saving. Nor did I mean Mayor Liu, as he was already out of my reach. I wasn't sure if it might include Zhao Zhong or not, but I was saving one man for sure, and that was Peng Guoliang. I would free him from his hideous wife, and use my love to make him understand that there is a power in this world that can call forth his tears, and that power was my love.

When I entered his office, he was sitting on the sofa, distracted by a photograph in his hand. There were several drawers' worth of photographs on the coffee table in front of him, and several new photo albums to one side. It appeared that my task would be to put the photos in the photo albums. I respectfully called to him. 'Mayor Peng!'

He awoke from his memories, a sweet smile on his face. When he saw me, his eyes lit up amiably and he asked me to sit, displaying none of a mayor's usual severity towards his underlings.

I was embarrassed by the seductiveness of his gaze, but I steeled myself and sat down next to him, asking, 'Mayor Peng, what photographs have got you so distracted? Are they of an old lover?'

Had it been Mayor Liu, I would never have dared flirt like this.

'Beibei, do you know what lovers signify?' asked Mayor Peng, his eyes dancing. 'I think real love only exists between lovers. Marriage is only a formality; any love that is limited by rules, responsibility and duty isn't true love.'

My dream was to become a famous consort. Even if I should be hanged at Maweipo like Yang Guifei, it would be worth it. So I looked directly at him and said, 'A moment can be the point of a knife!'

Mayor Peng chuckled. 'I like knife points! I've been waiting for the point of a knife for a long time, Beibei. Do you have the courage to be that knife point?'

This was bald provocation. Since you like knife points, I thought, why don't I give you a prick and see if you bleed?

'Mayor Peng,' I said, drawing near him boldly. 'Aren't you afraid of being bitten by a snake?'

'Beibei,' he answered, breathing heavily, 'is it the snake of the Garden of Eden? Don't forget, it was that snake that taught us to eat of the forbidden fruit. Be my forbidden fruit, I can't wait any longer!'

Then he pressed me to him, and I became his forbidden fruit. I had finally taken the first step towards realising my dream of becoming empress, and it thrilled me. I longed for the depths, the depths of love, to plunge into the depths of night, until I reached Peng Guoliang's heart. I wanted to sleep, rise and live within his heart, to kiss his heart every day.

Since I ran into Zhao Zhong at Ci'en Temple, the fatty won't leave me alone. He asks me to dinner at regular intervals, giving me a salon gift certificate one day, a Chanel handbag the next, sparing no expense. Two days ago, he treated me to dinner and told me some surprising news: at the end of the year, Liu Yihe will be replacing the old mayor. He is going to be appointed Vice-Secretary of the Municipal Party Committee, and become acting mayor.

If Liu Yihe becomes Mayor of Dongzhou, Peng Guoliang's position as a standing vice-mayor might no longer be safe. Everyone knows they don't get on. And if as a result Peng is transferred to another city, my empress dreams will be extinguished before they've barely begun.

There's nothing like a few drinks when you're feeling glum. Zhao Zhong was well aware of how his news had affected my mood, and was getting me drunk. In fact, I got completely blotto. Zhao Zhong took me to his car. I told him to take me home. He ignored me completely and drove the Benz to the Kempinski Hotel, where he'd booked a room in advance, and took me straight into the elevator.

The moment we were in the room, Zhao rushed to embrace me and carry me to the double bed, saying all the while, 'Beibei, I've wanted you for so long!'

I knew perfectly well that Zhao Zhong had long ago planned out tonight's dinner. I had drunk too much and had no strength to resist. Now that I knew that Liu Yihe would return to Dongzhou as mayor, I had no reason to resist either, because if Liu Yihe returned it was almost certain that Peng Guoliang would be transferred. Only Zhao Zhong could keep this from being a complete loss, as his relations with Liu Yihe meant that being with him would enable me to realise my dreams of becoming empress, or at least a respectable shopkeeper.

While my mind was racing, Zhao Zhong had rushed to undress me, but to my absolute surprise, after going through strenuous motions, that thing of his stayed limp as a dough stick. Being unable to perform with a woman as pure and ravishing as me – it was nothing less than an insult!

Incensed, my mind began to clear, and as I pulled on my clothes I said to him scornfully, 'Zhao Zhong, you call yourself a man?!' Then I went out, slamming the door behind me. It was after midnight when I left the hotel.

I followed the sidewalk aimlessly, feeling wretched. What was I . . . I wanted to live like an empress, I had the capability of living like an empress, but I was living like a prostitute. Cars streamed along Liberation Avenue, their lights cutting swathes through the fog, and people stood scattered along the roadside. I took a closer look at the made-up women on display, some standing solitary, some in groups of two or three. Sometimes a car would pull over and hail them, and I realised that they were what men called 'wild chickens'.

A black Audi pulled up beside me and a man rolled down the window and asked me how much for a night. A sense of humiliation washed over me and I hurried to flag a taxi.

Number Two Department, Director-Level Section Member, Zhu Dawei

SOMETIMES I THINK that if my spirit could skitter around the office building like a rat, visiting all the leaders of the Municipal Government, I would learn all manner of interesting things. If I'm not permitted to be a wolf, I could at least be a rat.

Even so, I would be a rat only in spirit.

Don't think that I never aspired to anything greater than rathood. But if you want to be a dragon, you must first learn to pass, rat-like, through the dark places. Actually, I once wanted to be neither a dragon nor a rat, but a fox. I think there are two kinds of people in the world: foxes who strut about in the company of tigers, and foxes who merely wish they knew a tiger. Some people, once they become officials and gain some authority, believe that they've become tigers or dragons. That's bullshit! The actual tiger or dragon is official position, and official power. Anyone who achieves position and power is actually only a fox in the guise of the tiger or dragon. Even a rat, once in the seat of power, can command the tiger's might, the way a clod of mud will sparkle brilliantly if gilded.

I was born in the year of the rat and because my spirit often goes wandering around the building while I'm working, my girlfriend gave me the nickname 'Rat'. She's called Shang Xiaoqiong, and has worked for the Provincial Disciplinary Committee for six years. Her job is catching crooked officials, so I gave her the nickname 'Cat', and that's what we usually call each other: Cat and Rat.

I came to work at the Municipal Government in pursuit of a grand career. In college I'd dreamed of becoming mayor or governor, creating wealth and happiness for the common folk, but my father told me that real success consisted only of winning respect from this world of power brokers. Without a position of respect, no one would take you seriously, and you would have to live by taking your hints from the power brokers. My father was in politics for nearly twenty years, and while he never made a name for himself, he learned a few things, and one thing he said stuck with me: a person without social status would never have 'nobility'.

Though his judgement was extreme, it spoke precisely to the world as I saw it. I felt in my bones that your social status was equated with your worth as a human being. That was beyond doubt. My father was never given the chance to shine, though he was extremely capable. This became clear after he left the Municipal Committee and single-handedly created the greatest real estate group in Dongzhou. Though he was unstoppable in business, he never forgot his dreams of politics, and before I'd even graduated from college, he was already pulling strings and concocting schemes to get me into the Municipal Government. At first he considered Number One Department, Combined Affairs, but the mayor, once the second part of his term was up, would become director of the Municipal People's Consultative Conference, and the one most likely to replace him would be Liu Yihe, then a standing vice-mayor. After nearly twenty years in politics, my father had great faith in his own judgement, so I went to Number Two Department, which served Vice-Mayor Liu directly.

My father's final exhortation was that if I wanted a future in officialdom, I would need to follow the right man. When my father was head of the real estate department of the Municipal Committee, he had followed the wrong man. He'd been thick with the vice-director but had offended the number one, and nothing went right for him after that. What I learned from his experience was that if you wanted to be a number one you had to follow a number one.

How to follow, exactly?

That was up to me.

There were only two 'number ones' I could follow in the Municipal Government at the time. One was Zhao Zhong, Department Head, and the other was Xiao Furen, Deputy Chief Secretary and Director of the Municipal Government. As soon as I arrived, I noticed the unusual relationship between Department Head Zhao and Mayor Liu – even Director Xiao had to bow to Zhao – but I never did figure out the exact nature of that relationship. I was lowest ranked and least experienced in the department, and I knew quite well that remedying that would take time. But I was in a hurry, and not everyone got ahead by waiting. Those who could make their own way were rare, but they went up like rockets. I knew there was some trick to it, though I didn't yet know what. I even wished I were a tapeworm in a leader's gut, so that I could learn all the different tricks people used to get ahead and employ them myself. My future would be guaranteed.

For the time being, however, I would have to be Zhao Zhong's tapeworm. I would first learn how he thought, then ingratiate myself with him and obtain more opportunities to improve myself. Zhao believed that one's talent corresponded to one's official grade: the higher the grade, the greater the talent. In Number Two, Zhao Zhong's grade was highest, and he therefore naturally believed himself to be the most talented. But since I'd arrived, I'd never once seen him write a document. Important materials were all written by Vice Department Head Xu Zhitai and Department-Level Researcher Huang Xiaoming. Huang was the only section member in the Municipal Government with a master's degree and the more theoretical assignments were all his to write. Even the most insignificant meeting minutes were more often given to Junior Department-Level Researcher Ou Beibei than to me, and her job was mostly administrative.

I became the most idle member of Number Two Department. Luckily the Deputy Chief Secretary who corresponded to Mayor Liu was Xiao Furen, and every time Xiao Furen was asked to arrange some business or attend a meeting on behalf of Mayor Liu, he would bring me along. I practically became Director Xiao's secretary. Zhao Zhong might have looked down his nose at Director Xiao, but my father constantly urged me to serve him well because he would have a crucial influence on my future. After a period of observation, I noticed that Director Xiao's greatest interest was in chess, so I secretly began to study the game. This plan paid off. Not only was I Director Xiao's secretary in everything but name, but I also became his favourite chess partner. This position brought me no small political advantage.

I discovered that when everyone is eager to cross the river and pan for gold, I could do better by building a bridge and charging them a toll than I could by joining them. I might have no greater role in the department than writing up the minutes of meetings – and only deputy chief secretary-level meetings at that – but if I had the chance to write something important, I know I could compare with Xu Zhitai or Huang Xiaoming. That kind of formalistic writing has a pattern. All you need is to grasp your leader's point of view and have a sense of how the political winds are blowing, and then address the problems your leader cares about. It never fails.

Mayor Liu's impending departure meant a change of dynasty was coming to Number Two Department. Zhao Zhong's visa to Japan arrived just as Mayor Liu was about to change jobs, and that night he – now Vice-Governor Liu – booked a private room at Beautiful World and treated everyone in the department to dinner to thank them for their hard work in his service.

That was the first time I met Mayor Liu face to face. During dinner he patiently enquired after me. I'd prepared for this beforehand. It was a rare opportunity. I would use it to create a deep impression, or at least to make him realise that a dragon had been crouching by his side all this time, and make him wonder what exactly Zhao Zhong was up to. I was determined to make the damned hog look bad.

Mayor Liu asked me about my education, and I answered that I'd studied politics. His eyes brightened, and he asked me in careful tones whether I might recommend a couple of classic works on politics to him. The blood began to rush through my body. I thought to myself that I had him now. Mayor Liu, you're in a high position but I'll bet you don't have time to read, particularly the classics. I, on the other hand, had read a whole series of political classics while I was at university.

I feigned modesty. 'Governor Liu, you've got a master's in law. You must have read Aristotle's *Politics*.'

He answered frankly, 'You overestimate me, Dawei. My master's was limited to reading Marxism. I learned neither law nor politics. To tell you the truth, I haven't read a single one of Aristotle's books.'

I felt a deep respect for Mayor Liu's confidence. Huang Xiaoming interrupted, saying, 'The core of Aristotle's political thinking is the "doctrine of the mean".'

Mayor Liu asked with interest, 'Do you mean Aristotle and Confucius had the same idea?'

I was afraid Huang Xiaoming would squeeze me out of the conversation so I stepped in hurriedly. 'They're not quite the same theory. Aristotle's "doctrine of the mean" meant finding a power that could mediate between the rich and the poor in order to maintain social stability. That was the middle class. Aristotle believed that the middle class neither had designs on other people's wealth, as the poor did, nor aroused the jealousy of those less fortunate, as the rich did. They lived calm lives, with few worries and healthy morals, and were thus ideal intermediaries between rich and poor.'

Mayor Liu said thoughtfully, 'Aristotle's theories are worth consulting as we build a socialist market economy! Dawei, can you recommend a slightly more practical book on politics?'

From his expression, it seemed to be a sincere question, not a test, so I gathered my courage and said, 'The most practical of all is Machiavelli's *The Prince*.'

Intrigued, Mayor Liu asked, 'What's practical about it?'

I had recommended that book both to show off my own political acumen, and even more to get a sense of Mayor Liu's political character. I answered, 'Because *The Prince* is the most honest portrayal of the specific techniques of political struggle.'

Mayor Liu suddenly became very serious. 'That sounds practical indeed. Tell us more.'

Everyone's ears had perked up. Even Huang Xiaoming, with his theoretical background, wore a look of intent curiosity.

I began my display. 'Machiavelli notes that there is only one goal in politics: victory. He believes that all means are acceptable in its pursuit, and if a prince is to protect his power, he must be capable of immoral acts. In attacking others, for example, one must do enough damage that one no longer has to worry about a counter-attack. Another example: evil acts should be committed once and for all, while good acts should be drawn out over time. He also reminds us that the prince should be fox-like in his ability to sniff out traps, but lion-like in projecting his authority. He gets right to the heart of the matter: "It is better to be feared than loved . . . for love is preserved by the link of obligation which, owing to the baseness of men, is broken at every opportunity for their advantage; but fear preserves you by a dread of punishment which never fails."'

Before I'd finished, Zhao Zhong broke in excitedly. 'Brilliantly incisive! This Machiavelli was a true connoisseur of politics!'

The normally mild Mayor Liu turned severe. 'So, Zhao Zhong, you support Machiavelli's point of view? Don't forget historical context when you're reading. Machiavelli lived in Florence at a time when the Italian peninsula had long been divided between five major powers: Milan, Venice, Florence, the Vatican and Naples. There were many smaller city-states and duchies besides, all of them embroiled in war, contending for supremacy, none of them able to achieve their goal of unifying Italy without greater political power. Considering this long-term destructive state of affairs, Machiavelli felt that only a concentrated centre of power would be capable of quelling internal chaos and fending off external attack, thereby preserving national sovereignty and national dignity. But Machiavelli was most in favour of a republican system, and his political career was tightly linked to the Republic of Florence. While working in the government of the Republic of Florence, he was often ordered to go abroad. As the ambassador of a wealthy commercial nation lacking the strength to protect itself against bullying from its more powerful neighbours, he felt deeply the humiliation of a divided fatherland. It was under these conditions that Machiavelli wrote *The Prince*. He hoped that the prince would be able to use strong centralised power to stave off foreign aggression and achieve unification of Italy. Now look at you, Zhao Zhong, treating this great political thinker as a scheming co-conspirator . . . Zhao Zhong, you ought to read the original, and remember that your political point of view is the basis for your world view.'

Zhao Zhong looked mortified at Mayor Liu's scolding, which satisfied me even more. Mayor Liu was obviously a great reader of the classics and deeply familiar with *The Prince*. I felt a bit abashed at having showed off in front of him, but luckily Ou Beibei picked up the thread of conversation. She'd been distracted and thoughtful all night, looking at Mayor Liu with eyes full of emotion. You wouldn't have noticed it unless you looked carefully, but the fact that I was in the midst of a love affair myself made me more observant. Cat often looked at me that same way. Inwardly, I sniggered at Ou Beibei's outsized ambition.

She had already picked up the karaoke microphone and was singing 'Seeing Off the Red Army' for Mayor Liu.

Moved, everyone else began to join in. As she sang, Ou Beibei didn't look at the screen, but fixed her gaze on Mayor Liu, and as she sang 'sea-deep feelings won't be forgot, oh Red Army, the revolution is victorious, come home soon,' tears rose up in her eyes. She sang as if she were bidding a lover farewell instead of the Red Army. That confused me. Could Ou Beibei actually . . . But how could that be?

Dinner concluded with a rendition of 'Camel Bell' by Xu Zhitai. As we left Beautiful World the moon had just reached the tops of the willow trees, and for some reason I felt a melancholy akin to lines from a favourite poem, 'on the balcony, the flute sounds thin, a swing in the yard, the night is deep'. I couldn't be bothered retrieving my bicycle from the Municipal Government compound, though it was just next door. I didn't take a taxi either. I wanted to walk in the night. My father was wealthy enough that I could have driven a Benz home from the office, but the mayor and vice-mayors only had Audis, and it would be disastrous for me to arrive in a Benz.

I like the night. As the darkness of night approaches, I feel a pleasure of escape perhaps related to my being born in the year of the rat. You never see a rat strolling down the street in broad daylight. That would be dangerous. Darkness gives me a sense of security, but I'm not willing to simply hide in the darkness, because I also need stimulation. The most pleasurable stimulation is terror, of course, and nothing is more terrifying than being on the street in daylight, because anyone crossing the street with their eyes closed is guaranteed to die in a pool of blood. If that's true for people, how much more so is it for an 'office rat' like me?

As I walked, lost in thought, my mobile phone rang. It was Cat.

The only time I could extricate myself from my rat alter ego's thoughts and become a human again was when I heard Cat's voice or saw her in person. That's what attracted me to her. Sometimes I'd even wonder: when such a beautiful woman comes face to face with corrupt officials, do they think improper thoughts? Perhaps her beauty might even encourage those officials to confess their crimes.

At any rate, she might only be a girl in her twenties, but she's participated in many high-profile anti-corruption cases and she says when she meets these officials, she feels like a cat facing a mouse. I hadn't seen Cat for more than a week and thought she might be missing me, wanting me to take her out to a disco or to a bar. She likes dancing, or going for a drink. She may be a real beauty, but she drinks booze like it's water.

I had just greeted her with a warm 'Xiong!' when she interrupted to tell me that she'd been assigned to a case in Changshan. Curious, I asked her what the case was, and she said it was secret, but Secretary Qi was leading the team herself and her whole office was involved. She told me to be good since she might be gone for a couple of weeks, then blew me a kiss and hung up.

I stood there dumbly, shaking my head and thinking that if Secretary Qi Xiuying were leading the team herself then it wasn't only a big case, but also one with far-reaching consequences, likely to shake Changshan City. Qi Xiuying might have been Secretary of the Qingjiang Provincial Disciplinary Committee for less than a year, but she had already unseated corrupt mayoral-level officials from three different cities, and the name 'Qi Xiuying' was making officials across the province uneasy. She had a nickname too. She was known as the 'Female Bao Gong' after the Song Dynasty official who executed members of his own family in his fight against corruption and even dared to indict the emperor's relatives too.

After that farewell dinner with Mayor Liu and once Zhao Zhong had left for Japan, Xu Zhitai could restrain himself no longer.

In the open letter he presented to us all, which was to be sent to the Municipal Party Organisation, the three characters 'Huang Xiaoming' were signed in a strong hand. Ou Beibei's name was in a much weaker one, as though she were hesitating even as she signed. To be honest, I wasn't enthusiastic about participating, because even if we succeeded it could bring me no advantage. A successful coup wouldn't result in promotion, and a failed coup didn't bear imagining.

When Xu Zhitai asked me to sign, I said I had to visit the restroom, and straightaway called my father's mobile phone and explained the situation. I often told him the news from the office, and he had a good sense of what went on in Number Two Department and the whole Municipal Government. He told me to go immediately to Xiao Furen and report on the situation. I felt much better.

I turned left out of the restroom and passed two doors to Xiao Furen's office. I hurried inside and found him reading documents. When he saw me coming in all flustered, he knew something must be going on, and motioned me towards a chair in front of his desk. I collapsed into it then hesitated. Wasn't I about to sell out my friends and colleagues? If Xu Zhitai, Huang Xiaoming or Ou Beibei found out, how could I stay in the department?

Xiao Furen wasn't Director of the Municipal Government for nothing. He saw through me right away. He took a sip of tea, smiled, and said, 'Dawei, Mayor Liu has gone to the provincial government, the new standing vice-mayor hasn't taken office yet, Zhao Zhong is on a trip abroad. I wonder if someone in your department is getting ideas?'

Your leader is your leader, and it was time to make good on my loyalty. I laid out all the details of the coup from start to finish, after which Xiao Furen chuckled and said, 'You must all have felt uncomfortable under Zhao Zhong's rule. With a backer like Mayor Liu, he doesn't even have to take me seriously, much less Xu Zhitai. Mayor Liu knows all this perfectly well. Why do you think he didn't leave Zhao Zhong any instructions before he left for the provincial government? Obviously Mayor Liu saw through him long ago. Just go with the group on this one, Dawei. But you've done the right thing. You should toe the party line in all things. Do you know why Xu Zhitai has been vice department head for a decade? Because he just keeps his head down and pulls his cart, he never looks up at the road ahead. If you don't raise your head from time to time, how will you know whose cart you're pulling?'

Xiao Furen's words came as a revelation to me. To me, the 'party line' in this case was Xiao Furen. Everyone in Number Two Department sought the favour of the mayor and vice-mayors, thinking only those officials could change their fates, but they'd forgotten that the real official in charge was Xiao Furen. I was as excited as Columbus discovering the New World, and rushed back to the office, where I signed the open letter without the slightest hesitation. I knew Zhao Zhong was done for, but I also knew that even if he left, Xu Zhitai would never become the new department head. Who would promote someone who didn't know how to toe the party line?

As he enjoyed the sights of Hokkaido, Zhao Zhong could never have imagined that Number Two Department, so firmly under his thumb, was preparing for revolution, and with the support of the municipal authorities, no less.

When he came to work the day after he returned from Japan, he showed off photos from his trip. He had only just spread them across Xu Zhitai's desk when the interior phone line rang. After he took the call, he went outside. We guessed it was something out of the ordinary, and sure enough Zhao Zhong was gone for two hours. When he finally returned, his face looked like eggplant skin.

After dropping into his chair, panting, Zhao Zhong smoked two cigarettes in a row, then his face darkened and he said, 'Seeing as everyone's here, let's have a department meeting. This may be the last department meeting I call. No need to be nervous, I'm not trying to take revenge, I don't have that right any more. I'd just like to tell you all a story by the great Ji Xiagang:

'One day, by way of a drinking game, a gathering of people agreed that they would confess their greatest fears to each other. Seated in their midst, heard but not seen, was a fox, and soon enough the fox's turn came. When they asked him what he feared, the fox said, "I'm afraid of foxes." The crowd burst out laughing. "There's nothing wrong with people being afraid of foxes, but what does a fox have to fear from its own kind?" "The only thing in the world one ought to fear is one's own kind," the fox sneered. "It is children of the same father who fight over inheritance; it is wives of the same husband who fight for his favour; it is nobles of the same rank who fight for power; it is merchants in the same market who fight for profit. It is those of similar station who obstruct one another, bringing one another to ruin! A hunter of pheasants seeks to lure pheasants, not chickens or ducks; a trapper of deer sets out for deer, not for sheep or swine. One who desires to sow mistrust within a group, or to spy on it, must naturally be of a kind with that group; otherwise how could he ingratiate himself and thereby penetrate it? Thinking this way, how could a fox not be afraid of foxes?"'

Zhao Zhong looked at us one by one. 'If even foxes fear their own kind, how much more should humankind fear?' he said. 'Drop your guard for a moment, and you'll fall victim to someone's scheme.'

'Xu Zhitai, we've worked together for five years and you've always been docile as an ox. I forgot that you're my own kind! You think if you get rid of me Number Two will be yours? You're dreaming. I'll tell you. You may have gotten rid of Zhao Zhong, but after me there'll be a Wang Zhong, a Li Zhong, or a Zhou Zhong. You've been a civil servant for years, don't you understand why this is? Or maybe it's no surprise: you've had a pitiful ten years as vice-head. How about this, before I go I'll give you a few words of admonition. Do you know why they sometimes call the world of officialdom the "seas of officialdom"? Because there are so many who want to be officials, that's why. Why do so many stand forlorn on the shore? Because they don't know how to get on the ship. We've been colleagues for five years, and you've been vice-head for ten, and it really pains me to see you still standing on the shore. Remember this, Xu Zhitai: if you're planning to turn the department into a democracy, you'll need to be clear on what democracy is first. "Demos" means the common folk, "Kratos" is the ruler. You're the common folk and I'm the ruler, and no ruler likes a mob. You won't get on the boat until you learn to love obedience. Rebellion is human nature; obedience is official nature. If you can't sublimate your human nature within official nature, you'll never be anything but an ant!'

With that, he abruptly stood and went out, slamming the door. No one moved. Xu Zhitai stared into space, Huang Xiaoming looked through some book, Ou Beibei read a fashion magazine. I flipped through a paper. It seemed no different from any other meeting, but each of us drew the same conclusion from Zhao's speech: though we'd succeeded in our revolt against him, nothing would really change in the department. No one felt the slightest sense of victory.

The Stapler and the Staples

THE STAPLER AND the staples were best friends. They told each other every-
thing. In the evenings, when everyone had left Number Two Department,
they discussed the life of a civil servant.

STAPLES: Do you know what the eternal subject of conversation in
the corridors of power is, brother?

STAPLER: The topics vary with the changing of the guard. How could
there be an 'eternal subject'?

STAPLES: Of course there is. It's politics!

STAPLER: If you really want to understand politics, there are six
books you must read.

STAPLES: What are they?

STAPLER: *Dramatically.* Aristotle's *Politics*, Machiavelli's *The
Prince*, Locke's *Two Treatises of Government*, Montesquieu's
Spirit of the Laws, Hegel's *Elements of the Philosophy of Right*,
Rousseau's *The Social Contract*, and Tocqueville's *Democracy in
America*.

STAPLES: *Mockingly.* Ha, I can tell right away you don't understand
politics. Those books are all out of date. The key to politics is actually very simple: follow your leader.

STAPLER: *Earnestly.* I know what you mean, and it certainly sounds simple, but actually it's the most difficult thing for a civil servant to do.

STAPLES: How is that?

STAPLER: You may only be a thin bit of wire, but actually you're a perfect symbol of the civil servant. Your clean silver colour is just like an official's uniform, you all look exactly alike, and when you're put together with me, your leader, you all fall into line. No matter how I bend and squash you, you don't complain; you're made to be shaped and used.

STAPLES: So you're saying civil servants don't have the courage to say 'no'? But didn't Number Two Department say 'no' as a group under Xu Zhitai?

STAPLER: You're wrong. They didn't say 'no'; they were actually currying favour. Xu Zhitai calculated that Xiao Furen was unhappy with Zhao Zhong, but he was unable to do anything about it because of Liu Yihe. Once Liu Yihe was gone, Xu seized his opportunity and gave Xiao Furen a chance to strike at Zhao Zhong.

STAPLES: That's not right. If that were true Xu Zhitai would have gotten into Xiao Furen's good graces. So why wasn't he promoted to department head?

STAPLER: Simply a matter of precedence. If Peng Guoliang hadn't personally chosen Yang Hengda, Xiao Furen would have promoted Xu Zhitai for sure. Actually, civil servants have the ability to say 'no', they just lack the courage when faced with the bureaucratic establishment. Who would be so careless about their official career? It's like Milan Kundera wrote: 'In the bureaucratic world of the functionary, first, there is no initiative, no invention, no freedom of action; there are only orders and rules: it is the world of obedience. Second, the functionary performs a small part of a large administrative activity whose aim and horizons he cannot see. It is the world where actions have become mechanical and people do not know the meaning of what they do. Third, the functionary deals only with unknown persons and with files. It is the world of the abstract.'

'In this world of obedience, of the mechanical, and of the abstract' – the world of the civil servant – 'where the only human adventure is to move from one office to another.'

STAPLES: I can hardly agree with Kundera here. Wang Xiaobo wrote of a 'maverick pig' that won its freedom after escaping from the pig pen, and even grew new tusks. There are staples too, who resist your pressure. Their legs bend outwards instead of in. There must be civil servants like that as well.

STAPLER: *Derisively.* You are too naïve, my boy. They drove that pig out of the village and left it wandering in the wild, and staples that resist my pressure come to an even worse end: the trash can. A successful civil servant sticks to his leader like a staple and paper; he thinks his leader's thoughts, concerns himself with his leader's concerns and takes pleasure in what pleases his leader.

STAPLES: Nietzsche wrote: 'Few are made for independence. It is a privilege of the strong. And he who attempts it, having the completest right to it but without being compelled to, thereby proves that he is probably not only strong but also daring to the point of recklessness.' I am convinced that politicians must be this sort of person. I'll admit that even I would like to let myself go, to live in freedom and ease, doing as I please even if it means I am cast away. I believe the best a staple can do is to be flexible and extensible like an elephant's trunk. Those who can be flexible and extensible in the pursuit of their careers are by no means weak. Precisely the contrary; they are strongest of all.

STAPLER: So if you're an elephant's trunk, what am I?

STAPLES: *Ingratiatingly.* Well, your ideal is to be like an open-minded person. A successful civil servant must be able to contain thoughts the way you do staples, within his broad mind and expansive heart. We two are one, as a matter of fact. We're a team, and that's why we work together seamlessly.

STAPLER: You're convincing me now. Without staples a stapler would

71

be an empty shell, useless, like a general with no soldiers. But without the stapler, staples would likewise be a heap of scrap wire. Truly we cannot do without the other, the way Number Two Department is a team.

That reminds me of something that happened once. Xiao Furen had just graduated and arrived at Number Two, still full of vigour, and idealism and literary dreams. He never anticipated the dullness of his daily grind.

One day he was given an assignment. The head of the reception and hosting committee needed some materials printed and bound for a meeting the next day. He repeatedly reminded Xiao Furen to prepare for the binding, but Xiao blew the warnings off. Later that night, of course, when Xiao was printing and binding the materials, he ran out of staples after only a dozen copies. He sauntered to the staple supply only to find the box was empty. He was thunderstruck. Everyone ransacked the office but there wasn't a single staple to be found.

It was already midnight. Xiao Furen had to take a taxi to a five-star hotel with a business centre. It was dawn before he finished. When the hospitality department head turned up in the morning and found Xiao Furen looking like a ghost, he patted him on the shoulder and sighed, 'Furen, the great war horse stumbles not on the craggy mountain pass, but while he's crossing the smallest stream. Remember this lesson of the staples. They may seem insignificant, but they have the power to determine success or failure. Great success is an accumulation of insignificant detail.'

STAPLES: Why are two tiny staple points able to penetrate a thick stack of paper? It's because their force is concentrated on a tiny area. If every civil servant could be like a staple – identifying the goal, concentrating force, never wavering, hesitating or flagging – I'm sure each one would find success.

STAPLER: Your reputation is even more glorious than mine, you know. You once defined an era!

STAPLES: How's that?

STAPLER: On the thirty-fifth anniversary of the founding of the new China, a group of college students wrote 'Hello, Xiaoping!' on a big banner and hung it where Deng Xiaoping would pass by. In fact, they made it by stapling big pieces paper to a bed sheet. So you see, you fixed an entire era in place!

STAPLES: It's a good thing they didn't have glue back then or we would never have had our chance. China went from 'Long Live the Emperor' to 'Hello, Xiaoping', instantly bringing our leaders back into the mortal realm. What does this tell us?

STAPLER: It tells us that society is progressing and the people are maturing. But reforms still have a long way to go, and the 'officials come first' attitude is still holding us back . . .

Chief of the Municipal Finance Bureau, Chen Shi

WHEN I CLOSE my eyes these days I feel darkness pressing in on me from all sides, and my head fills with thoughts of ambush and deceit. I've always felt that the vault of my soul was full of rats, packed in tight and struggling, gnawing at the cellar door with their front teeth in an effort to get out. But those rats could not stand the light, so I fought to keep them from breaking through the door. It exhausted me, this effort, it drained my spirits. They reproduced like cancer cells and my ears were filled with their squeaking and rustling and gnawing. The sound surrounded me, enveloped me and deepened my fear of ambush.

Over time the pack of rats grew so large that I could not contain them. They were going to burst out, wander the streets like human beings. When rats emerge, everyone's first instinct is to kill them. When the time comes, I thought, it won't be rats on the street that people are trying to kill. It'll be my tattered, rat-gnawed soul.

When the rats finally did burst out, however, they didn't go wandering the streets. They went straight to the vaults of the Finance Bureau. No one saw them enter, and once they were in, they didn't forget that my soul was their true home. Like ants moving house, they transferred the gold from the vaults of the Bureau to the vaults of my soul, which transformed from a dark and dismal corner to a golden, glittering palace. For the first time in my life I felt the riches of the soul. I took my place on the palace throne.

Still, I felt uneasy. Particularly after Liu Yihe had returned to Dongzhou to become mayor. He doesn't like me. But for the fact that Vice-Mayor Peng is responsible for the Finance Bureau, I think Liu would have had me transferred long ago. The reason he dislikes me is something that happened on the first National Day after he took office.

I'd heard he liked fireworks so, wanting to get in his good favour, I proposed to him that the Finance Bureau fund a National Day fireworks display in the name of the Municipal Government and hold it in the government square. Liu always jumped at anything that might make the people happy and agreed immediately.

I co-ordinated with Xiao Furen, Director of the Municipal Government, to set up a viewing platform in the broad space by the main gate of the government compound. We set out tables bearing fruit platters, sunflower seeds and tea. Mayors, vice-mayors and some head secretaries sat at the tables and waited for the fireworks. Mayor Liu was in high spirits and spoke and laughed with animation. But as the first firework climbed into the sky and the crowd was beginning to 'ooh' and 'aah', a scrap of burning cinder drifted straight down into the rest of the fireworks and the compound was abruptly transformed into a sea of fire. One of the largest shells exploded right on the platform. My office director called the fire department, but by the time the fire engines arrived, all the fireworks were ruined. It's lucky no one was hurt. I ran up to the viewing platform, hanging my head, to make my report. When I was done, Mayor Liu said nothing, just stood up and stalked off in a huff. From that time forth, he never once gave me a smile.

You try to kiss the horse's arse and your lips land on its leg. At least I hadn't gotten a fart in the face or a kick in the head, and that was only thanks to Vice-Mayor Peng standing up for me.

In Dongzhou politics, even the Municipal Party Secretary had to tip his hat to Mayor Liu, but Mayor Liu had to tip his hat to Vice-

Mayor Peng, for a very simple reason: Liu depended on Peng for his political success.

Mayor Liu made the development of foreign trade and investment one of the priorities of his tenure, and Peng was the vice-mayor in charge of that area. Also, in order to display his magnanimity, as well as his democratic leanings, Mayor Liu gave Peng the job of delegating mayoral duties. Peng took over everything related to finances and human resources, clearly intending to sideline Liu altogether. But then Mayor Liu leveraged the other vice-mayors' discontent with Peng Guoliang's power grab and put him on his back foot again.

Liu still relied on his underlings to get things done, however. This was particularly the case with Peng, who was his equal in terms of abilities and achievements. Mayor Liu was perfectly aware of this: he'd witnessed it when the two of them had been in competition for the position of standing vice-mayor. But in politics, a single misstep can lose the race. Liu was Peng's superior when it came to winning hearts and minds, and in the end he won on reputation. From the point of view of practical ability, however, I believe Peng is far the greater mayor.

Take foreign investment for example. Peng Guoliang took the first steps in this direction when he was still Bureau Chief of the Municipal Bureau of Commerce. He set up a representative office in Hong Kong and sent his own office director, Niu Yuexian, to head it up. This Niu Yuexian not only has near-mystical social skills, but she is also possessed of an otherworldly beauty. Peng's eye had lighted upon this gorgeous typist the moment he'd arrived at the Bureau. In no time, she'd been promoted to deputy director of the office, and six months later she was director.

Once he'd established the Dongzhou Representative Office in Hong Kong, he tasked Niu Yuexian with turning it into a base from which to make friends and connections throughout South-East Asia. Along with the advantages of beauty and personality, Niu Yuexian had a first-class brain. She soon earned a reputation as the social toast of

Hong Kong. Through her, Peng established links with many South-East Asian entrepreneurs and tycoons. Many of them called him 'brother', something Liu Yihe could only envy.

Peng was soon setting new records for foreign investment in Dongzhou. Several large shopping complexes that had been on the verge of collapse were resuscitated and returned to profitability. He was consequently promoted to the position of mayoral assistant, and soon after that became a vice-mayor. It is no exaggeration that Peng won the position thanks to his skill at attracting foreign investment. Liu might have made foreign investment one of his priorities, but when it came down to the painstaking work of making it happen, he relied entirely on Peng.

This was doubly unfortunate for Liu Yihe because he hated the sight of Peng, and now he had to give him face. That's also the reason Liu couldn't remove me from my position or discipline me after the fireworks disaster. I had Peng Guoliang's protection. In politics, tugging a single thread will often unravel the whole sweater, and no one in charge can afford to ignore the power of the clique. A clique is a political force. On your own, no one above will look out for you, and no one will follow you.

As top dog of Dongzhou, Liu had to balance the interests of many different cliques, and he was deeply cognisant of the fact that Peng did not operate alone. Not only was Peng at the heart of his own powerful clique, but he was also a key member of other, much greater cliques – cliques it would be very dangerous to rile up. All Liu could do was cultivate secondary power centres to balance out Peng's power.

To be honest, since throwing in my lot with Peng, I've not only reaped considerable benefits, but I've also learned a lot. He once said to me, 'For thousands of years, Chinese culture has emphasised loyalty versus betrayal, never truth versus falsehood. Loyalty means loyalty to the imperial power, and the imperial person. Most people think loyalty is one of the traditional Chinese moral virtues, that it means filial piety to your parents, but I'm telling you filial piety is just a mask. Who are your real parents? Government officials, of course. Why do we call it the "paternal state"? After thousands of years of the paternal state, how can we suddenly transform ourselves into a "civilian state" run by public servants? Even the people themselves would rebel – thousands of years of worshipping power has dealt a mortal wound to Chinese culture. That's hypocrisy and falsehood. The habit of falsehood is fatal to a culture. But to us, falsehood is the essence, and we can employ this essence to fabricate our own weights and measures. Doesn't the measure of justice exist within each of us? The Qin Emperor unified the standard weights and measures. Is it within our power to change them? So long as we can keep a thumb on the scales of justice, we can resolve all difficulties. Those who worship power must worship falsehood, and for that reason each and every profession has developed its own highly developed unwritten rules. Know this: preserving the unwritten rules means preserving yourself.'

I was struck by the last thing he said, and the cloud of fear and dread that had long accompanied me abruptly lifted. From then on, I railed publicly against corruption at every opportunity, and all cadres at the bureau level or higher received regular training in integrity and self-discipline. Actually, what Peng Guoliang had said about 'preserving unwritten rules' didn't go far enough. People often speak of 'fishing in troubled waters'. But as I preferred to say, 'In politics, the best way of protecting yourself is to yell "stop thief!" whilst picking your neighbour's pocket!'

Secretary of the Provincial Disciplinary Committee, Qi Xiuying

RECENTLY I'VE BEEN receiving some unusual letters. They're not mailed to me at the Provincial Disciplinary Committee but to my home. The contents are two or three pages of notebook paper, apparently torn from a full notebook. What's shocking is the notes seem to be written by Mayor Liu, and the moment he's finished them he's torn out the pages and sent them to me.

But that's impossible.

My guess is someone has stolen his notebook and is tearing out a few pages at a time and mailing them to me.

When I read these letters, my jaw drops open. Not only are the contents nigh unbelievable, but they would have earthshaking results if published. They appear to be a record of Liu Yihe's deepest secrets, and the notebook thief appears to be mailing them to me out of a sense of moral outrage. The only marks he leaves are a few typewritten words on a piece of photocopier paper attached to each batch of the notes as if they are a title: *The Civil Servant's Notebook.*

It's obvious the notebook thief is not only familiar with Mayor Liu. He must also be familiar with me. He seems afraid that I'll work out his identity. Each letter bears no return address and the postmarks show that each has been mailed from a different location. The earliest came from different districts within Dongzhou City, later ones from a county town under Dongzhou's jurisdiction and the most recent from other provinces. The most distant was mailed from Shenzhen.

Liu Yihe has made such important notes in this book that if he were to discover their loss he'd be jumpy as a cat on a hot tin roof. So why has nothing come of it? The whole business is strange.

Proper procedure would be to report the letters to the Provincial Party Committee, but such a report might alert the perpetrator. The first order of business is clearly to find the notebook thief. But how? My years of experience tell me that whoever it is must be close to Liu Yihe, likely someone in the Dongzhou Municipal Government.

After thinking it over, I decided the best course of action was to send someone to get close to Liu Yihe and see what they could uncover. But who? They'd have to keep a low profile and get close to Liu without attracting his attention. I pondered the question for a while and settled on Shang Xiaoqiong from the Sixth Office of the Provincial Disciplinary Committee.

Shang studied criminal investigation at the Public Security University. She's bright. In the three short years she's worked in the Disciplinary Committee, she's participated in many major anti-corruption cases. I'd been planning to send my secretary, whom I'd brought along from K Province (she'd worked with me five or six years), down to county level for some on-the-ground experience and replace her with Shang Xiaoqiong pro tem. I'd have to put that off for now. We needed to get to the bottom of the *The Civil Servant's Notebook*.

The next question was what position near Liu Yihe would be most convenient for her work. I thought about it for a whole week and couldn't find an answer.

At the end of the week the Provincial Disciplinary Committee held a standing meeting. I arrived at my office at dawn, much earlier than usual, to organise my work reports. I found a girl from the Janitorial Brigade cleaning my office. My eyes lit up. If I sent Shang Xiaoqiong to the Dongzhou Municipal Janitorial Brigade to clean Liu Yihe's office, she'd come into close contact with him without attracting suspicion. Given her motivated work habits, we might not only learn about Liu Yihe, but we might also find the notebook thief.

After the meeting I told the Director of the Sixth Office, Deng Hongchang, to come and see me. I explained the case and told him to send Shang Xiaoqiong to work undercover in the Dongzhou Municipal Janitorial Brigade. Deng is a senior inspector, loyal to the Party and deeply experienced. Before I'd finished, he'd caught my meaning as well as the fact that this might be an anti-corruption case of enormous proportions. He called Shang Xiaoqiong into my office and explained the mission to her in front of me. I emphasised the severity of the case and reiterated the importance of secrecy to both of them.

That's how Shang Xiaoqiong was sent to the Janitorial Brigade of the Dongzhou Municipal Government in the guise of an etiquette graduate from the local vocational school.

After a month undercover, Shang Xiaoqiong had discovered nothing. During that time I received another three chapters of the mysterious *The Civil Servant's Notebook*, each more shocking than the last. The most recent had me bolt upright in my chair. Its contents read:

'I had not realised that desires could be measured with cash. I've always thought of myself as someone with no greed for money. As Mayor I need many things: reputation, status, trust, appreciation, support, veneration, authority, power, love, flowers, applause . . . but I do not need money. I thought I was made of iron, because I did not doubt my ability to cleave to my one dream: to make the people of Dongzhou proud of me, and proud of themselves. But money was all around me like a damp breeze, impossible to ward off, like a pestilence imperceptibly encroaching on the body. Though I may be made of iron, I may yet rust . . . What is rust? It is convention, thousands of years of traditional reciprocity, and who could withstand that? If you were to equate reciprocity with corruption, wouldn't all of society be entirely corrupt? I've gone from vice-mayor to standing vice-mayor, then to vice-governor, and now to my position as Mayor of Dongzhou. An entire decade! And in that time, I've accepted as much as eight figures worth of gifts. As a vice-mayor, I could never have dreamed it. I'm a mayor, what do I need all that money for? The people choose me as Mayor, and as Mayor I act on behalf of the people: that was my original intent. That intent has grown weaker, but no matter how strong it was, it could never have resisted this exterior strength; the desires of society are far, far stronger than the desires of the individual. It's similar to the way we are terrified of death, yet none of us can escape death's clutches – the more I longed to be clean, the more I was driven to corruption. The harder I struggled to avoid my fate, the more surely I was ensnared in its net. What is it that caused loftiness to become base, uprightness to become corruption? I cannot fathom the answer. Last night Zhao Zhong came to see me expressly to give me a Juvenia wristwatch on the occasion of my daughter's birthday. My relationship with Zhao Zhong is one of father and son; I was obliged to accept. As we chatted I asked him, what was it that people needed most these days? He replied immediately that they needed the salvation of their souls. I asked him why, and he said that people's greatest unhappiness was their inability to break free. This sounded right to me. With such a firm grasp of human needs, human emptiness, it's no wonder he is able to make so much money running his temple. I asked him how people might break free, and he said: by believing in something. When I heard this casual remark I suddenly understood why the harder I strove for uprightness, the deeper I fell into corruption. After Zhao Zhong left I conducted a thorough self-examination and could come up with no single thing that I believed in.'

If these two pages of notes had really come from Liu Yihe's pen then he was one of the most corrupt officials in Qingjiang Province. If we could verify this, I would do everything in my power to make an iron-clad case out of it. But could someone be setting Liu Yihe up? I often conducted surveys among my subordinates, and I had asked for news of Liu Yihe's political reputation while he was vice-governor. Everyone said that not only was he a diligent leader, but he was also kind. Could someone like that be corrupt?

While I was secretary of the K Province Provincial Disciplinary Committee, I suffered all manner of misunderstanding, slander, rumour and abuse because of my anti-corruption cases. My son was even framed for using my power and status to make an illegal fortune. At that time reform was fully underway and all manner of conflicts were emerging at all levels. Could a diligent, kind leader such as Liu Yihe be framed for corruption?

While Liu Yihe was working in the provincial government, we attended a few meetings together, and though I didn't know much about him, I could tell from the tone of his speeches that he was someone who believed he had a mission and didn't hesitate in pursuing it, and also that he was someone who stood by his word. After he came to the Dongzhou Municipal Government, I heard that while working with secretaries or mayors he would often disregard their lead and express his own opinions. Someone like that is prone to a 'my way or the highway' mentality. They say absolute power corrupts absolutely, and the greatest flaw in the current system is the lack of effective checks or oversight against the depredations of 'Number One'. Power is a double-edged sword. Might the kind and diligent Mayor have two faces?

The notes said that desire could be measured in cash. You have to admit that in a market economy the value of the individual can be measured in his ownership of capital. This has shaken the idealism and changed the world view of some civil servants. From the notes, it was obvious that Liu Yihe was suffering spiritual torment. But were those his true feelings?

Former Head of the Real Estate Bureau of the Municipal Committee Office, Zhu Wenwu

ZHAO ZHONG AND I often get together to play mahjong, but he's never invited me out for a drink.

Until now.

When he was head of the Number Two Department and my son Dawei was under him, more than a few times I invited Zhao to go drinking. Not only a drink; we'd often move on to a sauna or massage parlour. I did this in the hope that he'd look after Dawei, give him an opportunity.

Back then, Zhao used to go around with his nose in the air because of his special connection with Liu Yihe. During the Cultural Revolution, Liu Yihe's father had been struggled against, and Zhao Zhong's father had brought him food. With such solid backing, it's no wonder Zhao Zhong was a tyrant inside the department. He behaved so badly his whole department was nearly up in arms. He never dreamt they would rise up against him.

We all learn from our mistakes, and although he was driven out of government with his tail between his legs, Zhao turned disaster into opportunity and has since made a mint from running temples. I've always wondered how he does so well.

In vino veritas. Once he'd had a few he told me.

'My friend, let me tell you why I failed as department head. It's very simple: I didn't understand the nature of control. Why did everyone say I was an autocratic department head? Because I controlled their sensibilities without controlling their thoughts. Control of sensibility is merely a restriction of one's physical body, but without controlling thoughts, people will start to feel discontent, and it was that discontent that defeated me. Reflecting on my failure, I see that the key to successful control is to make the controlled feel happy about it, to make them appreciate it, even worship it. You must create a deep connection between controller and controlled, to turn control into something irresistibly seductive, as though it were a drug, until even those who are beyond control still feel the *desire* to be controlled, and regret the lack of control.

'How is this done? By controlling not only thoughts but also souls. Those who tend towards discontent, in particular, are most vulnerable to control of their souls. That is, those who think most feel the most pain. We cannot fulfil everyone's desires, but we can employ control to bring solace to the desiring soul. How do we bring that solace? To give illusions to those who are full of desires, and to make them see hope. Hope is controlled by the soul. Submission to the soul leads to understanding, and thence to freedom. When people submit to the soul they acknowledge, trust and even worship control. And who does not wish for the solace of the soul?

'Thus, the highest form of control is control of the soul, and only religion is capable of that. In China today it is Buddhism that goes deepest into the human heart. My dear friend, running temples not only leads to good works and the salvation of souls, it can also earn income from incense money! Why wouldn't I do it?'

Incense money! I thought to myself, with grudging admiration. He's getting rich off souls!

But he hadn't asked me out drinking just to tell me about his business methods. He asked me about Robert Luo, the representative from

Wantong Property from Hong Kong, and I became wary. Robert and his project were close to Peng. Was Zhao Zhong gathering information for Liu Yihe?

Peng and Liu had been at loggerheads during their fight for the position of standing vice-mayor, and though Peng was now a lower grade than Liu, he wasn't one to accept defeat. It was only a matter of time before he counterattacked.

My son Dawei had told me that Peng's secretary, Hu Zhanfa, had an idea that Dawei should succeed him when he moved on, as he was due to soon. But Dawei seemed to think that Peng was more interested in Huang Xiaoming, who did have the advantage over my son in terms of ability. That's not to say that my son was inferior. I know better than anyone what he's capable of. But he lacked opportunities to test himself and grow.

A mayor's secretary is in an unusual position. He wields a hidden power, an extension of the mayor's authority that often has more force and room for play for him than it does for his boss. Becoming secretary to a mayor was a shortcut in one's political career, but if you followed the wrong man it could also lead to a fatal dead end.

Doing business in China, particularly real estate, meant cultivating contacts, and contacts meant politics. A real estate mogul like myself often had requests to make of Hu Zhanfa, and he had profited plenty in the course of helping me.

Hu Zhanfa had long ago become Peng Guoliang's crutch, and to a certain extent it was the servant who was in control. A secretary that powerful, who behaved so wilfully, had to have something dirty on his boss. He must have had his own reasoning behind wanting my son to take over his position, and probably thought he would be able to use Dawei to control Peng Guoliang even after he himself had moved on, whereas if Huang Xiaoming took the position he wouldn't be so easily manipulated.

In fact, Hu Zhanfa was wrong. He had forgotten that my son was a distinguished student of politics and, furthermore, if he became the mayor's secretary, he would be responsible to the mayor, not to the mayor's former secretary. He would know all too well that his future was in the hands of his leader.

For these reasons, I pressed Zhao Zhong to recommend my son to Liu Yihe. At the same time, I provided him with some information about the relationship between Peng Guoliang and Robert, including some rumours I had heard about 'under the table' handouts connected with the Hegang Gardens project, which I had been working on with Robert's Wantong Group.

There was one thing I didn't tell him, however. The Hegang Gardens project included a luxury villa development called Pear Blossom Garden. There were twenty villas, and they were the most expensive properties in Dongzhou. When they were still in the blueprint stage, Robert asked me to reserve one villa for him. I thought he was going to move his wife over from Hong Kong to live there and thought nothing of it. But after construction was completed and the villas were sold, I discovered that he'd sold that one to a woman named Miao Guizhen. I'd met Robert's wife before and that certainly wasn't her name, so I joked with him, 'Have you got yourself a mistress to ease the loneliness?'

Robert made no bones about it. 'My tastes aren't that low! To tell you the truth, the woman who bought the villa is the sister-in-law of Chen Shi, the head of the Municipal Finance Bureau.' I almost gasped out loud when I heard that.

I remained doubtful of what Robert told me, however, and meant to find out whether Chen Shi really had a sister-in-law. As it turned out, he only had a brother-in-law. I didn't know why Robert was lying to me. All I knew was that those villas cost ten million, but this Miao Guizhen had bought hers for only one. Even if she was Chen Shi's sister-in-law, Robert wouldn't give her such an enormous discount. This deepened my curiosity and I kept an eye out for exactly who this fairy woman was, but no one ever moved into the villa. The other nineteen were bought by some of the richest business owners in Dongzhou.

I was one of them, of course.

One evening I was out at a dinner and came home late. As I drove past that villa, I noticed an Audi parked out front, which immediately piqued my interest. I pulled over into a dark spot to watch what might happen. After waiting more than an hour, I saw two people emerge from the villa, a man and a woman, and by the streetlights I could see that the man was Peng Guoliang and the woman Ou Beibei. My heart leaped to my throat. A man got out of the driver's seat of the car and opened the door for Peng Guoliang. Ou Beibei got in first. The driver was Hu Zhanfa.

It wasn't until long after they had driven away that my heartbeat returned to normal. There was only one thought in my head: stop Dawei from becoming Peng Guoliang's secretary. I'd heard that Peng Guoliang was a womaniser, but you wouldn't expect him to choose his prey from his own office. The beast couldn't even pass up Ou Beibei. That was bad news for Wang Chaoquan. I'd heard Dawei say that Ou Beibei was very vain and looked down on her own husband, but Wang Chaoquan's feelings for Ou Beibei ran deep. If he knew he was being cuckolded by the standing vice-mayor, he'd be devastated.

I'd kept this whole business to myself.

There was one person I couldn't help mentioning it to, however, and that was my future daughter-in-law, Shang Xiaoqiong. My son's nickname for her was 'Cat', and I thought it very suitable, because her job was catching mice. She worked in the Provincial Disciplinary Committee under the notorious Secretary Qi Xiuying. I asked her if she could help me ascertain the identity of this mysterious Miao Guizhen. Not ten days later, Xiaoqiong told me that Miao Guizhen was an alias for Peng Guoliang's wife, Zhang Peifen, but the ID card of this 'Miao Guizhen' was genuine. It gave me a shock to hear that!

Dongzhou Representative of Wantong Property Group, Hong Kong, Robert Luo

GIFTING A VILLA worth ten million to Mayor Peng was a sweet deal because Wantong Group hadn't paid a penny of land usage fees for the hundred *mu* Hegang Gardens development on the Wujiazhuang section of the Blackwater River. A word from Peng Guoliang and it was all waived. Even our local partner, Zhu Wenwu, was surprised. When the previous mayor had taken a team to Hong Kong to look for investors, the incentive he'd allowed for that particular development project was a land usage fee reduction of twenty per cent. After Zhu Wenwu went to work on him, he'd agreed to a forty per cent, which the Wantong Group was already very happy with. But the board felt we could still do better, and asked me to continue working on Mayor Peng, who was the vice-mayor responsible for the project. I treated him to several dinners and even visited him at home, but Peng wouldn't budge.

One evening his secretary Hu Zhanfa invited me out to dinner. Hu Zhanfa was Peng's most trusted man and had a good deal of influence over him. I thought this would be a good opportunity to drum up support. I readily accepted the invitation.

Hu Zhanfa reserved the most luxurious private room at Golden Splendour, an entertainment venue that combined restaurant, karaoke and spa. By rights, I ought to have been the one treating Hu Zhanfa, but he made the reservation of his own accord. I was curious to see what he had up his sleeve since, as the saying goes, 'he who comes bearing gifts wants something in return'. We'd been acquainted for a while, and my impression of him was not so much that he was a hypocrite, but an 'honest crook', conniving to the point of frankness. You never had to guess what he was up to.

Sure enough, after three drinks, he cut to the chase. 'In fact, Manager Luo, there would be nothing difficult about a total waiver of the land usage fees. But there's just one condition.' He made a point of stopping there and taking a deep drink.

My heart leaped at the words 'total waiver'. I could hardly believe my ears. The board's argument for reduced fees was that the Hegang Gardens development was riverside property, without any basic infrastructure, and construction would necessarily entail many additional expenses. They were hoping that I would be able to secure another ten per cent reduction in the land usage fees, a total of fifty per cent off. That would be an extraordinary discount, as land usage fees generally go, and I never expected to hear the words 'total waiver'. That would practically be giving it to us.

I hastened to ask, 'Name the condition, Secretary Hu. I'm sure we can work something out.'

He smiled craftily, blew a smoke ring, and said, 'A total waiver of the fees would be a princely gift from Mayor Peng to Wantong. I'm sure he could expect some show of gratitude?'

'But of course, of course,' I said. 'Perhaps Secretary Hu could name a price.'

The corner of his mouth twisted down in something like a smile. 'It's not high, just set aside a villa for Mayor Peng in Pear Blossom Garden, and an apartment for me in Hegang Gardens.'

Obviously Peng had asked only for the villa and Hu Zhanfa had tacked on the apartment himself. Truly, it wasn't a very high price, but the figure was still high enough that I couldn't make the decision myself. I used my mobile phone to make a report to the CEO, who assented with no hesitation.

I hung up the phone and told Hu Zhanfa it was a deal. He was elated, and at a clap of his hands, two lovely young girls approached. I'm helpless before beauty, and when Hu Zhanfa saw the effect the girls had on me, he told them to sit next to me, saying, 'Manager Luo, this is the merest token of my regard. You're emperor for a night.'

I knew that this was his way of keeping me quiet about the apartment he'd asked for, and I assured him. 'Not to worry, Zhanfa. Boss Peng's business is his business, your business is your business, and I'm quite clear on the difference between the two.'

When he heard that, Hu Zhanfa toasted me. The girl on my left put a grape between her full lips to feed to me while the girl on my right wrapped her white arms around my neck and said sweetly, 'You must always take care when eating and drinking, Boss Luo, you could be in danger! An eighty-five-year-old woman got married to a twenty-five-year-old man, but the next day the young fellow died. Do you know why?'

I shook my head. She gave a snort of laughter. 'I'll give you a hint: the coroner determined the cause of death to be food poisoning.'

Confused, I asked, 'How was it food poisoning? What did he eat?'

The girl on the left said coyly, 'Still can't figure it out? He drank expired milk!'

Suddenly the answer dawned on me, and I burst out laughing.

Then the girl on the left said charmingly, 'Boss Luo, let's test how quick-witted you are, okay?'

I answered cheerfully, 'Sure!'

She asked craftily, 'Why is it that men use Viagra?'

I feared a trick question, so shook my head and said, 'I don't know.'

She clapped her hands and said, 'Congratulations, that's the correct answer!'

The girl on the right chimed in with a straight face. 'A very incisive answer indeed.'

I was still befuddled and couldn't see how I'd gotten it right. Hu Zhanfa pointed at me and shook with laughter.

I don't have much of a sense of humour. I only understand business, and to a businessman, truth can only be found in a deal, not in a joke. In this regard, I truly appreciate Dongzhou more than Hong Kong. I say this because all the business deals I've conducted in Dongzhou have given me a sense of accomplishment. I've been in the world of business more than twenty years and know full well that there's no charity in the markets, but that doesn't mean you have to scorn making friends with those who make you shine brighter. On the contrary, a businessman must make friends with those whose economic fates are tied most closely to his own, and search for reliable backers who are like him in character. That is the quickest shortcut to wealth, even more so on the Mainland. I became deeply aware of this fact only after coming to Dongzhou.

Former Head of Number Two Department, Zhao Zhong

I'VE HEARD A lot of rumours and slander about Mayor Liu recently. Ou Beibei has talked to me about it several times. I asked her who she heard it from, and she said most came from Hu Zhanfa, Mayor Peng's secretary.

When I was head of Number Two Department, Hu Zhanfa was always running Mayor Liu down in private. He was Peng Guoliang's lapdog. Without his master's goading, I couldn't see him having the guts to actually bite anyone. A politician who only engages in alliances but never in conspiracies will always be at a disadvantage. Mayor Liu is just the sort of straight shooter who would never conduct manoeuvres or deals behind the curtain. He brings everything on stage, out in the open, and wants to meet his enemies face to face.

That's harder than it sounds. Those driven by jealousy to plot against you will always hide behind the curtains. They don't have the guts to meet face to face. I have urged Mayor Liu more than once that when dealing with someone like Peng Guoliang, who always conducts his stratagems in darkness, you have to give them a taste of their own medicine.

Mayor Liu's face always hardens when he hears me talk like this, and he says, 'No wonder they called you the "false monk" in the office, Zhao

Zhong! You may have a Buddhist nature, but you haven't got a Buddhist heart! I like having enemies – it makes this work worth doing – but I hate internal strife. As Mayor, I work for the people of Dongzhou; I don't get caught up in conspiracies. So long as I'm steadfast, heaven will smooth my path. Jealousy has killed far more people throughout history than cancer ever has, and of course there are risks in politics. We've had thirty years of reform and opening up, and every step of the way was dogged with risk. Why is that? Chuang-tzu has a line in 'Carefree Wandering' that goes: "If one did not extinguish a candle when the sun and moon come out, wouldn't it be hard to discern its light?" I have my own saying: "The rivers and seas are broad, but only the lakes are deep."'

His eyes flashed like fire as he was saying this, and when he was finished, his face wore a smile that spoke of a deep knowledge of the world, and his eyes were once again as placid as pools.

Though Mayor Liu often admonishes me to stick to business and not get involved in politics again, I always feel responsibility to help him where I can. While I was head of Number Two, people took me more seriously because I had Mayor Liu's backing. Now I am making great strides in business, and while that isn't directly due to him, I know that my success comes in part because everyone knows of my connection to him. Not only has our fathers' bond made us closer than blood brothers, but he has practically become the totem of my public self-respect.

For the sake of that self-respect, there was nothing untoward about engaging in a little conspiracy. If Mayor Liu, lofty as a philosopher-king, didn't deign to glance behind the curtain, I'd never thought of myself as particularly lofty, and so I wanted to take a peep to see exactly who was crouching back there.

While I was head of Number Two, I was the boss and I stood by everything I said. They called me autocratic, arbitrary, even tyranni-cal, to the point where Xu Zhitai, Huang Xiaoming and the others ganged up to drive me out. Given my power now, it would be child's play to make trouble for them, or even ruin their futures, but if they hadn't conducted their coup, I would never have made it so far. In a sense, I should thank them. Though it was a bit of a sucker punch, it was carried out in the open. Now Xu Zhitai and Huang Xiaoming have boarded Peng Guoliang's pirate ship. It will be harder to get off than it was to get on.

Now I am in the business of saving souls – I've gone from boss to Buddha. Since my path led me to Buddhism, I've come to believe that all human hope comes from the concept of a far shore, and all human suffering comes from the exact same thing. Everyone is hoping for salvation, and believes that only the far shore can save us. But how often we destroy ourselves in trying to reach it. That's absurd. The far shore can save our souls, but it can also constrict our souls. It is the existence of death that allows us to taste happiness and to yearn for the far shore and a life of deathless happiness, with no vexations. But that's not the true far shore; that's heaven. That's one of the reasons why people worship gods, and want to become gods. So what exactly is this far shore? That's one of the eternal human questions. Is it power? Definitely not. Power is the source of suffering and can only lead to the confinement of thought and the stagnation of history. Though all life rushes towards death, it will never stagnate. Only a person who lives can be said to be alive, or be called a 'person'. Otherwise we'd be corpses, and corpses disappear amid stench and putrefaction. Thus, the far shore must exist within our lives. It must be our inextinguishable hope, whereas power can only build walls around us and stifle our fragile hopes. Neither can the far shore exist within any particular social science, because all social sciences come with their own walls, their own systems, their own features. Thus, humans can only rely upon religion to soothe their souls. Religion is the ark that humanity has learned to use in its search for the far shore. To me, the ark is not a ship but a temple. Fan Zhongyan said that whilst living in the temple hall, one thought of the people, but whilst living among the people, one thought of the emperor. I am far from the people now, but very near to the temple. There's nothing contradictory about this. It is fate, and Buddhahood.

But if I meant to become a 'fighting Buddha', I would need to see where Peng Guoliang was sailing his pirate ship.

A few days ago, I invited Zhu Dawei's father Zhu Wenwu to drink with me. The reason was that I had noticed a growing closeness between Peng Guoliang and the Hong Kong agent Robert Luo whose Wantong Group co-operated with Zhu Wenwu's real estate group to develop the Hegang Gardens project. The investment was nearly ten billion, Zhu Wenwu's largest project since he started doing business. Robert was merely the representative of the Hong Kong partner. The project itself had come about when the old mayor had led an investment attraction team to Hong Kong, and Zhu Wenwu had used the opportunity to get to know the CEO of Wantong. He'd secured the project only after a protracted period of negotiation.

After Mayor Liu took office, he took the Hegang Gardens project very seriously. It meant the banks of the Blackwater River would very likely become Dongzhou City's silver belt of economic expansion. That was also the reason that my own new real estate company began to make inroads into that area, and I had asked Zhu Wenwu to dinner both to learn from his experiences in working with the Hong Kong partner, and also to find out why exactly Peng Guoliang and Robert had grown so close.

During the drinking session, Zhu Wenwu made much of my relationship with Mayor Liu, and asked me to recommend his son Zhu Dawei to him. While I was head of Number Two, I had noticed that Zhu Dawei had dreams of becoming a mayor's secretary, but he was stymied by the lack of open positions. Zhu Wenwu had heard that Song Daoming, Mayor Liu's secretary, would soon be moving upwards, and he lost no time in expounding his son's talents and high morals to me.

The very next day, I'd had some business at the Municipal Government. Every time I visited the offices, I would drop in to Number Two to sit for a bit, and just as I had entered that day, Huang Xiaoming was calling his wife, arranging for plane tickets. I asked Yang Hengda who Xiaoming was getting tickets for, and when I learned that Mayor Peng was travelling to Hong Kong the next day, I became suspicious. Huang Xiaoming's wife worked in the ticket office of an airline, and when Peng Guoliang was going abroad, Hu Zhanfa would usually go to Huang Xiaoming to get tickets. I chatted for a bit with Yang Hengda and Huang Xiaoming, then bustled out.

That evening I called Zhu Wenwu and asked playfully if he and Robert would be up for a game of mahjong. I was hoping to find Robert's whereabouts, and sure enough Zhu Wenwu said in an irritated tone, 'Robert went to Hong Kong to collect a prize.'

Perplexed, I asked, 'What prize? He couldn't have won the lottery, could he?'

Zhu Wenwu grumbled, 'Goddamn it, the Hegang Gardens project was plainly my doing, if they were going to give prizes for attracting foreign investment, then I should be the one to get it. What the hell does it have to do with Robert? Now Peng Guoliang, as the mayor in charge of the project, has not only got his prizes mixed up, he's gone to Hong Kong to meet Robert in person. There's something fishy going on here, Zhao Zhong.'

Deputy Chief Secretary and Director of the Municipal Government, Xiao Furen

MY PRECISE JOB description is Deputy Chief Secretary serving Standing Vice-Mayor Peng Guoliang. But when Mayor Liu was a standing vice-mayor and I was in charge of Number Two Department, Combined Affairs before Zhao Zhong, Liu got in the habit of using me and he still comes to me to discuss most everything he does.

This puts me in a bind because both leaders often call for me simultaneously. To be honest, I would much rather serve Mayor Liu. I owe him my career, after all. But Mayor Peng keeps a tight grip on me, and grumbles about my having a foot in two camps.

'Having a foot in two camps' hardly does the situation justice. I'm being split in half by a tug-of-war! I say that because relations between Peng Guoliang and Liu Yihe are starting to resemble the bitter rivalry that existed between General Zhou Yu and Chancellor Zhuge Liang during the Three Kingdoms period. Peng Guoliang has Zhou Yu's resentment. 'Since there is a Zhou Yu, what need is there of a Zhuge Liang?' he says.

I swing between the two of them, as helpless as Lu Su did when dealing with the General and the Chancellor. Actually, Peng Guoliang doesn't have Zhou Yu's talents, and Liu Yihe doesn't have Zhuge Liang's strategic acumen, and of course I would never presume to be a Lu Su with a 'head full of stratagems and heart full of schemes'.

There is one aspect in which I feel I am handling this delicate situation well. I stick by Peng Guoliang in body, and Liu Yihe in spirit.

A strong personality can be a liability in politics, but Liu Yihe has a strong individual character. You could say that he has benefited from this over the twenty years of his political career, but when his position was elevated to vice-governorship, all the old petty personal conflicts and strife were elevated into deadly political struggle. That was precisely when he needed to be Lu Su, with a 'head full of stratagems and heart full of schemes', but there was never anything hidden about Liu Yihe. He goes about his work like a tank, rumbling straight ahead in contempt of any and all minefields. As he puts it, 'All can and should be boldly explored, so long as no national laws, regulations or directives are broken and there are no direct orders to the contrary. If there is flexibility in our superiors' policies, we must be creative in their application. The liberation of thought is a long and bloody road, and it is likely that some will be sacrificed as we walk along it. I would rather be martyred on that road than take a single step backwards.' That sort of person may typically keep quiet, but should they ever decide to act, they will shake the world.

These thoughts were prompted by a visit from Liu's secretary, Song Daoming, whom I had called in to discuss some personnel matters. Our conversation strayed to rumours that were circulating about Mayor Liu. Some government functionaries had been saying in private that Mayor Liu had divorced his wife and taken a programme host from Changshan Television as a mistress. Every long weekend he would drive to Changshan alone.

I have served Mayor Liu for many years, and I know that his wife is a bit of a shrew, but Mayor Liu never says a word against her and has never treated her harshly. Could this be a mere façade? In a marriage like that, any man would be prone to stray, so I didn't completely discount the rumours. I was even inclined to place some credence in them. On second thoughts, however, there was something calculated about them. Mayor Liu's wife may have been a shrew, but he seemed to take pleasure in her temper. The foundation of their love was strong – they had been college classmates – so how could they separate so lightly?

Song had just left my office when my mobile phone rang, and I was surprised to hear Deng Hongchang's voice. He and I were classmates at the Provincial Party School young cadre training course. I had been class monitor and he was the Party Branch Secretary. Though we had worked well together, we hadn't stayed in contact after leaving the Party School. It wasn't because there was anything wrong with him – he was an enthusiastic, honest and straightforward person – but rather because he became Director of the Sixth Office of the Provincial Disciplinary Committee, in charge of major cases. The most corrupt officials in the province fell at his hand, and because of his work, he had the habit of watching everyone with a judging look that made you uncomfortable. I'd kept my distance from him.

Now he was calling me out of the blue, asking me to dinner that night, and I honestly did not want to go. Who knew whom I might accidentally offend by dining with him? The malefactors he investigated were punished with disciplinary action, demotion, expulsion from the Party or dismissal from public service – that's if their case was minor. Major offenders would find themselves in jail, or even their heads on the block, literally. The family, friends and associates of these corrupt officials naturally bore deep grudges against him, and it was these people I feared offending by being seen with him. Those who knew us would know we were friends, but those who didn't might think I was making a report or being pumped for information.

'Hongchang, this wouldn't be the fox asking the hen to dinner, would it?' I joked. 'Why don't I treat you instead – I'll feel a bit more relaxed that way.'

Deng Hongchang didn't stand on ceremony. He agreed, saying he just missed our time together at the Party School and wanted a drink. I made a reservation in the Blackwater Room at Beautiful World.

Deng Hongchang arrived at the appointed hour. As we sat, he talked to me about the progress of anti-corruption work, and complained of the 'four bitternesses' of being a disciplinary supervisor: poverty, exhaustion, stress and emotional torment. This last one was most difficult. Placating 'public displeasure' often led to private grudges. Without a certain measure of flexibility and conviction, most people could not stand the pressure. I was moved by the sincerity with which he spoke, particularly when he talked about the five things that a good disciplinary cadre could not fear: death, imprisonment, demotion, expulsion from the Party and divorce. I couldn't help commenting, 'The path of the righteous is desolate.'

After Deng Hongchang's soliloquy, the thread of conversation moved on to the main topic. He clinked glasses with me and said directly, 'Furen, I wouldn't have asked you to come out without special reason. I have a favour to ask!'

As soon as I heard this, the knot of tension within me suddenly relaxed. I wouldn't have guessed that Deng Hongchang and his 'five things you can never fear' might lower himself to asking me for a favour. I suddenly felt well-disposed towards him, and said in the voice of an old friend, 'Hongchang, there's no need for "favours" between us. Just tell me how I can help and I'll be sure to do my utmost!'

Deng Hongchang lit a cigarette and said disconsolately, 'Furen, I've got a niece, my elder sister's child, who graduated from vocational school a year ago and still can't find work. I'm hoping you might be able to help find a place for her.'

He looked as miserable as if this niece were his own daughter, and I resolved to help him. But what could a vocational graduate do in the Municipal Government? Even the cafeteria ticket sellers had bachelor's degrees. I told him, 'Hongchang, with that little education there's not much she's qualified for besides the Janitorial Brigade.'

His face broke into smile. 'The Janitorial Brigade! Furen, my niece is doing a degree equivalency programme, and in a couple of years she'll have her BA. Once that happens, you can find her something better!'

It must have been embarrassing for him to even have brought this up, I thought. If I was going to help, I'd help all the way, so I said frankly, 'Hongchang, I said I'll help and I will. But the Janitorial Brigade just cleans the offices of the mayor and vice-mayors. Isn't that a bit low-level for your niece?'

'Not at all, Furen,' he replied with satisfaction. 'Cleaning the offices of the mayor and vice-mayors is just as prestigious as being an airline stewardess.'

I had to come completely clean. 'All right then, but there's still the question of appearances. The girls in the Janitorial Brigade are all real beauties.'

He replied, 'Furen, cleaning the mayor's office isn't a beauty pageant. Why is that necessary?'

I knew his professional ethics were kicking in and I hurried to forestall him. 'Serving the mayor requires a certain panache of course. You're representing the Municipal Government!'

Deng Hongchang burst out laughing, 'If you put it that way, I wouldn't be surprised if my niece became the star of your brigade!'

I relaxed when I heard him say that, and tried to be conciliatory. 'If that's the case, I'll assign her to Mayor Liu's office. What's your niece's name, Hongchang?'

He seemed more than a little proud of her as he answered readily, 'Shang Xiaoqiong.'

The Instigator

IN THIS WORLD, not even idiots are innocent. What could be more ridiculous than Liu Yihe's posture as the paragon of virtue and righteousness? There is too much orthodoxy in 'filing a report', too much that is shadowy about 'anonymity', too much opprobrium attached to a 'frame up'. I want nothing more than to return things to their original condition. The reason I want to do this is that I don't believe that there is such a thing as 'original condition'. Everything is enslaved to nihilism. In a world where you can't be sure what is black and what is white, who would dare dance beneath the sword of Damocles? That person might be able to climb a little higher up the ladder of official success. If anyone seeks to restrain my ascent, I'll brandish the sword of Damocles at him, and knock him off the ladder.

The sword is not in my hand, however – Liu Yihe snatched it first. What to do?

My boss, wise as always, told me that in these situations one must seek to prevail by wits, not by strength. As for how to do that, the only thing I could think of was making use of a proxy to attack Liu Yihe. But who had that power?

It wasn't until Qi Xiuying came from K Province to be Secretary of the Qingjiang Provincial Disciplinary Committee that it suddenly came to me. Qi hated wrongdoing above all else, and if she could be made to see Liu Yihe's wrongdoing, she would be sure to act against him. If the Provincial or Central Disciplinary Committee were to open an investigation into him, it would ruin his reputation and career even if the investigation produced nothing. And how could it possibly produce nothing? Catching Liu Yihe in the act would be the perfect first success in her new position in Qingjiang. Who would turn down such a neatly packaged gift?

So how could I go about presenting Qi Xiuying with Liu Yihe's wrongdoings? Once again, the boss had the answer. He noticed that my handwriting is very similar to Liu's. I'm a calligraphy enthusiast, skilled with pen and brush, and I took his hint at once. A little further direction and my path was clear.

I spent three months painstakingly learning to imitate Liu's handwriting. I can replicate many styles, the way actors do impressions of celebrities. Liu is quite a calligrapher, actually, with a bit of the famed Wang Xianzhi's style. Anyone who knows calligraphy could tell at a glance that he had studied the *Orchid Pavilion*, and studied it deeply. Though he had developed his own style, it still bore the marks of Wang Xianzhi in its firm, masculine grace. But still he persisted in his own development and in the end only retained Wang's shapes, replacing the spirit with his own overriding personality.

I like that personality, to be honest, because he and I are of the same sort. But my status is too low to allow me to express my personality. I must keep my true self hidden. The real difference, of course, is that he is a mayor, and I am not. It makes me feel like I'm some sort of forgery, like we are a pair of porcelain vases: Liu Yihe the unique and priceless original, me the clever copy.

Some people think that my boss was mistaken in 'buying' me, but he thinks he detected a misappraised treasure, and that's why I'll follow him to the grave. We take respect for talent seriously. I may not be a 'thousand *li* horse', but I at least can count as a 'hundred *li*' or 'ten *li*' horse, right? And who was it who decided that a man of talent had to be a 'thousand *li* horse' anyway? Couldn't a 'thousand *li* donkey' or 'thousand *li* ox' or 'thousand *li* mule' serve just as well? And besides these beasts of burden, couldn't there be a 'thousand *li* dog', 'thousand *li* wolf' or 'thousand *li* tiger'?

To hell with the 'thousand *li* horse'! I'd rather be a 'thousand *li* dog'. I will pounce without remorse or hesitation on anyone who dares stand in my or my boss's way. I'll sink my teeth into his crotch and show him what the 'thousand *li* dog' is made of!

Mayor Liu was born in the year of the dog, and he's a bit of a 'thousand *li* dog' himself, otherwise he wouldn't look down his snout at others. We've both got the dog nature. The difference is that Mayor Liu is a rebel dog. Dogs can live just fine without faith in anything, but a rebel dog is different. All that is sacred becomes orthodox, and there can never be such thing as a methodology. Methodology is philosophy, and everyone has their own philosophy. My philosophy is not to base my actions on values or principles. When has the advancement of the human race ever been based on anything but selfish interests? I simply didn't believe that Mayor Liu's value system and world view had nothing to do with self-interest. Even if it did, I would create self-interest for him. That was the wrongdoing that I would show to Qi Xiuying. I would do this by means of writing out all his dirtiest secrets in his own hand, in his own voice. I wrote a complete notebook for him, and when it was done and I'd read it from start to finish, I found I'd created something worthy of publication. If it were published, I knew it would be a bestseller. Who wouldn't want a peep into the dark secrets hidden in the depths of a mayor's heart? This book of notes would reveal all.

When it was complete, I gave it to my boss to read, and he once again praised my uncommon talents. I wanted to mail the whole thing to Qi Xiuying but he disagreed, telling me I should mail it to her a few pages at a time, giving her regular doses of stomach-turning medicine. It was a brilliant suggestion. In order to strengthen the impression, I gave my work a title, *The Civil Servant's Notebook*, and every time I mailed an instalment I printed this title out and pasted it at the top of the first page.

When I mailed the first part I didn't dare do it from within the city, so I drove to Changshan. As I tossed the envelope into a mailbox in the post office, my heart was nearly climbing out of my throat. The lady in line behind me thought I was having a heart attack. I sneaked back into my car like a thief, a terrible sense of guilt welling up in me. It was terrifying but also thrilling, as addictive as a drug.

These days, if I go more than a couple of weeks without mailing an instalment of *The Civil Servant's Notebook* I get terribly antsy, as if I were missing my fix, and I leap into my car and go looking for a mailbox or a post office.

I knew that once Qi Xiuying began receiving the *The Civil Servant's Notebook* she would do everything in her power to find me. I couldn't let that happen. I made sure never to leave fingerprints, and to mail the packages from random locations, ensuring they could never find a clue. The only clues they could possibly find were in the contents of the Notes themselves: the list I had written of Mayor Liu's 'wrongdoings'.

The earliest notes were quite creative, literary even. I guessed that if Mayor Liu had the chance to read them, he would stamp and grunt like a boar in heat.

The opening goes like this:

'Today I spent two hours accompanying Feifei shopping in the Changshan Mall. She couldn't bring herself to buy anything, though she had her eye on a particular skirt. She circled it for a while and I knew she liked it, so I told her to try it on. She wouldn't consider it, saying she would save the money to spend on my birthday. Working as I did from morning to night, I'd practically forgotten my birthday. I started looking forward to the weekend as soon as I started work on Mondays, thinking of how I would relax with Feifei. I said a skirt like that can't be more than ten thousand, and it's not like we're short of cash; I decided I'd buy it. She still wouldn't have it, and said it was me she loved, not my power or money. That's what enchants me about Feifei, she's just so pure, even naïve. She doesn't just love me; she actually worships me. And not for my wealth or status either. So long as my heart belongs to her, she thinks she's the happiest person in the world.

'There was something of love at first sight between Feifei and me. That was when I was still a vice department head. I'd gone to conduct a survey in Changshan, where Feifei was the host of a TV news programme. She came to my hotel to interview me, and while we were chatting I told her that she looked like the class beauty from my college days, then told her frankly that that class beauty had always had my heart, but I had felt so unworthy of her I'd never dared dream of possessing her. Feifei was just as frank, and told me that I looked to her like the white knight she'd always dreamed of in college. Our conversation grew warmer as we got to know each other, and we eventually exchanged numbers. Less than a week after I returned to Dongzhou I got a call from her, and I could hear from her voice that she had been thinking of me constantly. I told her I'd drive to Changshan myself that weekend to see her, and after that it was too late to change our minds about anything.

'Three years went by in a flash, and Feifei became my spiritual refuge. I don't think there's anything immoral or dissolute about extramarital affairs; I respect all that is beautiful about the human character. I was so busy I forgot that today is my birthday. I could never dare hope that my wife would throw a party for me since she's too thoughtless to remember even her own parents' birthdays. Besides my own secretary, the only people who remember my birthday are my lickspittle subordinates who hope to use my power to change their own fates. Only Feifei observes my birthday out of love.

'We returned to her little villa in the suburbs, and as soon as we got in the door she gave me a surprise: a thousand paper cranes of various colours were hung about the room. She told me that she had spent five whole evenings, working late into the night, folding those cranes. As the incomparably lovely Feifei spoke, the tinderbox of my heart suddenly burst into flames, and like Faust falling in love with Helen, the dawn broke over my spirit. If marriage could be compared to the sun, then the most glorious radiance is only found outside of the sun, not inside it. I think this is the truth that all successful men who pursue affairs live by.'

I had a very simple reason for starting with Mayor Liu's affair, rather than with bribery or corruption: Qi Xiuying was a Disciplinary Committee secretary who'd been a widow and single mother for more than ten years, and a woman like that would never forgive such a lofty public servant for straying from the marital fold. She would be sure to treat a corruption case like this one with as much severity as possible. He'd never dig himself out from under it!

After all was said and done my boss proved prescient. His most profound political theory was that if a person was to retain his official position, he needed a perfect understanding of how that position might be taken away from him. If someone wanted to advance, he would need a perfect understanding of the pleasures and weaknesses of whoever it was who could help him do so, and at the same time he would need to sweep away any obstacles to that advancement.

As I put the *The Civil Servant's Notebook* plan into effect, I realised something. If you want to achieve something in your official career, you have to brave death, imprisonment, demotion, expulsion from the Party, even divorce. Otherwise you will only live in fear.

Mayor of Dongzhou, Liu Yihe

I ONCE SAID that I had come to Dongzhou to be a boat-puller, and I wasn't just mouthing fine words. Reform doesn't come from going with the flow, but against it, and along the way we must face sand shoals, submerged reefs, whirlpools and the danger of capsizing. So I've always advocated tolerance towards reformers, even failed reformers. Lack of tolerance would be a tragedy for the nation. But when a boat-puller pulls, chanting work songs, he's often accused of flaunting abilities – a major taboo in Chinese politics. But to a real reformer, the target of reform is precisely these old taboos!

Recently I led a team to four South-East Asian countries to drum up investment. The media in Singapore claimed that the openness of my thinking came as a great surprise to the worlds of industry and commerce in the area, and even *The New York Times* gave me high praise. They called me the mayor 'who dared to be first'. Praise like that was unprecedented, and some feared that by showing my mettle I'd made myself a target for criticism.

After my trip, I'd attended a meeting of the Municipal Standing Committee where the old mayor, now director of the Municipal People's Consultative Conference, and a few standing Committee members gave me a friendly reminder in private that I should learn to protect myself. My secretary, Song Daoming, was also worried about poisoned chalices and knives in the night. It's not that I don't think about these things. But you can't do nothing simply because you're worried about poisoned chalices. I firmly believe that no matter what storms rock the official world, the basic principles of human society will still apply.

So during the meeting I told everyone frankly, 'I've got an advertisement for Dongzhou into *The New York Times*. Reform and opening up is not just the spirit of Dongzhou, it's the spirit of China. Reform and opening up has allowed China to show its mettle on the world stage. Dongzhou was already moving towards the world, and who can become mayor of a provincial capital of eight million people without a little courage, and the guts to display his own mettle? Dongzhou was once a manufacturing base for the People's Republic's armaments, but development has met with an unprecedented bottleneck, and if it is to continue it will require upgrades of industry and the attraction of foreign investment, all the while encouraging Dongzhou's enterprises to boldly "go out". This was my original motivation in promoting foreign investment at the start of my term.

'To tell you the truth, every time I go abroad to discuss investment deals and I see the clear skies and blue waters of Western countries, I find it as galling as the cadres at the beginning of reform and opening up did when they went abroad and saw the wealth of other nations. Last year when I visited Japan and saw the natural beauty of Hokkaido, I felt an enormous weight suddenly descend upon me. I don't know if Dongzhou has any place that beautiful, and even if it does it's probably only because we're industrially backwards and economically depressed. Meanwhile the Japanese are able to reach a high degree of industrialisation while preserving such a beautiful natural environment. It made me deeply envious, but more importantly, it told me I have a job to do! The environment our ancestors left us was beautiful to begin with, so when will we be able to return that beauty to our people, and to our ancestors? Seeing their environment, I suddenly blushed to think that Dongzhou has been praised as a forested city, an ecological city, a hygienic city and a model environmental city. I felt ashamed on behalf of all those officials who don't know to blush, and who instead gloat over the political points they've scored! Those points are not meant for taking credit for the work of others, or increasing one's own wealth and power; they're meant for benefiting the public. Only political achievements that can withstand the tests of practice, history and the scrutiny of the people can really be called achievements.

'Our investment attraction team stopped off in Hong Kong on our way back, and there I saw a news item on the television about how some people had encountered difficulties while mountain climbing near the city, and had been rescued by passers-by. I thought to myself that in terms of area and despite its high population density, Hong Kong is barely an ink spot, but after more than one hundred years of development it still has large areas of wild, forested mountains. We've only been developing for thirty years and we've more or less used up our land. The air we breathe, the water we drink, the food we eat: they're all polluted. The flames are lapping our toes, and we're still bashful about flaunting our mettle in public? We're not worthy of the people of Dongzhou!

'Some may think I have ulterior motives here, that I am thinking first of my career. I'll admit that I hope as much as anyone for a bright political future, but there's no contradiction between climbing the ladder and achieving something real. The higher your position, the more and the greater things you can do. The height of the position I occupy is the business of my superiors, but the height of my aspirations is my own business; therefore the greatness of what I achieve will be decided by us together. Reform in Dongzhou has always been conducted along three principles: market efficiency, democratic values and a harmonious society. In the pursuit of these three principles I do not shun the "rule of man". Today, when the ideals of democracy are not yet fully formed, I have the authority as Mayor to combine the rule of man, rule of law and rule of letters in the execution of reform. When I conduct surveys of the lower levels, I hear more boasting and empty talk than I do serious thinking about development. How will we change the situation without the "rule of man"? Frankly speaking, I will employ all methods and means in the pursuit of human development and social stability.'

Everyone was deeply moved by the speech, and all felt that in taking the team on our tour of South-East Asia we had promoted the advanced thinking, desire for change and 'dare to be first' spirit of Dongzhou not only to the media of South-East Asia, but also to *The New York Times*. This 'advertisement' had been perfectly placed.

Despite the warm reception, however, I felt a cold wind rustling at my back. That wind blew in from behind the backstage curtain, and keened as if it blew over a bare dagger blade.

Lyndon Johnson once said, 'It's better to have an enemy inside the tent pissing out than outside the tent pissing in.' My principle is, no matter whether these pissers are friends or enemies, they'd all better do their business in the bathroom.

Most people believe that if someone makes up a story about them that isn't refuted immediately, the story will become truth within the space of twenty-four hours. Though knives come at me from all directions, impossible to ward off, I still retaliate against each one. The means are simple: poke holes in each lie as it comes. In politics you can feel intuitively who your enemies are. They say that only the innocent are not afraid of rumours. After all, no wall can block all whispers. So I spoke frankly and fearlessly at the meeting, facing the rumours directly.

'There's been a lot of interest recently in my weekend trips to Changshan,' I joked. 'Some people think my wife is too fierce, and I ought to have a fling. They seem to think that if someone of my position keeps running off to Changshan, it must be for an affair, and so they've made up a beautiful soul mate to embellish the story. These folks really ought to have gone into screenwriting rather than politics. They have me giving my lover a dog as a present, worth several hundred thousand *yuan*.

'So what's my lover's name? It's Feifei. There really is a member of my family named Feifei: my wife's most beloved little dog, the apple of her eye.'

As I spoke, there was some embarrassed laughter in the room, and I continued my tale with gusto. 'If you're dissatisfied with my work, you may attack me however you please; even my wife doesn't mind being attacked. Everyone calls her a shrew behind her back. She's used to it. But attacking my wife's dog, Feifei . . . well, she won't have that. Not only does my wife dislike attacks on Feifei, but Feifei herself is not pleased.'

By this point the whole meeting room had collapsed into laughter. I continued, 'So why is it I keep going to Changshan? Everyone knows that filial piety is part of China's traditional morality. For me, a major criterion for choosing friends is whether or not they're filial. Who could be friends with someone who doesn't respect their parents? Though the pressures of work mean that I can't often visit my parents – a source of great guilt to me – I still think of myself as a filial son. I love my parents as I love my motherland. My mother's health has been poor, and she was missing her daughter. You may not know that my elder sister lives in Changshan. I sent my mother to live at her house, and I go to visit them on the weekends. Who knew that some people with ulterior motives would make up such elaborate stories? I hereby warn the slanderers: resort to such low tactics, and you're bound to give yourselves away!'

The moment I said this, several vice-mayors turned towards Peng Guoliang. It looked like my sarcastic counterattack had found its mark.

Chief of the Municipal Investment Promotion Bureau, Wen Huajian

CONVICTION IS FRAGMENTED by nature. Who takes it seriously anymore? Whoever says their conviction is strong is bound to be the world's biggest hypocrite. As top dog in the Investment Promotion Bureau, however, I'm obliged to stress in public the connection between Conviction – by which I of course mean faith in the Party – and the soul. Hypocrisy is one of the fundamental skills of the politician, and the most profound lesson of politics. It's most important to strike an attitude of great rigour. That's called sincerity. I know a secret to being sincere: surreptitiously swapping the spiritual body and the physical body. Some people are worried that in the process they'll confuse the face with the buttocks, and the key to this particular secret is showing people the buttocks of the soul. But that sounds awfully crude, so I usually keep it a secret.

The buttocks possess many advantages compared to the face, though we're in the habit of ignoring them in the same way we're in the habit of suppressing the talents of those under us. In terms of aesthetic appeal, the buttocks are far more beautiful than the face: smoother, softer, more tender. They do not wrinkle and they get fewer pimples, moles and age spots. They are not only simpler and more appealing in shape, but you also don't have to spend money on their upkeep. Also, according to the *fengshui* principles of physiognomy, they indicate good fortune. When it comes to character, the buttocks give an impression of sincerity, and never wear a false smile as the face might; no two-faced Janus there. They are humble and reserved, able to put up with humiliation when necessary, and accept hardship on behalf of the face. This is their most admirable quality. In truth, the buttocks' greatest advantage is their reliability. They can sit and stand, and they are a window of communication between exterior and interior. From a dialectical standpoint, they are thesis and antithesis, capable of resolving the two. For this reason I always reverse the body and the soul whilst I am stressing the importance of Conviction, always with excellent results.

Is there anyone in this world who doesn't live by their brains? So many brainless bodies sit in our meeting rooms, it would be impossible *not* to talk about Conviction. But what is Conviction? It's definitely not a political slogan; sermons are of no use whatsoever.

I have been inoculated against Conviction. I have antibodies in my body but even more so in my soul. The more antibodies, the weaker the Conviction, and the weaker the Conviction, the more one needs something to fill Conviction's role. In most cases, those who have Conviction are as addicted as a drug user. In fact, anything that causes addiction will make people dogged in its pursuit. I hate drugs because they destroy the body, but I like stimulation, especially stimulation that addicts the soul and completely replaces Conviction. After searching endlessly for stimulation, I unexpectedly found it in gambling.

After falling in love with gambling, I began to win every bet I made, in the casinos or in government, to the point where my wife joked, 'I've heard that people's brains are split into left and right, but I'm starting to wonder if your brain is six-sided like a die. How did you get so good at wagers?'

She was telling the truth. Just as the light of life burns more brightly for someone who has resolved to die, when a person is determined to gamble, a fire begins to burn in their hearts that is more powerful than any faith, so much so that it replaces all faith. I wasn't the only one who felt this way. The Mayor was the same, another indication that gambling and faith are in some ways interchangeable.

The Mayor once said something particularly incisive: 'When you've been in politics long enough, you start to feel like a giant panda living in the world's most luxurious jail. There's no thrill whatsoever, and after a while you're bound to get the 'three highs' (he was referring to blood pressure, blood sugar and cholesterol) and need a breath of fresh air, a little stimulation. Otherwise it's like you've got a corpse buried inside you, like your heart is a grave. You need to dig a little hole in the grave and release the spirit of the corpse or you'll suffocate inside!'

I once went with the Mayor to the Philippines, and the local mayor who greeted us drove a Jeep and was accompanied by more than ten bodyguards. He had two handguns strapped to his waist. He invited us into his home and called out seven or eight of his wives to keep us company. As he poured the wine, he told us earnestly that while he was mayor, we were welcome to invest wherever we liked, get rich however we liked, and he would see to it that nothing went wrong. But there was one condition: we'd split the profits fifty-fifty. On the plane back to China, the Mayor said a true word: 'If we were businessmen, we could strike it rich for sure: just open a casino in the Philippines!'

The greatest thing I learned from that trip abroad was what freedom really is. Our politics are too hampered by rules and regulations, Party discipline here, national law there. Not only are our hands and feet tied, but even our hearts are bound. What do we know of freedom? In truth, it's every man for himself. Why do we pretend to the people that it's all for one and one for all? It's as if we're putting on a show for the common people. What do you want them to believe? The only thing you can't do is to let them see things as they are – every man for himself – or do away with all false equality. Only the truth will prevent exhaustion at every social level and encourage the lower classes to wage a struggle against the upper classes, creating a force for social progress. This alone constitutes true freedom. In this sense, the rules of the casino are worth promulgating to society at large: small fry stay in the main hall, while big fish enjoy VIP treatment. They can borrow funds if they're broke, but they have to pay back what they owe, transparent and free. If you want to find out if you count among the powerful, walk into the casino and see where they put you.

You could say that the Mayor and I got to know each other best in Las Vegas. He was leading an investment attraction team to America and our time was tightly scheduled. At one point, he complained of exhaustion and asked where we could go to relax. I recommended we have fun at a casino and he agreed. To my surprise, he was hooked the first time he tried it, and soon after we returned to China, he started to feel the hankering. He wanted to gamble, but didn't dare be too brazen about the arrangements. He waited for someone else to broach the subject. My greatest strength is understanding the needs of others and taking the pulse of my leaders. As time went by, the Mayor began to feel that I was closer to him than anyone, and even his wife began to think it was strange that he took me with him every time he went abroad. But the Mayor didn't have a brain like a six-sided die. He lost continually, to the point where his funds began to run low, and I had to rack my brains for sources of cash.

Director-Level Section Member of the Provincial Disciplinary Committee's Sixth Office, Shang Xiaoqiong

I AM ZHU Dawei's girlfriend. He usually calls me 'Cat' while I call him 'Rat'. I'm working undercover in the Janitorial Brigade of the Dongzhou Municipal Government. I didn't tell Dawei about it at first. I wanted to get accustomed to the environment. The main job of the Janitorial Brigade is to come in early and clean the offices of the mayor, vice-mayors, chief secretary, deputy chief secretary and a few other directors of the Municipal Government. We start work around five in the morning and are done by seven. People start work at eight-thirty, so Rat isn't likely to see me.

Our work isn't done when the offices are clean, of course. We have to hang around for the entire day. Who knows when a leader might need us? We need to be on call.

A week after I started in the Brigade, I met Rat in a hallway and gave him a healthy shock. I dragged him into a corner and explained that I was on assignment and he was to pretend he didn't know me. Rat is sharp. Although he seemed perplexed, he complied without question.

This assignment brought me a lot of stress at first. Qi Xiuying judged that whoever was mailing the *The Civil Servant's Notebook* was hiding within the Municipal Government. That meant more than seven hundred possible suspects. One of the targets of investigation was

Liu Yihe, Mayor of Dongzhou, and with a target as big as that, being discovered could have unthinkable consequences. Then I thought of Rat and felt that I wasn't totally alone in my mission. With the help of the person I loved, my confidence was strengthened immeasurably.

When I was young, my family lived next door to Rat's. He is two years older than me and we were childhood friends. By the time he was going to university we had fallen in love, and we would long for the weekend when I would go to his school or he would come to mine. Our favourite thing to do was to see a movie. My degree is in criminal investigation and I like crime films, so Rat would always try to make me happy by getting tickets to the newest crime movies the moment they came out. Rat studied politics, where he learned to be cunning, but he's never been insincere with me. I think he's really got a head for politics, and if he ever gets the chance to take high office, I'm sure he wouldn't be your average politician. But since he arrived at Number Two Department, he hasn't had a single break. All he's allowed to do is compose the minutes of conferences and meetings; he's never had the chance to display his writing skills.

Rat is a thinker. He has a point of view and is a good writer to boot. What's most important is that during the time we've been together, he's been tremendously thoughtful and understanding, and if he can understand a girl's thoughts and desires, he should have no problem understanding those of his leaders. I've always believed that all he needs is an opportunity to write some materials for one of his leaders and he'll be a success.

But Rat's luck was no good. There was someone in Number Two Department with a master's degree named Huang Xiaoming, and a woman named Ou Beibei, who was as beautiful as a flower and fluent in English. What's more, both the department head and vice-head were excellent writers. Not the smallest opportunity to show off his writing ever came Rat's way. But he was a clever one, and knew that being secretary to a mayor was a shortcut to the top. He wanted to be Peng Guoliang's secretary, but I thought he was being a little rash in his choice – Peng might be powerful and his future bright, but we who work in the Provincial Disciplinary Committee are quite aware of how many reports are made of his misconduct. I advised Rat to go slow, pick his target more carefully. Rat usually listens to what I say. He had meant to compete with Huang Xiaoming for the position, but he took my advice to let it go.

Rat knew very well that in the two years I have worked on major corruption cases under Secretary Qi, I have seen and experienced far more than he. But I've always believed that Rat was made to work in politics, and that he would get the opportunity to make a future for himself one day.

Right now, however, my assignment was the most important thing.

Had the *The Civil Servant's Notebook* really been written by Mayor Liu? If so, then he was the most corrupt of corrupt officials! But after more than a month of careful undercover observation, I simply couldn't see Mayor Liu doing it.

In addition to our regular cleaning duties, the Janitorial Brigade was also responsible for servicing the major government meetings. Once during a Municipal Standing Committee meeting, I was assigned to serve the leaders. The committee meeting primarily focused on attracting foreign investment, and during the meeting Mayor Liu solemnly declared, 'I've always said we should rather change our thinking than change our personnel. The plan to attract foreign investment is a product of liberated thinking. Ideas dictate results, and so long as we focus on developing Dongzhou instead of our own personal interests, the cliff edge of risk can become a vista of opportunity!'

I was thoroughly convinced by Mayor Liu's speech, and I wondered how someone who thought that way could possibly be corrupt. Later, a mayors' office meeting was held to discuss environmental protection in the city. The head of Oldbridge District had been tipping the wink at polluting industries to bring in more income for his district, and the chief of the Municipal Environmental Protection Bureau had agreed to keep quiet in exchange for favours. Mayor Liu had already made a discreet investigation to confirm the situation, and during the meeting he banged the table and shouted, 'What have we got this cat for if not to catch rats! You're not worthy to be the Environmental Protection Bureau Chief! Don't think corruption only means taking bribes! Taking the taxpayers' money and doing nothing is just as corrupt – a corruption of the soul!'

The Bureau Chief's face turned bright red and he hardly dared lift his head. The atmosphere in the meeting room was deadly tense. Mayor Liu's words impressed me deeply. Such a display of outrage couldn't be a show. It had to be true sentiment! This is what began to weaken my suspicions about Liu Yihe.

Senior Reporter at the *Qingjiang Daily*, Lin Yongqing

MY RELATIONSHIP WITH Qi Xiuying is hard to describe in a nutshell. We were college classmates, together with her future husband. The three of us were in the same school and classes, we were also cadres in the student committee. Her husband was the chairman of the committee, not only handsome and elegant, but also an eloquent speaker. I thought of myself as a good writer, but I was an introvert, and not particularly attractive, and though I fell in love with Qi Xiuying the moment we began school, I never dared tell her. She was the most beautiful girl in our school back then and plenty of boys pursued her. Of course the one who pursued her most doggedly, and who had the best chance of success, was her future husband. I never gave up, though, and finally came clean to her just before we were going to graduate. When she'd heard me out she wept tears of regret, saying that I and her future husband both held important places in her heart, but because I'd waited so long she had already accepted his love, and decided to follow him to K Province. Thus my cowardice lost me her love. But the three of us remained good friends, and later I took a kind and gentle editor at the newspaper as my wife.

By then Qi Xiuying was working in the Public Security Bureau of H Town in K Province. Her husband worked in the Procuratorate.

122

He was a hard worker and had become a department head at a very young age, but fate was unkind, and he died in a car crash while on an assignment. Qi Xiuying was devastated but she was a woman of strong character. She raised her son herself without ever remarrying. She threw herself into her work, and ten years passed in a flash. During that time my own wife also passed away from lung cancer. Qi became a widow and I a widower.

We often talked on the phone, giving each other moral support, and even wrote letters. But because of her high official position and the fact that she was in distant K Province, I knew we'd be unlikely to come together even if we wanted to. But fate was either helping us or mocking us. I was shocked to learn that she was being transferred to Qingjiang Province to be secretary of the Provincial Disciplinary Committee. She'd hardly arrived in Qingjiang – we hadn't even had a chance to meet – when some of her limelight was shed on me, in a big way.

I mentioned I'm an introvert, and I've never been much of a talker. That meant I had little luck with girls in college, and fewer opportunities in work. When my wife was alive, she called me a wimp. She said I'd end up last in the line to eat shit. The thing that really got me fuming was my housing situation. I was living in a fifty-square-metre apartment, a place that my wife had cajoled from the newspaper leaders while she was alive. Other colleagues my age, department directors or editors, had places that were one hundred and fifty or sixty square metres. We'd gone through several rounds of housing reallocation, and given my seniority I should have been upgraded long ago, but I never did get to the front of the line. My colleagues with their three-room or four-room apartments got them just as housing reform was being instated. They hardly paid a thing, and shortly thereafter, the apartments became private property. They turned around and sold them, then took out a little loan and bought themselves split-level or two-floor apartments.

I, on the other hand, was spending all my savings looking for a cure for my wife's terminal cancer. My son was of an age to marry, and we weren't going to be able to squeeze into a fifty-square-metre hovel. It weighed on me day and night. But heaven provides, and the manna started falling the moment Qi Xiuying arrived in Qingjiang Province.

Saying 'heaven' is hardly an exaggeration. To me, a regular journalist at the *Qingjiang Daily*, a standing Vice-Mayor of Dongzhou City is God. My coming into contact with God was indirectly thanks to Qi Xiuying, and directly thanks to Xu Zhitai, Vice-Head of Number Two Department, Combined Affairs.

Xu Zhitai and I were good friends when he was a journalist at the *Qingjiang Daily*. Later, he got fed up with the hard work and loneliness, and finagled a place in the Municipal Government. Things went smoothly at first, but for some reason his luck soured and he was stuck as vice department head for ten years. We share a character flaw: we're too docile, too obliging. When we come under unfair pressure, the kind that cannot be rebelled against, we accept it, bear it and gradually come to feel that it is fair after all. For example, all the dirty business that was going on behind housing assignments at my newspaper. That dirty business was too much for me, and it was so often disguised as righteousness.

The only consolation that righteousness can bring us comes through suffering, and though that suffering might be noble, nobility only exists in fantasy, not in reality. Only basic human nature is real, and within human nature, all desire is reasonable. I had repressed my own desires for too long.

By the time I met Vice-Mayor Peng, my numbness had bereft me of everything but my humility.

Xu Zhitai drove me to Beautiful World that day, saying that Mayor Peng wanted to meet me. I had thought he was joking, that he just wanted to have a drink. He often took me for a drink when he was feeling down, not because he really wanted a drink, but for the chance to pour his heart out. I didn't believe him this time because he didn't say why Mayor Peng wanted to meet me. I couldn't think of any plausible reason beyond his wanting me to do a profile in my paper, and I had no plans to do a profile. Furthermore, if he wanted a profile done, he didn't have to treat me to dinner; we could have discussed it at the office.

When Xu Zhitai brought me inside, however, we were met by a smiling, capable-looking man in a suit who shook me warmly by the hand and addressed me as 'Teacher Lin'. He said that Mayor Peng had already arrived. Xu Zhitai hurried to make introductions. This was Hu Zhanfa, Mayor Peng's secretary. Only then did I realise it was real, and began to feel uneasy.

When Xu Zhitai and Hu Zhanfa bustled me into the private room, Mayor Peng stood up and shook my hand most ingratiatingly, saying, 'Teacher Lin, I've heard a lot about you! Your *Heart of the Blackwater River* series is a classic in the Municipal Government.'

Peng's flattery found its mark. That series had once won first prize in a national-level photography contest; it was my greatest pride. It really was a classic in the city and even throughout the province, and appeared at most important municipal venues. But the photographs themselves were far more famous than their author, and very few people knew I had taken them. I was a little embarrassed by Peng's praise. There had to be a purpose behind such flattery, but I couldn't imagine what a standing vice-mayor, in charge of a provincial capital of eight million people, could possibly want from me.

After a few rounds of drinks and dishes Mayor Peng said to me in matter-of-fact tones, 'I've always wanted to hang your *Heart of the Blackwater River* in my office. I think being able to see our mother river every day would be a grand encouragement to a public servant like myself!'

I knew this was more flattery, that an ulterior motive lay behind it, but I enjoyed it all the same. All of a sudden I felt much calmer, and I said with modesty, 'Mayor Peng, it's an inspiration merely to know that you appreciate it. I'll be sure to ask Zhitai to help arrange something.'

At this point Xu Zhitai pulled a fat, beautifully bound booklet from his bag and handed it to me, saying, 'Lin, Mayor Peng and I were chatting and the subject of your relationship with Qi Xiuying came up. Mayor Peng has a lot of admiration for Secretary Qi and hopes you might be able to make an introduction and help him get to know her better. This book is for her. It's a compilation of Mayor Peng's thoughts and theories on reform and opening up and the development of Dongzhou Municipality. We also hope you'll tell Secretary Qi all about Mayor Peng. You know all about his reputation as a fighter for what's right, as well as his capability and courage. He's achieved re-markable results in everything from municipal development to foreign trade, and he's beloved by the people of the city. But in China, anyone who tries to get anything done is sure to meet opposition. There's al-ways a small band of naysayers sniping at you from some dark corner. Mayor Peng's achievements are self-evident, Lin, and this compilation is evidence of the theoretical underpinnings of his actions. Dongzhou needs more leaders like Mayor Peng now, leaders who dare to risk all for the welfare of the common folk. We can't yield to those petty people who do nothing but drag down anyone more capable than themselves, who see reform as a joke. Let me toast you on behalf of Mayor Peng!'

Xu Zhitai had barely finished speaking when Peng raised his glass and added warmly, 'Zhitai, I can't let you toast on my behalf! With this glass, Teacher Lin, we become friends, and friends must treat each other with sincerity. I've heard from Zhitai that you've had difficulty with your housing situation.' He turned to Hu Zhanfa. 'Zhanfa, it's your responsibility to settle these difficulties. We can't allow an experienced news worker, one who's made such great contributions to the media of Dongzhou City and Qingjiang Province, to be treated this way!'

He drained his glass.

I was moved by Vice-Mayor Peng's sincerity and enthusiasm for my cause. At the same time, however, I felt a nameless anxiety. What

Mayor Peng wanted from me was actually very little, and he shouldn't be obliged to go to such lengths on my behalf. Xu Zhitai handed me the book and explained the situation, and I promised to fulfil my role. I couldn't help thinking, though, that there was no need to treat me so royally – even resolving my housing difficulties – merely for the sake of a few words in Qi Xiuying's ear. Could it be . . . ? But never mind. For the sake of the apartment, I would help even if Peng Guoliang were corrupt! I felt much more at peace after making this resolution. If he was corrupt, then I might be the floating spar that saved him. I had confidence in my relationship with Qi Xiuying. Besides her son, no one in the world was closer to her than I. And if he weren't corrupt, well that made things even simpler. None of the sniping would hurt him in the end. But I thought even Xu Zhitai didn't really know whether Peng Guoliang was corrupt or not. He was just using me to improve his standing with the Vice-Mayor.

One week later, I moved into a new apartment – one that belonged to me. Split-level, one hundred and fifty square metres and beautifully decorated. The first thing I did was hang *Heart of the Blackwater River* in a conspicuous place on the living room wall. I did this because Mayor Peng liked the photograph and had hung it in his office. I was able to live in such a nice apartment because of him. You could say that a palatial home like this was the greatest reward I could have hoped for after a life of struggle. Now my dream had come true, and I owed it all to Mayor Peng. Once, I'd felt proud of *Heart of the Blackwater River*. Now I was moved by the 'Heart of Peng Guoliang'. No matter what, I would tell Qi Xiuying that Peng Guoliang was a great official – the 'Heart of the Common Folk' – and that the Provincial Disciplinary Committee had a responsibility to see him safely through!

The Puppet Master

I MUST REMAIN behind the scenes. That way I can clearly see the flaws of the actors on stage. This is what nearly twenty years in government has taught me. In politics it is the hidden hand that is decisive. Some people call that person the 'black hand', but others call him the unsung hero. I'm neither a black hand nor a hero. I just know a plain truth: the bigger fish eats the smaller fish, and the biggest fish eats them all. So how does one ensure one is always the biggest fish? By lurking in the depths, in the darkness, and watching the other fish silently; by not making a move until you've grasped your opponent's weaknesses.

The secret to defeating your opponent is to attack from behind. Of course, you need to make preparations. Most important is to befuddle your enemy's senses. The means are simple: manufacture truth. Act the part of the humble servant of the people and the whole world will follow your act, believing that the truth is evident to anyone with eyes to see. They only look with their eyes, never with their hearts. How do the blind find their way? By looking with their hearts, not their eyes. All that stuff about the masses' eyes being snow-bright is complete nonsense. The masses' eyes may be bright, but their hearts are deaf, dumb and blind. They believe that what they see is real. They don't know that the world is absurd, and that absurdity is the true essence of reality.

Since they believe their eyes, however, we can make use of those eyes. Everyone has voyeuristic tendencies. No one believes what they see on stage. The snow-bright eyes of the masses believe that rumour is the most reliable truth. They put trust in information that comes by back channels, and thus they are not only the consumers of rumour, but they are also its creators and perpetrators. They say that a thrice-repeated rumour becomes unstoppable. If so, then a rumour repeated thirty times, three hundred times, three thousand times, thirty thousand times or three million times becomes a matter of resounding truth. Manipulating the thoughts of the masses is an easy thing, actually. Formulate those thoughts as rumour, spread them via back channels, and they'll be far more effective than words printed in a newspaper or broadcast on television.

Only by placing yourself behind the scenes can you see the stage clearly. Only by remaining in the darkness can you see the bright places clearly. That's politics. But my target suddenly turned his head, his gaze stabbing towards me like a cat spotting a mouse, freezing me to the spot in panic. He's a natural born actor who appears at first as nothing more than a mediocre bit player but then proves himself flexible and versatile during the play, creating a startling shower of sparks. Those sleep-swollen eyelids hang above friendly, welcoming eyes, yellow and catlike, a pair of glass balls. It's those eyes that seem to see straight into hearts, that look on the common people as though they look on his own mother and father, his smiling face awash in sunlight. But to me, that smiling sunny face is a shadow, and his public servant act makes me want to vomit.

But that shadow is also a diligent worker of extraordinary dedication. He is best at putting on a show of concern for the people's welfare. He never seems to tire of it. I doubt that the blood in his veins has ever flowed sluggishly. It probably boils even as he sleeps. Since he's taken the stage, he's spoken constantly of the need to 'blast away with the force of an atom bomb all outmoded thinking or institutional bottlenecks that obstruct development'. He boasted that 'I want nothing more than to be a boat-puller, to walk the same road as the people of Dongzhou, to think their thoughts, join in their labours, to pull the great ship of Dongzhou against wind and waves, to make steady progress forward.'

For a city mayor to compare himself to a boat-puller is sheer hypocrisy, obviously, and Liu Yihe is the worst of hypocrites.

But my biggest headache is that he seems to match his actions to his words, and with ferocious efficiency, leaving hardly a chink in his armour. He seems to have indefatigable spirits, inexhaustible energy and unbending willpower; the strength to stop a train with his hand. He talks about how true administrative ability lies not in what the government controls, but in what the government *doesn't* control. What was the consequence of the government insisting on monopolising everything? The poor suffered, the rich profited and the bureaucrats benefited . . . Nothing needed reforming more than the government monopoly!

Backstage, I'd long since tired of his fervent words, but I'd forgotten that those who cannot curb their tongues often bring disaster on their own heads. There's no such thing as a person with no weaknesses. The wise repeat no tales, they say, but no one realises that rumours may also originate with the wise. Paging through China's history is like being caught in a magic spell where nothing is solid, truth is distorted, rumours rule and danger lurks on all sides. We take pleasure in the misfortune of others, in adding fuel to the fire. So long as we ourselves are not harmed, each of us is a past master of the poison tongue, a consummate liar.

You want reform, you want achievement, don't you my friend? Well I've prepared a spell for you, one which you won't escape unless you can advance with utmost caution, watch your back as well as your front, walk on eggshells and ultimately fall on your own sword. Hearsay is a spider's web, one that stretches from horizon to horizon, and you're the fly who will not escape. Ice water is the way to deal with a hot-blooded one such as you, and my veins run with the ice of the Yellow River in February. Though it might be lava running in your veins, still I will freeze you solid.

But as it turns out, the bastard's blood was as impervious to freezing as oil. It burned hotter and hotter. I half wondered if he'd experienced some genetic mutation in the womb. Besides his work and career and the odd moment snatched for reading, he had no interests whatsoever. Neither women nor gambling caught his fancy, and he spent his days in his office, buried in documents; an archetypal workaholic.

He might be hot-blooded, but that was just an act for the common people and his colleagues. His hidden designs and plans would never show themselves beneath his heavy, red eyelids, and that was the most dangerous thing about him. His controlled calm gave you an impression of great power and made you watch yourself around him. I knew quite well that no one in government dared attack him. He was impervious to all manner of attack. I had worn myself out thinking of ways to defeat him but none were practicable. I realised that my strategy was flawed, and began instead to research all the methods by which a mayor protects his position. I believed that, once I had grasped those methods, I could use them to find a way to defeat him.

The best means of defeating your opponent, of course, is to strike using another's hand. Luckily I had found one, not a black hand behind the scenes, but a hand in the open, the hand of a goddess, the claw of a cat that catches mice. That claw was as sharp as the sword wielded by the 'Jade Cat', and as terrifying as the chopper of Bao Longtu. I knew this was playing with fire, but I said it was ice water that flowed in my veins, and I do not fear fire. In fact, I like playing with fire. Who in government doesn't? We only say those who play with fire will end up burnt as a way of scaring the cowards off. Who achieved anything without playing with fire? The anti-corruption effort was also playing with fire. The people could see no hope unless the fire were roaring, but if it leaped too high, they would not only lose hope, but even feel despair. That required deft control of the flame, and I was placing my hopes in this particular hand being unable to exert such control. So long as she was chasing a corrupt official she would pour more fuel on the fire, desperate to burn him to bone ash.

The female Disciplinary Committee secretary who had been moved to Qingjiang Province was obviously determined to start some fires, and at this critical juncture the best means of self-preservation was clearly to strike while the fires raged! Since Qi Xiuying was such a master of playing with fire, I would provide some kindling for her. Not only would my rival become the centre of the conflagration, but I would make sure Qi Xiuying was sacrificed on the flames as well.

When I was in high school I'd dreamed of studying directing at the film academy, and although circumstances led me into politics, this new profession required not only acting abilities but also directing abilities. *The Civil Servant's Notebook* was a documentary that I was directing, one that would draw in Qi Xiuying like a television serial and gradually spur her to action through the dastardly corruption of its main character.

After more than six months of mailing her the Notes I hadn't seen the slightest reaction. That means that I'd already hooked her; she was likely conducting secret investigations. They say that the thunder rolls in silent places. They also say that a person lives by their face, as a tree lives by its bark. If a woman like Qi Xiuying began investigating, she wouldn't rest until she'd uncovered a massive case, making something out of nothing if she had to. Otherwise she would suffer a massive loss of face.

I didn't always like the feeling of hiding in the shadows, however. While I am spying on other people, might someone also be spying on me? I often imagine someone suddenly clapping my shoulder from behind, which makes me come out in cold sweats. I've also developed a new tic. Every night, once I am sound asleep, I dream that I and Liu have become versions of the Monkey King, and we fight furiously with our golden staves, the battle raging all the way to the South Sea, where the Guanyin Bodhisattva becomes Qi Xiuying.

While Liu and I fight we ask her which of us is the real Monkey King. Qi Xiuying puts her palms together and smiles, saying, 'I only recognise corruption, not the Monkey King.' Liu Yihe and I have to continue fighting, all the way to the Western Heaven, where we meet the Tathagata Buddha. He turns out to be the Old Leader, and Liu Yihe and I both ask him which of us is truly the Great Sage Equalling Heaven? The expressionless Old Leader tosses each of us a book, the *Philosophical Reflections on the Urine Cure*. Unhurriedly, he says, 'The one who can understand this book is the Great Sage Equalling Heaven,' whereupon Liu and I sit on the ground and open our books. It praises urine as some sort of miracle cure, as though it can bring the dead back to life and bestow immortality. I can't tell if the book's claims are based in experience or idealism; all I know is that urine is the product of the body's metabolism. How can it be worshipped as though it is holy?

This book should actually be titled the *Theological Reflections on the Urine Cure*. We know that philosophy is divided between materialism and idealism, while theology belongs purely to idealism. Furthermore, there are many ways to ensure physical health. How could the book propound only the urine cure?

The Old Leader's point of view is a bit like the enshrinement of Confucianism over all other schools of thought. In my dream I give a disdainful laugh, and the book in my hand suddenly becomes two small turtles. Just as I am staring in surprise, Liu's book turns into an official chop. This instantly puts me into a rage, and I have just stood and pointed my finger at the Old Leader, about to accuse him of running a rigged game, when he suddenly roars, 'He's a false Monkey King! Lock him down, left and right!' The turtles in my hands suddenly become shackles around my wrists, and I wake in absolute panic.

I don't know what the dream signifies. I have pored through every book about dreams that I own, but find no answers. Remembering that the Old Leader's urine therapy could also cure convulsions, I forced myself to drink a cup one morning and, sure enough, after I started the therapy, I've never had the dream again.

Number Two Department, Junior Department-Level Researcher, Ou Beibei

AT FIRST I'D thought that I could get everything I wanted by following Peng Guoliang, but so far I hadn't even made bureau-level researcher. I had brought it up with him several times but he always answered noncommittally. I knew it was a woman he wanted, not a female civil servant, and once he had me and his desires were fulfilled, there would be nothing more!

I decided to show him my true colours. The bloom might be off the rose but he couldn't rid himself of it. So I began to meet with him more frequently in private. Once, when I brought him some documents, he shut the door behind me without a word and carried me to his desk. The sofa would have been fine, or the single bed in his retiring room which he used for his afternoon nap, but we'd done it too often in those places and the thrill was off, and Peng Guoliang liked a little variety.

Every time, I made Peng Guoliang weak and distracted with pleasure. He couldn't compare to Wang Chaoquan in terms of endowment, and Zhao Zhong wasn't even worth mentioning, but unfortunately Wang Chaoquan was as useless in his career as Zhao Zhong was in bed. If only Wang's career had been as powerful as his member, then he could have brought some glory to his woman, and I wouldn't have needed to exchange my body for it now!

For years I never understood why, despite Wang Chaoquan's power in bed, I never got pregnant. How could such a masculine man be unable to get me pregnant? If we'd had a child, I might have been a wonderful mother. But he couldn't even fulfil this dream of mine! How despotic is fate!

Since the night in the Kempinski Hotel when Zhao Zhong's sail had furled in front of me, he would shrink a bit whenever he saw me. All men's dignity relies on a little piece of meat. Otherwise how could they call themselves men? Since that time, however, Zhao Zhong had also been more devoted to me, and spent no small sums on me. Damn false monk, you really wanted to make me your nun, didn't you?

I hadn't wanted to reveal my relations with Zhao Zhong, particularly to the men in Number Two Department who all knew how much I used to hate him. I'd always curse him and call him hogshead, but now he'd become a hog prince. What could I do? All princesses love princes.

Though I kept my relations with Zhao Zhong a secret, Peng Guoliang's secretary Hu Zhanfa once saw us dining together at Datang Shifu. To be honest, I've never had a good impression of Hu Zhanfa. His eyes in particular seem made for voyeurism. Nothing that happened between me and Peng Guoliang seemed to escape those narrow eyes. He toasted Zhao Zhong and me with an unpleasant smile. We had been in a private room where he wouldn't have seen us, but Zhao Zhong had gone to the restroom and met him there. If he'd lied and said he was there with some business contacts, that would have been the end of it, but he had to boast that he was treating me to dinner, as though he were threatening Peng in front of Hu.

Hu Zhanfa of course wanted to see the situation for himself so he came in with his wine glass, and when he saw that I and Zhao Zhong were alone in a private room, he seemed to understand everything. I grew tense the moment he walked in, because he was quite clear about the relationship between Peng and me. After toasting us he uttered some pompous clichés of hospitality and left, throwing me a look as he went through the door. That gaze swept over me like an autumn chill, and I trembled inside.

Only a few days later Peng Guoliang had a meeting with some American businessmen in the foreign reception room, but he used an interpreter from the Foreign Affairs Office instead of me. Xu Zhitai was present at the meeting and was a bit confused, as Peng Guoliang never had anyone but me to interpret, and after the meeting he asked me why.

I laughed lightly, but I became wary. I knew it had something to do with Hu Zhanfa catching Zhao Zhong and me at dinner.

Sure enough, Peng Guoliang continued to pass me over as interpreter, while Liu Yihe sent a secretary to fetch me when he was meeting with foreigners. Soon, I'd practically become Liu's personal interpreter. I was hoping for an opportunity to talk to Peng Guoliang in private, but he kept making trips to Hong Kong and was otherwise too busy to see anyone, so I never found an appropriate chance.

Worst of all was that I was starting to feel morning sickness, and Wang Chaoquan noticed the first time I vomited. He didn't reveal his suspicions, however, and merely asked after me solicitously. I covered up by saying I'd eaten something bad the night before. He asked if he should take me to the hospital but I said there was no need, and he hurried off to work.

I was certain I was pregnant. Peng Guoliang had done this, and I couldn't let it go to waste. I would use my pregnancy to squeeze him. At the very least I would make department-level researcher. While he and his ugly wife were still married, there was no way I would bear his child. I wasn't that stupid. In fact, I could easily have faked being pregnant to fool him.

In the interest of certainty, however, I went to the municipal obstetrics hospital, and discovered that I was two months gone. After I'd received the results, I was walking along and reading them when someone tapped me on the shoulder. When I turned to look, I nearly choked. Wang Chaoquan yanked the test results from my hand and scrutinised them, then threw them in my face and hissed, 'Shameless!' Then he strode off.

Director-Level Section Member of the Provincial Disciplinary Committee's Sixth Office, Shang Xiaoqiong

WHILE I WAS sweeping up in the Mayor's office I happened across some real notes of Liu Yihe's. The fat black notebook was in the central drawer of his office desk, a drawer that had always been locked, but that morning was somehow unlocked. Perhaps Liu Yihe was so busy he'd forgotten. It opened with a light tug, revealing the fat black notebook.

I flipped it open and found this rhythmic and forceful line inside the cover: 'Liu Yihe, throw your whole soul into the execution of justice and the speaking of the truth!'

Thereafter, each entry consisted of thoughts or lessons regarding work:

'Since being transferred to Dongzhou I have emphasised acts over speech: doing more and saying less, doing first and then speaking, driving the development of government programmes in Dongzhou without controversy, needless dithering or ostentation. Some cadres, however, have consistently lacked vigour, trailed behind in motivation and are utterly missing the pioneering spirit. Not only are their wills weak, some simply don't have a thought in their heads. They fulfil their duties only perfunctorily, lost in bureaucracy, busy with meeting and greeting. Some simply make a show of getting work done and never accomplish anything, satisfied with being a 'mouthpiece', a 'transfer station', content to hold meetings about meetings, to write documents about documents. Some fight for profits and advancement, their eyes on the position above them instead of the work in front of them. The existence of these problems means that some things that might have been done are not done, some issues that might have been resolved are put off indefinitely, conflicts that might have been eased are instead exacerbated.

'I once said that I had come to Dongzhou to be a boat-puller, and no matter how complicated the environment or how pointed the conflicts, I would stand by the people every step of the way, surmounting their difficulties with them. Faced with problems of development that must be resolved, or problems of particular importance to the people, we will keep calm, not panic, not mouth empty platitudes, and resolve them earnestly. So long as we have confidence, resolve, perseverance and patience, there is no river we may not cross!'

This had to be the real Liu Yihe, writing from the heart. I was sure this was his true voice. It fitted perfectly with the man I'd observed in secret, a Liu Yihe who not only couldn't be a corrupt mayor, but who was truly a servant of the people. It was the good fortune of the people of Dongzhou to have such a great mayor.

Quite obviously, *The Civil Servant's Notebook* could not be the work of Liu Yihe's pen, though the handwriting was the same. I could now say with confidence that someone who had forged his handwriting was trying to set him up. Whoever it was, he or she was employed in the Municipal Government. They couldn't be someone in the service centre, but must be in one of the combined affairs or secretarial departments.

I guessed that Peng Guoliang was the man behind the *The Civil Servant's Notebook. He* would benefit most if Liu Yihe was to fall. I lacked proof, of course. The reason I thought Peng Guoliang was operating remotely, behind the scenes, was that his handwriting was full of loops and flourishes and was nothing at all like Liu Yihe's. Also, someone as volatile as Peng Guoliang would never have the patience to learn to imitate someone else's handwriting. So who was actually writing the *Notebook*? There were only two possibilities. The first was Huang Xiaoming, who'd just been promoted to be secretary to Mayor Peng, and the other was his predecessor Hu Zhanfa, who had left the Municipal Government to become Deputy Head of Oldbridge District.

I'd heard Rat say that Huang Xiaoming was originally transferred to Number Two Department because he'd attracted the notice of Liu Yihe, then a standing vice-mayor. That meant there was a bond of obligation between the two. If Liu Yihe hadn't been elevated to Vice-Governor of Qingjiang Province, Huang Xiaoming might have eventually become indispensable to him. Now he was secretary to Mayor Peng, but would he be capable of something so low as framing Liu Yihe? I didn't think so. Besides, he'd only been Peng's secretary for a few months and wasn't likely to be so deep in his confidence that he would be given a job like writing the *The Civil Servant's Notebook*. I'd seen a few theoretical essays that Huang Xiaoming had written and published in newspapers and magazines, and could tell from his style that he was someone with a noble spirit. How could someone like that do something like framing Liu Yihe?

On the other hand, most people in politics are not always free to act according to their own conscience. Could he be doing this against his will? Peng Guoliang was a ditch of filth, and it would be hard for Huang Xiaoming to remain clean in his service. Given Huang Xiaoming's educational background and sensitivity, however, he would in theory be quite capable of imitating Liu Yihe's handwriting and authoring the *The Civil Servant's Notebook*.

Huang Xiaoming happened to be accompanying Mayor Peng on a trip to Shenzhen at that time, so I asked Rat to work with me in conducting a full search of Peng's and Huang Xiaoming's offices. Beforehand, I made a special report to Deng Hongchang, Director of the Provincial Disciplinary Committee's Sixth Office, hoping that the organisation could help switch me with Lin Doudou, who was responsible for cleaning Peng's office. She would take over Mayor Liu's office, and I would henceforth be assigned to Peng. I was confident that the proof I needed was in that room.

Sure enough, when I went into his office one morning I discovered that since the last time I'd managed to get inside, he had hung on the wall a new calligraphy scroll in a red sandalwood frame. It was by Hu Zhanfa. He had written 'The Timely Blind Eye'. What was unusual was that where other calligraphers might have imitated the style of Zheng Banqiao, the original calligrapher, Hu's work showed traces of Wang Xianzhi. What surprised me even more was that the vigour of the work made it seem as though it had been done by the same hand that had written the 'Keeping Up With the Times' scroll in Mayor Liu's office. That particular scroll was done by Mayor Liu himself. Why did their calligraphy appear so similar?

My suspicions were aroused. This 'Timely Blind Eye' scroll was clearly something that Hu had given his boss as a parting gift. But a simple piece of calligraphy wasn't enough to prove that Hu Zhanfa was the author of the *The Civil Servant's Notebook*. It did, however, make me move Huang Xiaoming down the list of suspects and put Hu Zhanfa at the top.

In the lower left drawer of Mayor Peng's desk were several cartons of soft pack Zhonghua cigarettes. In the four cabinets under his bookshelves were seven or eight bottles of Hennessey and Louis XIII, as well as a light-green Chanel woman's handbag, a very delicate item, with the price tag still hanging on it: thirty thousand *yuan*. Beneath the calligraphy was a two-level safe that couldn't be opened without a code. I wondered to myself how much incriminating evidence might be hidden inside.

After 'cleaning' Peng Guoliang's office I went to 'clean' Huang Xiaoming's. Besides a wall full of bookcases, there was his desk with a computer on it. As I 'cleaned' I found nothing out of the ordinary, only a work journal in his drawer. Huang Xiaoming typically wrote everything on his computer and I'd never seen him with a fountain pen. This work journal was the first I'd seen of his handwriting. Though it was elegant enough, it was quite divergent from Liu Yihe's style, and more or less eliminated the possibility of Huang Xiaoming being the mysterious author.

The biggest result of my 'cleaning' expedition was to confirm Hu Zhanfa as my prime suspect. But Hu Zhanfa had already left the Municipal Government, so how was I going to get my hands on proof? I shared my thoughts with Rat, and he gave me a smile and said, 'Leave that up to me.'

Sceptical, I asked him what he could do, and he said that Hu Zhanfa had asked him over to his house that night to work on his master's thesis. It was a heaven-sent opportunity. Hu Zhanfa was studying for an in-office master's degree but it was Rat doing all the work. If Rat could make good use of the chance to visit his house and come up with some iron-clad proof, then my days of languishing in hell would be over. I gave him a firm, no-nonsense kiss, and told him I needed him to be a real rat.

He didn't let me down. At midnight he called me to say that he was parked outside my house and had a surprise for me. I rushed downstairs and leaped into his Benz.

'Qiong,' he said searchingly. 'How are you going to thank me?'

I replied disdainfully, 'Why would I thank you?'

He pulled a black notebook out of his document folder with great satisfaction and passed it to me. 'See for yourself.'

I hurriedly opened it and scanned the first few pages. To my shock I saw it was a copy of the *The Civil Servant's Notebook*. Hu Zhanfa was the true author, and he had kept a copy.

Thrilled, I asked, 'Dawei, how did you get your hands on this?'

He replied smugly, 'Seek and ye shall find. When he headed to the bathroom I went through all the drawers of the desk in his study and found this black notebook. I didn't even have time to look in it. I just stuffed it in my bag. I didn't glance through it until after I'd left his house, but I got a shock when I did!'

Early the next morning I paid a visit to the Provincial Disciplinary Committee. First I reported to Director Deng, who became very agitated as he looked through Hu Zhanfa's notebook. He took me off to report to Secretary Qi on the spot.

Director of the Hong Kong Representative Office of the Dongzhou Bureau of Commerce, Niu Yuexian

AFTER GUOLIANG WENT from the Dongzhou Bureau of Commerce to become assistant to the mayor of Dongzhou and the Bureau's Representative Office in Hong Kong was shut, I decided to stay on in Hong Kong to make a new life for myself. It was also Guoliang's wish that I use the foundations laid by the Representative Office to establish a venture capital and trading company, and of course I would be unable to sustain such an endeavour without Guoliang's support. He had far-reaching plans for the company. It would belong to him, and I would only be a caretaker. He often said that changes come fast and thick in politics, so if one day things changed for the worse, it would be good to have a stronghold to retreat to from the storm.

If Guoliang has a flaw, it's that he doesn't know how to read people. Since he began to depend on people like Wen Huajian, he's developed a serious gambling habit. And after he got to know Robert from the Wantong Group in particular, he began visiting not only the casinos in Macau, but also the gambling ship in Hong Kong. The money he so painstakingly saved up over the years all went to gambling. It's heartbreaking to think of it. Nonetheless, Guoliang is a real man, with the guts to stake everything on a single throw of the dice. If he left politics for business, I'm sure he'd take to it like a fish to water. He often says that life is just like a big casino.

You could say the same about love.

When we began our affair, we were making a grand gamble. I've always liked a life of risk, and after all these years of gambling, I've come to feel that my relationship with Guoliang is one of my great achievements. Guoliang often says I am a strange woman, who combines a man's wisdom with a woman's sensitivity, but I'm not strange. I'm simply a woman who knows what she needs.

I've never entertained dreams of marriage, but I do have dreams of love.

I should mention that after Guoliang fell in love with gambling, our relationship grew far more risky. You could say that I'd climbed a lofty mountain and now I was discovering it was actually an iceberg under my feet that was rapidly melting.

Although my liaison with Guoliang had brought me rewards, I had yet to achieve my original goal. Now the risks were growing greater. I guessed that his run of luck would come to an end sooner rather than later and that his love of gambling would be his undoing. Time had come for me to cash out, capital plus interest.

The Dongzhou Government had established a reward program for those who'd made significant contributions to attracting foreign investment. I made a proposal to Guoliang: why not put this money into the Hong Kong company? As standing Vice-Mayor he decided who to reward and how much to give them.

Guoliang picked up on the idea immediately. He also chose Robert Luo as a recipient of an award. In fact, Robert was neither an investor nor a target of investment. He was merely the representative of the Wantong Group in Dongzhou. But he was also the one who brought Peng Guoliang, Wen Huajian and Chen Shi to the gambling cruise ship. Giving him the award created the impression that he'd had something to do with the investment. It was also free money as far as he was concerned, and he would be thrilled with however much he was given.

Guoliang had generously agreed that I should be CEO of the Hong Kong company. He also gave me fifty per cent ownership of the company while Wen Huajian and Chen Shi got twenty-five each. They didn't protest because they were perfectly clear that my fifty per cent actually belonged to Peng. But they all miscalculated. I had made thorough preparations. Not only was my fifty per cent beyond Peng Guoliang's control, but their own quarter ownerships were actually mine to dispose of as I saw fit too.

The day the company was established, Peng Guoliang wired over thirty million Hong Kong dollars, then flew to Hong Kong with Wen Huajian and Chen Shi and checked into the Conrad Hotel. I had planned a banquet to celebrate the new company, but the three of them were taken by gambling fever and they insisted on cooling it in Macau first. I drove them to the ferry terminal and they boarded the express hydrofoil. They were gone for a day and two nights. When I went to the terminal to pick them up, there were dark circles under their eyes.

By previous arrangement, I had readied 450000 US dollars, and when we returned to the hotel, Peng Guoliang called Robert Luo to say that in light of his contributions to the development of foreign investment in Dongzhou, the Municipal Government had decided to reward him, and hoped that he would continue to make such contributions in the future. As elated as if he'd won the lottery, Robert came to the hotel to collect his 250000 dollars.

After he left, Guoliang took out the remaining 200000 and said with feeling, 'Attracting investment is hard work, my brothers. You will each take 50000 dollars – this is my reward to you.'

Chen Shi wasn't so sure. 'Many thanks to our leader for his generosity! But if this ever gets out, we should have our story in order.'

Guoliang puffed his chest out and said, 'I'm the one who decides the award amounts. If anyone asks where this 200000 went, I'll know what to say; you can relax.'

Secretary to the Standing Vice-Mayor, Hu Zhanfa

WHY DID I keep a copy of the *The Civil Servant's Notebook*?

For one thing, it represented an enormous labour on my part, and I wanted a copy as a keepsake. Moreover, if it really did result in the fall of Liu Yihe, I wanted a copy to hold over Peng Guoliang. So long as his star was rising, I would rise with it to my desired position. Politics is an ugly business. You always need to keep a knife in reserve, even for your own boss.

Lechery is a relatively minor sin for a politician. At worst it is a 'lifestyle problem', and once you've attained a certain status and power, it's no longer an issue at all. But addiction to gambling is a major sin. So long as you don't get deeply entangled, lechery will never lead to major expense. Gambling is different.

Eating and whoring are human nature. An affair or two won't wipe out your ancestral inheritance. But once you've become a gambler, you're liable to lose all you have, and more.

Gambling became Peng Guoliang's greatest flaw. It started out small, but now he was gambling more and more. While I was his secretary things were all right. At least we were birds of a feather. But then Huang Xiaoming succeeded me. He might have suited Mayor Liu, but for Mayor Peng he was a time bomb in the pocket. I urged Mayor Peng to choose Zhu Dawei, a born secretary, but he wouldn't listen, saying he already had plenty of people to wash his feet, and what he needed was someone to tell him what he needed to hear. It couldn't be helped. The decision wasn't mine to make. But surely you know that it's your secretary who wipes your arse each day?

And if he wanted to suck up to the Old Leader, had it really been necessary to make his former secretary head of his Number Two Department? The fact that Yang Hengda drank urine for five years for the Old Leader showed his undying loyalty, but they say a loyal minister won't serve a second master. You can insist on dragging him to your side, telling your political opponents that the Old Leader trusts you, but you're also revealing your entire hand to the Old Leader. Do you think Yang Hengda won't report your every move back to him?

Yang Hengda doesn't seem particularly reliable to me. He's been spending a little too much time with Song Daoming and Zhao Zhong recently. Doesn't Peng Guoliang know those two are as loyal as hounds to Liu Yihe? Yang Hengda is head of Number Two, not Number One. What could he want with Song Daoming and Zhao Zhong?

In politics, once you've decided to go on the offensive you've got to be heartless about anyone who stands in your way. Forget that nonsense about 'Trust those you use, don't use those you mistrust'. You need to both mistrust your friends and make use of your enemies. But there need to be reasons for your mistrust, and you need to take care in the use you make of others. Take Yang Hengda: if Peng Guoliang really wanted to get in with the Old Leader, he shouldn't have installed Yang as head of Number Two Department. He should have promoted him to a vice bureau-level leadership position. It wouldn't have been difficult to keep him close – just make him Vice-Director of the Municipal Government. He was a full bureau-level secretary and had served the Old Leader for years. Of course he would get antsy as a mere head of a combined affairs department. Liu Yihe might have realised this long ago. He might be using Song Daoming and Zhao Zhong to undermine

Peng Guoliang, via Yang Hengda. In an environment as complicated as this, it sends a chill up the spine just to see how carelessly Peng went gallivanting off to Hong Kong and Macau.

What worried me most was how it took so long for the *The Civil Servant's Notebook* to have its effect. How could someone of Qi Xiuying's character simply turn a blind eye? There's a line in a Lu Xun poem: 'discerning thunder amid the silence'. Could she have already begun secret investigations? That woman is crafty as a fox. Mayor Peng tried several times to invite her to dinner but each invitation had been tactfully declined. This struck me as an ill omen.

My friend in the Provincial Disciplinary Committee told me that they never received any anonymous letters reporting poor conduct on the part of Liu Yihe, whereas they got sacks of such letters about Peng Guoliang. The previous secretary had simply sat on them. They were all good friends and of course looked out for one another. But Qi Xiuying was different. She benefited from the anti-corruption effort. She climbed a ladder made of the bones of the corrupt, and that was why Mayor Peng instinctively grew worried when she arrived in Qingjiang Province.

That's why I thought of using the connection between Xu Zhitai and Lin Yongqing to get to Qi Xiuying, arranging for the 150-square-metre split-level villa in Hegang Gardens for Lin Yongqing. Once he'd moved into his dream home, he was firmly in our camp, of course, and did his best to sway Qi Xiuying, but never to any great effect. I began to worry on Mayor Peng's behalf, or perhaps it would be more accurate to say I was worried for myself. I've been deputy head of Oldbridge for less than a year, and if things get rocky for Peng, my dreams will begin to burst like bubbles.

What a horrible woman Qi Xiuying is. If I'd known, I would have written a *The Civil Servant's Notebook* about her instead, and mailed it to the Central Disciplinary Committee. It was too late for all that now, because my copy of the *Notebook* has been stolen for sure, and it can't have been by anyone other than Zhu Dawei, whom I had trusted so completely. This fellow's father has made the biggest contribution to foreign investment in Dongzhou, but Mayor Peng gave the award to Robert, the Hong Kong agent. Zhu Dawei has borne a grudge against Vice-Mayor Peng ever since, and his theft of the copy of the *Notebook* means he now has Mayor Peng by the throat. Not bad, Zhu Dawei! You might know a man's face, but you'll never really know his heart! I had to report this to Mayor Peng immediately and tell him to put the screws to Zhu Wenwu. We need to get that copy back. If it really ends up in Qi Xiuying's hands, Mayor Peng and I will become morsels in her chopsticks!

Deputy Chief of the Anti-Terrorism Unit of the Qingjiang Provincial Public Security Bureau, Wang Chaoquan

I AM LIKE Harry, the protagonist in the American movie *True Lies*. We both live a world of lies, and outside our organisations no one knows the truth about us, not even our wives. If I hadn't chosen this sacred and secret path, full of hardship, challenge and danger, I'd be a top professor in a university by now, teaching foreign languages. Or if I had gone into politics properly, I wouldn't have stopped at bureau-level researcher, leading even my wife to despise me.

But I am passionate about this sacred and secret path, because I am passionate about my nation. I have given everything to my work, and my work has made me into a true spy.

The demands of national security mean that Harry had to hide his true identity from his wife for many years, maintaining the fiction that he was a regular businessman. Likewise, the demands of national anti-terrorism and anti-drug campaigns have kept me from revealing my true identity to my wife, Ou Beibei.

I was chosen by the Anti-Terrorism Unit of the Public Security Bureau while I was still in college. I underwent secret training, and after graduation was sent to work in Qingjiang Province. The nature of my position meant that I did not actually work in the Provincial Anti-Terrorism Unit, but instead was sent to the Foreign Investment

Bureau of Dongzhou City, where I was to remain undercover by the side of Director Ning Zhiyuan. My organisation had determined that Ning Zhiyuan was the Dongzhou operative of a certain international terrorist group. His codename was Bald Eagle. The terrorist group relied primarily on drug trafficking to fund its activities. It had established drug smuggling channels and also formed a criminal network in the Dongzhou area that was developing outwards into large cities around the country. My mission was to feel my way out to the rest of the network, beginning with Ning Zhiyuan as the central node. When the time was right, we'd close the net.

Clearly it was a glorious yet also a formidable mission. While I was undergoing training I held to a single precept: absolute loyalty to the nation. I had given up my youth, my knowledge, my passion and my family to this one solemn oath, which had become my heart's blood, my faith and my conviction.

People like me need to 'sacrifice the dear, endure the unendurable, accomplish the impossible'. The battle lines of the hidden struggle will never be known, and the struggle is to the death. It demands of me not only a firm political faith, but also special skills and areas of knowledge that ordinary people would find quite surprising. Military science, politics, linguistics, law, psychology, social interaction . . . we must be adept at them all. My particular strengths are infiltration and investigation, including counter infiltration. My own training was focused on domestic investigation, and after years of experience in the hidden struggle, I have become a bright sword and a sturdy shield in the service of national security. It is my deepest pride.

How I yearn to tell my wife of my accomplishments, and to share with her the pleasures of my many victories! But my oath of absolute loyalty to the nation demands my secrecy and silence and the concealment of my true identity, and no matter what painful misunderstandings I might encounter with family and friends, I must accept them all! In my heart I keep a list of the named and nameless heroes who encourage me: Li Kenong, Pan Hannian, Qian Zhuangfei, Hu Beifeng, Xiong Xianghui, Shen Jian, Cheng Zhongjing . . . Their great deeds have mostly gone unknown and unrecognised, vanishing soundlessly into the dark heart of history. When I became a nameless warrior in the hidden struggle, I joined them in that darkness. Fighting on the front lines of national defence, no matter how intense or cruel the struggle, I am doomed to be a nameless hero. When I joined this grand and quotidian path, I knew this in my bones.

It is this that allowed me to laugh off my wife's haughty condemnations, regardless of what discomfort I was feeling, and to play the role of the useless husband. In fact, I'd already explained it to her a thousand times, in my own heart: 'I'm far from useless, Beibei, I'm a real man. If you love me, you should be able to feel the passion in me, you should be able to sense my strength, you should be aware of this burning heart that loves you. But you've changed, Beibei, you are no longer the pure and beautiful girl that I first loved. You've become opportunistic and vain. We once swore to live hand in hand, to love each other all our lives, but now your gaze is fixed upon money and power, and the eyes that were once limpid as springs have already lost their glow; they have become unbearably earthly. What temptations have made you forget our love, my dear wife? What devil has blinded your eyes to the sight of your own soul? Turn back, Beibei, the void is before you! You would leap in, leaving your husband behind, but I won't let you. I'll save you. But I cannot, because to save you would be to reveal my identity.'

After Beibei and I married, we planned to have a child, but she never got pregnant. When we went to the hospital to get checked, the doctor said the problem lay with me: I have a low sperm count. I took all manner of medicine, none of which was effective. It made me miserable.

I would never have dreamed that my wife could possibly stray from me. They talk about the seven-year itch but I never believed it. I was confident that the foundations of our love were strong. I never thought they might tremble or crack, letting the bitter groundwater seep up to the surface. If I'd known that my marriage would become a pool of stagnant water, I would have chosen to enter my profession as a single man and have become a lifelong monk!

I am not made of iron, however, and when I learned – thanks to my special channels – that it was Peng Guoliang, standing Vice-Mayor of Dongzhou, who was having his way with Beibei, I could hardly stand it. I wanted nothing more than to kill the sanctimonious bastard, but I couldn't. My calling demanded I drink that pool of bitter water to the last drop.

On the day Ou Beibei found out she was pregnant, I was promoted to the post of Deputy Chief of the Anti-Terrorism Unit. That day also happened to be my birthday. It should have been a happy day for me. I had planned to celebrate with Beibei under the guise of a birthday party because my superiors had already promised me that once I'd cleared up the gang of international criminals that was threatening the safety of the nation, I would be transferred out of the Foreign Investment Bureau and allowed to work openly as Deputy Chief of the Anti-Terrorism Unit. Then Ou Beibei would finally learn that her husband was an anti-terrorism warrior and an anti-drug hero. I knew she would be proud to have a husband with such thrilling credentials. But it was all ruined by the results of the pregnancy test from the hospital.

I was in agony. I ran blindly for more than two hours through the rainy night, howling like a wolf, but I knew that nothing would ever be the same.

I could not dwell on my personal tragedy, however. The very next day I had to fly to Macau to apprehend Bald Eagle. He had chosen the Casino Lisboa as his meeting place. The noise and chaos provided ideal cover. Because he was number two in the terrorist organisation, as well as an internationally known drug pusher, I guessed that he would have a security network deployed around the casino in case of emergency. I arranged for my own security dragnet. This was my first active mission since becoming Deputy Chief. I was determined the operation would be a success.

Despite my confidence that there would be no slip-ups, however, an unexpected situation did arise. The other drug pushers had shown themselves and entered our surveillance zone, strolling around the gaming tables as though it were a perfectly ordinary visit to the casino. Suddenly, three familiar faces appeared on my monitor. The one in front was wearing a red t-shirt and a gold chain, smoking a gold-tipped cigarette, with a gold bracelet on his wrist. Though he looked nothing more than a two-bit punk, I knew at a glance that he was that lofty, sanctimonious bastard from Dongzhou who had made me a cuckold. The two behind him were like a pair of clowns: Wen Huajian and Chen Shi. I'd heard the three referred to in Dongzhou political circles as the 'Iron Triangle', three brothers with a common love for gambling. If I hadn't seen the three of them with my own eyes, I would never have dreamed that a personage so grand as the standing Vice-Mayor and Municipal Party Committee member of Dongzhou City would so brazenly visit the casinos of Macau in the company of his two underlings. No wonder the Dongzhou business world was abuzz with sightings of the three of them in the casinos of Macau, Hong Kong, Malaysia and Las Vegas.

Once the three had moved into our surveillance zone, they fell in behind the drug pushers, and I knew immediately that our operation would be a failure. 'Bald Eagle', aka Ning Zhiyuan, was office director of the Dongzhou Foreign Investment Bureau, directly under the authority of Peng Guoliang. If he saw his Dongzhou superior wandering openly around the casino, right behind the people he'd come to meet, there was no way he would dare show himself. As a result, Bald Eagle was spooked and didn't appear, and the operation was a failure.

It wasn't a complete write-off, though. I had recorded Peng Guoliang, Wen Huajian and Chen Shi playing dice, losing thousands of dollars without blinking an eye.

After calling off the operation and returning to Dongzhou, I immediately reported to the Provincial Party Committee. Given the gravity of affairs, the Committee passed my tapes directly to the Provincial Disciplinary Committee instead of the Dongzhou Municipal Disciplinary Committee. Faced with such egregious corruption, I was very aware that Qi Xiuying, Secretary of the Provincial Disciplinary Committee, would never rest until she'd drawn Peng into her net.

When I thought that the criminal ringleader who had mistreated Ou Beibei was about to be swept up by the law, I felt the inexpressible satisfaction of revenge. During training our instructor had often said, 'Our work is of the utmost importance, it is tied to the fate of our nation! When personal feelings come into conflict with the interests of the nation or the country, you must not hesitate in sacrificing your feelings!' But sacrificing your feelings didn't mean forgetting them. The pain Peng Guoliang had caused me was like a knife wound. Even if he were cast into hell, it would not lessen my own suffering. But I will never forget that I am an anti-terrorist warrior, and no matter what suffering I feel, I can only gnaw on it in my dreams. For the sake of national security, I need to be at my best while I work!

Number Two Department, Junior Department-Level Researcher, Ou Beibei

I NEVER IMAGINED that Wang Chaoquan might follow me to the hospital, and I was amazed that I hadn't noticed him. I chased after him, wanting to explain, but he was gone. I stood stiffly by the hospital gate, thinking that the other shoe had finally dropped. I signalled tremulously for a taxi, and went to the office to ask Yang Hengda for two weeks' leave. He assented readily. I gathered up a few things and left.

I went to Peng Guoliang's office and pushed at the door but it was locked. Goddamn it, with all this going on he was nowhere to be seen. I gave Hu Zhanfa a call and asked him where Peng was. I needed to see him.

Hu Zhanfa said mockingly, 'Who do you think you are, Ou Beibei? You can't just see Mayor Peng whenever you please!'

I checked my rage. 'Hu Zhanfa, you tell Peng Guoliang I'm pregnant!'

Hu Zhanfa burst out laughing and said nastily, 'Zhao Zhong's good deed, I imagine?'

I was furious, and began shouting, 'Hu Zhanfa!' but he hung up.

Instead of going straight home, I wandered the streets, full of fury. I was like a lost sheep, searching everywhere for my fold, and I found myself walking into a Xinhua Bookstore, where there was hardly anyone. I felt confused and numb. It wasn't Peng Guoliang's avoiding me that was difficult, or Hu Zhanfa's insults. What really hurt was that Wang Chaoquan knew everything. That damned Wang Chaoquan had actually tailed me like a spy. He'd actually called me 'shameless'.

When Chaoquan had proposed to me he was full of promises about making me the happiest wife on earth.

What bullshit!

What wife could be happy when her husband was so lowly? It was men who couldn't fulfil their promises who were really shameless. Now you're upset about being cuckolded. Well I'll tell you: men who work and work with no achievement *ought* to be cuckolded!

I had meant to become the light of Wang Chaoquan's life, his fire, but he had never been able to ignite me. So I looked for someone who could, and what I found was that light and fire were both dark things. I kept seeing the image of Peng Guoliang's dashing face, full of power and lust, and I came to the painful realisation that once a person was possessed by lust, no incantation can exorcise it. I was feeling cold, and the dead atmosphere of the bookstore made it feel like a tomb. It wasn't a tomb I was looking for, but a sheepfold. I went back out onto the street in a huff. The sunlight stabbed down, passing through my body like a cold arrow.

It was time to show Wang Chaoquan my cards, but he wasn't at home, and his mobile phone was off. I waited up all night for him, completely unable to sleep. At dawn it began to rain heavily, and Wang Chaoquan returned home looking like a drowned rat. I didn't know what he'd done outside all night. Although he would occasionally come home after midnight, since we'd been married he'd never stayed out all night. But I wasn't interested in where he'd been. I laid the divorce papers I'd prepared in front of him and said coldly, 'Sign them!'

Chaoquan glanced over the papers, then said, 'Ou Beibei, you've sunk too deep in your dream. It's time to wake up. Don't think that divorce will solve everything. You should think this over carefully.'

With no hesitation I answered, 'Sign them! I made my decision long ago.'

Without emotion he said, 'You've made your decision, but I haven't made mine. Leave me alone, I've got something pressing to do and I don't have time to waste with you!' He pushed me away and went straight to the desk in the study, pulled out a document folder, put it in his bag and turned to leave.

I blocked his way, shouting, 'Wang Chaoquan, what right do you have not to sign!?'

He laughed, 'Ou Beibei, your brains have turned to water,' and slammed the door as he went out.

I couldn't hold back any longer and screamed at the top of my lungs, 'Your brains aren't water! They're piss! They're shit! All men are the pillars of their family! You must be the most useless man in the world! You're barely a man!'

The neighbours must have heard me, but Wang Chaoquan didn't. He had vanished like a spirit, leaving my heart suffering as though it had been filled with lead, so heavy I could hardly breathe. I resolved to see Peng Guoliang that day, one way or another. I was sure that Hu Zhanfa would have told him about my pregnancy, but still he hadn't called me, and I grew even more distraught. I knew perfectly well that threatening Peng Guoliang was playing with fire and that I'd likely scorch myself, but I had to come out of this with something. I took a moment to calm myself, then took an umbrella and left, heading for the Municipal Government building through the rain.

I went straight to Peng Guoliang's office, but the door was still closed tight. I could only retreat to a corner of the corridor and call Hu Zhanfa. He asked me what I wanted. I calmly asked him when Peng Guoliang would be returning. Hu answered that he'd gone to Hong Kong. I knew that Peng Guoliang was avoiding me. I snapped my phone shut. The moment I did, I received a text message, a joke from Hu Zhanfa: 'Miss Radish wanted to lose weight, and dieted until she was skin and bones. Her mother said, "Who will marry you when you're so skinny?" Miss Radish said scornfully, "White Liquor has his eye on me. He wants to pickle me and call me Ginseng."'

I knew Hu Zhanfa was trying to humiliate me, and I was nearly bursting with rage. I wanted to call him back but my phone was nearly out of power. I felt worse and worse. If my husband were a mayor's secretary or even just head of something, if my husband were a boss like Zhao Zhong, or if I myself had some kind of official post, would I have to suffer humiliation from someone as lowly as Hu Zhanfa?

The more I thought, the worse I felt. I went back to Number Two Department in a stew, and picked up the phone to call Wang Chaoquan. Everyone was in the office, watching me. I swore bitterly at him over the phone, telling him I was divorcing him for sure. Yang Hengda waved everyone out of the office and came over to me, meaning to say something comforting, but clearly didn't know what to say or how to say it and in the end just shook his head and went out. I hurled the phone down in a temper, a sense of deep grievance washing over me. It was the first time in my life I felt I'd been used like a rag. I knew it was over between Peng Guoliang and me, and I would need to get an abortion if I were to keep my job and prevent the situation from worsening. I steeled myself and left.

I hailed a taxi in the rain and went to the hospital, where I endured the suffering of an abortion. Afterwards, instead of going home I went to my mother's house. I turned off my phone and rested there for two weeks, during which time the only two calls that came to the house were from Wang Chaoquan. My mother picked up both times. The first time he asked how I was recovering, and the second he reported that he had quit his job and was going to work in a company in Shenzhen. He also said that he'd signed the divorce papers. When I heard that, I collapsed into my mother's arms and cried.

After two weeks I returned home. The divorce papers were signed, on the coffee table, and Chaoquan had left me a letter as well. I opened the envelope with shaking hands and pulled out the letter: 'Beibei, you have suffered by marrying me. I have not brought you happiness, so I will give you freedom. But a word of advice, as your elder. We live our life. We don't live our position or our status. There's a film called *True Lies*, with Schwarzenegger. It's a pretty good movie – you should watch it. After you do, I think you'll understand.'

No kidding. Who doesn't know that life is precious? But if you don't have status, if you don't carry weight, if you have no position, then what's the point? Women in particular will never be privileged without status or position. All women want to be women of privilege. Why would I watch *True Lies*? That line, 'We live our life. We don't live our position or our status', sounds like a true lie to me!

To be honest, Wang Chaoquan and I hadn't seen a single movie together since we were first married. You can see what a dull life he leads. Marrying him was like a blind woman marrying a blind man. We live in our own worlds. It was fine that we were separating. I'll use it to establish a dictatorship over him. Since love has been twisted out of shape by life, then let us lead twisted lives. A crooked thing only appears straight if you look at it crookedly.

As it turned out, however, even a thing that has burnt itself out may still bear heat, and we'd lived together all those years . . .

I held Chaoquan's letter, tears rolling down my face. At that moment, though Wang Chaoquan and I were now separated, I felt no sense of freedom.

Why?

Why?

I realised that I needed to end things with Peng Guoliang. If you're going to keep avoiding me, I thought, then I'll have to write you a letter. I decided to do it, and explain exactly what I'd suffered on his account. Whether he responded or not, that would be an end to it.

Ou Beibei might not be a golden phoenix, but you're certainly not the *wutong* tree on which I'd perch, Peng Guoliang. Henceforth I'll go my way, and you cross your bridge. When I'd finished with the letter I finally felt a little ease. I'd been under so much pressure recently, I could hardly bear it. Perhaps Chaoquan had been right to say after all that without true life, status meant nothing.

Standing Vice-Mayor of Dongzhou, Peng Guoliang

WHEN HU ZHANFA told me that the copy of the *The Civil Servant's Notebook* had been stolen, I could hardly believe my ears. That guy was a little too clever for his own good. I told him countless times that he shouldn't keep a draft or a copy of the notebook, but not only did he keep a draft, he also made a copy! What could he want a copy for, if not to have a weapon in reserve? Even my own personal secretary, who I trained myself, wanted something on me. Could I trust anyone?

Hu Zhanfa wanted me to use Zhu Wenwu to force his son to hand over the manuscript, but yesterday evening a vice-secretary I know at the Provincial Disciplinary Committee called to say that Qi Xiuying has got her hands on the copy of the *Notebook*. She's already held a preliminary meeting on the matter with several vice-secretaries and made a report to the Committee. They have decided to take action against me.

This is a real case of being hoist with your own petard! I meant to use the *The Civil Servant's Notebook* to get rid of Liu Yihe, but instead Hu Zhanfa has handed him a victory. Now he gets to sit back and watch the show.

When I was considering secretaries, Hu Zhanfa had recommended Zhu Dawei but I didn't like the look of his shifty, ratty features. I thought they concealed a calculating mind. Sure enough, Hu Zhanfa has fallen right into the little bastard's trap.

The way I see it, Zhu Dawei must have acted on orders from Qi Xiuying, otherwise how would the copy have found its way into her hands so quickly? Or perhaps it was Liu Yihe, the old fox, who set a trap for me and made Zhu Dawei his snitch? Zhu Dawei stole the notebook and gave it to Liu Yihe, who passed it to Qi Xiuying. That son of a bitch Liu!

My biggest headache right now, though, isn't actually the copy of the *The Civil Servant's Notebook*. It's Niu Yuexian.

My wife has turned a blind eye to my relationship with Yuexian all these years because she knows that I planted Yuexian in Hong Kong to act as a money launderer. Our family's money can be sent abroad thanks to Yuexian's services. Ever since I used part of the investment attraction prize money to start the company in Hong Kong, I've felt there's something a little strange about Yuexian. I didn't think much of it at the time. I assumed she was just annoyed about my gambling habit. How could I have guessed that the bitch was willing to forget our ten-year relationship for the sake of money. Now she's swept up all the money and fled Hong Kong. I haven't been able to get in touch with her for days.

No wonder she was so enthusiastic about urging me to start the company, imploring me to make her the CEO. Why not, I thought at the time. She herself belongs to me. I'm not surprised at the tricks Liu Yihe plays on me, but how could I expect the same from a woman I'd been sleeping with for ten years!?

The greatest danger now is the thirty million. If Qi Xiuying gets wind of it, I'll be obliged to blame it on Liu Yihe. He always hoped to gather all Dongzhou's best real estate together into a package and put it on the market in Hong Kong. I made many trips there to mediate this process, and that required money at every step. Setting up a company was only a pretence. It made it more convenient to make regular visits to Hong Kong. No matter what, we would need some flexible reserve funds. I actually discussed this with Liu Yihe, but he neither accepted nor rejected the idea. All he said was that he didn't need to hear about means or process, he just wanted to see results. In that case, I thought, I'll just do it my way. Either way, I'd made my report to Liu Yihe.

What Chen Shi and Wen Huajian once said to me was right, of course. The three of us made all those trips to Hong Kong for the sake of Dongzhou's foreign investment. We poured out all that blood, sweat and tears. It is only natural that we should be rewarded. What's wrong with that? Nothing bothers me as much as the current system where they make horses race but give them no hay to eat. If giving a horse hay to eat is corruption, then call me corrupt!

We're always so suspicious of the 'rule of man', as if the rule of law is a panacea for our ills, when in fact the main thing is the 'rule of corruption': helping the horse both to race and also to get a mouthful of hay. I know there's no point in saying all this, but it comes from the heart, and more importantly, it's what all civil servants are secretly thinking. Our expectations for our civil servants are far too high, far too grandiose. The pressure is far more than their flesh and blood bodies can withstand.

I, at any rate, cannot withstand it. Nor do I want to. Qi Xiuying, haven't you become addicted to bullying others? Bring it on then! Who deserves hell more than I? But don't think I'll go easily. Most people in politics have their little ups and downs, but things have always gone right for me, so bring on the storm. I'll be damned if I can't weather it!

Though I am fairly sanguine about the whole thing, my wife is quite the opposite. Last night she didn't sleep a wink, just wiped away her tears all night long. I kept telling her, 'Don't you worry, I'm not made of mud. Even if I do get nabbed, I won't talk. They can't pry my lips open!'

My wife made a solemn pledge. 'If you do get nabbed, Guoliang, I'll get you out of there if it means my own life!'

That's my wife. People say that husband and wife are like two birds in the same forest: when disaster comes they fly in different directions. But my wife's attachment to me is more like that line from Zheng Xie's poem: 'Still standing strong and firm after many storms. No matter what direction the wind blows.'

I'll tell you the truth. Since entering politics, I haven't done right by my wife. Of all the people who once clustered around me, some of them have broken off relations, some have beaten a strategic retreat, some have saved their own skins, and some have taken pleasure in my defeats and kicked me when I was down. My wife must have suffered through every day of all this. Just thinking about it brings tears to my eyes.

My wife couldn't stand to see me unhappy, and she held my head and cried. Crying would solve nothing, however, and after she'd cried for a while, I suddenly thought of Lin Yongqing. I wiped away her tears as I said, 'Peifen, if Qi Xiuying moves against me, you need to ask Xu Zhitai to put you in touch with a certain person. His name is Lin Yongqing. He's a journalist at the *Qingjiang Daily*, and he's got a special relationship with Qi Xiuying. Two things: get him to persuade Qi Xiuying to go easy on me, and also, work our old connections in the capital. Don't worry about expenses, just get them to put pressure on her from above. She's not made of iron.'

My wife listened earnestly, but was still worried. 'But what if this Qi Xiuying really has no humanity. What will we do?'

I sighed, 'Then, my darling, we'll just have to accept our fate!'

She ground her teeth. 'Who says I'll accept it? She may be made of iron, but is her son, too? If the son sinks into the mud, won't the mother follow?'

Who knew that when the chips were down my wife would remain even more resolute than me? That night she helped me go through all my vulnerabilities, all the chinks in my armour, and come up with justifications and explanations for each one. Soon the sky was lightening, and when Huang Xiaoming, my new secretary, came to pick me up, my wife had still not slept. By that point my mood had reached its nadir, and I had no desire whatsoever to go to the office.

Still in her nightgown, my wife led Huang Xiaoming into the bedroom. He looked quite nonchalant but I could tell he already had an inkling of what was going on. If I got in trouble it would go hardest for Huang Xiaoming. It was his poor luck to follow the wrong person. If he'd followed Liu Yihe he would have been standing on his own two feet in a couple of years. Politics is cruel. People can't help assuming that birds of a feather flock together, and if something really were to happen to me, I'm afraid that would be the end of this fellow's political career. But given how things were going, I didn't have much time to worry about him.

My wife called him over to my side and asked, 'Has your elder brother treated you well?'

Huang Xiaoming was evasive. 'What is there to say? What's going on?'

My wife sighed and said, 'I guess I'll have to tell you the truth, Xiaoming. Some petty people are out to get your elder brother, but I can promise you that whatever they say about him, he's completely innocent. You admit he's been good to you, right? Now is when he needs your support the most!'

After she'd said her part she wanted me to add something, but I was too lost and disoriented to know what to tell him, and could only pat his shoulder helplessly and say, 'Call Xiao Furen and ask him to buy a paper shredder for my office this morning.'

Huang Xiaoming nodded.

I waved a hand and said, 'Okay, wait for me downstairs. I'll just wash my face and we'll go to the office.'

Once he was gone my wife asked me anxiously, 'Can we rely on him?'

'When it comes to character,' I said solemnly, 'he's way ahead of

Hu Zhanfa. Plus he hasn't been with me that long, he doesn't know so much. At the moment I'm more worried about Hu Zhanfa. Once I've gotten to the office, I'll find him and give him the necessary instructions.'

I usually move my bowels first thing, but I didn't have the slightest urge that morning. My gut was as empty as anything. Our nanny had prepared breakfast, but I didn't have the slightest appetite. I washed my face, got dressed and went out without even tying my tie. The morning sun seemed to lack vitality. I staggered into the car. The most important thing to be done in the office today was to destroy all the documents that needed destroying.

I worked in the office until noon, when the paper shredder was full. I heaved a sigh and moved slowly to the window. There were always so many people idling in the square below. Where did they come from? Some were discussing matters of love, others sang or made music, some played chess, and others were there to paint portraits for money. To my eye, the Municipal Government office building was just like a golden imperial palace, and all the souls moving to and fro on the square before it were terracotta warriors.

Huang Xiaoming came in to call me to lunch at the cafeteria, but I told him I had no appetite and didn't want to eat. I wanted a car to send me home. While Huang Xiaoming sent a text message to the driver, I opened the safe and passed him a bundle that I'd earlier sealed with packing tape, telling him, 'This is some spending money I keep around, Xiaoming. Keep it safe for me until I need it, all right? For God's sake, don't keep it in the office – it won't be safe there. Keep it in your home.'

It was actually fifty thousand US dollars that I had prepared for the Old Leader. When I'd visited him over the Spring Festival, he'd indicated that he'd like a small expense account to hold a nationwide seminar on health and therapy for retired cadres, to be held in Hong Kong. It had taken me no small effort to prepare the cash for him, but when I brought it to him he wouldn't accept it, saying that the retired cadres themselves had put together the cash and he had everything he needed. I couldn't force him to take it, so I brought it back and had kept it in my safe ever since. Now it had become a time bomb. I couldn't put it in the bank and it was too dangerous to keep in the office, so my only choice was to give it to Huang Xiaoming for safekeeping. If I made it through this calamity, I swore I'd take the money to the casino and enjoy a good round of gambling. Huang Xiaoming stuffed the package into his document folder without saying anything. In silence we locked the door and left the office.

I was in a hurry to go home and talk to Wen Huajian and Chen Shi about the incentive reward money we'd received. At the door to my house I told Huang Xiaoming to have them come to my place immediately, and went upstairs.

Around half an hour later Wen Huajian and Chen Shi arrived, looking like orphaned sons of a fallen family. Seeing their flustered, panicked faces and the state of mind they were in, there was little point in swearing some kind of blood pact between us. It would be hard enough for us to keep from attacking each other. I instructed Wen Huajian to find Robert as quickly as possible so that we could each give to him the money we'd kept for ourselves. Both their faces went pale. They told me they'd gambled that money away long ago, and it would be difficult to produce a sum like that on a moment's notice. I told them sternly that they were to give the money to Robert before nightfall, then handed to Wen Huajian the hundred thousand I'd prepared in advance. Seeing I meant business, they took the money and left with no hesitation.

After they were gone, I dropped to the sofa in exhaustion and fell asleep.

The Government Square

THE FAMOUS LOCAL writer Huang Xiaoguang once wrote a fantasy short story called 'The Government Square' in which he turned me into a mirror that, beneath the daily sun, reflected all of Dongzhou City. In the story, three students from the art academy come to the square every day to paint portraits for passers-by. While they were idle, they drew scenes of the Municipal Government office building next to the square. One student often portrayed it as a castle, another turned it into a mountain in a nature scene, and the third generally drew it as a temple. Onlookers praised each of the students, saying the castle, mountain and particularly the temple somehow all looked very like the government office building, but what they didn't know is that I am a magic mirror. The three students' drawings really are of the government office building, but within my reflection their drawings have become twisted. When the sun saw that my magic reflections were stealing her limelight, she used her brightest rays to crack me with heat, and I shattered into countless fragments. The government building the three students had been painting regained its true appearance. Huang Xiaoguang was trying to use me to tell people that what appears in the mirror is not necessarily the truth. The truth is often staring at us from the other side of the mirror.

Actually, I am not only a mirror. I'm also a thick book. Specifically, I am a single page out of *The Book of Sand*. I may only be a single page from a book, but I am extraordinarily important. I am neither the first page nor the last page – *The Book of Sand* has neither a first nor last page – but though I am only one of its pages, my contents are infinite. I represent history: the history of Dongzhou, naturally. The history of Dongzhou is but a single leaf in the great forest of human history. Of course 'the best place to hide a leaf is in a forest', but I'm actually only one part of one page. Each page of *The Book of Sand* is printed with a mask, and I am that mask. I represent Dongzhou as its 'coat of arms'.

When each new incarnation of the Municipal Government decides to rebuild me, however, they don't realise that I am a page, that they should protect me the way a library protects its rare collection. They build me neither as a mask nor as a coat of arms, but as a Tower of Babel, exactly the sort that was set down in Kafka's 'The City Coat of Arms'. 'The essential thing in the whole business is the idea of building a tower that will reach to heaven. In comparison with that idea everything else is secondary. The idea, once seized in its magnitude, can never vanish again; so long as there are men on the earth there will be also the irresistible desire to complete the building.' And: 'There would be some sense in doing that only if it were likely that the tower could be completed in one generation. But that is beyond all hope. It is far more likely that the next generation with their perfected knowledge will find the work of their predecessors bad, and tear down what has been built so as to begin anew.'

This same point of view can be found in Borges' *The Book of Sand* as well: 'If space is infinite, we may be at any point in space. If time is infinite, we may be at any point in time.' A point cannot be infinitely big, only infinitely small. Thus, so long as a tower is a point, it can never reach heaven. Strictly speaking, humanity is one component of a point, but even so, some people believe that this 'point' is 'heaven';

they can't understand that a 'point' is only a grain of sand. And books, like sand, possess neither beginning nor end.

Just as Kafka wrote in 'The City Coat of Arms', each time the city government changes they decide to build me anew. In the past ten years alone, three separate sculptures have stood at my centre. The first was a sceptre with a roc, a sunbird that was a totem of the ancients five thousand years ago. This bird is recorded in Chuang-tzu: 'In the darkness of the Northern Ocean there is a fish named K'un. The K'un is so big that no one knows how many thousands of *tricents* its body extends. After it metamorphoses into a bird, its name becomes P'eng. The P'eng is so huge that no one knows how many thousands of *tricents* its back stretches. Rousing itself to flight, its wings are like clouds suspended in the sky.'

Isn't this simply another form of the Tower of Babel? Soaring ninety thousand *li* – and yet to heaven. Isn't that simply a 'point'? Of course I understood that this government simply wanted to display the spirit of the roc and leviathan, but what does that mean exactly? Chuang-tzu's original meaning was distance, naturally, that what the people truly needed was distant journeying. But how could they do that if you stuck a sceptre into my kidneys? Soon after came another change of government, and this one felt that the sunbird, the totem of the ancients, smacked of feudalist superstition, and could not represent the spiritual vigour of the Dongzhou people who had undergone the baptism of reform and opening up. So they tore down the sunbird and put up a sculpture in the shape of an enormous thumb. They said it was modelled on the thumb of the mayor at the time. It was supposed to symbolise the self-reliant spirit of the Dongzhou people, but it somehow smacked of autocracy, and the people weren't having it. They felt it symbolised nothing but the boasting, self-congratulatory spirit of the actual mayor, a monument to himself.

The next government naturally couldn't abide a monument to the previous mayor, so they got together and decided to rebuild me altogether. The thumb, like the sunbird, was consigned to the dump, and soon it was a *huabiao*, a traditional ornamental column exactly like the ones in Tian'anmen Square, that adorned my kidneys. The symbolic significance of a *huabiao* is enormous, descended as it is from the wooden pillars that emperors erected at crossroads and important causeways as early as the age of Yao and Shun. According to a Han Dynasty philosophical treatise, those pillars were 'a tool of Shun's slander', 'words fair and foul were recorded in the wood of the *huabiao*'. What that meant was that the masses could write what they actually thought of their kings and emperors on the wood of these columns called *huabiao*. The columns were crested with a carving of an auspicious animal, a carnivorous beast both like and unlike a dog, called a *hou*. The pair of *hou* atop the *huabiao* at the back of Tian'anmen are facing north, towards the Forbidden City, indicating a hope that the emperor would not sequester himself within his palace, but come forth and know his people, and so they are said to be 'awaiting the Prince's emergence'. The *hou* atop the *huabiao* in front of Tian'anmen face south, meaning that the emperor should not stay too long away from home, and are said to be 'awaiting the Prince's return'.

After the *huabiao* was erected at my centre, however, harsh criticism of the mayor at the time began to be heard, saying he was ambitious and had his sights set on Beijing. At any rate, it is the hope of everyone in politics to make it to Beijing, and the successive government accepted the significance of the *huabiao* and refrained from wasting more money and labour on razing and building, building and razing.

I am often dressed in new clothes of a very unique sort. Huang Xiaoguang praised me for it in his story, saying that I am a mirror, an opera, a face, a painting, an essay, a corral, a gathering, a political victory, a kaleidoscope, a stage, a brand name tag, a seal, a coin, a well, an 'Aleph' ... But in the end, I am still a heavy book, one page out of *The Book of Sand*.

The reason no one realises I'm a book is that those in power still don't understand that a city is actually a library. There's no need for us to build Towers of Babel, because the library is higher than those towers. Each civil servant is actually a librarian, and each urban resident is a book. There's a superstitious term, 'Man of the Book', though actually it's not superstitious at all. People are books by nature. They say life is a book. But no one is able to see their own nature clearly and they continue to rack their brains for arguments that they are regular people and not 'Men of the Book'. So what's the argument? It's that they are not 'Men of the Book' but 'Men of Things', and they offer involved explanations of why they are so.

'Men of Things' 'felt themselves to be the masters of an intact and secret treasure', and so 'abandoned their sweet native hexagons and rushed up the stairways,' but they don't know that the 'Library is a sphere whose exact centre is any one of its hexagons and whose circumference is inaccessible.'

'These pilgrims disputed in the narrow corridors, proffered dark curses, strangled each other on the divine stairways'. As a result some of them were pushed over the stairs. Their grave would be the fathomless air. 'My body will sink endlessly and decay and dissolve in the wind generated by the fall, which is infinite.' Others went mad. In the hallway there is a mirror that, in its limited way, faithfully duplicates the unlimited nature of the world. This is the natural home of the 'The Man of Things', the way a grain of sand belongs in the desert. This can't be compared to the return of a drop of water to the ocean, because a drop of seawater can reflect the brilliance of the sun, while a grain of sand cannot.

That is the teaching of *The Book of Sand*. I think *The Book of Sand* is the sum of all other books, and for that reason I am only part of the contents of one single page within it. Each day I lay stretched before the Municipal Government building, serving the people of Dongzhou, unflagging and uncomplaining, like the most dedicated of civil servants.

There's one civil servant in particular who crosses me twice a day, once in the morning and once in the evening. That's Song Daoming, the Mayor's secretary. He lives on my east side, very close to the government building, and so he walks to and from work every day along my central axis.

He seemed to have something serious on his mind when he went to work this morning: his head was down and he was lost in thought. As he walked, a mouse suddenly scampered out from behind the *huabiao* and ran past his foot, giving him a turn. Not stopping to wonder how a mouse could live at the foot of the *huabiao*, he gave outraged chase. The crafty mouse took two turns around an enormous flowerbed and then dashed into a hole and disappeared. A huge, ancient pine stood in the centre of the flowerbed – they said it had been transplanted from nearby an emperor's tomb – and next to it stood an old gentleman out for a stroll, his hands behind his back, looking up at the tree. 'Originally there are three points of view we might have on an old pine: practical, scientific and aesthetic. What a shame we've only been left with one.'

Curious, Song Daoming asked him, 'Which point of view is that, old sir?'

The old man gave him a glance and said, 'Don't you think this old pine looks like a Tower of Babel?' So saying, he shook his head and left.

Song Daoming looked up at the towering old pine, the glare of the sun dizzying him.

Secretary to Mayor Liu Yihe, Song Daoming

MAYOR LIU SHOULD have hosted the dinner for the Minister of Finance at Beautiful World himself, but he asked me to call Peng Guoliang and pass the job to him. I'd just put the phone down when someone knocked at the door. I did a double take when I opened it because there were six people standing outside. I knew only one of them, Shang Xiaoqiong, from the Janitorial Brigade. But today she didn't look like a cleaning girl. There was something heroic in her mien. First through the door was a bald, middle-aged man.

'Are you Secretary Song? I'm Deng Hongchang, Director of the Sixth Office of the Provincial Disciplinary Committee. I'm looking for Mayor Liu.' I ushered them into Mayor Liu's office, and once they were inside Shang Xiaoqiong closed the door behind them, shutting me outside.

Shang Xiaoqiong was actually with the Disciplinary Committee! So why had she been working in the Janitorial Brigade all this time? The sudden appearance of all these unexpected guests made my heart leap to my throat. Intuition told me that earthquakes would be felt in the Dongzhou Government that evening. I even had a guess as to who they were after, and understood why Mayor Liu was not treating the Minister of Finance personally.

It was past eight p.m. The six of them had been in Mayor Liu's office for more than two hours. The Municipal Government building was empty. I'd heard of detention but had never seen it in effect. Only two sorts of people had that experience. First were those who worked in the Disciplinary Committee and thus were responsible for detaining others. Second were those who had been detained, who generally didn't come back to tell the tale. After they were detained, they were mostly delivered directly into the mechanisms of the law. Once that happened to a civil servant, or a politician, you can imagine his fate.

My office was silent. I knew that the six of them must be reporting their proposed plan of action to Mayor Liu. I had no idea what they were planning, but one thing was for sure: Mayor Liu was going through unbearable suffering.

Suddenly the door opened and he emerged from his office with beetled brows. His expression severe, he gestured to me and said, 'Come in, Daoming, Director Deng wants to have a word with you.'

Perplexed, I followed him inside. I couldn't guess what the office of the Provincial Disciplinary Committee wanted with a mere mayor's secretary. Deng Hongchang stood up from the sofa, took my hand and drew me down to sit next to him. He spoke earnestly: 'Comrade Daoming, the Disciplinary Committee has conclusive proof that Peng Guoliang, Wen Huajian, Chen Shi and Hu Zhanfa have been gambling abroad, embezzling money and accepting bribes. The Committee has established a special investigation team for this case, and we've decided to detain the four of them tonight. We're also asking for Huang Xiaoming's co-operation in the investigation. As leader of the investigation team, I'm asking for your help. Please call each of them and tell them Mayor Liu has something urgent to discuss, that they should come to his office as soon as possible. If they ask what he wants to discuss just say that you're not sure. At any rate, do whatever is necessary to get them to take the bait. Also, tell them different times. We want them to arrive one at a time.'

I knew the Disciplinary Committee didn't go around nabbing people like police officers do. I always wondered how they got their detainees. Now I knew. They were going to dangle bait in front of them. I knew a few commanders on the municipal police force and we'd often drink together. They called this kind of thing 'fishing'. So the Disciplinary Committee people wanted me to be their fisherman.

I thought they should have taken action against Mayor Peng and his crew long ago. They were nothing more than termites gnawing at the foundations of government, termites that should have been exterminated long ago. I only felt regret about Huang Xiaoming. I couldn't believe he was really one of them. But seeing how serious Deng Hongchang and his team were, I could only ask, 'Who should I call first?'

He thought for a moment and said, 'Call Wen Huajian first, then Chen Shi and Hu Zhanfa. Peng Guoliang is at a dinner with the Minister of Finance. I think by the time the first three arrive, the dinner will be over. Lastly call Huang Xiaoming. According to our intelligence he's asked for time off for family business and didn't accompany Peng Guoliang.'

Mayor Liu hadn't said a word the whole time and I knew his feelings must be even more complicated than mine. Suddenly his red telephone rang, the one for direct communications between provincial-level leaders. Mayor Liu picked it up and said, 'Hello Comrade Xiuying!' He handed the phone to Deng Hongchang.

After a few minutes Deng Hongchang put the phone down and said gravely, 'Comrade Xiuying has indicated that we must allow for no sympathy towards the corrupt. Comrade Daoming, please begin.'

I nodded solemnly and returned to my office, my head spinning. I knew what the results of these calls would be. They say that when you pull up a carrot you get a fistful of mud. If these people were locked up, how many more would suffer along with them? And if word got out that I had done this 'fishing', what would it do to my reputation?

I really didn't want to be the 'fisherman'. I was neither on the Disciplinary Committee nor was I a corrupt official. But I kept my resentment to myself and didn't say anything. I thought of all the craven tricks Peng Guoliang and Hu Zhanfa had played against Mayor Liu.

The bait was on the hook and I had no choice but to cast it into the water. I dialled Wen Huajian's number.

Wen didn't question my reason for calling. He said he would come over immediately. It sounded like he was driving. Sure enough, once he'd parked his Audi in the government compound he forgot to lock it. As he stepped into Mayor Liu's office, an armed policeman came in after him, carrying a leather case. The policeman told me the Audi downstairs was unlocked and he'd noticed the case on the back seat. Afraid it might be stolen, he'd brought it up with him. After the policeman had put the case on my desk, he gave me a salute and left. I took a good look at the case and noticed it had a combination lock. I couldn't get it open, so I brought it into Mayor Liu's office.

There was no one there so I went through to his personal conference room, where Deng Hongchang was solemnly stating, 'Wen Huajian, beginning this moment you are under detention, and will be required to answer our questions at an appointed time and place.'

Wen Huajian's face paled and sweat appeared on his forehead when he saw me come in with the leather case. I put it on the tea table and explained where it had come from.

Deng Hongchang thundered, 'Wen Huajian, what's in this case?'

Wen Huajian hemmed and hawed, and wouldn't say. Deng Hongchang threw Shang Xiaoqiong a glance and she ambled over to the case, inspected it for a moment, and popped it open with ease. The moment she lifted the lid we were all flabbergasted. The case was filled with neatly wrapped stacks of dollars, ten stacks of 20000 dollars each, in crisp new bills.

Wen Huajian's legs gave out from under him and he collapsed in a chair. Two burly guards hoisted him up and out of the conference room. Deng Hongchang and Liu Yihe exchanged a crackling glance, then Mayor Liu motioned to me and I returned to my office to call Chen Shi.

Sitting in front of my desk, I felt that the Municipal Government office building had turned into a giant mousetrap. I made the calls, and Chen Shi and Hu Zhanfa came scampering inside, according to plan.

It was time for the most crucial call. I couldn't help feeling a little nervous, but I calmed myself and dialled Mayor Peng's mobile phone. He had just finished his meal with the Minister of Finance and was in his Audi on his way home. When he took my call he seemed a bit cautious and ventured to ask, 'What exactly does Mayor Liu want to talk to me about, Daoming?'

I chuckled, feigning calm, and answered, 'I really have no idea, Mayor Peng. He just said it's important.' I tried to speak in a tone that conveyed how important it was for Mayor Liu to have Mayor Peng's opinion, without giving him the sense that anything was out of the ordinary. He was obviously aware of the possibility that he might be in trouble, but he was willing to take his chances and agreed to come.

Around fifteen minutes later he came in, looking exhausted and bedraggled. As he stepped through the door he asked, 'Where's Mayor Liu?'

I led him through Mayor Liu's office and into the conference room. When Mayor Liu saw him come in he stood up, looking as though a burden were being lifted from him, and said, 'Guoliang, allow me to introduce you to Comrade Deng Hongchang, Director of the Sixth Office of the Provincial Disciplinary Committee. Director Deng will introduce the others.'

Deng Hongchang didn't even stand but only said, with a dark expression, 'You must know why we're all here, Peng Guoliang. I guess I don't have to tell you about Party discipline or national laws. At any rate, both discipline and law are without pity for the individual. You are now under detention. Is there anything you'd like to say?'

Still tipsy from dinner, Peng Guoliang spoke disdainfully. 'Liu Yihe, I have shed my heart's blood and broken my bones for the sake of Dongzhou. This Deng might not know that, but you? Look at you, attacking others and exacting revenge in the name of counter-corruption!'

This clearly struck home with Liu Yihe. He had long been aware of the problems with Peng Guoliang and he had warned him more than once that he was straying perilously close to the edge. But Peng Guoliang had seen it as mere jealousy and personal attack. Now things had come to a head. Liu spoke with pain. 'Peng Guoliang, look into your heart and ask yourself what is right and what is wrong. You've thrown away thousands in public money at the gambling tables. Is that me exacting revenge?'

Peng Guoliang huffed, 'That is base slander, Liu Yihe! Deng Hongchang, Comrade Xiuying understands me. I want to make a call to her.'

Deng Hongchang surged to his feet and raised an arm. 'No need! You will see her at the appointed time. Secretary Qi is currently appreciating the gambling skills you displayed at the Casino Lisboa in Macau.'

Peng Guoliang asked, 'What do you mean by that?'

Deng Hongchang laughed scornfully, 'Your little performance at the casino was recorded by the Public Security Bureau. Are you going to hold out until the bitter end?'

Peng Guoliang's face went white. Deng Hongchang motioned to two guards. Peng hung his head and left the conference room. Huang Xiaoming arrived soon after that, and after the six people from the Disciplinary Committee had shaken hands with Mayor Liu and me, they and Huang Xiaoming left the room together.

I couldn't help going to the window. More than twenty cars appeared below it. The convoy left the compound in a long, snaking line. The neon lights of the municipal square burned like spirit lamps, and I suddenly recalled something that Huang Xiaoming once said to me: 'Depravity is nothing more than our ignorance of heaven.'

Number Two Department, Junior Department-Level Researcher, Ou Beibei

WANG CHAOQUAN LEFT with nothing. He left our apartment to me, and while it wasn't big, loneliness made it feel like a whole empty world. It had been a long time since anyone had touched me. The son of a bitch who had ruined my marriage didn't lack for women, and after the abortion I didn't have the slightest contact with him. That irresponsible bastard didn't even have the most basic 'sexual morality'. I cursed him to the lowest level of hell.

I sat naked on my bed. The mirror on my wardrobe reflected my beautiful body. My breasts, which Chaoquan had always loved to touch, stood between my naked shoulders. Each time we were about to make love, he would bury his angular face between them, seeking my nipples like a small newborn dog that hadn't yet opened its eyes. My nipples were like a pair of cherries, pink and delicate, and Chaoquan would look at them as if they were rubies. He sucked at them greedily, nuzzling them like a pig at the trough, and when he'd had his fill he would thrust at me over and over, the two of us grappling like wrestlers as we rolled on the bed, sometimes onto the floor. Those were our happiest moments, but I could never understand how a man who was so virile never managed to make me pregnant. At first we had blamed each other, but later Chaoquan secretly went to the hospital, and in the end he hung his head before me since the problem lay with him.

At the time I simply couldn't accept the fact. How could my man's semen contain no sperm? I went online to research causes and discovered something terrible: the Y chromosome possessed by men is unable to repair damage caused to it by genetic mutation, and is gradually de-evolving as mankind develops. Calculations of the rate of the Y chromosome's gradual disappearance indicate that the male gender will almost certainly go extinct. Scientists believe that the earliest version of humans was female, and males were only a by-product of female genetic mutation. In theory, men are simply mutated females. Therefore, the earth will become a 'woman's kingdom' in the future. Scientists are learning to make 'artificial sperm' from women's bone marrow, and once they've succeeded, women will be able to reproduce asexually. But since the sperm created from women's bone marrow cells all lack the Y chromosome, their offspring will all be women.

When I read that report I felt very strange. Chaoquan was without a doubt a forerunner of this future de-evolved man. Scientists claimed that over the past fifty years the average sperm count has experienced a steep decline of twenty per cent. The result of Chaoquan's hospital test was a declaration that there could be no crystallisation of our love. How much I longed for a child! If we had one I would dedicate myself to my family. I wouldn't think for a moment of straying. But in the end, I lost husband, chastity and honour.

I approached the mirror, examining my snow-white skin and lushly furred crotch, and felt a sudden revulsion for this body in which I'd once taken so much pride. It seemed horrid to me; I had lost not only my soul but also my confidence. It vanished along with the newly conceived life that the doctor removed from my belly with his steel forceps. Before all that, I'd wanted to embrace the entire world.

There are only two kinds of people: those who weave nets and those who cast themselves into them. There is no third kind. While I was thinking that I had escaped the net, perhaps I was simply waiting for another net to leap into. Occasionally I would ask myself why people wanted to cast themselves into a net. Because of depravity?

Depravity fills us with a kind of despicable pleasure. But thinking it over carefully, I decided it was because of fear – fear of death. From the moment of birth we are closely tailed by the angel of death, drawing nearer and nearer, telling us that there is no escape. And so we build a labyrinth in our imagination and seek to lose ourselves, telling ourselves that the labyrinth is heaven when in fact it is a net, or even a grave. Put this way, depravity seems to be an ignorance of heaven, but it isn't. Depravity comes mostly from raging desire.

People use dreams as wings. We come into the world tainted by original sin, and none of us can escape the vast web of heaven. We are all punished. The punishment only differs in degree. What determines that degree? The strength of our desire.

My desires are nothing compared to those of Peng Guoliang, and thus fate would naturally administer a lighter punishment to me than to him. But what was beyond my comprehension was that fate had so far only punished me and had yet to raise a hand to the mighty Peng Guoliang. Did even fate fear the strong and bully the weak? Impossible! Faced with powerful villainy, fate had to nurse its strength before it struck. I had the sense that fate's strength was growing by the day. Never mind that Peng Guoliang seemed to command the wind and rains. He was no more than a john who had been drained dry by a prostitute, his face sunken and sallow, tottering on his feet. I'd once pronounced a curse: anyone who harmed me would die a horrible death! I could already smell a change in the weather, and it gave me a nameless pleasure. For some reason, that nameless pleasure made me think of Chaoquan.

Since he'd broken up with me, I'd had no news, as though he'd vanished from the face of the earth. Every time I met Zhao Zhong he would tell me that he'd seen him once for sure in the Casino Lisboa in Macau, not only dressed to the nines in a Western suit and gold-rimmed glasses, but with a huge entourage, like a mafia boss. This was completely ridiculous. The false monk must have been reading the wrong scriptures and gotten his eyes crossed; he couldn't even tell who was who! And what was he doing in a casino in the first place? But that was the only news I had about Chaoquan after he left me.

Even when Zhao Zhong had been head of Number Two Department, he had never liked Chaoquan, and now that he was a wealthy boss with Mayor Liu at his back, he was more scornful of Wang Chaoquan than ever before. Actually, before he witnessed this so-called Wang Chaoquan in the Casino Lisboa, he had barely spared him a thought; he never even brought him up during our meetings together. But now Chaoquan seemed to have taken on the image of some mythical hero in his mind. I thought Zhao Zhong must have seen a ghost. In the casino, the only ghosts were bound to be the ghosts of gamblers.

When I was studying at the Administrative Academy, I heard from the teachers there that the vice-principal and Peng Guoliang's wife, Zhang Peifen, often said that men who liked gambling weren't lechers, and I remember one teacher in particular railing against this absurd theory in class. The teacher felt that eating, drinking, gambling and womanising were all related sins, and that gamblers were also born womanisers. I believed Zhang Peifen had to know that her husband was a gambler, but she might not know he was a womaniser. Of course, I knew – better than anyone.

Not long ago, Zhao Zhong told me that Peng Guoliang was nothing but a winter grasshopper, hopping out his last few days. It was a meaningful thing to say. Everyone knew that Mayor Liu hated evil with a passion. But a man like Peng Guoliang wouldn't go down easily, and he wouldn't go down cleanly. That's why I was so looking forward to a final showdown.

One day when I was in the office, Zhao Zhong invited me to see a show. I hadn't been in a theatre for ages, and I asked enthusiastically, 'What show?'

Zhao Zhong said, *Officialdom Unmasked.*

My heart skipped a beat. I had noticed that Zhu Dawei had spent the afternoon reading the very same book, and now Zhao Zhong wanted to see this show. Could it be a coincidence?

I asked him, 'Are you putting me on? I haven't heard anything like that was showing in Dongzhou.'

Zhao Zhong giggled. 'It's not a trick, I'll explain everything tonight.' I hung up the phone and couldn't help glancing at Dawei's book where it lay open on his desk.

Not long after, Zhao Zhong arrived. As usual, he practically began to drool when he saw me. While we drove, he drew out the suspense. As we passed the Qingjiang Theatre, I saw no sign that anything was playing at all. But he was as excited as ever and I knew we were bound to see something worth watching that night. The damned fatty's 'carrot' might be useless, but he did know how to cheer me up.

While he often took me to the Jinchongcao restaurant, he'd never ordered grain liquor before. But tonight he ordered a fifty-year-old bottle of Maotai, worth thousands. This struck me as odd, and I joked, 'Hey false monk, have you cured your diabetes? Has your limp carrot come back from the dead?'

Zhao burst out laughing. 'Beibei, I promise that when we've drunk this bottle, the carrot will become a golden cudgel, and I'll show you how the Monkey King wars with the spirits and demons.'

'Zhao Zhong,' I said mockingly, 'you're just the landlord of a little temple. Don't start thinking of yourself as Buddha!'

He replied with a straight face, 'You wound me, Beibei. "The lost Buddha is mortal; the enlightened mortal is Buddha." "One who's true to himself is a true Buddha; one who's committed the three sins is a true devil." But it's true: though I have spent much time in temples these past few years, the stink of money is too strong on me. I'll never be a true Buddha, but a false Buddha is still a Buddha. After all those years in politics I understand "enlightenment", and with the protection of "enlightenment", at least I'm assured of never becoming a true devil.'

His words were sincere, but there was an element of sophistry to them. As I saw it, Zhao Zhong was neither a false Buddha nor a true devil. He was half-Buddha, half-devil. Half-Buddha because, after he'd made his money, he'd done many good deeds. Half-devil because he'd made his money from lay followers. Some of them came to the temple out of helplessness, some out of greed. In order to part them from their money, Zhao Zhong had made up all manner of stories about the mysterious efficacy of worshipping at the temple, so wondrous that they compelled belief. On the other hand, however, all temples pull in this kind of income. Fancy incense cost more, regular incense cost less, as if Buddha were counting out how much everyone spends on him and dispensing his blessings accordingly. Thought of this way, Zhao Zhong's income seemed quite acceptable.

Ever since Zhao Zhong had tried to show me his golden cudgel and revealed a limp carrot instead, he'd treated me with great deference. Was there anything more debased than a manly man who behaves like a eunuch in front of a woman who's willing to be conquered by him? Now, no matter how I mocked him, he was all smiles.

I smirked and asked, 'So which sort of person is a true Buddha, and which a true devil?'

Zhao Zhong poured himself a cup of Maotai and drained it, smacking his lips heartily. 'As I see it, Mayor Liu is a true Buddha, one who is watching over the people of Dongzhou, and Peng Guoliang is a true devil, stricken by the "three poisons". I want to tell you the story of a true lie, Beibei. Want to hear it?'

When I heard that, I couldn't help thinking of the movie Chaoquan recommended I watch when we parted. I'd never said anything about it to Zhao Zhong because it was a secret that I felt I needed to work out for myself. It gave me a real shock to hear his question.

'I'm all ears,' I responded.

Zhao Zhong stared into my eyes, and began speaking in the cadence of a storyteller.

'They say there was an undercover detective in the Anti-Terrorism Unit of the Provincial Public Security Bureau who, because of the demands of national security, had to keep his true identity secret from his wife, though they'd been married for many years.

'He kept this secret due to the demands of his superiors and of his job, and also out of a desire to protect his wife and avoid a life of fearful worry. In order to better fulfil his mission, this undercover detective disguised himself as a grovelling little civil servant in the Foreign Investment Bureau office. He sacrificed pleasures enjoyed by regular people, and gained some unusual joys and sorrows in return. His wife always believed that he was a run-of-the-mill minor civil servant. The greatest hope of this wife, who hoped for great things from her husband, was to gain honour by his accomplishments.

'He only ever marched in place, however, even letting his wife pass him by, and after years in politics he was still only a director-level researcher. His wife was deeply dissatisfied. When they'd been in college she had practically worshipped this brilliant, capable man who was now gradually turning into a mediocre, humdrum waste of skin.

'Still chasing her dreams, she betrayed her husband and allowed herself to be seduced by an arrogant, powerful vice-mayor, even becoming pregnant with his child. None of this escaped her husband, the special agent. After she became pregnant she was terrified, and hoped for the support and protection of her 'lover'. Once that 'lover' learned of what had happened, however, he sent his secretary to mock her and freeze her out, hoping to coerce her into getting an abortion, all while avoiding any direct contact with her. Things went on that way until she was finally obliged to go to the hospital and have the abortion, but while there she ran into her husband.

'Helpless, she could only propose they get divorced. Though he was torn apart inside, he didn't want to divorce. He knew that he'd failed her completely since they'd married, and that once they were divorced there would be no opportunities to make amends. The wife insisted on divorce, however, and right then the husband was given a special mission that would take him to Shenzhen. He had no choice but to sign the divorce papers, after which he vanished with no word. What the wife didn't know, of course, was that the husband whom she thought was a grovelling little civil servant was actually a daring hero. When he was in the Casino Lisboa in Macau leading his team as they lay a security net to catch terrorists, three figures wandered into his surveillance zone, led by a man draped in gold necklaces and jade rings.

'At first the hero thought the terrorists had called for reinforcements, but looking more closely he saw it was none other than the very corrupt official who had stolen his wife away. He never expected to see a vice-mayor of his own city here in the casino, throwing away cash in the company of his underlings. Was this a servant of the people? Clearly he was nothing but an enormous rat who had yet to be discovered. To rid the people of this vermin, he unhesitatingly ordered his team to follow this false public servant in his every move, and record the insolent faces of all three of them as they leaned over the gambling tables. Then he handed the recordings over to the Provincial Disciplinary Committee, and that's why we've got a fine rat-catching show to watch tonight!'

Every word he spoke rocked me. Obviously I was the 'wife' he was referring to, and the 'rat' was Peng Guoliang. But how could the 'husband' be Chaoquan?

I stared at Zhao Zhong as though poleaxed, hardly knowing where I was. His story was convincing and I couldn't help but believe it, but if it were true then I was the stupidest, most wrong-headed woman on earth! But everyone – students and teachers, from elementary school to college – had always praised me for my intelligence. I had become a foolish, blind, vain and grasping woman!

Suddenly I grabbed Zhao Zhong by the throat, tears standing in my eyes, and asked, 'You fat bastard, was that the truth?'

Zhao Zhong calmly pressed me back into my seat and said evenly, 'You'll soon see for yourself, Beibei, whether it's true or not.'

He'd hardly finished speaking when the mobile phone he'd placed on the table rang. He hurried to answer it, first saying, 'Beibei, after I take this I'll tell you the result. The show has just begun.' He pressed his phone to his pig's ear and asked with some anxiety, 'What is it, Daoming?' Then his piggy little eyes opened wide as his head nodded continually, as if he were hearing sensational news. The phone call lasted a full ten minutes.

After hanging up, Zhao Zhong drained another cup, as though he were congratulating himself on some ill-gotten gain. Then he leaned close, his little eyes boring into me, and said with almost sensual relish, 'Beibei, the "rat" who hurt you was just detained by the Provincial Disciplinary Committee. Wen Huajian, Chen Shi and Huang Xiaoming were detained with him. That was Song Daoming who called. Believe it or not, but Wang Chaoquan's true identity is Deputy Chief of the Anti-Terrorism Unit of the Provincial Public Security Bureau. The "hero" I was talking about just now is none other than your ex-husband Wang Chaoquan.'

I stared at him expressionlessly and kept staring until he grew uncomfortable and asked, 'Beibei, are you all right?'

I lowered my head and said, 'Take me home!'

He smiled obsequiously and said, 'I wouldn't feel right leaving you alone like this. Let's stay a little longer. We should drink a toast to Peng Guoliang's detention!'

I surprised even myself by shouting, 'Take me home now!'

Zhao Zhong had never seen me on the verge of hysteria. Flustered, he said, 'All right, all right! Home it is!'

When the car reached my house, Zhao Zhong wanted to see me upstairs. I turned him down flat and he crawled sheepishly back into his car. The car horn sounded once, and his Benz disappeared into the night.

I went inside, feeling as though my soul had left me, as though some great wrong had been done to me. I threw myself onto my bed and burst into sobs. After crying for a while, I instinctively got up and opened my dust-covered photo albums, pulling out Chaoquan's photos and tearing them up. After I'd torn up most of them, I had a change of heart. I found some tape in a drawer and began piecing them back together again, and once I was done, I examined Chaoquan's handsome, smiling face. Disgusted with myself, I tossed the photographs on the floor, then kicked the photo albums off the bed.

I curled my legs up, held my head, and began crying once again. I didn't know why I was crying. The divorce had been my idea and I'd practically forced him to sign the papers. Now he'd suddenly transformed into what – a detective? A deputy chief? What did that have to do with me? Of course it had something to do with me, how could it not? If I'd had eyes to see, I would never have mistaken the treasure in my hands for mud, and cast it aside. It was heaven's will that Peng Guoliang should blunder into Chaoquan's surveillance net. Heaven was using him as an agent of its justice. There was nothing pitiful about Peng Guoliang paying for his crimes. What was pitiful was my own confusion.

I would cry no more. I had no right to cry, and certainly had no courage to keep crying. I needed to think carefully about what it was I really wanted.

Secretary to the Standing Vice-Mayor, Huang Xiaoming

I WAS CONFINED to a standard room on the third floor of the hotel attached to the Provincial Military Headquarters. Before he left me, Deng Hongchang clapped me on the shoulder and told me to have a good hard think about my problem, and then he was gone, leaving two men behind. I did have a problem – but what exactly was it? I spent three days thinking about it. My guards were changed every two hours, but no one came to interrogate me.

During those three days I went over my every act of selfishness since the beginning of my political career, but selfishness alone is not a crime and I would need to confess real crimes to be of use to the investigation team. So back I went once more, poring over the things I'd said and even thought, and after a fierce internal struggle I concluded that not only had I committed a crime, but it was a very serious crime indeed.

Before the investigation began, Peng Guoliang had given me that package, saying it was spending money he wanted me to keep safe at my home. From its size, if it contained notes of Chinese *yuan* it was somewhere around forty or fifty thousand. If it were US dollars, it was certainly worth several hundred thousand *yuan*. My God, if that's dirty money, then aren't I an accessory to the crime?

I was getting nervous. But I thought of Confucius's words: 'If a man's father were to steal another's sheep, should he report his own father? If he did, that would be unfilial.'

Confucius also said, 'The father conceals the wrongs of his son, and the son conceals the wrongs of his father, this is Righteousness!'

Well, Peng Guoliang may not have been my father, but he was the next best thing. Giving up the package wouldn't exactly be 'unfilial', but it would certainly be bad faith. Even the sainted Confucius believed blood is thicker than water. Could I really bring myself to sell out my leader, to kick him while he was down? This 'blood is thicker than water' was no different than the Westerners' concept of 'tolerance', one of the highest expressions of humanity. To me, convicting someone for being an accessory to a crime because they won't give up a relative was the grossest inhumanity. Peng Guoliang was not my kin, but I was his personal secretary. You could call us relatives with no blood connection, close enough to demand we cover for one another. I made a firm decision that I would not sell him out.

Soon my terror began to ebb, and shortly thereafter an unusual calm came over my panicked mind. Even so, I hadn't seen the sun for a week. I spent all day lying in bed, reliving my political career as though in a waking dream. I had gone over every detail of my actions and behaviour, no matter how insignificant, and I had to conclude that my only real problem lay with that package. I wondered why Peng Guoliang might have given it to me before the case broke, and only one answer presented itself: Peng Guoliang was prepared for the worst. If he went in for good, all his wealth and property would be confiscated, so he'd left me that 'spending money' to give to his son! In that case, my responsibility was even greater. But I was quite aware that the safety of the money depended not just on me, but also on Peng Guoliang keeping his mouth shut. I also asked myself, if this money came from questionable sources, what would happen to me if Peng Guoliang buckled and confessed? I began to get nervous again, but no matter what, I was no Judas. I'd rather Peng Guoliang let me down than I let him down.

After breakfast on Monday, Deng Hongchang and Shang Xiaoqiong came in. Deng asked me how my reflections were coming along. I said I'd thought about everything I was supposed to, and he said, so let's talk then. I asked what about, and he said, let's start with yourself. I told him the whole story of everything I'd done since I entered politics. Shang Xiaoqiong took notes as I talked. When I was done, Deng Hongchang was silent for a moment, then laughed and said that my soul-searching still hadn't touched my soul. What I had done looked like self-examination, but was actually self-praise. Given my attitude, I needed to continue with my reflection. I said no thank you, I've been at this for a week, I truly have conducted a self-examination and exposure of my inmost soul. Scornfully, Deng asked, 'Have you? And you found no problems at all?'

He may have been sitting in front of me, speaking calmly, as a leader might to an errant subordinate, but every word he spoke bore the weight of absolute power, and every time he opened his mouth I shook with fear.

That's why I had turned the confession and self-criticism I'd prepared into self-praise at the last minute. I painted a rosy picture of my actions not to protect myself, but to protect my dignity. But I could tell that if I persisted, Deng Hongchang would assume I'd secretly yielded. To him, anyone who put on a show of strength was revealing their cowardice by instinctively relying on deception to get them through. I felt that righteous indignation would carry the day. I couldn't trot out my character flaws as if they were sins, nor could I manufacture sins for myself. And as for the business of 'keeping it in the family', I wouldn't breathe a word unless it really came to the very end. I would abandon everything before I abandoned my humanity.

So question by question, answer by answer, I began to find a strange and crafty pleasure in the interrogation. Never mind that to Deng

Hongchang this pleasure was merely a laughable sort of fear. He seemed to understand me well and didn't spend too much time on me. His primary target was still Peng Guoliang. I could sense that from the thrust of his questioning. In the past week he hadn't gotten anything of real value out of Peng Guoliang. I was young compared to Peng Guoliang, Wen Huajian, Chen Shi and Hu Zhanfa. He was picking on my youth and trying to get me to break first!

I knew all about Peng Guoliang's gambling escapades abroad, as well as some other illegal behaviour on his part, but I'd never taken part directly. Every time he went to Macau, he left me behind in Shenzhen, and what I knew came from the mouths of the so-called foreign trade representatives he was in contact with – crumbs they dropped unwittingly that I'd carefully pieced together.

To be honest, before becoming Peng Guoliang's secretary I'd looked up to him as a hero, but after I fell in with him I regretted it and blamed myself for being too eager for advancement. I was even more distressed that I'd chosen a con man as my leader, one who would ruin all the political ideals and aspirations I'd so carefully nurtured. Every time I recalled this, I was seized with resentment. He had abandoned his responsibilities towards me, even more so towards his parents and family. He had no sense of loyalty, filial piety or justice!

Nonetheless, from the moment I was shoved into that black Audi, I had determined not to cause harm to anyone. Whatever evil he got up to was his own business. The sum total of my responsibility had to begin and end with my actions as a human being. I needed a clear conscience later in life. I had done nothing I was ashamed of, at any rate.

Deng Hongchang was patently uninterested in my clever tricks. He was only waiting for me to slip up or drop a clue. I had just begun to praise Peng Guoliang's political achievements when he stopped me. Apparently Peng had also started out by praising himself, but Deng only wanted to hear about Peng's problem. He said that the organisation was setting a test for me. If I actively co-operated, they might take that into consideration and allow me to continue my reflection at home. If I tried to be smart, I could keep doing it here. I wanted to get home as soon as possible, of course. I had disappeared with no warning, my wife and child were no doubt worried sick. My mother, in particular, was nearly seventy and in poor health, and I hoped that my brother and his wife had told her nothing. But it's impossible to keep the cat in the bag.

It mattered little that the investigation team had set our arraignment in a military headquarters and made a big mystery out of everything – stuffing us into cars, circling around for two hours in order to disorient us. These days the more mysterious a thing is, the more certain it is to be known to the whole world. I guessed that at this very moment Peng Guoliang's detention was being discussed in every alley and lane of Dongzhou, and as they gossiped about Peng, they'd be sure to touch on his secretary. Seeing as the secretary had been swept up along with Peng, well, who could doubt his guilt? Not only would they not doubt it, but they would assume it was guilt to a heinous degree, guilt requiring instant retribution. No need to ask questions or verify facts, just take him out and shoot him. It's what he deserves!

I often think that while people's lives may be better these days, they're also angrier about more things: angry about the rich, angry about the powerful, angry in particular about corrupt officials. As the saying goes, 'hate me, hate my dog', and in this case, of course, I was the dog.

After a long bout of intense thought, I finally came up with a way to both co-operate with the investigation team and avoid hurting those I didn't want to. That was to shunt Deng Hongchang's attention onto Wen Huajian and Chen Shi. I went on at great length about my unfavourable impression of those two, but everything I mentioned involved things they'd done at Peng Guoliang's behest. I spoke with great indignation for three hours that morning, but never touched the heart of the matter.

After Deng Hongchang and Shang Xiaoqiong left, I learned from the two guards watching me that Shang Xiaoqiong's boyfriend also worked in the Municipal Government, in the combined affairs department that served Peng Guoliang. I asked what his name was and they told me it was Zhu Dawei. It was stupid of me to ask, as he was the only unmarried man in Number Two. I learned that Shang Xiaoqiong worked in the Sixth Office of the Provincial Disciplinary Committee, and had been sent undercover into the Municipal Government Janitorial Brigade. That meant that more than a year previously, just after I'd taken over from Hu Zhanfa, the Disciplinary Committee already had their eye on Peng Guoliang, which meant in turn that Zhu Dawei knew at that point what was going on.

No wonder he hadn't competed that vigorously with me for the position of Peng's secretary, later giving up the fight altogether and putting on a show of yielding to a superior opponent. He really had his strategies mapped out well! I had always thought of myself as someone with abilities and strong moral fibre, as well as a certain subtlety, but here I was, defeated before I even got a chance to compete, all because I'd followed the wrong man.

After two more sessions with the investigation team, they finally released me from detention.

Before I left, Deng Hongchang delivered a half-hour political lecture, mostly about the political situation in Dongzhou. He asked me to keep mum about everything I'd heard, seen and experienced at the Provincial Military Headquarters. This was for my own safety and to keep Peng's people from interfering with the case. Furthermore, it was to avoid negative influences on the progress of reform and opening up in Dongzhou. It was political probation. If they discovered that I'd let slip something I should have kept secret, I'd be right back inside. Since I was the first person related to the Peng case to be released, my return to freedom was bound to cause a stir, so the investigation team had arranged time off for me. Until the case had wrapped up completely, I could rest at home. But I had to stay within their immediate reach and could not leave the province, not to mention the country, without permission.

Deng Hongchang arranged a car to bring me home, where I promptly lit a cigarette and collapsed exhausted on the sofa, feeling like my brain was thoroughly empty. Lifting my head and seeing my wife's fashion photos on the wall, I suddenly realised that she'd had no news of me and must be mad with worry. I needed to call her right away and tell her I was out!

To my surprise, when she answered the phone she didn't sound anxious, as I'd imagined, but was quite calm. She was happy to hear from me, of course, and said that the night we'd all been taken in, many friends had called the house to ask what had happened and how I was. Just after she'd heard the news, she was beside herself with panic, but after she'd called my brother she was much more at ease. My brother was particularly calm, feeling confident that I would be okay, and he told my wife not to worry. When my father died my brother became the pillar of the family – tradition dictates that the eldest son has the authority of the father. My brother urged my wife not to tell our mother the news of my detention, and also to use our connections to get word of my condition. My wife therefore knew early on that I was being held in the Military Headquarters.

When my wife mentioned my mother, my eyes grew wet. Though my wife, my brother and his wife didn't say anything, my mother still learned from our neighbours what had happened to me, and she'd been worried sick about me, terrified that I'd gotten involved in some illegal business with Peng Guoliang. She hadn't had a single night's sound sleep since. I told my wife I'd take a taxi to her office to pick her up, and then we'd go together to see my mother.

After hanging up I called my brother's mobile phone and told him that all was well. He was elated to hear my voice and said he'd take me out that evening to soothe my nerves. From his voice I could tell he was full of confidence in me, but I still felt a weight like a boulder on my chest. My wife didn't know it, but I'd taken the package that Peng Guoliang had given me before the case broke and, without her knowledge, had hidden it in the kitchen, in a cabinet near the sink. Though I had been freed from detention, that package could very well send me back in again. Despite the risk it posed, I resolved to keep it a secret and keep it safe, so that I could keep my promise to Peng Guoliang.

At dinner that night my brother could tell I still had something on my mind, and when our wives went together to the bathroom he poured me a drink and told me that I shouldn't keep anything to myself. I insisted repeatedly that nothing was the matter and he finally, albeit sceptically, joined me in a toast.

Vice-President of the Municipal Administrative Academy and wife of Peng Guoliang, Zhang Peifen

I SPEND MY days tormented by worry. We've transferred all the family cash and savings accounts overseas, but the house itself is still full of things. Our ten golden Buddha statues alone are worth nearly a million. It's impossible to transfer several truckloads of stuff on a moment's notice. Luckily I called Guoliang before I left work and he said that all was well, and that he was sleeping at home. Only then did I begin to relax a little.

When I got home after work, however, Guoliang wasn't there, and the nanny said that he'd left after getting a call from Mayor Liu's office. Apparently he'd been asked to host a dinner for the Minister of Finance. Suddenly my heart began pounding once more. I called my younger brother and asked him to drive right over. We could at least move some of the most valuable things out of the house.

My brother and I worked until ten that night. A friend of Guoliang's in the Provincial Disciplinary Committee gave me a call on the sly to tell me that Guoliang was in trouble, that he'd been detained immediately after the dinner. Incredibly, he'd been picked up straight from Mayor Liu's office.

To be honest, I'd always felt terribly anxious that something like this would happen. Now that it finally had, I was able to relax a little. I was actually surprised at my own calm. I hadn't expected to feel quite so fearless in the face of danger. It's true that the larger a crisis, the more one needs to remain calm. I needed full control.

I put down the phone, gathered my strength and decided without hesitation that I would simultaneously defend Guoliang and attack Qi Xiuying, who I knew was behind all this. Corrupt officials are as common as sparrows.

Hey! Qi Xiuying! What right do you have to single out my husband for punishment? And you, even if you've got no real dirty laundry, I'll bet there's something in the basket that still stinks! I'll take you on, 'Iron Maiden'! You may be the 'Iron Maiden' but I'm the 'Steel Maiden'. You may be the 'Female Bao Gong' but I'm the 'Empress Dowager'. Let's have a battle across the ages, and we'll see if heaven stands on your side.

Our friend in the Disciplinary Committee told me that Guoliang was being detained in the guesthouse of the Provincial Military Headquarters. We would be unable to meet face to face for the time being. It was crucial that I remain in contact with him, but that would be impossible unless it were through one of the investigation team members.

After making extended enquiries I learned that Peng Guoliang was being held on the sixth floor of the guesthouse. The whole building was locked down by armed police, with two guards watching the elevators at each floor, and everyone was required to sign in and out, even to go from floor to floor. The investigation team consisted of two people per shift, changing shifts every two hours, watching Guoliang by turns. He was like an animal in a cage now, and couldn't even leave the room. The weather was so hot. Would they have given him air conditioning?

In a flash, it was nearly two weeks since Guoliang had been detained, and I hadn't had the slightest news from him. The day they'd taken him he had been wearing a suit, with only one shirt underneath. He usually changes his shirt every day. After so many days of hot weather, he must have been desperate for a fresh one. But no one came on behalf of the authorities to speak with me. During that period, I visited Liu Yihe's office and wept as I said to him, 'Mayor Liu, Guoliang's in detention, and I dreamed of him in there, telling me that only you, Mayor Liu, could save him. Mayor Liu, I believe it was a true dream, and I beg you to save him! You are the Mayor of the city, you must know about his situation. Please tell me, how is he? Whether or not he's guilty, please tell me, and I'll repay the debt though it means I'm reborn as a beast in my next life.'

My eyes and nose were streaming; even a stone would have been moved by my plea. But Liu Yihe said, cold as ice, 'Zhang Peifen, don't forget you are Vice-President of the Municipal Administrative Academy. Look at yourself! This case is in the hands of Qi Xiuying, Secretary of the Provincial Disciplinary Committee. It was not I who went gambling at the casino. The authorities have not directed me to go in to see him, so how would I know his situation? This is not something I can help with.'

If he wasn't going to lift a finger, then there was no point giving him face, so I stopped my tears and said rudely, 'You think I don't know you're in cahoots with Qi Xiuying? You've lit the fire, now be careful you don't burn yourself! Justice is evident for those with eyes to see. Guoliang has done so much for Dongzhou. You had better believe heaven will see it.'

I could tell my words had given him goose bumps. I wanted him to know that Guoliang and I would give him no peace, even after our deaths.

A few days after that conversation I received an unexpected phone call from Yang Hengda, head of Number Two Department. He told me someone from the investigation team had visited him, and he instructed me to prepare a change of clothes for Guoliang. I realised that if Yang Hengda were speaking with the investigation team then he must know about Guoliang's situation, and as head of Guoliang's office, he should be firmly in Guoliang's camp. Furthermore, he'd once been secretary to the Old Leader. Why not try to reach the Old Leader through Yang Hengda, get him to speak on Guoliang's behalf? The Old Leader was a heavyweight not only in Dongzhou but also at the provincial level. If he were to make an appearance, all the old cadres in the province were likely to go along with him. That would put enormous pressure on the Provincial Party Committee and Disciplinary Committee. I doubted even Qi Xiuying could stand up to the Old Leader.

I prepared ten sets of clothing for Guoliang, and Yang Hengda came to collect them. I reminded him of the debt of gratitude he owed Guoliang, before asking him to speak with the Old Leader. He agreed but surprised me when I asked him what news he'd had from the investigation team. He said only that Huang Xiaoming had already been released, and that he'd heard nothing more. I sensed that he was putting me off. He was already beginning to forget about Guoliang.

I was unable to reach Huang Xiaoming. He'd been locked up for more than two weeks and of course had to know what was going on inside, but the moment he was detained, his mobile phone was confiscated by the investigation team, and incoming calls were being monitored. He probably didn't have his phone with him now, his wife's phone was off and no one answered the home phone, so all I could do was send a text message to his wife's mobile phone, asking her to contact me soon.

Since Guoliang got in trouble, I've been worried about my own mobile phone being monitored, so I dropped the old number and got three new ones. I used three separate phones to send text messages to Huang Xiaoming's wife. Sure enough, Huang himself called back, and we arranged to meet at the Jingyesi Teahouse. I got there early to wait in the private room.

Huang Xiaoming hadn't been Guoliang's secretary for that long, but the moment I saw him I felt choked with emotion and couldn't help the tears running down my face. Huang's feelings must have been strong as well. His eyes were wet. But he was as wary as a wounded fox. I had no idea what had happened to him during those two weeks, but I could be certain of one thing: he, like Guoliang, had been cast from heaven to hell in the space of one night.

I said a few words of comfort then told him in a firm tone: 'Xiaoming, Guoliang's been unjustly accused. We've got to think of a way to save him!'

His face turned grave and he asked earnestly, 'How?'

I held nothing back. 'It was Liu Yihe and Qi Xiuying who did him wrong. You don't need to worry about Qi Xiuying, but in Number Two you've worked under both Peng and Liu. You know both of them. Now do something for me, quick as you can: find proof of Mayor Liu embezzling, taking bribes or womanising, write up what you find and give it to me. I'll take it to Beijing and get justice for Guoliang.'

I spoke with the fervour of outrage, but Huang Xiaoming stayed silent for quite some time before speaking. 'I may have to disappoint you, sister. I can tell you anything you like about work-related matters, but beyond that I really know nothing.'

Huang Xiaoming's refusal surprised me. He was different from Yang Hengda – he was Guoliang's personal secretary, after all – and I had expected to get something out of him. But talking to him was even more disappointing than talking to Yang. I asked him what the investigation team had asked about when he was inside, and he told me they hadn't asked anything. Then he looked at his watch and said, 'My mother's ill, I've got to go see her. If there isn't anything else, I'm going to go.' Then he left.

From the window I could see his brother Huang Xiaoguang standing next to a white Toyota, smoking. When Huang Xiaoming emerged, the two of them exchanged a few words and then got in the car and drove off. I felt like my heart had been dipped in ice water. The sense of abandonment knocked the wind out of me. I drained my teacup, steeled myself and left the teahouse.

I wiped away my tears as I drove. My phone rang. I picked it up.

It was Xu Zhitai, who I had just been thinking I should speak to. Here he was calling me of his own accord. There is a heaven.

Xu said, 'I've been vice-head for more than a decade, sister, in the service of many standing vice-mayors, and only Mayor Peng ever appreciated me. I'm loyal to the death and can't just sit by while Qi Xiuying ruins such a diligent, hardworking, capable mayor. My old colleague and friend Lin Yongqing has an unusual relationship with Qi Xiuying, and it shocked him to hear that she has had Mayor Peng detained. Your husband has been good to old Lin – the 150-square-metre split-level apartment where he lives is thanks to him – and as they say, he won't forget the hand that's fed him. Lin wants to meet you. He says he'll do everything he can to save Mayor Peng.'

I felt warmth spread through me when I heard that. Some people will kick you when you're down, but I guess others really do remember who their friends are. I'd heard Guoliang mention this Lin Yongqing before. He was Qi Xiuying's college classmate and an old lover to boot. Before Guoliang was detained, he'd talked to me about making good use of Lin, and now Lin was in a position to repay a debt. If only we'd known, Guoliang could have promoted him to head editor of the *Qingjiang Daily*, and Xu Zhitai to deputy director of the Municipal Government. Now I knew what it was to have had power but not used it. If we ever overturned this case and restored Guoliang to his rightful position, we'd be sure not to forget our friends.

I arranged a time and place with Xu Zhitai, then withdrew a large sum of money from the bank. I meant to turn Lin Yongqing into a time bomb, under my control. Qi Xiuying had better behave herself, otherwise we'd be meeting our makers together!

Senior Reporter at the Qingjiang Daily, Lin Yongqing

THE MOST PERPLEXING question for philosophers is this: where do we come from and where are we going? I've always felt that I come from 'nothing' and will return to 'nothing'.

Since I met Peng Guoliang through Xu Zhitai, however, I think I've gone from 'nothing' to 'something'. Not only do I have a 150-square-metre apartment, but yesterday his wife Zhang Peifen gave me thirty thousand *yuan*. Now I really do have 'something'.

After Zhang Peifen and I parted, on my way home I wondered what this 'something' meant, and after chewing on the problem I decided that the 'something' was a mission. Though I've come from 'nothing', I am here to complete this mission of 'something', and only once I've completed it can I return to 'nothing'. There is no doubt: my present mission is to convince Qi Xiuying to go easy on Peng Guoliang.

I accepted this mission entirely out of sympathy and in the belief that Peng Guoliang's merits outweigh his crimes. Men are not saints. Who has not sinned? But if you exaggerate that and exaggerate a person's flaws, then who among us cannot be counted a criminal?

Zhang Peifen insists her husband is innocent. She wept as she told me all that Peng Guoliang has done in the service of the people of Dongzhou. In terms of foreign investment alone, he has achieved ten times as much as Liu Yihe did when he was standing vice-mayor, and there is no end to the examples of his love for the people. I myself have been a beneficiary of Mayor Peng's 'people first' principle. Is it really necessary to be so petty and vindictive about a reformer with such a glorious political reputation and record of achievements?

So I was feeling indignant when I went to visit Qi Xiuying. I called ahead and, although she was perfectly friendly, there was a note of caution in her voice. I had intended to visit her office, but she asked me to go to her home that night. It would be more convenient to speak there. A warmth spread through my body.

I always thought the best character for a politician was no character at all, but even after she had become Secretary of the Party Committee and the Disciplinary Committee, Xiuying's unyielding character still didn't change. Back in college she hated all wrongdoing and never kept her opinions to herself. You'd think a person like that would be fundamentally unsuited to politics. I've never understood how she's got as far as she has. She has iron self-discipline, of course. She is revolted by extravagance and empty fashion, and excels at keeping her private life and emotions hidden. Perhaps her character is a help after all.

This was exactly why our relationship was a bit muddled. I knew perfectly well that she wished we could pass the rest of our lives together, but that lofty position of hers made everything difficult. It seemed to put a barrier between us.

And was that official position really so great? She's made enemies of practically everyone. In the end you retire, same as everyone else, and are forgotten. She's always had a weak heart, and the strain of researching Peng Guoliang's case over the past few days has caused her angina to return. An ambulance was even called. I can't understand why she is so dogged in pursuing these cases. Quit while you're ahead; that's what people say. In fact, that's what Lao-tzu meant by 'inaction': the avoidance of excessive or unnatural action. All things must have their 'measure'. Doing everything in the name of faith or conviction – who would buy that?! Look at all the Party cadres who have become Buddhists.

Last New Year I went to the Ci'en Temple in the Western Hills to photograph the bell ringing ceremony, and was surprised to see a large red banner hanging at the gate of the Western Hills Park that read, 'The Ci'en Temple Bell Ringing Renewal Ceremony Wishes Good Fortune and Popular Support for All Leaders and Cadres'. I'd heard Xu Zhitai say that the Ci'en Temple had been taken over by Zhao Zhong, the former head of Number Two Department, and that he was raking it in by the bucketful. Obviously, the 'Gods blessing the Cadres' really meant the 'Cadres blessing the temple'.

If all those leaders are ignoring the human world in favour of the spiritual world and only Qi Xiuying is left to care for the human world, what will the human world care for her efforts? When all is said and done, the 'blessings of the Gods' all give way to the 'blessings of the people'.

Peng Guoliang blessed me, and if Qi Xiuying really loves me, she ought to find it in her to bless Peng Guoliang in return, and to go easy on him. Everything can be forgiven. If you couldn't even see your way to doing him this favour, then what will be left of your humanity? You go on about ideals and convictions; would you betray your kin for the sake of those convictions? What good is an ideal that demands such betrayal?

These thoughts rioted in my head as I pushed open the door to Qi Xiuying's home. She'd quite clearly made herself up and thrown off her usual 'Iron Maiden' image. She led me demurely into the dining room. A bottle of red wine and four dishes were on the table. Usually her maid cooked for her, but the maid wasn't there that night. She must have sent her away on purpose.

'Xiuying, these dishes look vice provincial-level,' I joked. 'You must have cooked them yourself.'

She chuckled. 'I've been so tired recently. I was mostly just hoping you'd have a glass of wine with me.'

Seeing she was in a good mood, I teased her. 'Usually your maid's here, Xiuying. Now that it's just us, it almost feels like we're having an affair!'

She gave me a playful shove. 'Listen to you! Here, let's have a drink!'

I thought of the female bureau chief Kalugina in the old Soviet movie *Office Romance*, and felt I was just like the male lead Novoseltsev, and Qi Xiuying was exactly like Kalugina! What I envied about that story was not only the love between Kalugina and Novoseltsev, but also the way that two lonely hearts came together. Qi Xiuying caused me no end of grief, though. Perhaps it was because her official position was so much higher than Kalugina's. Novoseltsev had to leave behind his customary cowardice before he won love. It seemed that I, too, would have to depart from my normal character.

After we'd finished a first glass of wine, Qi Xiuying said, 'Yongqing, once a woman's worked for a while in a disciplinary department, everyone starts to see her as a cold-blooded animal. Do you know how long it's been since I simply went shopping? Probably more than ten years. In the Disciplinary Committee I'm the first in the office in the morning and the last to go home. My life takes place on a line between two points: home to the office, office to home. I have barely any social interaction, not to mention dinners or parties. I know you secretly blame me, Yongqing. If it weren't for my official identity, how I'd love to sit around in cafes and bars with you!'

It was rare for Qi Xiuying to talk like that about her feelings. I saw my opportunity and took it. 'Corrupt officials are everywhere these days. How many can you crush all by yourself? Why be so hard on yourself? People are weak. Who would want to become an official if it wasn't to profit by corruption? The people all say that they'd prefer a corrupt official who gets things done to an upright leader who only keeps his seat warm. Even during the feudal dynasties they said that officials watched out for one another. A few years from now you'll retire, Xiuying. Do you really need to make so many enemies? What good is it to cut yourself off from friends and family and the masses? You're only as good as your official position. Why not spare a thought for what comes after, and for what will happen to your son? Take Peng Guoliang's case, for example. This is nothing but a political struggle between Liu Yihe and Peng Guoliang. I'm a journalist. I hear things from all sides. The struggle between the two of them isn't a new thing. Both have done great things for the people, haven't they? No one is perfect, Xiuying. Shouldn't we think about going easy on someone like Peng Guoliang, who has done so many great and useful things for the people? Shouldn't we leave an out for someone like that?'

Qi Xiuying's face hardened as I finished speaking, and she asked pointedly, 'Tell me the truth, Yongqing: has Peng Guoliang done anything for you personally?'

She'd struck right at the heart of the matter and my face reddened, but I steeled myself. In my whole life, no one *but* Peng Guoliang had ever done anything for me. They say that a drop of kindness should be repaid with a river, and for the sake of that 'room of my own', I was willing to compromise in front of Qi Xiuying.

'Xiuying,' I said, trying to keep calm, 'I'm speaking to you sincerely. Think carefully – who else would say these things to you? You don't need to suspect me just because I'm telling you the truth, telling you what I feel.'

Her gaze swept me like a hawk, and there was disappointment in her voice. 'I wouldn't have thought it of you, Yongqing. Was it Zhang Peifen who sent you? She's a vice bureau-level cadre, yet not only does she ignore national law and Party discipline, but she even interferes in criminal cases, in some insane hope of restoring her husband's position . . . What a joke. You say the connection between Liu Yihe and Peng Guoliang is unusual, Yongqing, and that may be true. But Liu Yihe is a straightforward and upright man, while Peng Guoliang is a devious snake. When I first came to Qingjiang Province, I began receiving notes written in Liu Yihe's voice and hand. They were titled *The Civil Servant's Notebook*, and they were filled with fabrications and slander. We investigated and discovered that their true author was Hu Zhanfa, Peng Guoliang's former secretary. You could say he is really stopping at nothing to get rid of Liu Yihe, including using some truly underhanded tricks. How could a person so cunning and deceitful really be thinking of the common people? The national Public Security Bureau has already taped him gambling thousands at casinos in Macau. In the face of cold, hard facts he's still acting the loyal minister and dreaming of overturning the charges. Yongqing, you mustn't let yourself be used!'

To be honest, I'd come with high hopes. I thought that the depth of feeling between the two of us would oblige her to give some ground, and couldn't have guessed she would still be the 'Female Bao Gong'. It looked as though she wouldn't take it seriously unless I hit her where it hurt.

'I'm not a three-year-old child who can't tell the difference between right and wrong,' I said. 'Look at everything that reform and opening up has brought. What you're doing isn't serving reform, it's just disturbing stability and harmony. Xiuying, so long as your feet are on the ground, you're bound to step in the mud. Even the hands of a tough anti-corruption crusader like you might not be quite as clean as they say in the papers.'

Qi Xiuying's gaze crackled with electricity. 'What do you mean by that?'

I replied darkly, 'I heard your son has started a real estate company. Never mind that children of officials at your level are not allowed to run companies, but even if they were, the bit of land he's working with is at the disposal of Peng Guoliang. Why would Peng Guoliang hand over the best bit of land to your son? Even an idiot could see the answer.'

This bit of information had come from Zhang Peifen. I didn't really believe her at first, but the arrow was on the bowstring and I didn't have time for scruples. To my shock, the words were hardly out of my mouth when she pounded the table and shouted, 'Lin Yongqing you despicable bastard! Get out of my sight this instant!'

I'd gone too far. I'd only make it worse if I kept talking, so I stormed out, slamming the door behind me.

For a full week following that, I was in a desperately bad mood. I didn't know how I could face Zhang Peifen. I'd promised her the sky, but not only had I not improved Peng Guoliang's chances, I'd made the situation worse.

Former Standing Vice-Mayor of Dongzhou, Peng Guoliang

AFTER A MONTH-LONG battle of wills, I still hadn't made a peep to the investigation team. If that idiot Wen Huajian hadn't had the two hundred thousand dollars in his car the day he was detained, our mutual pact of silence would have denied the investigators even a scrap of evidence. But that ill-gotten cash was a break in our defensive line.

Then I was brought from the guesthouse of the Provincial Military Headquarters – where I'd been originally detained – to an interrogation room at the Provincial Procuratorate. There I was interrogated simultaneously with Wen Huajian, Chen Shi and Hu Zhanfa. Those three idiots were completely cowed by the severity of the questions. Their fingers fidgeted on their knees and they practically quaked in their boots. Wen Huajian and Chen Shi immediately owned up to taking fifty thousand each. Hu Zhanfa instantly gave me up as the instigator of the *The Civil Servant's Notebook*.

They say real friendship is proved in adversity. Well, I wasn't seeing an ounce of friendship. We were turning on each other like dogs.

I'll admit that when I saw our defences break down I began to sweat, but I didn't lose my head. I was able to keep calm because I knew I was the mainstay of foreign investment in Dongzhou. Never mind about 'embezzling' a hundred thousand dollars. Giving me that as a reward would have been entirely within reason. Then I had the inspired idea to blame the fifty thousand on the Old Leader, who had actually come to me to ask for it when he was planning to hold the seminar in Hong Kong about the health benefits of the urine cure for retired cadres. When he didn't need the money, I'd passed it to Huang Xiaoming the day they came for me. Greatness demands ruthlessness, and in the interest of my future restoration to power, I was willing to risk everything. I'd let them take me for now. I doubted they would go head to head with the Old Leader.

Worst of all was the damned biddy Niu Yuexian, running off with all that money. And why couldn't she have run a little farther? The investigation team, working with the Hong Kong Police, found her in Malaysia. That put me in a real bind. Luckily, I'd prepared my strategic response and blamed the entire thing on Liu Yihe, saying we'd deposited thirty million Hong Kong dollars in flexible reserve funds for when we might list H shares on the stock market in Hong Kong. At worst, that was a breach of discipline, and I really had made a report to Liu Yihe about it. He hadn't actually given me the nod, but he hadn't objected either. Then there was all the reciprocal gift-giving associated with courting foreign investors. It all took money!

Though I had answers for every question, the Procuratorate still decided to hold me for further interrogation, so I was locked up in the Dongzhou Detention Centre. There I was questioned at irregular intervals by the investigation team. I knew Peifen was doing everything in her power to overturn my case, and after twenty years of marriage, I knew perfectly well what she was capable of. Soon the interrogations became less frequent.

After all my years in politics I know that any problem can be solved with the right skills, and I am entirely confident that so long as Peifen doesn't give up, I am sure to see the light of day again. I will not let myself fall apart.

I was lucky to be in the Dongzhou Detention Centre. When I was in office, I'd taken care to do right by the police authorities and give them regular bonuses. Now that I was in trouble, a few police officials who still had consciences felt sympathy for me. Hoping to boost Peifen's confidence, I sent a letter to her care of one of them. I'll admit that as I was putting pen to paper, my tears flowed freely, even wetting the letter. Thinking of Peifen struggling out there all alone, I began to hate Qi Xiuying, Liu Yihe and all the people who were against me, who counted the destruction of a family as a victory.

Tears in my eyes, I wrote:

'My dearest Peifen, it's been one hundred days since we were parted, but it feels like a hundred years. During these hundred days and nights you haven't once left my thoughts! After more than twenty years of marriage we've become as one, our hearts united. We've weathered countless storms, but this one came so much more suddenly and cruelly than I could ever have anticipated. In my darkest hour, your incomparable love still supports me, consoling and strengthening me like a goddess of love. Every time I think of you, I feel power flowing into me. What moves me most is that from the very beginning, you have never uttered a word of complaint or blame, not only staying by my side, but abandoning all else in your struggle to win me justice and restore my honour! One hundred days have passed, and your love has proven to me that you are both my most cherished wife and an angel who will deliver me from darkness into light. I am not yet going to congratulate myself on possibly turning misfortune into fortune through your unremitting efforts, but I am going to congratulate myself on having made the right choice more than twenty years ago, choosing you as the one who would accompany me through the wind and rain. I have complete faith that with you beside me, any miracle is possible ... '

I knew that when Peifen read this letter and saw my spirits were still strong, she would feel comforted, and would continue the struggle to overturn the case at any cost.

My police officer friend soon had good news for me. Peifen's efforts had begun to bear fruit. First, she'd hired two top lawyers from Beijing with strong political backgrounds to cause trouble for the investigation team. They demanded to see the case materials. According to legal procedure, the counsel for the defence could only learn about the charges; they had no right to be shown the case materials. But in addition to getting hold of the materials, the two lawyers also discovered plenty of flaws in them. Indications were that my darkest hour was passing and the dawn would soon break.

A few days later, however, the situation changed again. I was abruptly transferred to the detention centre in Changshan. Being transferred to another town was a bad sign. Experience told me it had to be the work of Qi Xiuying because she was infuriated by the pressure from the Beijing lawyers. I knew that Qi Xiuying was a woman of steadfast character, and she wouldn't deviate from her chosen course even if dragged by wild horses. No matter how strong her spine, though, it couldn't be stronger than my will.

Once in the Changshan Detention Centre, I was cast into deep solitude, with no information from outside. Compared to the officers in Dongzhou, my guards here had nothing but stern looks for me. I was determined that the shift in location wouldn't cut me off from the outside world, however. I knew Peifen would find a way to breach these castle walls. In an unfamiliar place, one is obliged to make new friends. I once told Peifen that so long as she has the spirit of a spider, she'll be able to weave her web ever wider. All of China, in fact, is nothing but an enormous spider web, and all of us spiders upon it. Though I am behind impregnable walls, I am still within that web which, after five thousand years of weaving, is as unbreakable and sturdy as the Great Wall.

A philosopher once said, if you believe that no one can make absolute use of power, then you've failed to study history. I am hoping to see what absolute use Qi Xiuying will make of her power. Justice is merely a street lamp that is entirely insufficient to illuminate Dongzhou, particularly when you consider that politics is a dark and ancient world.

Moving me to Changshan is an obvious sign that they were beginning to falter. They think the detention centres of Changshan and Dongzhou belong to different worlds. Why else transfer me here? What a colossal joke, to speak of justice while lacking so deeply in confidence.

In the Changshan centre, my isolation from the outside world makes my memories seem even more real than life as I'd lived it. Of course, it is most pleasant to recall women. The tenderness of Ou Beibei, the freshness of Niu Yuexian . . . it all comes back to me. But what comes home most powerfully is that all that dallying was not star-crossed. It wasn't fate that was lacking, but love. All that is left to memory are some clouded, insipid, half-painful traces. The only woman who can give me real power now is my own wife.

She hasn't disappointed me, either. The other day a tall police officer led the other inmates on a janitorial detail to the latrines, leaving me alone in the room. Suddenly another guard passed me a mobile phone and told me to call Peifen. I could hardly believe it was happening, and I was so thrilled my hands shook. I nearly dropped the phone.

I spent five minutes talking with my wife, but her news was not optimistic. Although she continues to give me encouragement, she hasn't made much progress in overturning my case. But at least I once again have someone inside the detention centre that I can rely on and use to get news from the outside. Even so, my spirits have sunk low.

The Old Leader

I WAS TAKEN quite by surprise to hear Peng Guoliang had been detained by the Provincial Disciplinary Committee. I learned of this from my erstwhile secretary Yang Hengda. He came to my house that day all in a fluster, looking thoroughly distracted.

Of all my secretaries, Hengda has the strongest grounding in theory. Not only is he an excellent writer, but he's also got a top-notch brain. He was born for politics. When Peng Guoliang hired Hengda, I thought he would see to his advancement and entrust him with important tasks. I'm surprised now to discover that Peng Guoliang has done little but engage in sensual pleasures without a thought to his duties, his head stuffed with bourgeois Epicureanism. I hear he split up the prize money for foreign investment attraction amongst his cronies and they blew it all in casinos. That amounted to a betrayal of my hopes and expectations for him, and of course it slowed Hengda's advancement as well.

Above all, though, it was a neglect of study.

Hengda tells me the copy of the *Philosophical Reflections on the Urine Cure* that I presented to Peng Guoliang has never left the shelf. He's never read a single page, though he's claimed to me that he's read it twice. Guoliang is the son of a common labourer, and he advanced to his position one step at a time. Now he's descended, one step at a time, into criminality. There are a multitude of reasons for this, and many lessons to be learned, but there's one core reason: his modes of thought have gone astray.

Some people think reform is a means of renewing modes of thought: out with the old, in with the new. They think everything old must be bad, and everything new must be good. But they can't actually tell what is old and what is new, just as some people believe that urine is a waste product of the body.

Every time I drink my morning urine, I feel my soul is ablaze and I forget I'm an old man of more than eighty winters. Chinese medicine identifies the kidneys as the key to the body's health. Long life depends on strong kidneys, but how do we strengthen them? Urine is the best tonic, of course: it not only strengthens the kidneys, but it also improves the brain, promotes intelligence and clears away spiritual pollution. Only when the spirit is healthy can the body be healthy. Thus, I advocate dispensing with all other health trends and relying on the urine cure alone. This keeps the thoughts in line. Only with a healthy body can we resist the lusts and temptations that besiege us and lead to spiritual pollution.

This connects to political truth.

In theoretical terms, the principal end of politics is unification. This requires politicians to have a profound understanding of how something is created from nothing. Creating something from nothing is best achieved through cycles, like the urine cure. So long as you persist in imbibing in the morning, you can achieve the virtuous cycle of water becoming blood, blood becoming urine and urine once again becoming water.

I emphasise yet again, urine is the crystallisation of the metabolic process, and if we do not drink it, it will be lost. That would be not only a material loss, but also a spiritual loss. Thus, the urine cure is paramount to our health, and we must follow its directives for the sake of our physical health. It is the quintessence of traditional thinking on health and of traditional culture in general.

Those who don't know how to use the urine cure end up like Peng Guoliang, attacked by all manner of bacteria and viruses.

No wonder he became corrupt!

So how did Yang Hengda, who serves Peng every day, avoid infection?

It's simple: he worked with me for five years, during which time my urine cure gave him a very healthy body, but more importantly gave him a strong sense of loyalty to authority. He was deeply aware of the fact that he would be nothing without the Old Leader, and so he has always taken the Old Leader's will as his will, and whether or not he was serving Peng Guoliang, or Liu Yihe, or whoever, he knows that the interests of the Old Leader are paramount, and that the meaning of the Old Leader is that the Old shall lead the Young, otherwise the Ship of State will stray from its course. He's not like Guoliang, who forgot everyone else the moment his wings were dry, with the result that he is now digging his own grave.

Most galling is how Guoliang refused to admit his crimes to his higher-ups, and even tried to dump his garbage on my doorstep. I once spoke to him about funding for a seminar on the benefits of the urine cure for retired cadres, but later the cadres raised the funds themselves and we didn't use his money at all. Yet he has slandered me, saying I'd accepted fifty thousand dollars from him, thereby agitating the investigation team so much that they arrived at my house to verify the information.

Is that the way to treat an old leader such as myself?

I was so put out I didn't even let them in the door. I raised my cane and drove them off. I wanted to teach those young hotheads not to disturb the giant's slumber. My heart started giving me trouble again that day. Luckily my wife handed me a cup of that morning's urine, which eased my chest considerably.

My wife's quite right: there's no need for me to get in a temper about a bunch of young hotheads. If I'd ended up going to meet Marx, there's no telling where this great ship of Dongzhou might have drifted off to.

As long as I'm alive, I have to keep this ship on its course. Some people think reform is nothing more than a chance for them to play some clever tricks, to throw off discipline.

So I called Liu Yihe and warned him not to play so many clever tricks, and do a little more of substance. Otherwise Dongzhou will end up with diarrhoea, or an intestinal blockage.

Yang Hengda has visited me often over the past few days, hoping that I will make some calls and get him transferred to Number One Department, under Liu Yihe.

He's not been telling me the whole truth.

Once I'd given him the silent treatment, he came out with the real situation. He's antsy about his low grade, and no wonder. Peng Guoliang has treated him as an errand boy, forgetting whose secretary Hengda used to be.

People like Peng Guoliang, who don't understand politics, are bound to come a cropper sooner or later. Hengda tells me Guoliang's wife Zhang Peifen is hoping that I will make an appearance and speak up on Guoliang's behalf.

Who do they think they are?

If they want to frame me, that's their business. If they want to make use of me, then go ahead. Where are their principles? This Zhang Peifen is even more brazen than Guoliang himself. She'll stop at nothing to save her husband – she'll end up on the inside herself, sooner or later. There's only one real rule in life, universally applicable: you reap what you sow.

I gave Liu Yihe a call, telling him Yang Hengda shouldn't be left to rot in Number Two. He took my hint and said he's always had a special appreciation for Yang Hengda. The Vice-Director of the Municipal Government just happens to be moving to a position as Director of the Municipal Research Office, leaving his post vacant. Yang Hengda couldn't be better suited to it. When you got right down to it, the reason Liu Yihe is such a star among this crop of leaders, and the reason why he's made mayor, is that he understands politics.

I am old. Age has no mercy. There is much I want to do, but my strength fails me. If it wasn't for the urine cure, I'm afraid I would have gone to meet Marx long ago. My greatest hope now is to spread the word about the cure far and wide. A city has its municipal tree, its municipal flower – I believe it should also have its 'municipal book'. The book best suited to be the municipal book of Dongzhou is, of course, *Philosophical Reflections on the Urine Cure*.

Department Head, Number Two Department, Yang Hengda

WHOEVER HOLDS THE upper hand holds all.

Liu Yihe is clearly in this position. He has rammed one end of the seesaw into the earth, leaving the other high in the air. Peng Guoliang looks like he is about to fall to earth, and I can't afford to fall with him. What can I do? The only thing is to push him, give him a kick, knock him all the way down. I need to turn the seesaw into a bridge by which I can crawl across to Liu Yihe.

Why crawl? That way I'll present the smallest target, and by the time anyone notices, I'll be on the other side already. Then no one will dare curse me for a traitor; they'll be too busy praising my perspicacity in coming out of the darkness into the light, and they'll all have smiles on their masks. Why masks and not faces? Because they long ago lost their true faces. All they have are masks, or faces like masks. In an environment like this, the art of self-protection is to see the true expression behind the masks.

While serving Peng Guoliang, I studied his political skills and tactics. Though he is adept at exerting control over others, he has little in the way of self-discipline, otherwise he would never have been seduced by gambling.

But he did have one particularly clever trick: he always took care to remain in the shadows, and he was skilled at staying there. He didn't like others spying on him, discerning his motives. On the contrary, he liked to see everything from within the darkness. It's a pity he wasn't content to stay there and run things from behind the scenes, but he meant his backstage role only to be temporary – preparation for his taking centre stage. This was a fatal error on his part, and in this sense Liu Yihe is his superior. As Liu Yihe sees it, there is only the solid potentiality of power, nothing else. Though he is already the Mayor of Dongzhou, he still sees all the flashy posturing associated with power as so much worthless filth. That's precisely why Peng was never a match for Liu. Faced with a true statesman, he was nothing more than a professional gambler with some skill at political intrigue. In the course of his rivalry with Liu, Peng was defeated at every turn, and could only take out his resentment at the card table.

Everyone knows that Huang Xiaoming and I were Peng Guoliang's left and right hands. So if Huang Xiaoming goes down, what will happen to me?

The more I thought about it, the more I felt I needed to get out of Number Two. But even if Liu Yihe set me up as head of Number One Department, I still wouldn't be content. One way or another I needed to turn Peng Guoliang's case into a springboard for my career.

I'd had my eyes on the position of Vice-Director of the Municipal Government for a while. I needed to capitalise on Peng Guoliang's troubles to get the current incumbent, one Li Yumin, out of the way and take his seat. But I had to think about how exactly to do it. Success would depend on Liu Yihe, of course, but luckily I had the backing of the Old Leader. What I needed to do now was to adopt Liu Yihe's thoughts and worries as my own, and what had to be worrying him most at the moment was that his right-hand man had been detained by the investigation team. This was nothing less than an earthquake in Dongzhou politics, and he was probably desperate to know exactly how this earthquake scored on the Richter scale.

He knew that if Qi Xiuying was running the investigation it had to be a sizeable earthquake, but if it was too big it could inflict heavy damage on Dongzhou's politics and economy, which he would hate to see. What he needed most of all now was information about Peng Guoliang and the others on the inside.

It came to me: Number Two Department was Peng Guoliang's office, and now that he was detained I might, as the director of his office, become a bridge between the investigation team and the Municipal Government. If the team came to talk to me I'd have plenty of information to give to Liu Yihe, enough to make him sit up and take notice of me. Seen this way, Peng Guoliang's detention transformed itself into a rare opportunity.

Just as I'd anticipated, Deng Hongchang, the leader of the investigation team, called Xiao Furen, the Director of the Municipal Government, and asked the departmental Party organisation to arrange someone to contact Zhang Peifen and ask her to ready a few changes of clean clothes for Peng Guoliang. Without hesitation Xiao Furen passed the duty to me.

After I'd made a call to Zhang Peifen, I decided to be big about the situation. I mentioned what I was doing to Song Daoming, Mayor Liu's secretary, who was in his office arranging documents.

When Song heard I planned to meet Zhang Peifen, he said, 'Hengda, I've always thought of you as the Old Leader's man, never as Peng Guoliang's. Mayor Liu has said before that putting you in charge of Number Two is a waste of your abilities, but he needed to give Peng Guoliang face, so he couldn't shift you. Now that you've spent some time in Number Two, I'm sure Mayor Liu is prepared to do right by you and the Old Leader. As a matter of fact, after Deng Hongchang called Xiao Furen, Xiao also made a report to Mayor Liu, and it was he who decided you'd be the one to contact Zhang Peifen while Peng Guoliang is in detention. He did this for two reasons. One is that you were once Peng Guoliang's right-hand man and Zhang Peifen trusts you and two, you were once the Old Leader's secretary, and your higher-ups, particularly Mayor Liu, trust you even more. Mayor Liu is unhappy that things have gone wrong with Peng Guoliang, but what has made him even more unhappy is that Zhang Peifen is ignoring all questions of right and wrong, crime and punishment. She is running around proclaiming that he's been wronged, doing everything in her power to accuse and slander others, even hoping to bring Mayor Liu himself down. The more complex the situation, Hengda, the clearer our heads must be!'

Song Daoming's words were frank and well informed. It was a good thing I'd taken the first step in coming to talk to him. Who knew there was so much going on behind the scenes!

Zhang Peifen treated me like a long-lost brother the moment I entered her house, dragging me into the sitting room with tears running down her face. Her appearance stirred a melancholy pity in me, but the way she cursed heaven and earth and all their inhabitants, swearing she'd get justice if it meant her life, lessened my sympathy somewhat, and made me nervous on her behalf. She was clearly prepared to play with fire.

This reminded me that only if I appeared to stand with her would she be likely to reveal her next move to me. And so it was. I joined in her complaints about injustice, and slowly found that she knew everything that was going on inside the detention cen-tre where Peng Guoliang was being held, even down to what his meals consisted of.

I couldn't help being impressed. Clearly someone on the inside was feeding her information. She wasn't revealing all this to me by accident. She was giving me a message that her husband wasn't done yet, that there were many people still prepared to stand up for justice, and the end was still in question.

'So long as you do the right thing, Yang Hengda, my husband will do right by you once he's out!'

Peng Guoliang had been in politics for years and had a broad network of dependencies. There were those who protected him as they did themselves, and they were the ones prepared to take risks. Under the present system, the outcome of the law was in the hands of individual people, not in the hands of institutions, and the law often gave way to favours, connections and even public opinion. The 'iron fist of the law' only frightened the small fry, not the big fish.

But even if Peng Guoliang managed to escape with his life, he'd be greatly weakened. Only someone as pathetic as Xu Zhitai would believe Zhang Peifen's promises. I used to work alongside Peng Guoliang every day, and though I didn't know him as well as his personal secretary, I couldn't help but be influenced. Just take the business with Ou Beibei. He'd behaved like a beast. I didn't know what Zhang Peifen would think of that if she knew, whether she'd still rant on about heavenly justice. She had the courage to play with fire? Fine, maybe she'd burn clear my path to the future.

Zhang Peifen's maid had packed several changes of clothes. I took the bag and prepared to leave, but Peifen took my hand and begged me in confidential tones to visit the Old Leader and speak to him on Peng Guoliang's behalf. I didn't say I would and didn't say I wouldn't. I made some conciliatory noises and left.

It was the first time I'd driven into the compound of the Provincial Military Headquarters. Though the reception centre was only fair-to-middling in quality, it was clean and well appointed. Many cars belonging to Disciplinary Committee members were parked out front, two armed policemen watched the door and everyone who entered and exited wore a special tag. Xiao Furen had given me a phone number for the special investigation team, telling me to ask for a director-level researcher named Shang Xiaoqiong. After calling that number I got out of the car and had just lit a cigarette when a pretty girl with a certain heroic mien came out of the building.

'Did you bring the clothing, Department Head Yang?' she asked with a smile.

My jaw dropped. 'You? Don't you work in the Janitorial Brigade at the Municipal Government?'

The girls in the Janitorial Brigade were each one prettier than the last. During municipal or mayor-level meetings they were responsible for pouring tea and water. I had a vague impression of each of them, though I didn't know their names.

'That's right. So you remember,' she replied, her eyes flashing with pleasure. 'Actually, I was in the Janitorial Brigade hunting rats, and now that the rat is caught, it's time for me to leave. Thank you, Department Head Yang, for taking care of Dawei. One of these days we'll treat you to dinner.'

My eyes widened. 'How do you know Zhu Dawei?'

'He's my boyfriend, didn't he tell you?' She looked happy.

When she said that, it was like a thunderclap going off in my head. Zhu Dawei could certainly keep his secrets. I always thought Huang Xiaoming was the subtle one, but it turns out I was wrong.

Thinking about it now, Huang Xiaoming's 'subtlety' was nothing more than a certain stolidity of character. The truly subtle one was able to conceal enormous secrets, and as I considered the little duet performed by Zhu Dawei and Shang Xiaoqiong, the hair stood up on the back of my neck. Perhaps Peng Guoliang's demise at the hands of Wang Chaoquan was only a prelude to a greater tune. Extrapolating from the date when Shang Xiaoqiong began her work in the Janitorial Brigade, it could have been her and Zhu Dawei who brought down Peng Guoliang. No wonder Zhu Dawei had been visiting Song Daoming so frequently. He was a step ahead of me in shifting his loyalties to a safer berth. He may have been young, but he was subtle enough to make me nervous. Come to think of it, Zhu Dawei had been sucking up mightily to Hu Zhanfa for a while now. Could he have been searching for evidence for Shang Xiaoqiong? Hu Zhanfa, now in detention, must be curdling with regret.

'With such a beautiful, capable girlfriend,' I joked, 'isn't Dawei worried about who'll wear the pants in the family once you're married?'

'What's wrong with someone else wearing the pants?' she replied, giggling. 'A man who lets his wife wear the pants probably won't end up in detention!'

We chatted a bit further, then I handed over the bag of clean clothes for Peng Guoliang and she gave me another bag with dirty laundry, waved to me, and went back into the reception centre. I threw a glance at the grey, unprepossessing centre, which looked like a huge tombstone.

After returning from Zhang Peifen's home having dropped off the laundry, I thought back carefully over the interactions I'd had with her and Shang Xiaoqiong. At work the next day, I visited Mayor Liu's office. He sat me down beside him and asked solicitously, 'Hengda, what is it?'

I gave him a complete account of everything I'd thought over the night before. When I was done, I added the finishing touch. 'Mayor Liu, the Old Leader often used to say to me that there was only one real rule in life: you reap what you sow. Zhang Peifen doesn't think that way, however. All signs indicate she is trying to frame you. I think she, not Peng Guoliang, is the key figure in this case. So long as Zhang Peifen is free to act, the investigation team will suffer interference, and you yourself will have no rest. So I believe it would be better if Zhang Peifen were inside as well.'

When I was finished, Mayor Liu sat with knitted brows then said, 'Hengda, if a person contracts a terminal illness, their spirit can live on. But if someone contracts a disease of the soul, they cannot save themselves no matter how they blame others, or switch right for wrong. The path of righteousness is narrow indeed!'

I felt I hadn't fully expressed my loyalty, so I deepened my tone of concern, saying, 'Mayor Liu, we mustn't do others harm, but we must defend against harm from others!'

He laughed and said, 'You weren't the Old Leader's secretary for nothing, Hengda! Your political understanding runs deep. The deeper the political risk, the more it tests a person's political perspicuity, and in this sense you're far more mature than Xu Zhitai. These are unusual times, Hengda, and they will test our political mettle. You're going to have to withstand some trials as head of Number Two Department!'

He was obviously using Xu Zhitai as a warning. What had he done to make Mayor Liu hold a grudge against him?

After leaving Mayor Liu's office, I thought back over everything he'd said and felt there was something behind his last words. He didn't completely trust me yet, otherwise he wouldn't have mentioned 'withstanding trials'. How could I make him trust me the same way he trusted Song Daoming? By positioning myself opposite Xu Zhitai? No, Xu Zhitai had climbed on board a pirate ship and wouldn't disembark. What I would need to do is draw a clear line of separation between myself and Peng Guoliang. But I was still directly employed in Peng Guoliang's service. I was right to strike a blow at him, but perhaps my 'finishing touch' had been too much. I'd been pleased with myself at the time, but now it seemed not only excessive, but even unnecessarily cruel. If it were someone else it might be different, but I was Peng Guoliang's right-hand man. It would be acceptable to make an objective report, to express my point of view in a natural way, but I'd been in too much of a hurry to show my loyalty, and I might have given the impression of being in a hurry to sell Peng Guoliang out. What trials could be in store for me otherwise?

The more I thought, the worse I felt.

Since Peng Guoliang had been detained, Number Two was sealed and we had little to do. Each of us had gone his own way. Zhu Dawei spent his days researching chess and Ou Beibei spent hers studying make-up or flirting with Zhao Zhong over the phone. Only Xu Zhitai had vanished altogether. At first I had hardly noticed, but Mayor Liu's mention of him made me feel that his disappearance probably had something to do with Zhang Peifen.

I'd learned from Zhao Zhong about Xu Zhitai's friendship with Qi Xiuying's old lover, someone named Lin Yongqing, a journalist at the *Qingjiang Daily*. Is that what Xu was busy with? Could this Lin Yongqing really influence Qi Xiuying?

It seemed unlikely. They might be old lovers, but even if they were married, I doubt Lin Yongqing could influence Qi Xiuying. She was known as the 'Female Bao Gong', and Bao Gong was willing to put his own nephew's head on the block for the sake of the law. Not only would Qi Xiuying not be influenced, but chances were she would take care of Lin Yongqing, Xu Zhitai and all the rest as well.

Why had Xu Zhitai never gotten anywhere in politics, even after all these years? He couldn't read the shifting winds. As the peasants say, you piss with the wind and shit against it. He, on the other hand, seemed to make a point of getting it backwards, and now he was piss-drenched and stunk like shit. He should have considered his own abilities more carefully before deciding to become Peng Guoliang's saviour!

Number Two Department, Department Vice-Head, Xu Zhitai

I DON'T KNOW if it was my intuition that was wrong, or if there really are people in the world whose hearts are made of stone: Lin Yongqing told me he had failed to move Qi Xiuying.

When Peng Guoliang was transferred from the Dongzhou Detention Centre to Changshan, Lin and I felt ashamed to meet Zhang Peifen. But Lin is someone who doesn't take defeat lying down, and since things had turned ugly between him and Qi Xiuying, then let them be ugly.

He came to me to discuss our next step, and we talked for a whole afternoon in a private room in a teahouse before deciding that our pens would be our weapons. It was mostly my idea. Lin Yongqing was a senior reporter and well known in his field. He would be able to place an article in the internal reference section of an influential newspaper where the central leadership would be sure to see it.

When he heard my idea, he thought it was a good one. If he could attract the attention and interest of the central leadership, there was a good chance that Peng Guoliang could be saved.

We were elated to have thought of this, though Lin was still a little concerned about his lack of materials. He thought if he was going to write this kind of article, he should write three at once to ensure they drew interest. I laughed slyly and said, 'Lin, you've forgotten than I'm the Vice-Head of Number Two Department, Peng Guoliang's office. I know his achievements better than anyone, and I know the political situation of Dongzhou better than anyone. How could you lack for materials? You'll have the most complete, accurate and convincing materials possible!'

When he heard that, he said enthusiastically, 'If that's true, then there's really hope for Mayor Peng!'

After we parted I couldn't wait to call Zhang Peifen and tell her I'd hired a 'bounty hunter' who would be sure to win justice for her. Zhang Peifen was at home, stewing over a nationally known journalist who had accepted bribes but done nothing in return. She was a little sceptical about my news. She admitted that Lin Yongqing was an ideal 'bounty hunter', but he'd already failed her once. Would his articles be authoritative enough to make it into the internal reference section?

She was still worried, and asked me to visit her house, saying she had something important to entrust to me. Ready to do my part, I went to see her.

She was crying when I saw her, saying Qi Xiuying was determined to wreck her home and destroy her family. When she talked about the suffering Peng Guoliang had endured at the Dongzhou Detention Centre, her expression was so miserable, my heart trembled. I struck my chest in indignation and said, 'Whatever you need me to do, sister, just speak up, and I won't deny you.'

She was deeply moved, and took a package from her maid's hands to give to me, saying warmly, 'Your brother sent word from the detention centre. He sends his greetings and thanks you for all you've done in his cause. He's proud to have a brother like you, and believes that with you fighting for his cause, justice is sure to be done. He told me that, with winter here, spring cannot be far behind. This is his darkest hour and I cannot leave Dongzhou even for a moment. We're in our greatest need, but we've been abandoned by everyone. You're the only one I can trust, and I'm begging you: visit Beijing for me, and give this package to this official.'

As she spoke, she handed me a photograph of three people: the official, his secretary and Peng Guoliang. I gasped when I saw the official. He was a powerful leader, someone whose reach extended from heaven to hell. Though he was retired, a word from him carried equal weight to that of a member of the Political Bureau Committee. With an old cadre like this speaking and acting on our behalf, Peng Guoliang's case would be overturned for sure! And once it was, I would be his right-hand man. He would be sure to reward me!

My heart was filled with hope and enthusiasm, and I swore to Zhang Peifen that I would complete my mission. Honestly, at that very moment, I was moved by my own devout chivalry. Who would have known: not only am I a man who would die for his friends, but I'm also staunch in the face of danger.

Zhang Peifen drove me to the airport herself. On the way, she instructed me to find a place to stay in Beijing where the official's secretary would contact me. She'd arranged everything. The black bag she handed me was locked, and as we drove I couldn't help imagining what was in it. It was a big bag, and if it held money, it would be two or three hundred thousand. Zhang Peifen seemed to guess what I was thinking and she spoke directly. 'I'll tell you the truth, Zhitai. Peng Guoliang has always struggled in his official position, and we don't have much savings. I've spent what little we had on this struggle to clear his name, and I've had to borrow some from friends. I've got no choice. I'd be willing to go bankrupt to save your brother.'

Her sincerity moved me deeply. I'm helpless to resist someone who really trusts me. The minute someone speaks their heart to me, I'm bound to respond in kind. I boarded the plane to Beijing.

I was in Beijing for two whole days without contact from anyone. Eventually I was obliged to call Zhang Peifen, who told me to wait patiently. An official of that level was busy, but someone would contact me for sure. I waited another two days, then one evening a thin, tall man in his early thirties arrived, wearing a Western suit and shoes. He was the secretary from the photo Zhang Peifen showed me. After I'd verified his identity, he left with the bag. I called Zhang Peifen to tell her, and she congratulated me excitedly, thanking me for my work and asking me to fly back from Beijing the next day.

From her mood I guessed that the acceptance of the bag was a guarantee that we'd receive help, and I was deeply happy for her. The thought that my mission to Beijing might result in Peng Guoliang's restoration reminded my soul – which had hid for so long in loneliness, in darkness – of the value of existence.

One afternoon, about a week after my return to Dongzhou, I was reading the newspaper in my office when I got an excited phone call from Lin Yongqing saying that his articles had been published. He asked me to come out. He was waiting for me at the gate of the government compound. I hurried into the elevator.

When I left the government building I saw Lin Yongqing waving to me from the mail building. I trotted over, gesturing that we should go to the government square to talk, and he followed me over to the *huabiao* at the centre of the square. He pulled out his internal reference articles and handed them to me excitedly. I tore the paper open and the title of the first, 'Avoid Negative Influences from the Powers Behind the Corruption Allegations Against Peng Guoliang', leaped off the page at me. It was written in a sharp, incisive style, amply backed up with evidence, with a fresh new point of view; an article of substance.

When I'd finished, I couldn't help calling Zhang Peifen's office on the spot. All I said was that Lin Yongqing and I wanted to meet her, and we were heading over to the Administrative Academy immediately. I didn't say any more on the phone because I wanted to give her a surprise.

Zhang Peifen seemed to know why we were coming and was waiting at the gate of the Administrative Academy. When we got out of the car I passed her the newspaper, my face expressionless, and she took it, obviously beside herself with pleasure. She read the article from start to finish, then took off for a photocopy shop near the academy, holding the newspaper lovingly. She made ten copies, then returned the original to Lin Yongqing gratefully, saying, 'Lin, Zhitai, I'm going back to my office to gather my things, then let's all go to the Dongzhou shopping mall. I'll buy you both a full set of Zegna clothing, then we'll all go to Jinchongcao for a celebration.' Lin Yongqing and I couldn't turn her down.

A single stone will create a thousand ripples. Lin Yongqing's article provoked a strong response in the Dongzhou Government, which wrote a letter directly to the newspaper that ran Lin's article, arguing in their defence. He kept up the attack, publishing two more articles in quick succession which attracted the attention of the top leadership in Beijing. Zhang Peifen, elated, treated me to dinner and told me that many influential leaders had begun asking about Peng Guoliang's case, particularly the top official who'd accepted the bag I'd brought to Beijing. He'd made a special trip to Zhongnanhai. It was clear from Zhang Peifen's news that holes were starting to appear in the case against Peng Guoliang.

But nothing turns out the way you hope. The high-level attention failed to bring Peng Guoliang's case to a new turning point, and what's more, the investigation team retaliated by transferring Peng Guoliang from the Dongzhou Detention Centre, where conditions were relatively lax, to Changshan, where he knew practically no one. Zhang Peifen was once again thrown on the defensive.

About this time, I received an unexpected phone call. It was Wang Chaoquan. I'd been trying to contact him ever since he'd effected his glorious transformation into the Deputy Chief of the Anti-Terrorism Unit, but the phone number he'd left me before going to Shenzhen had passed on to a new owner, and I had no other means of contact. Since Peng Guoliang got in trouble, a rumour had been going around that Wang Chaoquan, while on an anti-terrorism operation in Macau, had filmed Peng Guoliang gambling in the casinos there. I didn't know what to think, and had wanted to ask him directly, but could never get in touch. Now he'd re-emerged of his own accord. I agreed to meet him at the Apricot Village Hotel near the Provincial Public Security Bureau.

When I entered the private room, I found that Wang Chaoquan had already finished ordering. He looked much better than he used to: he was natty in a Western suit, and even his face had changed. It was more heroic. As soon as I saw him I thumped him on the chest and said, 'You sure kept your secrets well, you bastard!'

Wang Chaoquan was my best friend among the civil servants. I am quite a bit older than him, so I spoke to him as if to a younger brother.

He laughed lightly and said, 'Brother Xu, people in my line of work only know one principle: "ultimate loyalty to the country". For the sake of loyalty we can, and do, sacrifice everything.'

Hearing that, I felt a little moved, and patted his shoulder, saying, 'No need to explain; I understand everything. I once thought that *True Lies* was just some Hollywood producer's way of squeezing cash out of moviegoers. Who would have guessed that sort of stuff happens in real life? And right under my nose . . .'

He gestured for me to sit, then poured out two beers and toasted me, saying, 'I'll tell you the truth: I'm carrying out a mission right now. I just made a little time to come from Shenzhen to treat you to a meal and a drink. Do you know why?'

'Not because you think I'm a terrorist?' I joked.

He answered in all earnestness, 'In my eyes, there's no real difference between a terrorist and a corrupt official. They both pose a threat to national security, and I think the threat from corrupt officials is actually the greater. Given our friendship, I can't watch you throw yourself over a cliff! I'll tell you straight: I came back to save you!'

My heart lurched when I heard him say that. I knew he was perfectly serious, but I still didn't know why he should say all this, so I asked, 'Chaoquan, what do you mean?'

His face drew long. 'Do you know what kind of person Peng Guoliang is?'

I said, with some displeasure, 'I worked with him. Of course I know. He's a man of uncommon talents and capabilities.'

Wang Chaoquan replied, 'I'm not denying that Peng Guoliang has done a fair amount of good, but he is corrupt to the bone. To me, he's like a rotten mackerel under the moonlight: bright and shining, and reeking of putrefaction.'

I finally understood why Wang Chaoquan had suddenly reappeared and invited me to dinner. He'd always suspected that it was Peng Guoliang who had gotten Ou Beibei pregnant, and he hated him for stealing his wife. Now he was hoping to stop me from helping Peng Guoliang. Yes, that had to be it.

Now that I knew what he was up to, I replied calmly, 'Chaoquan, you shouldn't make baseless accusations!'

He swept me with an eagle's gaze and said, 'Very well. First I'll describe for you what Peng Guoliang looked like while he was gambling at the casino. At the time I would never have guessed this was a man who acted as standing vice-mayor over a city of eight million. He was wearing a gold Dharmachakra around his neck, diamond rings on his fingers, a gold necklace as thick as your thumb and had a gold cigarette holder between his teeth. I was leading a field operation at the time and he suddenly appeared within our surveillance area. Do you know how much he lost at that one sitting?'

He paused here and clucked his tongue, then held out five fingers and said in tones of contempt, 'Fifty thousand dollars. And do you know where that fifty thousand came from? Even if I didn't say, you could probably work it out for yourself. That alone would be grounds for his wearing out a cell bench in jail, but it's only the tip of the iceberg. He's been keeping a mistress in Hong Kong called Niu Yuexian, who he sent there back when he was head of the Municipal Bureau of Commerce. Do you know why he sent her there? To launder money for him. Right before his case broke, this woman took all his money and fled. Do you know how much she took? More than thirty million Hong Kong dollars. Brother, I hear you've teamed up with a journalist to help Zhang Peifen interfere with Peng Guoliang's case, and that he's written a series of articles for internal consumption that severely violate his professional ethics as a journalist, not only twisting the facts to an enormous degree, but also slandering and personally attacking the members of the investigation team. I just want to ask you, my brother: what are you trying to accomplish? I can't believe your goal is simply to help overturn the case against Peng Guoliang. We've known each other for years and I know how you've suffered. You've been vice-head of the department for years with no opportunity for advancement, but even so, you can't imitate Peng Guoliang and start gambling. What gambler comes to a good end? I'm speaking from the heart here, my brother, though I know you won't like hearing it. I just can't watch you take the road to death.' He poured himself another glass of beer and drained it.

To be honest, his words really did find their mark. When we'd been friends before, he'd always seemed so weak and pathetic. I'd always been the strong elder brother. I'd never seen him behave so forcefully before, but perhaps this was the real Wang Chaoquan. I was cowed into silence and didn't know what to say; I had never imagined that Peng Guoliang had been so far gone.

If what Wang Chaoquan said was true, then it was impossible that Peng would keep his head. What hope was there of overturning the case?

'What's the matter with me?' I kept asking myself. Had I really been led astray? Wang Chaoquan had hinted that my purposes in helping Peng Guoliang were not pure. What about his purpose in treating me to a drink? Could someone who kept his own identity secret from his wife – his mate and companion – really speak from the heart to me?

I argued back. 'So there's nothing behind your words, huh? You don't hold any grudges over what happened with Beibei?'

He shook his head with a bitter smile. 'It looks like you'll hold out to the very end, my brother. If you're determined to dash yourself against the wall, then there's nothing I can say. You're right: I hold a grudge against Peng Guoliang because of Beibei. He ruined my marriage, didn't he? We call each other brother, yet you have so much sympathy for the person who ruined your brother's happiness? Do you still know the difference between right and wrong? No wonder you and Zhang Peifen get along so well. I'll tell you the truth: no one can save Peng Guoliang. The door of hell is always open for those rash fools who thought they would never end up there. I've said everything I can to you. Don't try to excuse yourself with this 'my leader, right or wrong' attitude. Before we part, my brother, I have just one thing to say to you: you're on the brink of the precipice, but there's still time to turn back. Do the right thing!' He shook his head in disappointment and then stood, saying, 'I've paid the bill already, brother. I've got something I need to do so I'm going. I hope you think hard about what I've said.'

He left without a backward glance, leaving me sitting there stunned, not knowing what to think. It was as if Wang Chaoquan had woken me from a dream and I'd suddenly discovered that different truths existed in different parts of the body: some in the heart, some in the liver, some in the kidneys. Furthermore, some of the truths that hid within the body were hidden within dung. When it came to the error I'd committed, I didn't know in which part of the body the truth in question was hidden. Were the truths hidden in stinking dung more true, or the truths hidden inside the heart and its beating blood? Apparently I'd misunderstood Chuang-tzu when he said that the *Dao* was in dung and urine. I'd thought that every part of the human body has its conscience, but I'd forgotten that dung is just dung, and urine is just urine; they are mere waste products and only stay within the body temporarily. Sooner or later they will be excreted. At that moment I had the feeling that I was being excreted, and flushed down the toilet, spiralling into the sewer.

Since I'd got a scolding from Wang Chaoquan, my spirits were low. The reason was that I felt my 'saviour' had come too late, and I'd already sunk into the mud.

I remembered something a Japanese writer once said: 'Between a high, solid wall and the egg that breaks against it, I will always stand on the side of the egg. Yes, no matter how right the wall may be and how wrong the egg, I will stand with the egg.' Clearly he saw the egg as truth, but he forgot that an egg can become putrid, it can be hard-boiled, turned into a hundred-year-old egg by lime. If any of those were hurled against a wall, they certainly wouldn't leave behind a bright yellow smear of yolk.

I was no longer a fresh egg – though I once thought I was – and that's why I chose Peng Guoliang, that rotten egg. All eggs, before the shell is broken, appear whole, but now Wang Chaoquan had smashed all the eggs before my eyes and I could smell a rotten stench. It wasn't the stench of rotten eggs, however. It was the smell of a human soul. Peng Guoliang's soul, to be precise, reeking amid fragments of broken shell. On the wall was a stain, as though dung had been flung against it, and flies circled incessantly.

The flies helped me understand the three fates of eggs: hatching into chicks, being eaten or rotting. Aren't those the very fates of man? Don't think it's good fortune not to be eaten or not to rot. Even if you hatch into a chick, you can't avoid a fate of being eaten, or getting some fatal disease like avian flu. Even chickens that lay eggs like crazy end this way. I'm already unsure whether I'm a chicken or an egg. All I remember is what my grandmother said to me when I was a child: 'Flies will ignore an egg with no cracks.' If I was an egg, then I was a cracked egg. But I didn't know when I had cracked, or how.

I was not corrupt; I was just someone who had helped the corrupt. It was just a pity that, because I'd put my money on the wrong square, my official career never made it past vice department head. That didn't seem right.

First-Level Superintendent of the Changshan Detention Centre, Wu Wenzhong

I'VE BEEN WORKING at the detention centre for ten years and I'm still only a first-level superintendent. We get all sorts here: naïve students, stubborn repeat offenders, irredeemable murderers and, of course, corrupt officials of various ranks and grades. This is the first time we've had one as high-level as Peng Guoliang, though.

Around a month after he arrived, I got a phone call from Xu Zhitai, the husband of an elementary school classmate, asking me to dinner. I hadn't spoken to him in years, and I guessed he had a favour to ask. In a job like mine, you often hear from friends or family of criminals on the inside, and I guessed that had to be the reason for this particular invitation. I was right, but I hadn't anticipated that he would be asking for my help on behalf of Peng Guoliang, the former standing Vice-Mayor of Dongzhou.

The dinner was actually arranged by Zhang Peifen, Peng Guoliang's wife, who arrived together with Xu Zhitai. We ate shark's fin soup and abalone, and drank Remy Martin. She spent the meal insisting that her husband was innocent and then tossed me twenty thousand *yuan*. I didn't want to take it, but it was nearly the equivalent of a year's wages for me. Anyone would consider it. I grew up in the countryside, and if I hadn't been accepted at the police academy and sent to work in the detention centre, I'd be a farmer right now. My parents still live in the village and support themselves off the land. Both are in poor health, and twenty thousand would mean the world to us. With Vice Department Head Xu urging me as well, I decided to take it.

Xu was not only the husband of my elementary school classmate, but he was also Vice-Head of Number Two Department, Combined Affairs, in the Dongzhou Municipal Government, so he was essentially the vice-director of the office that served Peng Guoliang. He went on and on about how Peng Guoliang served the people with heart and soul, and the reason he had encountered difficulties was because of a political struggle. Though I only half believed what I was hearing, I was truly moved by Zhang Peifen's determination to save her husband, and I agreed to provide what help I could. Xu had thought of everything. He even had a pair of mobile phones prepared for me and Zhang Peifen.

When I went home that night and handed twenty thousand *yuan* to my wife, her eyes shone as if they were electrified. In the eight years since we've been married, we'd never seen twenty thousand together in one place. The next day I went to the cell where Peng Guoliang was being held, called him to the door, and asked him if he knew anyone called Zhang Peifen. His dull gaze abruptly brightened as he nodded and said that was his wife. I expressed my concern in a few words and told him in a reassuring tone, 'If you need anything, just let me know.' When he heard that, the rigid muscles of his face relaxed a little.

A few days later, when I was leading a work detail of prisoners to clean the latrines, I found Peng Guoliang alone in his cell and passed him the phone Xu Zhitai had prepared for him, telling him to call Zhang Peifen. I opened the door to let him out for some exercise, and he took the hint, dialling Zhang Peifen's number excitedly.

In order to thank me, Zhang Peifen made a special trip to Changshan to treat my wife and me to dinner, even making a present of an Omega watch to my wife. In my ten years at the detention centre, I'd never seen such a valuable gift, and my wife fawned over it. I like people who are generous in their dealings, and Zhang Peifen was the most generous person I'd ever seen. I couldn't say whether Peng Guoliang had ended up in the slammer because he was framed, but I hoped to hell that he had been. If it were true, I'd be the one who had come through for him in his moment of crisis, and when it came time to show their gratitude, it would come to a lot more than an Omega watch and twenty thousand *yuan*.

I needed to prove my capability, of course, and couldn't disappoint Zhang Peifen, so I brought her a letter Peng Guoliang had written to her. Her hand was shaking as she took the letter, and her eyes filled with tears as she read it, as if she wanted to inscribe its contents on her heart. I could tell she wanted to keep the letter, so before she could ask, I stopped her, saying, 'Sorry, but you can't take that with you. It would be a disaster if anyone were to find it.' Despondent yet understanding, she pulled out a notebook to copy down the contents and then burnt the letter in front of me.

On the way home, my wife began to worry. 'Are you sure this won't cause us any trouble?'

I gritted my teeth. 'You've got to do a little extra to get a little extra. I'll be careful. Anyway, politics is just a big web. If there are people who want to hurt Peng Guoliang, then there must be people who want to help him. Can't you tell that Zhang Peifen is a woman who gets things done? If Peng Guoliang really does come out of jail as a martyred hero, things will be pretty good for us!' I really believed what I was saying, and I guessed that Xu Zhitai, who had accompanied Zhang Peifen, was thinking the same thing.

Later, Zhang Peifen made another visit to Changshan, and the two of us met alone. Before she came, she called me and said that the two lawyers she'd hired for Peng Guoliang wanted him to write a self-defence. When I told Peng Guoliang, he wrote a five-thousand-character self-defence on the spot and gave it to me. When I passed it on to Zhang Peifen, she gave me another five thousand *yuan*. Then, with tears in her eyes, she passed me Peng Guoliang's freshly laundered clothes and a picture of his son, who was in middle school. I'm a father myself, and I could imagine how much Peng Guoliang was missing his son.

When I brought the photograph into the detention centre and gave it to Peng Guoliang, his lips trembled and tears wet his glasses as he looked at his innocent son. He didn't keep the photograph, however. Eyes still full of tears, he turned it over and wrote, 'My son, learn true abilities, and become a noble man! Whatever you do, don't go into politics! Don't you worry about your father, he can take care of himself.' Then he gave it back to me and asked me to give it to Zhang Peifen.

As it happened, I was summoned to the city reception centre by the investigation team of the Provincial Disciplinary Committee before I could give the photograph to Zhang Peifen. I had a bad feeling. When I entered the room, I found six people waiting. Their leader introduced himself as Deng Hongchang of the Sixth Office of the Provincial Disciplinary Committee, leader of the team investigating Peng Guoliang. He invited me in a not unfriendly way to sit down, and poured me tea. A pretty, self-assured young girl introduced herself as Shang Xiaoqiong. Then they got straight to the point, asking me about the 888 mobile phone. That was one of the two phones Xu had prepared for me and Zhang Peifen. The two numbers were the same except for the last three digits. Hers ended in 777.

I've seen plenty of big shots in my ten years in the detention centre, but I've never had a slip of a girl come over as hard-boiled – Shang Xiaoqiong's demeanour was unflinching. But I didn't think much of her and played dumb. 'What 888 mobile phone? What do you mean? I think you've made a mistake.'

The next thing I knew, the friendly expression had vanished off Deng Hongchang's face, replaced by a glower. 'Wu Wenzhong, we wouldn't have talked to you without incontrovertible proof. If you're not willing to talk now, we can find a place to discuss things at length.

I hereby inform you that the Provincial Disciplinary Committee has authorised your detention. You must now come with us.'

I could only ask, stupidly, 'Where are we going?'

He laughed coldly and said, 'You'll know when we get there.'

The six of them escorted me out of the reception centre, and I was stuck in the back of a Santana between two big guards. An Audi drove ahead and our Santana followed behind. We drove straight out of Changshan and onto the expressway to Dongzhou, and I knew that was where we were going. My heart leaped into my throat and I cursed the situation. Things were going from bad to worse. If we'd stayed in Changshan I might have stood a chance, given all my contacts in public security, but I had no friends in Dongzhou. If I disappeared, my wife would go crazy with worry, and if my parents found out, their health would suffer for sure. 'What now?' I asked myself. 'What now?'

After less than two hours on the expressway we entered Dongzhou, and after a series of twists and turns we entered a military compound and pulled up in front of a reception centre. I was taken to a room on the fourth floor.

Before we entered the room, the pretty female investigator gave me a hard look and said, 'Don't get any smart ideas, Wu Wenzhong. We've got Zhang Peifen upstairs, and she's already told us all about the 777 phone.'

I had no idea if the girl was telling the truth, but it truly surprised me that she knew the last three digits of Zhang Peifen's number. Once we were inside, they didn't start right away with the interrogation, but instead left me to think things over, with two guards to watch me.

Before he left, Deng Hongchang spoke frankly. 'Your case is a serious one, Wu Wenzhong, but there's a chance we can go easy on you. If you tell us absolutely everything about how Zhang Peifen asked you for help in interfering with the Peng Guoliang case, our higher-ups will consider giving you a second chance. I hope you'll take the chance to do something for yourself. Think clearly now!'

His words reached me, and for the next couple of days I was hardly able to eat. It wasn't that I was weakening, but suddenly none of it seemed worth it. I had both young and old to look after, and if I happened to catch ten years, how would my old mother and father survive? My wife had lost her job and hadn't found another, our son was still young and I was the mainstay of our household. If I fell, wouldn't that mean the end of the family?

By this point the tears were running down my face and I turned to the two investigators guarding me. 'I want to see Director Deng. I want to make my report to the organisation.'

When the two disciplinary cadres watching me heard that, they exchanged glances and smiled in satisfaction.

Secretary of the Provincial Disciplinary Committee, Qi Xiuying

FOR YEARS, LIN Yongqing has been my only spiritual solace. Never in my wildest dreams would I have imagined he could disregard twenty years of feeling for the sake of an apartment, and speak to me on Peng Guoliang's behalf.

'Leave an out,' he said. 'Go easy on him.'

When I flatly refused his mad request, he betrayed his journalist's principles and his own conscience by writing internal reference articles, three of them, full of slander and calumny. Under the banner of 'reducing negative influences', he accused the investigation team of disregarding the larger picture of reform and opening up in Dongzhou, discounting Peng Guoliang's record of political achievements, and taking incorrect 'detention and interrogation' measures against him. Not only that, but he also aimed his spear at my son and me, saying that I was the force behind my son's real estate ventures, and that when my son became interested in a plot near the zoo, I personally made a phone call to Peng Guoliang asking him to grant that plot to my son. That land, so Lin wrote, was designated green space, so Peng Guoliang staunchly refused my request. During that time, my son reportedly continued to nag Peng Guoliang, who would not compromise, and so I decided to make use of my authority to strike out in revenge.

My lungs were bursting with anger once I'd read all three articles. How could I have been so blind? That someone I'd regarded as a soul mate could be twisted beyond recognition by the prospect of personal gain was a torture to heart and mind.

I was also angry with the man who'd dragged Lin Yongqing down, someone named Xu Zhitai, the Vice-Head of Number Two Department, Combined Affairs in the Dongzhou Municipal Government. He'd previously been a journalist at the *Qingjiang Daily* himself and was a petty man who took every opportunity to claw his way upward. Peng Guoliang was already in detention, yet Xu refused to climb down from the 'pirate ship'. Not only that, but he had also pulled Lin Yongqing on board with him.

Xu thought he could use the relationship between Lin Yongqing and me to overturn the case against Peng. Once Peng was restored to his rightful position, Xu would enjoy status as a benefactor in time of trouble, and could use his so-called loyalty to advance himself. It was sheer opportunism, a pitiful, petty move by a pitiful, petty man.

Unfortunately, it was a petty move that made things very difficult for us.

Zhang Peifen understood the importance of public opinion and she used the internal reference articles to support her efforts in Beijing. She beseeched retired leaders with connections in Zhongnanhai to 'seek justice' for Peng Guoliang. In fact, one of them, after reading the articles and at Zhang Peifen's urging, actually made a personal trip to Zhongnanhai to plead for Peng Guoliang's case, even calling the secretary of the Provincial Party Committee and interfering in the case.

Luckily the Qingjiang Party Committee is a principled group that listens to all sides of an issue and isn't easily fooled. The secretary came personally to talk to me, saying, 'Comrade Xiuying, I've seen the internal reference articles and the anonymous letters slandering you, and I think these people's methods are despicable. They have only one purpose in doing this, and that's to shake the Central Government's faith in the Qingjiang Party Committee and Disciplinary Committee and to keep the case from moving forward. But remember this: the Central Government and the Central Disciplinary Committee have faith in the Qingjiang committee and in you personally. It's precisely because you are unflagging in your duties that others wish you harm. I've looked into your son's situation and learned that he's a highly regarded university lecturer. He's never run a company at all. Comrade Xiuying, with the Provincial Party Committee and the people of Qingjiang at your back, you must persist in the prosecution of this case, no matter how Peng Guoliang tries to derail it.'

This was a tremendous support to me. What more could I say? All I could do was to use cold, hard facts to make the case against Peng Guoliang rock hard and airtight. You want to have this case overturned, do you Zhang Peifen? Not in this lifetime.

At the same time, I couldn't help admiring Peng Guoliang's wife. Despite standing alone against the whole investigation team, she had used bribery to swiftly build a massive 'rescue team' that reached from Dongzhou to Beijing, from the Party to the courts, from the media to universities. I had underestimated her abilities. Peng Guoliang had been incredibly arrogant at first, as if the Dongzhou Detention Centre was his own personal luxury spa, and I had him transferred to Changshan as a way of puncturing that arrogance. But after less than a month there, Zhang Peifen still managed to get a mole inside. She began her back dealings from the moment the investigation team was formed, paving her road with gold and making use of all her contacts, planning her attack and spreading lies and slander. Peng Guoliang was just as stubborn. He refused to confess, denying the case any breakthrough. If we were going to make progress we'd have to dissipate his dream of resisting the investigation and overturning the case, and the only way of doing that would be to cut off his and Zhang Peifen's communications. After a period of research and planning, the team decided to detain Zhang Peifen, Xu Zhitai and Lin Yongqing.

I didn't sleep the entire night before making the decision to detain Lin Yongqing. Who would have thought that twenty years of friendship and feeling would end like this? If it hadn't been for his silent support for me and my son after my husband passed, I truly don't know how I would have made it. Recalling that time, my tears began to flow. The past is not smoke. They say I'm made of iron, but it's not that which makes me strong. It's that the law is blind. And this life-and-death struggle was growing steadily fiercer. The complexity of the case had long ago exceeded the bounds of imagination.

Wu Wenzhong was the opening which allowed us to detain Zhang Peifen. For quite some time the team had known Zhang Peifen had a mobile phone with a number ending in triple seven which she used to call another phone whose number ended in triple eight. The first eight digits of the two numbers were the same. Deng Hongchang guessed that something fishy was going on and reported the matter to me. I directed the team to look up which city the triple eight number was registered in, and they discovered that both were registered in Changshan. Deng Hongchang felt there had to be a connection between Peng Guoliang being held in Changshan and Zhang Peifen's regular calls. I asked him if we had any other clues, and he mentioned that the triple seven phone, besides making regular calls to the triple eight one, had also made a few calls to a landline in Changshan. I instructed the team to head to Changshan at once and lock down the owner of that phone, and was surprised to learn that it was this Wu Wenzhong, a first-level superintendent at the Changshan Detention Centre.

After Wu Wenzhong was detained, I directed the team to detain Zhang Peifen, Xu Zhitai and Lin Yongqing, an order that they carried out with alacrity. While searching a cabinet in Zhang Peifen's office, Shang Xiaoqiong discovered a package of original and photocopied letters reporting complaints against me and Liu Yihe to various government offices. Her plan was clear: she intended to muddy the waters and use sleight of hand to keep Peng Guoliang from the block.

The team also found a big notebook in Zhang Peifen's bag, which, in addition to a large quantity of phone numbers, also contained regular occurrences of the word 'his'. I especially arranged for Deng Hongchang and Shang Xiaoqiong to speak with Zhang Peifen about it, but she craftily replied that the notebook contained her jottings for a novel she was planning. She felt she'd led a rich life, one that could make for an interesting novel, and the notebook's contents were fictional details. Who would have guessed she could be even more stubborn than Peng Guoliang?

I was obliged to detail team members to work on cracking the contents of the notebook. Once they'd succeeded, our case suddenly became a lot clearer. The notebook was in fact a record of everything Zhang Peifen had done to overturn Peng Guoliang's case since he was taken in, including the names and relationships of the people she'd dragged into her plans. The 'his' which appeared so often in the notebook marked the directives which Peng Guoliang issued to Zhang Peifen from within the detention centre. The notebook was a Pandora's box for the Peng Guoliang case, which had so stubbornly refused to progress. It was also 'open sesame'.

Director of the Sixth Office of the Provincial Disciplinary Committee and Leader of the Special Investigation Team, Deng Hongchang

ONCE ZHANG PEIFEN was detained and I informed Peng Guoliang of the fact, he seemed to realise that the situation was slipping beyond his control. In response, he adopted silence as a method of resistance. Though he was as recalcitrant as ever, the destruction of his contact network by the investigation team meant I could face him with a quieter heart. I knew that although he was outwardly calm, his inner world was in uproar. Years of investigative experience have taught me that anyone in detention goes through a three-stage process of resistance, inner struggle and then confession. Without a doubt, Peng Guoliang had entered stage two.

These past few days I've been studying the records of my clashes with him. The scene of our first encounter is still fresh before my eyes.

He began singing his own praises as soon as he opened his mouth, a common trick among those in detention. He said, 'I've never claimed to be spotless, but I am absolutely not a corrupt official. I have examined my own conscience, and found that I am a public servant with integrity, dedication and political skill. In terms of foreign investment alone, I pulled in more than thirty billion for the people of Dongzhou. I have not let down the Blackwater River which bore me and raised me.'

'So your visits to the casino in Macau were to attract foreign investment as well?' I asked him pointedly.

'All my trips to Macau were solely for the purpose of attracting foreign investment,' he insisted. 'I went to the casino for pleasure, because the work of negotiations was so tense. It was purely for relaxation; never took a trip solely to gamble.'

'Do you mean to say that using the investment attraction reward money to set up a private company was also in the interest of foreign investment?' I tightened the noose.

'That was entirely part of government policy – preparation for H shares going on the market,' he said craftily. 'I made my report to Liu Yihe about this matter. It was done with his approval, for the purpose of attracting more funds for Dongzhou.'

'Do you mean to say that your higher-ups have wronged you?' I asked mockingly.

'At any rate I've never done anything criminal. If my superiors won't let me serve my people then it's not my loss, it's the people's loss,' he said, arrogant as ever.

'Wen Huajian, Chen Shi and Hu Zhanfa have all come clean, Peng. Why won't you see the light? If you didn't have suspicious financial dealings, would the Provincial Party Committee and Disciplinary Committee have set up a special investigation team for you?'

'Deng Hongchang, was Jesus guilty of a crime? Yet he was nailed upon the cross all the same. I'm sitting here today for no other reason than that my political opponents have seen fit to put me here.'

That's Peng Guoliang's attitude. Since he's been detained, we've crossed swords countless times, and each time he has been thunderous in his self-defence and supercilious in his attitude. Added to this is Zhang Peifen, who at Peng's direction leveraged the connections they'd painstakingly cultivated over the years to make a nuisance of herself. On the one hand, she enticed some unprincipled officials into corruption, and on the other, she spent vast sums on bribes and destroying criminal evidence, impeding the investigation at every turn.

If the decision hadn't been made to take timely action against Zhang Peifen, the investigation team would likely have been further stymied.

I should mention that since the investigation team was established, it has worked under highly secretive circumstances, but after we detained Zhang Peifen and went through her notebook, we found she'd written down each team member's mobile phone number, home and office numbers, as well as some details of the investigation. She'd even recorded testimony from people who'd co-operated with the investigation. The enormous energy of Peng Guoliang and Zhang Peifen is far beyond anything I expected. The two of them are almost lunatic in their desperation to overturn the case.

The first time I crossed swords with Zhang Peifen I took a lesson from my first meeting with Peng Guoliang and held tightly to the issue of her and Peng Guoliang's false confessions. At first she blew a smokescreen of stories, hoping to distract me, but I stuck to the question of false confessions until the holes in her stories became painfully evident and finally fell apart.

Shang Xiaoqiong was particularly adept at using other cases to illustrate Zhang's situation, and she described two wives of two corrupt officials, one who co-operated with the investigation and got off without criminal charges, and another who was obstructionist and went to jail. These stories had a powerful effect on Zhang Peifen. She began to move from the resistance stage to that of inner struggle.

On the thirtieth day of the New Year, Zhang Peifen suddenly made a request. She said this was Peng Guoliang's zodiac year and she wanted the investigation team to buy red underwear for her husband. I braved the snow to visit several stores, and at last found some red underwear in a box that read 'Zodiac Year'. That satisfied Zhang Peifen. When I handed them to Peng Guoliang, he was quite moved.

This incident had a considerable effect on me. The idea of the humane prosecution of cases has long hovered in my mind. To someone like Peng Guoliang, who once commanded the wind and the rain, nothing was more unbearable than being shut out in the cold. If I were to show respect for his character and consideration for his condition, perhaps it might ease his misgivings and wariness towards me. After I braved the snow to buy him underwear, I saw a real difference in his attitude.

From that point on, every time Peng Guoliang and I crossed swords, I didn't address him by his full name, but showed my respect for him by calling him 'Old Peng'. Knowing his biggest worry in life was his son, who was born with severe gastroptosis and about whom he fretted constantly, I arranged for a few phone calls between them. He was also a heavy smoker, so I bought him cigarettes with my own money. We even chatted a bit together about family and life, and I gradually worked in some stories to illustrate the law. Deprived of his external supports, Peng Guoliang's spiritual defences began to crumble.

When we met two days ago, he suddenly asked me, 'Director Deng, is the Central Government determined to have my head?'

I didn't miss my opportunity. 'Given the quantities of money you've embezzled and the bribes you've made and accepted, according to national criminal law, you could be given a limited sentence, a life sentence or possibly even the death sentence. Why so uncertain? It will depend on the specific circumstances and the severity of the consequences. There was a report in the *Qingjiang Daily* today about a Vice-Mayor of Xizhou who accepted vast bribes and was given a suspended death sentence. Based on the amount of bribes he accepted, he should have been executed on the spot, but because he confessed and showed good behaviour and also returned the bribes, he was allowed to keep his neck.'

Peng Guoliang was silent for a while, then finally worked up the courage to ask, 'If I come clean first, is there a chance they'll go easy on me?'

Apparently my 'brink of death' strategy was having its effect. I slowly pressed my advantage. 'Your case will have a major influence on society. In the end, exactly how it turns out will depend on you.'

The floodgates were finally starting to open. He realised he could make things easier for himself by dropping a few hints. And so by fits and starts he spoke, sometimes restraining himself, sometimes letting go, as if we were trying to squeeze toothpaste out of him. The story of his criminal behaviour emerged as silk is spun from the silkworm cocoon, bit by bit.

While Peng began to come clean, Zhang Peifen steadfastly clung to the story the two of them had worked out between them. One day, Shang Xiaoqiong reported a new development. Since Peng's case broke, his son had become the subject of scorn in his school and he was refusing to go classes. I felt this was quite a serious situation and reported it to Qi Xiuying immediately. She went to Liu Yihe in person to discuss how to get the child back into school. After I'd told Peng Guoliang about this, he seemed quite shaken. Tears in his eyes, he asked for pen and paper and wrote Zhang Peifen a letter that came from the heart.

'Peifen, my dearest, dearest wife. In deepest remorse I come before you to repent. My wife, I am not worthy of being your husband, nor of being father to our son. I could kneel before you now and never rise again, but still it would not erase the harm I have done to the two of you. Since the case against me began, I have not looked to myself as the cause of my own difficulties, instead blaming heaven and earth. I have failed to take correct stock of the situation and to co-operate with the investigation, instead demanding your help in obstructing and attacking it, until at last I brought us to our current predicament, hurting you and our son, and so many of our friends. Most unforgivable is the damage I've done to the image of the Party and the Government. At this point I have no choice but to face reality, abandon delusions and actively co-operate with the investigation.

If I can work to earn the forgiveness of the authorities, I may win myself some leniency.'

Once Peng Guoliang had finished the letter and handed it over, he made a complete confession.

After I gave the letter to Zhang Peifen, she spoke in a trembling voice, as if to herself. 'More than a year, all that money, all those people . . . Who knew we'd end up exactly where we started? Guoliang, I've let you down!'

She put her hands to her face and began to weep in despair. People talked about the deep commitment between the two of them, and I could hear it in the sound of her weeping. She knew perfectly well that once her husband started to talk, the two of them might not meet again in this world.

Zhang Peifen's family had a strong political background, but she had none of the little princess's manner. Peng Guoliang had once boasted to me, 'After Peifen and I were married, she would wait up for me at home, no matter how late I got off work, with a midnight meal ready. Particularly in the winter, no matter how late I was, she would get up and pour a steaming hot foot bath for me, and after I'd soaked my feet, she would warm them against her bosom.'

Looking at this woman who was mad to save her husband and thinking of all that Peng had done, I couldn't help wondering, what kind of love is this? The two of them had pushed each other into the abyss. Especially Peng Guoliang, who had kept Niu Yuexian and impregnated Ou Beibei, all behind his wife's back. Was he thinking of how she'd warmed his feet then? Only when faced with death did his conscience reawaken!

This stage of the investigation was finally complete, and my superiors allowed me a few days' rest. After my vacation, when I'd just returned to work, Secretary Qi called me into her office and told me to arrange for a *Qingjiang Daily* reporter to visit the Changshan Detention Centre and interview Peng Guoliang. To my surprise, the journalist turned out to be Huang Xiaoguang, the elder brother of Huang Xiaoming, Peng Guoliang's secretary.

I knew that Huang Xiaoguang was a well-known author, and I asked him with befitting humility, 'What evil do you think we are inheriting and perpetuating in this case?'

He replied scornfully, 'Officials First.'

Author and Senior Reporter at the *Qingjiang Daily*, Huang Xiaoguang

'XIAOGUANG, WHAT'S THE opposite of darkness?'

That was the first thing Peng Guoliang asked me.

I knew he liked to smoke soft pack Zhonghua cigarettes. Most of Peng Guoliang's material needs were satisfied in the Changshan Detention Centre, but the rules stipulated that those under detention could not smoke, although Peng Guoliang could ask for a smoke when he happened to be in an interrogation or a meeting. Before I came, my brother told me to buy him a pack, and I figured these Zhonghua cigarettes might be the last luxury he would enjoy in this life. According to my brother, he'd needed a quick hand and eye to light Peng Guoliang's cigarettes for him. Peng never struck his own light.

I figured Peng Guoliang would be on his way within a few days, and before I visited him I interviewed Qi Xiuying, Secretary of the Provincial Disciplinary Committee, and made a point of asking how Peng was likely to be executed. The answer was lethal injection, a little more humane than a bullet.

How could I answer that kind of question from a condemned man?

To stall him, I lit his cigarette as my brother would have, saying, 'All I know is that light is something akin to darkness.'

Peng Guoliang laughed despairingly. 'To someone about to die, the opposite of darkness is darkness. Thank you for visiting me, Xiaoguang, and giving me the dignity of a cigarette before I die.'

I didn't want to spend the interview going over every detail of Peng Guoliang's crimes, and I didn't want to gloat over a dastardly criminal brought low. I knew that he had become a condemned man practically overnight, and a host of imponderable questions must be crowding his soul. What might those questions be? That's what I really wanted. That was most valuable. To treat him with scorn, or kick him while he was down, or revel in his misfortune? If I treated him that way, he would tell me nothing. Allowing him his dignity was my only choice.

We often say that life is worthless. Since Peng Guoliang was about to use his worthless life to redeem his own crime, he would shortly be without crime. In that sense we were equals, and this seemed to be real humanity. What is it we're all struggling for? Many people believe it's power, position, glory, wealth, but in truth these things are all adjunct to dignity. It is dignity that is most important to us in life. How could Peng Guoliang, who would shortly lose his life, have any dignity? But I would give it to him. He would see a thread of light in the darkness. There was no need for him to believe that the opposite of darkness was also darkness.

I admit that Peng Guoliang's fate was a tragic one, but no one seemed aware of the greater tragedy; that under the present system, anyone who reached Peng Guoliang's status was liable to follow Peng Guoliang's fate. What right did we have to look down our noses at him? Was it true that the opposite of darkness was darkness? That those who ostensibly stood on the side of light were equally dark? That the only difference was that they had not yet been exposed? If so, then the 'light' was truly horrible. Perhaps it was the 'light' that had pushed Peng Guoliang's world view into the abyss.

The opening of the *Three Character Classic* reads, 'Man at birth is good by nature.' I've never believed that to be true, but neither do I believe that we are evil by nature. What I think is, 'Man at birth tends towards the good'. Someone like Peng Guoliang couldn't have been born a rotten apple, so how did he get that way? That was the crux of the question.

In order to find the answer, I lit another cigarette for him, and asked him respectfully, 'So what do you think light is?'

He drew in a greedy lungful of smoke and said, 'Light is the present system and the most maddening of political symbols. I was once a worshipper and a follower of the light, and later became both a beneficiary and a creator of the light. Now I am being sacrificed to the light. To tell you the truth, in my "*Reflections on my Crimes*" I said I'd been influenced by the money worship of capitalism, and let my world view, life principles and values begin to slide. All that was actually bullshit. What does that have to do with their capitalism? Our system long ago got in the habit of blaming everything on the capitalists. My world view, life principles and values were actually twisted by the light. It was too bright, it dazzled my eyes, and that's how I lost my way. Not only did the light dazzle me, but it also seared my soul. You might think that the light is great, but that's because we are in different positions. If you were standing where I stand, you would see that the noble light illuminates the most despicable filth. But I see that filth as a part of the light, or the very light itself. In fact, that filth is fragments of the darkness that is hidden within the light. Only now have I come to understand that light is but another disguise of the darkness.'

I'd once thought that only a very few people could have real insight into the complex nature of light, and that those people must have passed through some torturous purgatory of the soul. Though I didn't agree with Peng Guoliang's point of view, one thing was for sure: though his body was still on earth, his soul was already suffering the tortures of hell. From the moment I learned that he would be given the death penalty I had been asking myself: could such severe punishment really halt corruption and crime? If so, then why was the Emperor Zhu

Yuanzhang, with his cruel methods of skinning and drawing tendons, unable to halt the depredations of corrupt officials? Our existing backward system provides no answers. A backward system could turn any normal person into a rat, and that is probably the key reason that Peng Guoliang felt he was a sacrificial victim of the system. I couldn't imagine how someone on the brink of death could be so horrified by the light. Could that thing that would come so suddenly actually be a disaster in disguise?

'If you're a sacrifice to the light, then what is Liu Yihe?' I asked tentatively.

'Someone who understands the darkness. That's what I admire most about him,' he answered in a heartfelt voice.

My brother had told me long ago that in the political arena Peng Guoliang had always seen Liu Yihe as his opponent. The two of them had started together, but from then on Liu had always been a step ahead, and Peng resented him for that. I was surprised that at this stage Peng could speak of Liu with admiration.

'What is it you admire about him?' I asked.

He answered directly, 'He knows that, to a certain extent, light is even darker than darkness. Light cannot be illuminated by light, and it is meaningless without darkness. I learned it too late, only after I was given my death sentence. Now it's too late for everything; I can only descend into the eternal darkness of hell, and remember the light.'

He seemed to relish the thought of darkness. I wanted to know more about his idea of hell, and asked, 'In your opinion, what is hell? And what is heaven?'

Peng tossed his cigarette butt on the floor and stamped it out with his foot, then spoke scornfully. 'Don't believe there's really any such thing as heaven or hell. That's all utopian thinking. Don't worry about whether I'll actually go to hell when I die. That's just a trick to frighten people. They say you go out like a light. Death is death. Death is oblivion.' He held out his hand for another cigarette.

I thought there was something bitter about his despair, and asked, 'Do you have any regrets?'

He was silent for a long time before answering painfully, 'Leaving me alive, leaving me to repent for my sins in jail, letting the years wash my soul, serving as an example to others; wouldn't that be more meaningful to society than exterminating my body? Have you heard of any developed Western countries wresting life from their citizens for the crime of corruption and bribe-taking? Expecting the death penalty to awe officials out of their corrupt ways is a laughable fallacy.

'If you want to talk regrets, I have done wrong by your brother. He shouldn't have lowered himself to be my secretary. If at some point in the future our mayors and governors are not appointed by their higher-ups but are instead voted into office by a democratic election, that will be Xiaoming's time to shine. But I'm afraid he's never going to be able to compete under the present system.'

While he had regrets regarding my brother, he clearly didn't know that he'd actually ruined his career in politics. A leader and a secretary rise and fall together. People can't help but think that birds of a feather flock together. In the old society, the illumination of the light proclaimed its complete possession of body and soul, and once you were cast out of the light into shadow, that meant you'd entered a darkness as complete as the abyss. My brother was bound to continue on the Wheel of Life, otherwise he would never get a chance to be reborn. Rationalism, particularly the present utilitarianism, had already enshrined the teachings of the light as truth, but it had also obscured a basic fact: that the source of light was precisely the darkness of human nature.

'My brother is going to resign,' I told him. 'After things went wrong for you, he feels tortured and unhappy. If he stays in politics he'd just have to go on the way he was before, which seems to him no better than waiting for death. I won't lie to you, it was my idea that he quit. He has to pass through death to be reborn.'

Peng Guoliang clearly felt guilty at hearing this news, and he spoke with deep regret. 'I had thought he hadn't been with me for too long, that he might not be dragged into it. I didn't think . . . Does he know what he'll do next?'

I pinched out the cigarette in my hand and said heavily, 'I think the lessons of this experience will last him the rest of his life. Given his talents, if he turned to writing fiction he could be as good as or better than me.'

He sighed. 'Your brother was born for politics. What a shame! But being a writer would be good too. He could tell my story, as a warning to others. It might be a way to put all this behind him as well.'

A glint of light had appeared in his otherwise dull gaze. I lit one more cigarette for him and he inhaled greedily as if, instead of simply smoking, he were using the dim spark of the cigarette to unite himself with the darkness. He already knew that black was the colour of existence. It was only a pity that he'd learned it too late.

Newly Promoted Vice-Director of the Municipal Government, Yang Hengda

PENG GUOLIANG'S CASE shocked all of Dongzhou, but what shocked me most was that while he was in Macau gambling, he was videotaped by public security units beside a group of terrorists, and the one doing the videotaping was Ou Beibei's ex-husband Wang Chaoquan. It was simply unbelievable!

The simpering yes-man of the Foreign Investment Bureau had transformed himself into the Deputy Chief of the Anti-Terrorism Unit of the Provincial Public Security Bureau. It was the sort of thing you only see in movies or read about in books. He became a legend in no time. Some said he never missed with a pistol, others that he could take on a dozen opponents at once, and was able to vanish or skip lightly over rooftops. In a nutshell, the little director-level researcher had suddenly become an invincible hero.

No one was more shocked than Ou Beibei, now his ex-wife. This vain and pitiful woman, who had so longed for honour that she'd fallen into the arms of Peng Guoliang and Zhao Zhong, had come up empty-handed. Life was simply too cruel. The combination of Peng Guoliang's fall and Wang Chaoquan's rise came as a terrible blow to her, and also made her a major laughing stock. Though she gritted her teeth and bore it all in silence, I could tell she deeply regretted hurting Wang Chaoquan and driving him away.

What I learned from this was if you want to avoid living a life that's merely a rough outline, you need to use the first half of your life to rehearse, and the second half to perform. Though living this way has its costs, it is worth it. At the very least, you will not complain like Tomas in *The Unbearable Lightness of Being*: 'If we have only one life, we might as well not have lived at all.'

If Ou Beibei could see her past as a rehearsal, draw the appropriate lessons and throw herself into the second half of her life, I was confident she'd be able to turn the rough outline into a full plan.

In order to ease her suffering as best I could, I used my birthday as an excuse to treat the whole office to dinner. During the meal Xu Zhitai spoke out in defence of Peng Guoliang. Ou Beibei, uncharacteristically, put up an argument, saying Peng Guoliang was a stinking heap of dog shit. Their argument raged viciously, but I didn't interject. What I found quite shocking was that Zhu Dawei very obviously stood with Ou Beibei, nearly goading Xu Zhitai into real anger.

Xu Zhitai spoke indignantly. 'Don't forget that we all once stood in Mayor Peng's camp, and we served him for many years. If even we kick him now that he's gone, we'll just become a joke to others. Ou Beibei, heaven gave us our faces, and we can't go making ourselves a new one, can we?'

This last shot deeply wounded Ou Beibei's pride. He was essentially calling her shameless. When Wang Chaoquan had been at the Foreign Investment Bureau, he and Xu Zhitai got along well, and Xu Zhitai was clearly speaking on his behalf. When she heard that, Ou Beibei rushed out of the restaurant as if she'd gone mad. Xu Zhitai hadn't expected that and was struck dumb. In the ensuing silence, Zhu Dawei quietly said to me, 'Sir, you should go and talk to her, make sure nothing happens.' I hurried out.

A fine rain was drifting through the night. Ou Beibei was running for all she was worth. I ran after her, finally catching her by the arm.

'Beibei, it was all just talk, don't take it seriously.' She fought to free herself; she wasn't listening. I could think of nothing to do but to press her against me and say, 'Beibei, I know how much you hurt. It's just me here now. Go ahead and cry; you'll feel better.' To my surprise, she held me tightly and really did begin to sob.

It was time for me to talk to the Old Leader again. I had learned from Song Daoming that the Director of the Municipal Research Office had reached retirement age and Mayor Liu was considering Li Yumin, Vice-Director of the Municipal Government, for the post. This would mean Li's position would be vacated, a heaven-sent opportunity!

What I hate most about visiting the Old Leader is that every single time, we have to talk about the urine cure. I drank my own urine for the entire five years I acted as his secretary, until my very eyeballs were yellow, and I hoped that once I left him I would never have to drink it again.

While I was with the Old Leader, I might have been sincere and assiduous in recording my thoughts on the urine cure, but actually I was thoroughly revolted by this 'cure' that I saw as nothing more than a joke. But since my resumption of the cure – at my wife's insistence – did lead to the resumption of my manhood, I've started to feel better about it, though I am still only half convinced. I'm not actually sure if it's the result of the urine cure or my fantasising about Ou Beibei during lovemaking. I hate having the lights on too brightly during lovemaking. Whenever I look down and see it's my wife I am embracing and not Ou Beibei, I end up once more with a 'limp riding crop'.

I spent two whole days rethinking my conclusions about the philosophical implications of the urine cure, and once I felt I'd done enough reviewing, I bounded off one evening, full of enthusiasm, to the Old Leader's house in Shady Nook. The Old Leader was in his study, bent over his desk and writing something. I drew closer and found he was annotating the text of the work on the urine cure that I'd authored, as earnestly as though it were a government proclamation.

When he saw me he took off his spectacles, praised my work on the urine cure tract and asked, 'Hengda, have you come to any new realisations about the urine cure recently?'

The review I'd done paid off, and I rattled off my prepared answer. 'I know you'll criticise me, but since I went to the Municipal Government, the pace of work has left me without a scrap of time to record my experiments with the urine cure. But in terms of progressing with the cure itself, I haven't slackened in the slightest. These days in particular, I've been especially moved by seeing how much progress you're making in promoting the urine cure throughout the province, including giving away your opus on the cure for free to people in your hometown. I have complete faith that, under your care, the people of this province will soon set about building a host of urine cure spas. Sir, you are truly spreading the good word about the urine cure, relieving poverty and difficulty, creating happiness for the people; all good deeds indeed!'

Seeing my confidence in the future of the urine cure in the province, the Old Leader said happily, 'I've been in good health since I retired and I've got some pep left. It's only right that I do a little something for the good of the people. It's been a while since you thought to drop in on me, Hengda. Is there something you need from an old man? Peng Guoliang's case must have had some repercussions for you . . . Tell me, what are you planning?'

There was no fooling the Old Leader. I laid out my ideas frankly, holding nothing back. He said nothing, but directly picked up the phone and called Liu Yihe. Who knew that something that had caused me sleepless nights could be resolved with a single phone call? If I'd known it would be this way, why would I have waited for Peng Guoliang to get in trouble? On the other hand, if he hadn't gotten in trouble, the Old Leader might not have agreed so readily. He was actually helping me out of a bind, unwilling to see me continue floundering. In fact, as I was the Old Leader's man, my floundering could reflect badly on his reputation as well.

I was hoping to use the opportunity to hear the Old Leader's opinions on Peng Guoliang's case, so I gave him a full report about Zhang Peifen's activity while it had been ongoing. To my surprise, he became angry and bitter. 'They brought all their troubles on themselves. That Peng Guoliang even dragged my name through the muck just to save himself! There must truly be something wrong with our system of promotion!'

I was a little surprised, and quite happy, to hear him say this. It was a good thing I hadn't listened to Zhang Peifen and asked the Old Leader to speak up on Peng Guoliang's behalf, otherwise I could have kissed the vice-director position goodbye. Everyone knew the head of Number One Department had had his eye on that position for a long time, but luckily I had foreseen the change in the winds. The people who are good at predicting the weather will be able to sail the farthest! I listened to the Old Leader pour out his resentment against Peng Guoliang, chiming in where appropriate, and left him quite satisfied.

Leaving the Shady Nook compound, I noticed that the moon seemed particularly large and round that night. Since Peng Guoliang had been executed, I'd felt terribly anxious, and thought I was the unluckiest person in the world. But now, looking up at the moon like a woman's buttocks, I felt as refreshed as if I'd just taken my pleasure in that woman's bed.

When time came for the annual audit of the Municipal Party Committee officials, I was surprised to hear Song Daoming say that the only blemish on my otherwise satisfactory performance audit had come when the audit working group had spoken to Xu Zhitai. He hadn't had a single good word for me, instead making all manner of wild accusations, two of which were quite severe and obviously aimed at interfering with my promotion. First, he said I had no sense of higher objective, that while with my inferiors I simply ate and drank with no thought for the suffering of the people. Second, my political conviction was not firm, and while in the office I'd often voice doubts about whether communism could be realised. Both accusations were obvious lies, but they were maliciously aimed. I truly would not have expected it of him.

Since I'd taken over Number Two Department, Xu was the one who'd benefited most: I'd given him practically all the opportunities to go abroad. Not only was he not returning the favour, but he was actually turning traitor at the most crucial moment. According to common logic, if I was promoted and my post was vacated, it would create opportunity for him, so he ought to sing my praises to ensure that I'd be on my way. Yet here he was doing it backwards. I tried to figure out what he was thinking, and guessed that he'd already seen the general shape of things. Even if I vacated my position, he wouldn't be promoted, and getting a new boss to lord it over him might be worse than the status quo. It would be a Pyrrhic victory for him. Couldn't he see that if he spoke well on my behalf and I was promoted, he could reach his own goal with a few well-placed words of flattery? Now here you were thinking you could stop me single-handedly, Xu Zhitai. Not only would you fail in that, but you'd also annoy someone who was about to become vice-director of the whole office. What were you thinking?

Xu Zhitai had wasted his moment of pious self-sacrifice for Peng. He had really believed that his connection with Lin Yongqing would be enough to pluck Peng from the fire and that he could work hand in hand with Zhang Peifen to overturn the case. When he had been detained himself, the Municipal Government had gone into an uproar. If someone from Number Two was to be detained, it ought by rights to have been me, not first Huang Xiaoming and then Xu Zhitai. But I had remained as free as ever. And now I've been promoted. This has caused a lot of perplexity.

After the Party organisation came to talk to me about my new post, my promotion took effect immediately. On my first day, just after the Janitorial Brigade had finished tidying my new office and I was admiring the calligraphy the Old Leader had written for me – 'If as an official you are beset by obscurity, remember that as a man you can always see clearly' – the internal phone rang. It was Xiao Furen, saying that Deng Hongchang and Shang Xiaoqiong had arranged to go with Huang Xiaoming to remove Peng Guoliang's effects from his office, and that I should receive them.

I put the phone down and swore. Xiao Furen was playing games with me on my very first day. He had been classmates with Deng Hongchang at the Provincial Party School, and no matter what the occasion, it should have been him doing the receiving. But he'd made some ridiculous excuse about a meeting and shoved me out in front.

As I left the office, I could see Deng Hongchang, Shang Xiaoqiong and Huang Xiaoming standing in front of Peng Guoliang's office. I'd spoken to the investigation team several times during the case, in addition to passing on Peng Guoliang's changes of clothes, and I was quite familiar with all of them.

I hastened to greet them, slapping Huang Xiaoming on the back. He clearly already knew about my promotion and said mockingly, 'Congratulations, Director Yang, you've finally realised your dream of pulling boats.'

There were two meanings to his words. One: needling me for having got off Peng Guoliang's ship and joining Liu Yihe's boat-pullers. Two: mocking me for having successfully moved against the current. While Peng's people had been swept downstream, only I was moving upstream. Clearly, he was accusing me of having sold out my master!

I couldn't bicker with him in front of Deng Hongchang and Shang Xiaoqiong, so I only said self-deprecatingly, 'Xiaoming, Mayor Liu says that he came to Dongzhou to be a boat-puller, and if someone like him can have a dream like that, it's my good fortune to have found a place on his team.'

Now it was his turn to slap me on the shoulder as he laughed. 'Director Yang, you'll go far!' Then he took an envelope out of his document bag and handed it to me. 'I had meant to deliver my resignation to Director Xiao, but since he's out at a meeting I'll deliver it to you, the managing director.'

The martyr act was a little too much, and I said, 'Is now the right time to resign?'

To my surprise, Deng Hongchang interrupted. 'Xiaoming, you should think twice about resigning. It would be a shame to lose such a good job!'

Shang Xiaoqiong added from the sidelines, 'That's right! If you resign, how will you get by?'

Huang Xiaoming laughed lightly and said, 'The French poet Rimbaud has a line that reads, "Life is elsewhere." As I see it, my "ideals are elsewhere". Li Bai said it even better: "I was born to be of use." Too many people want to be boat-pullers these days; I'm steering clear of the fad.'

Who knew that Huang Xiaoming would become such a bitter old man overnight! I wouldn't spar with him further. For him, life was elsewhere, but for me it was right here, under my feet, and of course that included my ideals, too.

Former Department-Level Researcher, Huang Xiaoming

DURING THE PENG case, my wife saw the pressure I was under and knew that I was keeping something from her. She asked again and again until I exploded and cursed her for a madwoman. I withdrew into my study every day, scribbling furiously as a way of releasing my tension, until one day I found I'd written three hundred thousand characters. When my brother came to visit me he read some of what I'd written and praised it, saying that with a little editing it would be highly successful as a collection of essays. He even thought of an appropriate title for me: *Spiritual Torment*. My brother's enthusiasm helped me forget my fear for a while, and the two of us found ourselves caught up in a discussion about literature.

I told my brother that for some reason the disaster had given me the desire to write. But I couldn't calm myself down, and I'd never written fiction. I wouldn't know where to start.

My brother's eyes lit up when he heard this, and he said excitedly, 'I'm thrilled to hear you're feeling the desire to write, Xiaoming! Our father's greatest wish was that we might become writers, and it always galled him that you'd gone into politics. If you've really decided to write fiction, I can help you.'

I was starting to get excited, and I asked for further advice. 'If I want to write fiction, where should I start?'

He thought before answering, 'Start with your own experiences. This mess with Peng Guoliang has put your soul through the tortures of purgatory. Why don't you write it down, as a warning to others? I've already thought of a name for it. Call it the *The Civil Servant's Notebook*.

When I heard this name, I was even more thrilled. This was an age when everyone was clamouring to squeeze into government, and every year millions of new college graduates were taking the civil service exams, the competition even fiercer than their original college entrance exams. If I put my political experiences and lessons into the form of fiction and they read it, it might change how they thought about their new profession. But . . . I heaved an involuntary sigh.

My brother saw my high spirits suddenly droop and knew there was something I wasn't telling him. He spoke with a sternness I'd never heard from him before. 'You were Peng Guoliang's personal secretary, Xiaoming, and though you weren't with him long, the two of you were together night and day. Since you came out of detention, you've had something heavy on your mind, so tell me the truth now: have you done something you regret?'

Seeing how anxious my brother had become, I was powerless to continue keeping secrets from him so I told him everything, going to the kitchen and pulling out the tape-wrapped package of money. Once my brother knew the truth he was perfectly calm, and after examining the package carefully he remained silent for a while, before saying, 'I understand how you're feeling, Xiaoming. Technically you haven't done anything wrong, but you've forgotten that this nation's laws are not tolerant. The law would not tolerate this concealment even if you were Peng Guoliang's family member, never mind his secretary. You can't keep this package at home. You need to hand it over to the authorities immediately.' After further consideration he said, 'The package belonged to Peng Guoliang, and he gave it to you before the case broke. If you voluntarily hand it in there shouldn't be any problem. Xiaoming, did Peng Guoliang ever tell you exactly how much money was in here?'

I shook my head. 'No.'

Sizing up the package, I guessed there was fifty thousand dollars. Peng had trusted me not to take the money and run. He had been confident I would give it back after the case was concluded. His son's health was poor and they had spent large sums on treatment. Recalling this, I let my emotions get the better of me. 'Brother, I can't hand this money over unless I absolutely have no other choice. This is clearly money Peng Guoliang was keeping for his son. He trusted me. I can't think only of myself.' My decision made, I put it back in the cupboard next to the sink.

Seeing that I was resolute, my brother sighed. 'Xiaoming, I understand how you're feeling, but you've got to think more carefully about this. Now's your chance to act!'

It was obvious that Peng Guoliang had said nothing to the investigation team about the money he'd hidden with me, but I'd mentioned it to Zhang Peifen. Would she say anything about it one day? Her case was still ongoing. Or would she also be relying on me to keep it for when she got out? What should I do? Hand it over or not? I was caught up in a raging internal struggle, the result of which was: 'wait'. I would see how the case progressed against Zhang Peifen and then make a decision later. Peng Guoliang had remained stubborn to the end. My feeling was Zhang Peifen was even more stubborn than he.

To my surprise, a mere week after Peng's execution the investigation team called me and told me to report the next morning. My wife and I were eating dinner at my mother's house at the time, and as soon as I put down the phone, I picked it up again and called my brother, asking whether he thought the investigators might be calling to ask about the package.

He was nearly hopping with anxiety. 'Whether they are or not, you need to hand it over! Why should you sacrifice yourself?'

I prevaricated. 'They call Qi Xiuying the Iron Maiden, but Zhang Peifen is a Woman of Steel. She ought to be able to hold out. I can't believe she's told them everything. I'll talk to them tomorrow and feel the situation out before deciding.'

My brother practically yelled over the phone, 'You're crazy, Xiaoming! Zhang Peifen dreamed of overturning the case but got herself detained instead. Do you want to be another Xu Zhitai?'

'I know what I'm doing!' I replied stubbornly, and hung up.

My mother was trembling with anxiety after listening to our conversation. I didn't want to tell her too much, so I called a taxi and went home with my wife. Once there, I closed myself in my study and thought back over everything. I sat in my leather swivel chair, my eyes shut tight, scenes passing before my eyes like a film reel. But no matter how carefully I thought, it seemed to me that I'd confirmed everything I possibly could. This had to be about the package.

The old fear pounded at my heart like ocean breakers. All I could think of was the word 'responsibility'. Not only my responsibility towards Peng Guoliang's widow and son, but more so my responsibility to my wife. Thinking of my life after I'd begun serving Peng Guoliang, the thing that infuriated my wife most was his irresponsible treatment of me. Even if it weren't for the package, my political life had come to an end as a result of his treatment.

The next morning, as I left my building carrying the package of money in a satchel, I felt that the sun was brand new. Someone once said that the sun is new every day, but as far as I was concerned, it was only this morning that the sun glowed with a new light. Since the sun was no longer yesterday's sun, then I should no longer be yesterday's me. So who was I?

Perhaps I would only know when I stopped thinking, but there wasn't a single instant when my thoughts were not running. I was not me while I thought. I was not me while I dreamt. The myriad details that flashed in and out of my conscious mind might be fact, but fact is the jumping-off point of fabrication and speculation. No matter what, I had jumped off.

I took a cab in the direction of the Provincial Military Headquarters. I knew that by the time I emerged from that compound once more, I would be free.

I went into the reception centre where I'd been detained and pushed open the door of the appointed room. I found Deng Hongchang himself waiting for me, together with two other members of the investigation team. Before Deng Hongchang had a chance to speak, I pulled the sealed package from my satchel.

'What's that?' asked Deng Hongchang.

Calmly, I described the situation. After he'd heard me out, Deng Hongchang asked me to open the package, and after I'd struggled through three layers of packing tape, the envelope that had so deeply impressed me finally emerged. I opened the envelope, revealing the mouldy green bills, and noticed that under the sunlight's bright rays, the whole room glowed with green light.

Deng Hongchang threw a glance at the other two investigators, chuckled coldly, and said, 'Count it.'

I feigned surprise and made a show of being nervous as I pulled out a stack of bills and brushed the mould from it, then began counting with extreme care. The stack was exactly ten thousand dollars. I counted the four other stacks, one by one, then put all five stacks back the way they'd been, and said with some trepidation, 'Exactly fifty thousand dollars.'

Deng Hongchang sprang up off the sofa and began pacing in a circle. Then he halted and gave me a piercing glance, saying, 'Huang Xiaoming, Huang Xiaoming . . . That's definitely a brain with a master's degree. You certainly pick your moment! Do you know how close this fifty thousand was to ruining you? Zhang Peifen kept perfectly clear notes about this money in her notebook. Don't think she didn't know how much was in there. This money had been a part of their plan since before the case broke. Lucky for you that you came around in time. If you hadn't, I think you can guess what would have happened to you! Well then, young man: give us a complete written description of the whole thing, and learn what lessons you can from Peng Guoliang's case. I hope those lessons will serve you well as you make your way in the future.'

He turned to his two colleagues and said, 'You two can handle things from here.' Then he slapped my shoulder and left the room.

One of the investigators brought me a pen and paper, and I began to write. I wrote not only the facts as they'd occurred, but also why I had taken so long in coming clean. Mostly I talked about the promise I'd made, and my desire to keep faith, and how I hadn't realised how severe the situation was to begin with.

When I'd finished writing I read it over twice and, feeling pleased with both its structure and its tone, I passed it to the investigators. They both read it, then one of them gave me an ink pad and told me to leave my fingerprint on the signature line as well as on a few of the edits before telling me, 'That's it, you can go.' I bowed and scraped and shook their hands, then left the room, a great weight lifted from me.

It was nearly noon by the time I left the military compound, and I hurried to call my brother. Elated, he told me to take a taxi to a Xiaojiangnan restaurant near his office, saying we would celebrate the beginning of my new life. I hung up the phone and looked at the sky. The sun was too bright to look at directly.

As I entered the restaurant's main dining room, my brother waved to me from a seat near the window. I saw the food and drink already laid out, and my brother poured me a beer as he said, 'What have you got planned, Xiaoming?'

I drained my glass at a gulp and told him something that surprised him. 'I'm going to write novels.'

To be honest, I'd decided this when my brother told me to write *The Civil Servant's Notebook*, but the business with the fifty thousand dollars had me so on edge that I never got around to discussing it more with him. Now the fifty thousand had been put to rest and I was feeling unutterably lightened, so I'd decided to broach the subject.

What had I done for society in my ten years in politics? Not a thing. I could no longer be a parasite, and if I'd gained anything from Peng Guoliang's case, it was discovery of my self, discovery that I, as a thinker, was none other than me.

And for that reason I said firmly, 'Don't try to talk me out of it, brother. People must pass through death to be reborn. I've already wasted a decade of my life in politics. How many more decades remain to me?'

My brother remained silent for a while, then solemnly filled two glasses and, picking up his own, said, 'I feel ashamed, Xiaoming, to hear you say that people must pass through death to be reborn. Perhaps it's because I've always lacked the courage to pass through death that I've never become a truly great writer. Actually, in the face of the soul, literature itself must pass through death! Come, brother, let's drink to having the courage to burn our bridges!'

After draining my cup, I glanced out the window and saw that the endless river of cars flowed not along the street, but along time itself.

Ou Beibei

AFTER PENG GUOLIANG'S detention, trial and execution, Wang Chaoquan became a legend within the Municipal Government.

There was also no doubt that the case influenced the fates of everyone in Number Two Department. Our office became the focal point of the whole Municipal Government.

We kept our thoughts to ourselves, hoping to avoid becoming a pawn sacrificed to the greater struggle. Each of us had once been proud to work in Number Two. Now all we hoped for was escape.

Yang Hengda and Zhu Dawei hoped for it most. The pressure was greatest on Yang Hengda, of course. Although he'd been the Old Leader's secretary, he'd been placed in Number Two by Peng Guoliang, and everyone thought of him as Peng's man. Now Peng had been tried and executed, Huang Xiaoming had resigned, and yet Yang Hengda was still sailing along peacefully.

The rumours flew thick and fast. Everyone felt it was unreasonable, as if Yang Hengda should naturally have gone down with his boss. Yang was perfectly aware of his predicament, but he also knew how to get out of it, and even more how to turn it to his favour – a skill a little woman like me would never be able to learn.

Yang Hengda seemed to have gone over to the other side without kicking up the slightest fuss. During the investigation he had made use of his unusual status, on the one hand pretending to care for Zhang Peifen, on the other feigning eager co-operation with the investigation team. At first no one saw his true face, right up until he got promoted.

When I heard that news, I understood. No one who made a living in politics could be truly just. They would turn traitor the moment it served their purposes. I had to privately admire Yang's move, though, and I learned from it that those in politics had to learn the art of abandonment if they ever wanted to find a firm footing. The key to this strategy, however, is that you must be qualified to be taken in elsewhere, you needed to bring with you something of value, and those who didn't understand this would always be caught in a bind. Yang Hengda was without doubt extremely skilled at increasing and utilising his value. In this sense he was as much a gambler as Peng Guoliang, though smarter in his wagers.

By comparison, Xu Zhitai held far more of value than Yang Hengda, and yet he was still cast about like an ant riding a twig through flood waters thinking he directed the twig's progress when, in fact, the twig was in the grip of the tide. The reason he'd remained department vice-head for ten years without the slightest progress was that he never learned to sail with the wind, let alone to sail before the wind. Even more pitiful, his political aspirations never rose any higher than the seat in front of him, and he never turned his gaze outside the department, let alone outside the Municipal Government.

Huang Xiaoming had once brought a pop psychology test to work. He drew four points on a paper and we had to use three continuous, non-overlapping lines to connect the four points. Only Xu Zhitai and I couldn't do it, and when Huang Xiaoming showed us the solution I realised that I could learn something important from the psychology test. If you think outside the box, the world can become very wide.

Xu Zhitai, on the other hand, felt the test was just a clever trick. He actually wished he was adept at clever tricks. After Peng Guoliang was detained, he expended every effort in helping Zhang Peifen interfere with the case, feeling this was the most important trick of his political career. That's exactly why he was using righteousness and loyalty as a cover for his own weakness. He was mocked by other cadres as a Don Quixote, but I thought that was an overestimation of him.

In my view he was more like Sancho Panza, the crafty fool, who acts from experience only, and knows nothing of ideals. All he wants is wealth and position, and that is precisely why he could be roused by the dreamer with his head in the clouds to follow him on his adventures. But Xu Zhitai truly did have something of Don Quixote's courage in tilting at windmills. Xu's courage came from his stubborn dream of becoming department head and, even more, from the rewards that Zhang Peifen dangled in front of him.

Even more subtly calculating than Yang Hengda and Xu Zhitai was Zhu Dawei. His hidden advantage was the advice he got from his father, who was experienced in politics and business. This, added to natural aptitude, meant the son would likely surpass the father. Then there was the inside information provided him by his beautiful, dedicated, hardworking girlfriend in the investigation team. Whoever got their information in advance had the drop on everyone else. In this whole case it was obvious Zhu Dawei had the newest, most direct, most accurate information; enough for his wily, plotting old father to lay out his strategy for him.

The fact that his girlfriend Shang Xiaoqiong had worked undercover in the Municipal Government for so long and Zhu Dawei had never made a peep also helped Mayor Liu see him with new eyes. Add to that the appreciation of Xiao Furen and Song Daoming, and it seemed likely that Zhu Dawei's dream of becoming secretary to the Mayor might come true. Even Yang Hengda slapped him on the back and called him brother when they met, and that was another signal that before long, Zhu Dawei would be climbing the ladder.

You could say that for Yang Hengda, Xu Zhitai and Zhu Dawei, Peng Guoliang's case represented a chance to show their mettle, and only I was left behind, forgotten as a leaf in autumn.

The dream of Wang Chaoquan was now ruined and I had no desire to return to it. So I rejected both return and ruin, and insisted there was a third way. What I hadn't anticipated was that Xu Zhitai would re-awaken my desire to return to my dream state. Towards the end of the case Chaoquan had invited Xu Zhitai for a drink. While I don't know what they discussed, the next time I saw Xu he handed me Chaoquan's new contact information. I got the feeling that Chaoquan had given it to him expressly to give to me. This turned my heart completely upside down. I even thought that he was trying to send me a sign. Though I knew this was pure fantasy, I was somehow very willing to surrender myself to it.

I should say that there was nothing arbitrary about the love between Chaoquan and me. We were together for all four years of college, and while I couldn't figure out when during that time he had been chosen by the Public Security Bureau, he most definitely did undergo secret training. In those days, love was my religion and I dreamed that I in turn would become Chaoquan's religion. No matter how sacred his work for the country, there was one fact he had to face: he had been lying to me, from the time we first fell in love until we divorced. He was loyal to the nation but he had lied to his wife. It was he who had laid the groundwork for my infidelity. Though I appeared to be Peng Guoliang's victim, I was in fact Chaoquan's. I wasn't done with him yet; the 'great hero' owed me an explanation and an apology.

Since Xu Zhitai gave me the contact information, I have been plagued by ideas like these. I've even dreamed, more than once, of Chaoquan embracing me and rolling about on the bed. Since we got the divorce, he had turned to ashes in my heart. Could those ashes spring into flame again?

My days pass not like a sliding stream, but in an ever-repeating cycle, like the hands of the quartz clock that hangs on the wall of Number Two Department. My life is slipping from me within this pointless cycle. It seems that this is my 'truth'.

The Municipal Party Committee sent an audit team to the office to audit Yang Hengda. For some reason, Yang Hengda's impending promotion made Xu Zhitai deeply unhappy. By rights Yang Hengda's promotion would create a vacuum Xu Zhitai could fill, but he seemed to have already realised that even if the position became vacant, the new standing vice-mayor would not choose him. He would already have someone else in mind.

If nothing had happened to Peng Guoliang, I was sure that Yang Hengda's promotion would have given Xu Zhitai a chance, and perhaps that was precisely the source of Xu Zhitai's unhappiness. He felt that Yang Hengda owed a debt of gratitude to Peng Guoliang, and when the leader had been in danger, that debt ought to have been repaid.

Now Yang Hengda was saying one thing but doing another, creating an out for himself, and treating his dead leader's disgrace as a chance to advance himself – a truly despicable action.

Thus, Xu Zhitai had nothing good to say about Yang Hengda to the audit team, and, what's more, even tried to get the rest of us to work with him to push out Yang Hengda, the way we'd pushed out Zhao Zhong. I hemmed and hawed and prevaricated. Zhu Dawei, contrary to his usual tactfulness, stated very clearly that he would not participate, and even put forth a long list of Yang Hengda's qualities. Xu Zhitai's mouth was hanging open. He went out in a huff, slamming the door. I cast a glance at the self-satisfied Zhu Dawei, thinking that he must have known long ago that Yang Hengda was bound to be promoted. But now he was speaking with an uncharacteristic self-assurance. He must have been close to taking over from Song Daoming.

I cast a glance at the clock on the wall and had the sudden feeling that everyone else was just passing through Number Two, while only I and the clock really belonged to this office.

I asked Zhu Dawei what he thought of Xu Zhitai's unusual behaviour, and he said with a disdainful shrug, 'People who won't accept failure and keep trying will never become leaders, Beibei. What kind of future can await people who throw themselves away? Like they always say, a wise man submits to circumstances. What are our present circumstances? Department Head Yang's promotion to Vice-Director of the Municipal Government, for one. He's been tapped by Mayor Liu personally, so this is immutable fact. Xu can't even see that much. No wonder he's spent ten years as department vice-head.

'What's worse is that Peng was obviously done for, and Xu was still running around insisting he'd been unjustly accused, colluding with his wife, teaming up with Lin Yongqing to interfere with the case. What was he after? Did he never stop to think whether his own two hands were enough to stop the wheel of history? I've said enough, Beibei. Xu was possessed. He was determined to follow the others into detention.'

I thought to myself, what had Xu Zhitai done besides run a few errands for Zhang Peifen? Zhu Dawei told me, 'For his help in convincing Lin Yongqing to write those articles, Xu Zhitai accepted fifty thousand *yuan* from Zhang Peifen, and even went to Beijing to deliver bribes in person. I told you once that he was determined to get himself locked up. He's got no one to blame but himself.'

Just after Yang Hengda was promoted, Huang Xiaoming handed in his resignation. This news was shocking. No one in the Municipal Government could understand why he'd done it. He could easily have pushed through, and Xiao Furen would have found him a post as head of one of the combined affairs departments. Xiao Furen had always thought highly of him, and if Peng Guoliang hadn't snatched him first, Xiao Furen would have been sure to recommend him to Mayor Liu as a replacement for Song Daoming.

Even if the Peng case had made that impossible, he could have found another job. But he chose to quit while he was ahead. No one who'd been in that position could understand his decision. Besides, this was an age of power worship. Everyone knows that power determines the direction of society. I was sure that Huang Xiaoming was experiencing all manner of suffering, but in an age of power worship I was even surer that he could find no one to whom he could pour out that suffering.

Never mind Huang Xiaoming. Whom could *I* pour my heart out to?

I always longed to fly, and to fly in the company of the one I loved, but now I only had one wing left.

I rebelled against my misfortune because my husband appeared to me in a false image. The brilliant, capable husband I loved was hidden from me, and I'd lived for years with a false Wang Chaoquan. I couldn't be held fully responsible for the end of our marriage. I wanted to find the real Wang Chaoquan and ask him what love really was. I became more excited the more I thought, and couldn't resist dialling the mobile phone number Xu Zhitai had given me. And just like that, easier than I could have imagined, I heard Wang Chaoquan's rich voice say, 'Hello?'

Secretary to the Mayor, Zhu Dawei

I ALWAYS THOUGHT that becoming a mayor's secretary would be a fast track for my career. For a mere director-level researcher like myself, to climb rung by rung up to bureau-level would take fifteen years or more. Most people were like Xu Zhitai. Even after fifteen years, they still got stuck around the vice bureau or bureau-level. Being a mayoral secretary was different. Given my current level, becoming secretary would automatically raise me to vice department-level, then full department-level within a couple of years. Once there, it was only one step away from vice bureau-level, and in two more years I'd be given a concurrent post as Vice-Director of the Municipal Government. That way, within five years I'd be assured of following Song Daoming's path in going down to the district-level as head of a local party committee, becoming the youngest full bureau-level leader in Dongzhou. Actually, that had been my dream since I'd entered the Municipal Government. I was amazed to think that I might achieve it so soon.

Over the years, Cat has described to me the scenes of many detentions, but that night when she called me and said they'd detained Peng Guoliang, Wen Huajian, Chen Shi, Hu Zhanfa and Huang Xiaoming, it still made my skin crawl. Someone once said that politics was a game. I acted accordingly. But when Cat told me how the investigation team had informed Peng Guoliang of his detention in Mayor Liu's private meeting room – Peng Guoliang looking like a morsel of food someone had picked from between their teeth – how could I still think of it as a game?

When Peng Guoliang was promoted to vice-mayor, his whole family must have rejoiced at the honour. He couldn't have imagined then that he would end up as a criminal. Any politician would hope to advance as smoothly as climbing a staircase. Shouldn't Peng's downfall serve as a warning?

I've seen and heard people rejoicing in Peng's misfortune, as if this sort of thing could never happen to them. I don't understand it. They say that the fox weeps when the rabbit's dead. Now the rabbit's dead and everyone's thinking of meat. Why did no one stop to think of why the rabbit died? I've been thinking about it, and I've concluded that without someone supervising the supervisors, there would be no true sunlight. This was the reason why corruption had spread everywhere.

I'd paid special attention to what happened to Huang Xiaoming. I asked Cat to keep a quiet watch on him as well. For some reason, I felt guilty about him. I thought about early on, how we'd competed for the position of Peng's secretary. I might have got it if I'd held out a little longer. Then it would be me who'd have been swept up. Luckily, my father saw from the beginning that Peng Guoliang was a bad egg and resolutely opposed my becoming his secretary. Not only that, but I also made secret use of Hu Zhanfa to 'help' Huang Xiaoming achieve his goal smoothly. That's why, after Huang Xiaoming was released from detention, I hadn't the courage to call him. Luckily, he hadn't gone in deep, which was to say he'd held himself back carefully, neither gambling himself nor holding the wallet as others gambled. He hadn't even gone abroad with Peng Guoliang. At first the investigation team was going to label him 'suspect six' and use him as an entry point to break open the case, but after a little more research they found that Huang Xiaoming was a fellow traveller but not a partner in crime. They were surprised and impressed, so Huang Xiaoming was restored to freedom.

When Peng Guoliang's case first broke and everyone learned that Cat was my girlfriend, rumours flew thick and fast, and I felt a little sheepish, as if it had been I and not her who'd gone undercover. Some cursed me for a turncoat behind my back, and others flat out called me a traitor. At any rate, the general consensus was that my character was flawed. Luckily, the news that I might replace Song Daoming as Mayor Liu's secretary started soon after, and those who had pointed accusing fingers behind my back began to bow and scrape when they saw me. That taught me no small lesson in human nature.

I saw my impending position as Mayor Liu's secretary as a kind of escape, because he called himself a puller of the great ship that is Dongzhou. Boat-pullers are always going against the flow. Only by doing so is it ever possible to find the source of the river. I like that kind of life. It is reminiscent of Columbus discovering the New World, particularly since Mayor Liu's label for himself was a humble one. In fact, he was the captain of the great ship of Dongzhou. As his secretary, even if I were forced to descend into hell, I would end up in heaven. But someone like Mayor Liu would never descend into hell. At the very worst, he would take a turn through purgatory before ascending to heaven. This was why I wanted with all my heart to follow him. Seen this way, I was far more fortunate than Huang Xiaoming.

The worst thing in politics is to end up following the wrong man, and that's what happened to Huang. The worst thing in love is to fall for the wrong person. Ou Beibei had fallen for the right person, but then got divorced. She'd always thought that she'd fallen for the wrong person when in fact the problem was that her inner world had been distorted by power. Once the vanity shut up in her heart was set loose, it was bound to derail the progress of love. Ou Beibei had always been proud of her beauty and was ashamed of having married a small man. She wanted honour from a powerful husband and was possessed by envy of any woman who had married better than she.

From this, avarice was born, and the decision made to exchange her beauty for wealth and honour. Fate seemed to be mocking her, forcing her to reap what she sowed.

How much worse her suffering must have been than that of Huang Xiaoming, though luckily there is repentance and hope. I believed that even Wang Chaoquan, now known as a hero of counter-corruption and anti-terrorism, couldn't be happy. His soul is also suffering in purgatory; perhaps it will meet Ou Beibei's in the earthly paradise at the top of the mountain.

I thought about this because although Wang Chaoquan was outstanding as a counter-terrorist agent and anti-drug hero, he wasn't fit to be anyone's husband. I believe that if a man can't bring happiness to the woman he loves then he shouldn't marry her. Ruining a woman's happiness is a man's greatest shame. I thought Wang had to feel the same way, otherwise he wouldn't have remained so calm in the face of Ou Beibei's infidelities, or fought against the divorce. I'd heard Ou Beibei say that she had forced him to sign the divorce papers, and I could understand how she was feeling at the time. She was still hoping for something from Peng Guoliang, and she hadn't yet discovered that to someone like him, she was nothing more than a few nights of pleasure. The stronger the desire for power, the stronger the desire for possession, and when the road to power is blocked, the desire for it is often sublimated into the need to possess women. A strong desire for possession is an incurable illness common to all who worship power.

Although Wang had a secret identity, the life he gave Ou Beibei was mundane, even mediocre, which eventually put Ou Beibei onto the wrong path. His sudden transformation into a hero was unfair to her. No wonder Ou Beibei came to the office every morning with eyes swollen from crying when everyone around her was abuzz with the news of Wang's real identity.

From Ou Beibei my thoughts turned to my own fiancée Shang Xiaoqiong. This woman with the cat-like nature seemed fated to chase after me, her 'rat'. I didn't know why I was so willing to submit to her, to become her prey. All I knew was that I was the weight she longed to bear. The greater my weight, the more content she felt. Amid her contentment I not only found love, but also the meaning of life. Without Cat I would be unable to face Mayor Liu with self-assurance. It was her secret investigation of him that showed me exactly what he was made of. I'd never understood why he demanded that a sign reading 'Serve the Citizens', not 'Serve the People' as is usual, be hung in the Municipal Government Standing Committee meeting hall. It was Cat's investigations of him that showed me that he was trying to educate the officials, to tell them the so-called 'modernisation of people' was the transformation of 'people' into 'citizens'. It was also under Cat's direction that I made use of Hu Zhanfa's trust in me to steal the copy of the *The Civil Servant's Notebook* from his home. That, with the addition of Wang Chaoquan's recordings, instigated the largest political earthquake in Dongzhou's history. And that, in turn, was what let me walk into Mayor Liu's villa with confidence.

Of course, when I first discovered that Cat was working undercover in the Janitorial Brigade, I felt a certain excitement. I'd been kept down too long. I hated a life as leisurely as that in the sanatorium atop the mountain. I yearned for thunder and wind and passionate emotion. More importantly, Cat needed someone to work with her. I was the obvious choice, and I did it willingly. The reason for my excitement was that I knew that whatever Cat discovered, I could turn it into political capital, and perhaps even change my fate.

Working in politics was akin to playing the stock market: a certain minority was always able to rely on its superior vision to make wise investments, while the majority followed blindly. An even smaller minority believed itself highly intelligent, when in fact they were stupid in the extreme. They snatched up stocks that everyone else saw as junk, losing the shirts off their backs or their entire households in the process. Some even lost their lives.

Official word soon came down that Yang Hengda would be promoted to Vice-Director of the Municipal Government. Because of the fierce competition for the newly vacated position of standing vice-mayor, it was unclear who would succeed him as head of Number Two. He was therefore obliged to temporarily fill both his old and new roles, though he had already moved to new and spacious offices. Only Ou Beibei and I were left in the office, and since Xiao Furen had prohibited my taking on additional responsibilities until I was officially promoted to Mayor Liu's secretary, I sat around the office reading chess manuals.

At noon my colleagues from the other combined affairs department came to play chess with me, and there was often a small crowd of spectators. Among them, some of the bigger mouths repeated the gossip of the day. Once, I would have chatted with them, but now I didn't say a word, focusing instead on my play.

Ou Beibei noticed this and gently mocked me. 'Dawei, you're awfully grumpy! I heard that in the Municipal Government alone, more than twenty people want to be Mayor Liu's secretary, each of them with a strong background. If you just sit around and wait, some dark horse is going to upset you!'

It made sense, what she said, and I was definitely sick of waiting. My father said that if someone important needed their glass filled, you had to be the first to fill it if you wanted to succeed. I believed that I hadn't given my opponents the slightest opportunity. There might have been a lot of them, but I had filled my glass and put it right in front of Mayor Liu. I didn't believe anyone had the guts to go into his office and switch their glass for mine.

I remember something a Western politician once said: 'An honest politician is one who, when he is bought, will stay bought.' In politics, what besides honesty counts as loyalty? I believed in Mayor Liu's honesty, not only because I'd received his promise, but also because I was the best choice.

Eventually Song Daoming was promoted to Oldbridge District as the Vice-Secretary of the District Party Committee and acting District Chief, and the public discussion again focused on who would replace him as Mayor Liu's secretary. Names were floated and dismissed. Of course, my name appeared most regularly. Every day, Ou Beibei would relate to me what people had been saying, and I spent a week in terror of public opinion. When I came to work one Monday morning, Ou Beibei told me that she'd just received a phone call from Xiao Furen, telling me to see him in his office. I was seized with anxiety. It seemed impossible that they'd already made a decision. I steadied myself and went into Xiao Furen's office.

Sure enough, the moment I was inside he told me the good news: at Mayor Liu's direction and by decision of the Municipal Party Committee, I would be serving as Mayor Liu's secretary.

The moment the words were out of his mouth I experienced an exhilarating sense of pleasure. Then Xiao Furen told me a joke that made me think.

In ancient times there was a forgetful bailiff who was charged with escorting a monk who'd committed a crime to the prefecture seat for judgment. Before they set off, he worried that he would forget something, and so he made himself a little ditty: 'Umbrella, shackles, and robe; documents, monk, and me'. The whole way, he repeated this ditty like one possessed, terrified that he would lose something along the way and be unable to fulfil his duty. The monk, seeing his strange behaviour, got him drunk while they'd stopped for a rest, then shaved the bailiff's head, placed his own shackles around his neck and scampered off. When the bailiff woke, he felt that something was missing. But the umbrella, robe and documents were there, as were the shackles around his neck. And when he rubbed his head and found himself bald, he knew the monk was there too. But he still felt something was missing, and so he recited his ditty and suddenly shouted in a panic, 'Me! Where am I?'

I wanted to laugh but I held it in. Xiao Furen told me to think carefully about the meaning of the joke, and instructed me to go report to Mayor Liu's office.

I thanked Xiao Furen, feeling that a great burden had been lifted from me, and went proudly forth from this office. That moment marked a new beginning for me, but I would never become that bailiff, much less the monk. I was myself, my own master!

The Name Card

I'VE DISCOVERED A secret: the higher the official position, the sparser the text on the name card. The converse is also true: the lower the position, the more is written on the card. There's a new trend among cadres of bureau-level and above: adding the title 'master's student' or 'doctoral student' to their card, demonstrating the depth of their educational background. Some even add 'visiting professor of such-and-such university'.

An actual professor once asked for a meeting with Liu Yihe, Mayor of Dongzhou, and the name card he passed over had more than ten titles on it, printed in tiny type. Mayor Liu looked it over at length and exclaimed, 'A mere professorship is an insult to someone of your qualifications!'

Even better is the abbot of Ci'en Temple, whom Zhao Zhong introduced to Mayor Liu. They met and the monk presented his card, which read not only 'Abbot of Ci'en Temple in the Western Hills', but also 'Member, Standing Committee of the Dongzhou Municipal Political Consultative Conference'.

Why do people take the name card so seriously? The reason is simple: everyone wants to be able to boast of their status. No good things come to those of mean stature. This is why we call those with honour and power 'big men', and the ineffectual and powerless 'little people'. You can see how the humble little name card reflects the broader world beyond it. The card represents an entire life. Without our social status to prop us up we'd all retreat into insignificance. Thus, an individual's power and prestige are his most essential and personal belongings. So how does one show off these belongings to strangers?

Simply print yourself a box of name cards.

People assume that name cards came into use where social interaction was common. But my master Zhu Dawei, who has been promoted to secretary to the Mayor of Dongzhou, was browsing history books recently and discovered that as early as the time of the Qin Emperor people had begun writing their names down on cards to hand over during visits and meetings. But paper was not in use then, so they wrote them on slips of bamboo.

After Cai Lun's invention of paper, the bamboo slips were gradually replaced by paper cards, following which they were referred to as 'names' or 'name papers'. After the Tang and Song Dynasties, with the appearance of the bureaucratic classes, they were called 'doors'. During the Ming and Qing, another kind of card, used by subordinates when meeting their superiors, or students when meeting their teachers, were called 'hand books'. In the Republican era, China began to have large-scale commercial contact with the West, and the Western-style name card appeared. These Western cards were manufactured according to the golden ratio. Westerners believed that the rectangular shape produced by the golden ratio was the most beautiful. Thus, Chinese, too, began shaping their name cards according to the ratio.

Since entering the Municipal Government, Zhu Dawei had longed for a name card he could be proud of, but as he was merely a director-level researcher, which wouldn't look very eye-catching on his cards, he'd never bothered to have any made at all. But now he was secretary to the Mayor, and in urgent need of name cards appropriate to his station. At Ou Beibei's suggestion he visited the

'Master of Name Cards', a print shop favoured by Dongzhou civil servants.

As Zhu Dawei entered he greeted the proprietor, who was of middling build, around fifty years old and dressed in black Tang-style attire. His eyes were small, his nose broad and flat, his lips thin, and he had a long black beard. He looked much like a fortune teller.

Zhu Dawei said, 'I've heard that name cards from this shop are popular with civil servants. Perhaps there's some secret to them?'

The owner said with satisfaction, 'I wouldn't call it a secret, but it's true. Everyone from the Mayor to the department heads buys cards here. False modesty aside, our print shop is not only the most technically advanced, but we also provide the greatest selection. We not only have regular printed name cards, but we also have all the waves of the future: laser colour printing, colour photographic printing, electronic name cards, digital cards and more. What kind would you like?'

Zhu Dawei said meekly, 'Sir, I'm only a common civil servant. Perhaps I'd better look at the printed name cards.'

The owner said, not without pleasure, 'We have an enormous variety of printed name cards: gilded, coloured, scented, folding . . . The choice is yours. Particularly popular with civil servants these days is this colour folding card, as well as the model with gold and silver lettering. Some bureau chiefs are partial to the luxurious look of the gold leaf card. But for an up-and-coming young lion such as yourself, I would recommend our exclusive *fengshui* card. It was precisely this *fengshui* card that made us so popular with you civil servants. I do not exaggerate when I say that each and every *fengshui* card is a protective talisman. A box of one hundred means one hundred times the protection.'

Zhu Dawei was amazed to learn that a mere name card could have *fengshui*. He wanted to hear more, and said with feigned earnestness, 'No wonder this shop is called Master of Name Cards. Could it be that the owner is a *fengshui* master?'

The owner winked craftily and said, 'The art of making name cards, my friend, works according to this simple principle: everyone wants their card to make a lasting impression and create a favourable reaction, a sense of admiration and even longing. No one who catches a glimpse of your card will ever forget you. But in actuality, that is not the card's most important function. A *fengshui* card will attract luck and repel calamity, bring success in your career and happiness to your home. It makes use of the heavenly trunk and earthly branches, *yin* and *yang* and the five elements, the *Book of Changes* and Eight Trigrams, all to enhance the bearer's innate characteristics. A card with a highly unusual layout, it employs principles of unity between heaven and man, its primary and secondary hues chosen according to the indications of the five elements found in the eight characters of the hour of his birth. That same balance of elements is used to determine the proper typeface, colour and placement of the name, title and telephone number. This sort of card creates the greatest influence when it is handed out, leading to further harmony between celestial timing, earthly luck and human harmony.'

The proprietor's words came in a torrent, and Zhu Dawei listened with a measure of scepticism, thinking, no wonder this print shop is so successful. There are secrets concealed here. It must be the *fengshui* cards that draw the civil servant trade. Who wouldn't want their career to prosper and their position to advance?

But seeing is believing. Zhu Dawei wanted to know who had been promoted or gotten rich because of their *fengshui* cards.

He asked craftily, 'What proof do you have for all this?'

The owner could tell Zhu Dawei was hooked, and passed him a large booklet of beautifully designed name cards, saying, 'You're in the Municipal Government, friend, and you must know some of the people in here. This gentleman, for instance, was only vice bureau chief of the human resources department when he arrived here. After using my *fengshui* name cards he was soon promoted to bureau chief, and is now vice department head.'

Zhu Dawei said, 'I know this man well, but I don't remember anything special about the name cards he had when he was vice bureau chief.'

The owner laughed. 'They were very special indeed! The element of wood was lacking from his eight characters, and I employed brown and grey-green, colours belonging to wood, in the design. The characters were all black, which belongs to water, and water gives rise to wood. I chose a long and narrow typeface based on the *songti* font, which has characteristics belonging to wood, and can strengthen that element. As for the placement of the name, I chose the location of the *Xun* trigram, also belonging to wood. These four decisions combined to completely counteract his lack of wood. The five elements now in balance, his career naturally took off.'

Zhu Dawei paged through the booklet and caught sight of Yang Hengda's name cards. He asked, 'And do you mean to say that this Mr Yang was promoted from department head to a Vice-Director of the Municipal Government with the help of *fengshui* cards too?'

The owner replied, 'But of course!'

These plain-as-day examples served to win Zhu Dawei over.

Just as he was flipping through the booklet and considering whether or not to tell the proprietor the eight characters of the hour of his birth, he caught sight of the name cards of Peng Guoliang, Wen Huajian, Chen Shi and Hu Zhanfa on the last two pages. They were clearly *fengshui* cards they'd had made before they were detained, and as Zhu Dawei stared at the cards he chuckled. The owner, uncomprehending, looked at him curiously. Zhu Dawei pointed with silent significance at those few name cards and the owner, suddenly understanding, instantly flushed red.

Zhu Dawei closed the booklet and said with a smile, 'Thank you for all this information; I feel I've really learned quite a bit. Since you claim to have the greatest variety and choice of name cards of all print shops in Dongzhou, you've probably got environmentally friendly name cards, yes? I'd like two boxes of "green" cards.'

The owner knew that he'd embarrassed himself. Hoping to dispel the awkwardness, he enthusiastically passed over paper and pen, saying, 'Of course we do! Made with the best recycled paper. If that's what you'd like, my friend, please write down your name, position and telephone number here.'

Zhu Dawei wrote, 'Zhu Dawei, Secretary to the Mayor of the Dongzhou Municipal Government'. When the owner saw that his eyes widened and he said flatteringly, 'The world belongs to youth, truly it does!'

Zhu Dawei studied the words 'Secretary to the Mayor'. He felt something was amiss. With some reluctance he crossed out the words 'to the Mayor' and left only 'Secretary'.

Mayor of Dongzhou, Liu Yihe

WHEN I FINISHED reading Huang Xiaoguang's reportage piece, 'Conversations with Peng Guoliang's Soul', in the *Qingjiang Daily*, I felt as though a heavy stone were pressing on my chest, choking off my breath. That stone was none other than the boulder that Sisyphus pushed up the mountain with such back-breaking effort, only to see it roll back down again. The boulder was corruption itself, and everyone who hated and fought it was Sisyphus. So who were the gods he had offended?

Without a doubt, the gods were the backward system. Those who fought corruption couldn't help but offend the old system, precisely as Sisyphus had offended the gods. Qi Xiuying was just one Sisyphus among many, and I was no different. But the old system did not permit you to stop supporting it, just as the drafts of the speeches that I delivered at meetings had been marked by the secretary: 'applause here', 'warm applause here', and 'sustained applause here'.

The old system was spurred on by precisely this 'hearts surge as applause swells' sort of cliché. The most fundamental tool of the counter-corruption effort was reform of the system, the equivalent of turning applause into pure noise. But 'sustained applause here' had long ago become a legally mandated form of democracy, and it could not be challenged. Without challenge, however, the boulder of corruption would grow larger and larger. Someone needed to be Sisyphus, to continually roll the boulder uphill even though it was bound to roll back down every time. But so long as we persisted, we might be like Sisyphus and find a new meaning within our lonely, painful, absurd and despairing lives. As Sisyphus pushes it, the boulder takes on a certain beauty, and the energy of his struggle is as graceful as dance. Lost in this pleasure, Sisyphus feels no more suffering, and once the boulder no longer causes him suffering, it will never again roll down from the mountaintop. Thus, Sisyphus becomes stronger than the boulder itself, and he finds that the struggle to conquer the peak is enough to satisfy his soul. That's the myth of Sisyphus. It will also be the myth of the counter-corruption effort. In that myth, Peng Guoliang's soul will no longer fear the light, and he will see the firm gaze of Sisyphus, looking up at the boulder from the bottom of the mountain.

That is what welled up in my heart after reading Huang Xiaoguang's article. Some people wondered if Peng Guoliang's case would implicate the entire government of Dongzhou, perhaps even me. I needed to consider it carefully. Without a doubt, Peng Guoliang's corruption was shocking, and it had infuriated the people of Dongzhou and damaged the masses' faith in their civil servants. It was perfectly natural that public opinion should turn against me as well. As the head of the Municipal Government, it was not enough that I should keep my own nose clean. I needed to make sure that no one strayed. Achieving that while also moving the work of government forward required open-mindedness and magnanimity on my part.

Thinking back on Peng Guoliang's road to corruption, I saw that it was directly related to my own lack of tolerance and broad-mindedness. Our struggle began the day we both became vice-mayors. If I'd been a little more tolerant of him back then – talked to him more, communicated better, helped him – Guoliang wouldn't have strayed so far. After I became Mayor, in particular, the evidence of corruption in him and his cronies was obvious, but I did not put a stop to it in time, even enjoying a little subconscious *schadenfreude*, until Peng Guoliang was lost completely.

In Huang's article he quoted Guoliang as saying that I was someone who understood the darkness. Not only was I someone who understood the darkness, but I was practically a man of darkness myself. As Guoliang was sliding towards corruption, I did nothing to help him.

Now, after the case, the civil servants of Dongzhou seem to have contracted the post-counter-corruption blues. Some departments are adopting the 'inactive' strategy of 'a smiling face, an open door, but nothing doing', and work efficiency has dropped off dramatically. Discussing the cause of this, some civil servants lump 'being corrupt' in with 'getting things done', thinking that if you were going to make an omelette, you have to break eggs. This goes to show how little they think of themselves as public servants and how far they've strayed from the people. They think of nothing but their advancement, not the practical problems of the people, and they are responsible to no one but themselves. This is the shadow that Guoliang's case has cast, and if we are going to get out of that shadow, we have to reform from the ground up.

That's why the Provincial Party Committee convened an educational conference for all the Party and government cadres in Dongzhou. After the meeting, Qi Xiuying asked me to come by her office, saying she had a souvenir for me. I had hardly got through the door when she pulled a black notebook out of her desk drawer and handed it to me solemnly, saying, 'This is for you. Keep it near you, as a warning bell!'

I flipped through the notebook and found that it was a copy of the *The Civil Servant's Notebook* that Guoliang had ordered Hu Zhanfa to write in my voice. Hu Zhanfa had kept this copy to hold over Guoliang's head, perfect evidence of the alienating effects of power upon the soul.

I put the notebook in my document folder and said, 'Comrade Xiuying, thanks very much for thinking of me. When it comes to the environment, the mistake we generally make is to pollute first and clean up afterward, usually at a high price. If we do the same thing in politics, the price will be even higher! The counter-corruption effort isn't a simple process of eliminating corrupt officials, but of establishing flexible and uncorrupted institutions. Thus, we should be turning 'counter-corruption' into 'corruption-prevention', and establishing institutions and a system that inoculates civil servants against corruption from the beginning. Only then can we avoid tragic lessons like that of Peng Guoliang! Otherwise, any sudden campaign to sweep away corruption will only mean a curtain call for a few old corrupt officials and a hearty welcome for the new ones!'

Qi Xiuying was silent for a moment before saying, 'There's plenty we can learn from a case like Peng Guoliang's. What you said about switching to corruption-prevention sounds to me like 'an ounce of prevention is worth a pound of cure', but anti-corruption isn't simply dusting the corners, nor is it equivalent to managing the natural environment. The likely result of any radical counter-corruption revolution is the destruction not only of the corrupt parts, but the body as a whole, whereas a gradually progressing anti-corruption reform can pose grave risks. I've come to accept that this is a life-or-death battle we cannot afford to lose, no matter what the price. I have long been prepared to sacrifice everything, for no other reason than to let the people live beneath a clear sky.'

Though her words were encouraging, they were also melancholy, and I punctured her mood. 'You'll need a hero to fight giants, and the hero here must be healthy institutions. The ancients tell us, "Officials must be removed 800 *li* from home". That's what's meant by institutions. Your transfer from K Province to Qingjiang proves the wisdom of that saying. No one is born a villain; we must judge by intentions. Peng Guoliang truly did wonders for reform and opening up in Dongzhou, even though he became corrupt and has paid the price with his life. In the course of educating and making examples, we often place total responsibility on the shoulders of the individual, saying that he's relaxed his world view and his values, that he did not build a defensive line against corruption in his mind. This is not only irresponsible, but it also shunts responsibility. Frankly speaking, it defends a system that's rusted into immobility, and it demonstrates a lack of courage to innovate the system. If we'd had a good system, Peng Guoliang wouldn't have slid into the abyss of corruption. But in our municipal team there seem to be many who have yet to understand that. Many of us are not corrupt ourselves, but take no action against it, and adopt a short-sighted *'après moi le déluge'* attitude, or preside over 'peace preservation associations' like the puppet organisations set up by Japan during the War of Resistance. They even go so far as to believe that corruption can be a lubricant for a rusted system, and that without it, all market reforms will be suffocated within the walls of the old system. Thus, they decide to go easy on corruption, creating a situation where 'those with spoons may eat', and even proclaiming that the corrupt may avoid the sudden collapse of the old towers. You can't refuse to look in a mirror, much less smash it to pieces, just because you're ugly.'

Qi Xiuying's brow furrowed, and she said, 'Comrade Yihe, what you say reminds me of something that Mr Bo Yang wrote in *The Ugly Chinaman and the Crisis of Chinese Culture*: "In order to conceal a mistake, the Chinese will expend extraordinary effort in committing additional mistakes, all to prove that the original mistake was not in fact a mistake." That hit the mark. I've always thought that having the courage and strength to criticise yourself is the best measure of the true greatness and confidence of a nation.'

I carried my heavy thoughts with me as I left Qi Xiuying's office and got into my Audi. The car slowly proceeded out of the Provincial Party Committee gate, and I cast an involuntary glance over my shoulder.

I'd been in and out of that gate countless times, but I'd never noticed that the decorative screen wall bore the following four words in bright red: 'Seek Truth From Facts'. In the light of the setting sun, those four words shone with particular brilliance . . .

The Government Car

IT'S NO BOAST: every civil servant dreams of possessing me. Why?

I am proof they have made it. I am a symbol of their status, their achievement, their success.

We often say that the 'grand wheel of history rolls forward', and ancient China was a nation of the wheel. When Confucius wandered from state to state he rode a horse cart, when our armies went to war they drove chariots, and up until the Wei and Jin Dynasties, the wheeled vehicle was the main means of transportation for officials and nobles. Even so, the horse cart, ox cart, donkey cart and mule cart are not my ancestors, and neither am I descended from the sedan chair.

My true ancestor is the grand palanquin. Officials began using palanquins in the Tang Dynasty, and since the Song Dynasty, their size, shape and usage have been regulated. By the Qing Dynasty, central government officials of the third rank and above would be carried on a four-man palanquin inside the city, or an eight-man one when travelling beyond it. Members of the royal family were seen on palanquins carried by twenty or even thirty men. A man's status could be measured by how many men bore his palanquin.

But times have changed, and the palanquin has become the sedan car. Even children know that 'the rich drive a Benz, and the powerful drive an Audi'. Any official of bureau-level or higher is given a car. At a certain level it comes with a police escort.

So how did palanquins come to be translated into sedans? They say that at the end of the Qing Dynasty, when the Empress Dowager Cixi celebrated her sixtieth birthday, Yuan Shikai spent ten thousand silver ingots on a German-made Benz as a present. The Dowager looked it over and felt that although it was clearly made of superior materials, it was little more than a dressed-up sedan chair. Fearing an imminent attack of imperial displeasure, Yuan Shikai hastened to have the German driver demonstrate the vehicle's abilities, and Cixi was mollified. She asked Yuan Shikai what this foreign-made curiosity was called. Struck by inspiration, Yuan Shikai invited her to name it. Observing that it was high in the middle and lower at front and back, like a sedan chair, Cixi decreed that it would be called a sedan car.

At that time the Empress Dowager was in the habit of riding a palanquin to various locations outside of Beijing. The first time she rode her Benz outside the Forbidden City, she discovered that her driver was none other than Sun Fuling, her old master of horse. He was seated at an equal height to her, and furthermore in *front* of her – nothing less than an upset of the natural order of things. She insisted that he kneel while driving, and he had no choice but to obey, nearly resulting in disaster. Cixi was eventually persuaded by her terrified courtiers to emerge from the car and board her customary sixteen-man palanquin. While the sedan car itself was a failure, the name stuck.

'Raising someone's palanquin' has long been a term for sycophancy in China, though what was once a matter of physical strength now requires creativity and cunning. Those who 'raise the palanquin' are typically those closest to their leaders, most favoured, and most likely to benefit by their leader's good fortune.

Hu Zhanfa is one of the best palanquin raisers I've ever seen. I became Vice-Mayor Peng's car at the same time as Hu Zhanfa became his secretary. Mayor Peng had a penchant for seeing women. His official position, unfortunately, made it a bit inconvenient. After a week of racking his brains, Hu Zhanfa invented a 'face-changing' licence plate for me. When attending important official events I wore my special vice-mayor's plate, when going out for a meeting I 'changed my face' to a common civil plate, and on trips outside the city I was disguised as a People's Armed Police vehicle. Even more impressive was that these face changes were controlled electronically from within the car. At the press of a button the licence plate would change. Vice-Mayor Peng was delighted.

One day when he was still Mayor Peng's secretary, Hu Zhanfa and Mayor Peng rode in with me together. I remember their conversation.

Peng Guoliang said, 'Zhanfa, simply sending *The Civil Servant's Notebook* to Qi Xiuying won't do. You should also spread some of your stories in the departments and offices of the city, and even let the common people hear them. You must learn to use public opinion as a weapon!'

Hu Zhanfa answered with a crafty, self-satisfied laugh. 'I'm planning to spread the "Miss Feifei" story around first, boss. It's a lively story, the kind that everyone wants to believe and likes to repeat. If it gets around, it will really put Liu Yihe's nose out of joint!'

Peng Guoliang asked darkly, 'That story's so lifelike, Zhanfa. Does Liu Yihe really have something going on with this Feifei?'

'He certainly does, boss,' replied Hu Zhanfa, almost giggling.

Peng Guoliang's eyes brightened and he asked, 'Do you mean it's more than just rumour?'

Hu Zhanfa replied, 'I'll tell you the truth, boss. Feifei is Liu Yihe's wife's pet dog.'

When he heard that, Peng Guoliang nearly died laughing.

CHINA LIBRARY

HE JIAHONG

HANGING DEVILS
Hong Jun Investigates

Set in the mid-nineties, *Hanging Devils* is a true-to-life story of cold-blooded murder and corruption from one of China's foremost legal experts.

Hong Jun, a recently-returned lawyer from the US, opens a practice in Beijing intent on helping ordinary people defend their rights. His very first case leads him to the hinterland of China's snowy northeast where the brutal killing of a local beauty took place ten years earlier. In his quest for justice, Hong Jun revisits the buried secrets of the recent past, and delves deep into the underbelly of the provincial police and court system in a case that proves to be anything but ordinary.

www.penguin.com.cn

CHINA LIBRARY

SHENG KEYI

NORTHERN GIRLS
Life Goes On

Qian Xiaohong is born into a sleepy village far
from China's headlong rush towards development.
A scandalous love affair launches the buxom but
unwordly sixteen-year-old on a journey to the southern
boomtown of Shenzhen. There, released from the
stifling conservatism of her rural upbringing, Xiaohong
must navigate a strange new world with unfamiliar
rules and values, and learn to go on in the face of great
adversity. Along the way, Xiaohong finds support and
solace from her fellow 'northern girls', with whom
life's challenges and pleasures can be shared.

Northern Girls explores the inner lives of a generation
of young, rural Chinese women who embark on life-
changing journeys in the search of something better.

www.penguin.com.cn

CHINA LIBRARY

DIVERSE STORIES
UNIQUE PERSPECTIVES

Comprising literature and narrative non-fiction,
twentieth-century classics and contemporary bestsellers,
the China Library brings together the best of writing on
and from China, all in one dedicated series.

www.penguin.com.cn